WILL YOU
BE MINE?

Library of Congress Control Number 2006905568

ISBN: 0-931761-59-X

Beckham Publications Group, Inc.
P.O. Box 4066, Silver Spring, MD 20914
987654321

WILL YOU BE MINE?

Barry Beckham

PUBLICATIONS GROUP, INC.
Silver Spring

Also by Barry Beckham

Fiction

My Main Mother
Runner Mack
Double Dunk

Nonfiction

The Black Student's Guide to Colleges
The Black Student's Guide to Scholarships
Beckham's Guide to Scholarships:
For Black and Minority Students

The College Selection Workbook:
Self-Paced Exercises to Help You Choose
the Right College

For Monica, Sidney, and Hughlyn

Chapter 1

No, no, no, no, no. No, no, no. You must sit still. Sit up straight and stop falling. There.

I turn almost too abruptly into the curve and brake slightly to keep from going off the winding road. There are several ways I could drive through the park to get to the other side of the city before reaching the interstate that dumps you onto the artery to the beach. I could drive at a steady forty-five, fast enough to send your heart racing as the road twists like a worm, but slow enough to stay in control. Or I could speed up on the straight-aways, brake slightly as I approach the curve, then accelerate as I take the turn. Or many times I have had to slow down because I wanted to look through the woods beyond the road to see the movement of the creek, wanted to see the water glide over the rocks before it swirls and foams up into a stream. I am not certain how I want to drive on this day.

Doctor Phoenix had suggested—no he had been quite adamant, far beyond the level of merely making a suggestion—that I should not drive at all. He had grabbed me as I was walking dazedly down the intimidating corridor of whiteness that is the hospital's hallway. Through the fog of my consciousness, I heard the metallic echoes bouncing off the ceiling and declaring that *Doctor Braverman* should *please call the switchboard,* that *Doctor Zees, Doctor Zees please, Doctor Zees* obviously needed desperately to *call in,* and *Line One needed a callback, needed a callback.* Was I staring when he found me? My mouth was wide open as I saw the blur of an approaching couple who were pushing their grandmother leaning lopsided in a wheelchair. They said something about she was doing much better. Was I glaring at them, painfully jealous of their uninhibited glee?

The weight of his arm around my shoulder was strangely overpowering, mighty enough to dissolve my resistance, my urge to run away. It was not only strong, but it was also encapsulating, possessing a force that seemed to have a physical quality of its own. I may have wanted to, but I did not run away. And I was so spent emotionally that each step felt as if it were encased in a ten-pound shoe. So I was glad that his arm had stopped me, had slowed me, for then suddenly, captured, I could capitalize fully on his comfort, turning now and facing him, folding myself into his embrace. Our cheeks touched for a second and then he whispered, "I know how much you loved her."

With that statement he had opened a harbor for the full-scale release of the overwhelming sense of loss I had quelled. Was this what my friend Harvey meant when he described how he—beset by the discovery that his wife was leaving him, facing a bank teller who had simply asked how things were going—broke down into an unintelligible, tearful babble? He found himself crying without control, his forehead in his hands. The teller spoke to him softly, then counted out Harvey's dollar bills.

Yes, I loved her, she's gone, I'm here with you and WBLK playing our favorites. Sit up. Why couldn't it last? Sit up. Of course WBLK would be playing the one about soul mates. A romantic Caribbean crooner's baritone insists that spending the day with her is like spending a lifetime in spring. A lifetime in spring. Something about her eyes makes him think that she had known him before, known him for years— perhaps before the world began. And now she was back to rescue him. Because she might be his soul mate. Could you be my soul mate? he asked. It would be unbearable to be without her, fatal for him to be alone. He asked again if she was his soul mate.

And now Frieda Sagen interrupts with a special bulletin. The police are engaged in a shootout near the zoo. Booby, do we care about a shootout right now? Do we? I push the button.

The doctor had warned me that I would be in mourning and therefore incoherent. "Your friends and relatives may say that you aren't making a great deal of sense. Even you may think that you aren't making a great deal of sense."

I'm not making any sense? Fiddlesticks, as my Aunt Clara would say. On the contrary, my good fellow, I maintain that I'm making plenty of sense. It's the nonsense of the world as it turns that isn't making any sense. "Hell is here on earth" is what my aunt always said.

And did he know, the good doctor, that Chinita—my sweet beloved butterfly, my *Che-Nee-ta* with an accent heavily and resoundingly on the last syllable, my *Neeta* in moments of special bliss and sometimes *Che-Neet* during a sportive instant—that last month, the sheet up to her nose, her sallow eyes looking straight at me, she had said, "I'm sorry that I had to disappoint you, my love; I didn't plan to leave you"?

Something had squeezed my heart suddenly. A warm, surging current of sadness charged through my insides. And then her eyes closed for an instant and reopened to stare again.

"You deserve a good woman, darling. I'm sorry I couldn't be here for you."

No, no, no. Sit up. There. Why won't you sit up and be still. What is it? What is it about? Who knows? I said who knows?

"I'm not sure if it is such a great idea to go back to the beach house," Dr. Phoenix had told me. "But on the other hand, you must accept the necessity of grieving. You should not fight the obligatory phenomenon of mourning." His hands were spread out in front of him, and he stood with his legs straddled as if he were on his home lawn awaiting his pet dog to run between them. "Come with me, young man," turning but waiting so that we could walk shoulder-to-shoulder down the hallway. I hoped that he would take me to a door that would open to a magical room, a space filled with an amnestic brilliance able to erase death from memory and send my precious butterfly flitting back to alight on my palm. I wanted an amnesia room. Upon entering, you would forget that death had occurred just as you would forget your first spanking or the first word you mispronounced in the third grade during show-and-tell.

God, I was so glad when Dr. Phoenix put his arm around my shoulder. I could hardly see. Everything ahead of us was as blurry as if I were swimming underwater. Well I could cry, couldn't I? Wasn't that my right? After all, she was my wife—my *wife*. I stopped, my eyes blinking quickly, the tears creeping down the sides of my mouth. Then, through the cloudy blur, I held Dr. Phoenix's arm, and pointed to the door. Here was the answer, my heart told me as its beat accelerated to loud thumps. This was the room that would bring on forgetfulness and erase death.

"Is this the room?" I asked, looking at the sign on the door.

"Oh, we are going to my office," he said, with sadly curious eyes. "This is anesthesiology. Why on earth would you want to go in there? Come on, just around the corner," and then, opening the door, "you know where the bathroom is."

I was relieved to sit down on the leather sofa facing his desk. I could see clearly now, cold water having shocked my facial muscles. The mirror had reflected a man with wild, puffy red eyes. I blinked rapidly. So did the man in the mirror. I rubbed them. So did he. He was I all right. The doctor moved with deliberation, but with swift, short movements of his hands to a pad, a desk drawer, a pen, a clock. It was the same set of

movements that I had seen three months earlier when he first told me of
Chinita's condition. He turned to open a closet door.

"Ah, here he is. Hey there, little man. How's my little man? Here is
what I've been looking for," his voice hollow in the bottom of the closet.
Then he was standing above me. "I want you to have this. He will be
good for you. Look at those ears. Here, hold him."

I did. I took you at the waist, Booby, and held your stuffed bear-
brown body up to my face and stared back at your beady eyes. Your
waist was almost the size of Chinita's after she had shrunken. I thought
back to the time I had lifted her in a similar position. I had been feeding
her baby food—sauce, her favorite—with a spoon. But she couldn't
control her mouth, and the sauce kept dribbling over her lips and down
her chin. Frustrated, she kicked up her little feet. Her eyes blazed. It was
a rainy Saturday afternoon. She turned her head toward the window. I
looked out too: a blue-gray pane of bubble spots, and beyond, a mirage
of tree limbs bending in the wind.

"I don't want to hear that anymore," she said, head falling back on
her pillow, dismissing my next spoonful with a hand flying upward.

"But baby, we love that piece," I said.

"Right. That's exactly it. That's all I *am* is a damn baby. Eating baby
food. Dribbling like a baby. I'm not me to enjoy anymore. I'm somebody
else," she moaned.

I slid my hands under the sheet, picked Chinita up and held her at the
waist just as I held you, Booby, when Dr. Phoenix placed you in my
hands today. Then I circled her with my arms in a delicately tight hold,
her gown large as a raincoat now, and nestled my cheek against the
antiseptic fragrance of hers.

I said, "Isn't that lovely still—*After the Rain?*" And we both must
have, through some vibratory connection that the Caribbean romancer
had just sung about, made the gray, soapy window a motion-picture
screen of our past. There we were just last summer walking on the hard
wet sand of the beach we are driving toward now—where a bright band
of red yellow suddenly appeared across the horizon line: it was near
sunset. I used black-and-white film, so the prints were horizontal bands
of black, gray and white gradations. The air was thick with a sea incense
of saltwater and wind. A four-legged quarterback, pursued by two
hysterically waving children cheering him on with "Come back, come
back, Buddy!" ran a zigzag pattern toward a touchdown. And an old
prospector dutifully swung his metal detector over a spot that a family
had inhabited earlier as if it were another dog on a leash.

The composition embodied that and all the other moments we had
enjoyed after the rain. Its slow tenorish introduction never evolved into a

full melody. Instead, the tune was filled with expectation—expectation never realized. It was about potential, what could be after the rain. The melody began as a long, lone wolf call in the dark, frozen night and then slowly eased its way to a stop. Its casual, skipping rhythm slowed itself gradually to a crawl. And you realized that the tune didn't really end. There was just a break, an interruption, as the bright sun inevitably intrudes upon the bleak rain.

Chinita's whisper, before her shoulders heaved and then shook mightily, was this: "What was the name of that puppy. It was Buddy, wasn't it?"

Now on this Friday afternoon when ordinarily we would be picnicking, I drive through the park without her. At the beach house in an hour, I'll lie down and listen to the sounds of the surf, then think about the funeral plans. I slow down for the knot of cars ahead of me. Aw hell, Booby, look at this damn traffic. God, we could be here for decades.

Chapter 2

We were almost a quarter century apart when we met. It was two years ago at the banquet in Iowa. She was in her mid-twenties, I was in my forties—late forties if you will. But I didn't think of her age. Age, what was that? "Age is just a number," Aunt Clara would say. Oh no, the only consideration was that hers was a face I could watch forever. The hue could not be described in one word. It was a combination of red and brown—red like the clay of Southwestern ground, brown like the dust flying over it. Her cheekbones poked out exquisitely, far prouder and resolute than any I had ever seen. Oh Booby, you should have been there.

"How old do you want me to be?" she had giggled when I asked.

"A child, man" is how Harvey re-described her for me. "You robbing the cradle this time."

I had just been in Washington with *Ontime* magazine for only a month when my editor called me into his office where I could see the magnificent Capitol building through the large window behind him. His painful frown—with lips so tightly pursed that they were nearly invisible—reminded me of the discomfort my Aunt Clara expressed when she was constipated.

"We need somebody with real sensitivity, a real feel for character...the sense of the dramatic," Taney explained. "Heck," everybody has shot Truman Washington. We need something arresting...mesmerizing... captivating. He's giving a major presentation in Cedar Rapids next week. We want to send you." He leaned forward with hands clasped on his desk and stared at me. Did my face reflect the surge of disappointment that had just shot through my insides?

"Who, me?" I asked, drawing a map in my mind. "You mean Iowa?"

I could visualize Pennsylvania and Ohio, but then the rest of the country became a stretch of white space until I got to...Nevada...then California. I looked down at my fingertips. This was my big assignment for *Ontime*?

It must have been almost a decade—for most of my thirties it seems—I had scuffled as a freelancer in a small Virginia town sitting on the Chesapeake Bay. I had gone there thinking that I would be allowed to shoot breathtaking portraits for a new magazine, but what was supposed to be wasn't what it was, to use Aunt Clara's phrase. So I left to freelance on my own.

I had exhausted myself. I had burned out. Or maybe they had burned me out. On several evenings, sitting on my deck, I wondered what was I doing. Why had I thought that Gahtsum's suggestion that I leave the Apple and come down to replenish my creative spirits was a good one? I had been the leading photographer of the movement for the country's leading weekly magazine, I kept telling myself. Now? a nearly starving director of blushing couples, restless twins, crying puppies? Where were my great landscapes? Architectural studies of angle and light? Brooding introspections of the nude form? Where? The truth is that I had to spend so much time on survival work that I was too exhausted at the end of the day to do more than fall on my bed, listening to the surf outside my beachfront condominium and staring at the ceiling.

God, the portrait of little Vixoria, the cum laude graduate of Helen's Day Care Center, took an entire afternoon. Our little vixen would not sit still. She had to pee, that's why she kept squeezing her legs together. She wanted to adjust my tripod. She wouldn't smile because "that man was looking at her." She didn't like her yellow dress, oversized, a miniature tent. And then, two weeks later as I presented the packet of thirty-six proofs to her mother, she smiled and tangoed around me toward the door. She was out the door. Next the vixen's leg was crawling into the back seat of their car, they were both waving, and as the passenger's window rolled down, Mother leaned forward, promising, "I will send a check next week, don't worry." I did though, and she did not.

I had faith in my art, but I was losing faith in my being able to pursue it.

"What the heck are you trying to prove down there anyway," shouted Harvey in the phone one night. "You've been there long enough. Come on up to the big city. You can help on the project."

"Who, me? I just want my work to be recognized," I said. I had envisioned assignments for photographs illustrating engrossing feature stories of people passionately involved in their work. Then, hanging in galleries would be my stunning portraits—head shots, candids and nudes—of my signed, limited editions. Eventually I would be represented in galleries throughout the world. And sometimes my dreaming would escalate to the scene where I (in a stunning tuxedo with white vest and standing against a black-curtained wall) accepted an international artistic award. And suddenly I would be the one facing the cameras as their bright lightning cracked and popped in *my* eyes this time.

Instead, what? Nothing. Assignments like these: a local retired teacher dressed as a clown to tantalize little children like Vixoria on the weekends. I shot him as you could only shoot a jester: making faces, gesticulating with his hands in front of his face, and of course juggling those balls so deftly that their wild little eyes nearly exploded. Mrs. Dempsey, the magazine's photo editor, had recently lost her mother to a sudden heart attack, and several of the other staff members suggested to me that she would be in a testy phase for many months as she struggled to overcome the sadness of that loss.

Her consideration of every story that had a semblance of happiness reduced her to a dour funk, and she, remembering her own melancholy, would reject it with a tearful intake of breath. "It's too...it's too...it doesn't have the mood I'm looking for," she would say. The jester's frown ruined the glee of the moment. The little darlings with their eyes popping out looked... "they look like extraterrestrials...God, look at this one in the middle with that ugly big yellow dress." Yet she continued resolutely to assign me to stories that were thematically encapsulated in the joyful splendor of special little moments we all treasure. And then she would reject them.

Editor Dempsey preferred to feature the painful rather than the heartwarming. Jumping out of the window of a burning apartment, they looked too much like paratroopers, she said about the rejection of what I considered one of my most dramatic catches: two men holding hands and leaping, the hungry tongues of red-orange fire lapping at the necks of their backs—and all this against the stark black of the building itself.

You could not see where they were leaping because I framed the shot to eliminate the ladder, the fire truck and the dazed neighbors looking upward from across the street behind the police line. You saw only the two of them—lovers who had been together for ten years, I heard one neighbor say. "Too much fear," she said later when we discussed my work over coffee. "We can't frighten the readers. The clown, what's-his-name, looked devious too I thought. Didn't you?"

And so the assignments were never published. Something was always just a little wrong, a little off from being perfect, not working for her.

Nor was my vision working for the owners of the few local art galleries. Mr. Finkel's assessment, in my last presentation before giving up on that strategy, echoed all of the previous attitudes. I caught him at Finkel's Fine Art and Custom Framing as he was finishing a sandwich. When he smiled, food particles stuck to his teeth. He licked his lips between sentences.

Finkel looked carefully enough at the prints that I thought represented my best work: the evening silhouette of several boardwalk hotels with a giant red sun sitting above them; portraits of a dozen community leaders, half of their faces bathed by afternoon shadow since I had deliberately placed each by a window in their office; and some candids of various faces I had encountered in my scouting of assorted neighborhoods and events.

"A little too dark. I like the composition, but the tones are too deep," he said about the silhouettes, shaking his head authoritatively. The portraits did not convey enough character. The candids? Needed more originality of approach.

Or, people couldn't pay. Or wouldn't pay me. I had accumulated many more rejections than paid assignments, and my stack of unpaid bills were becoming increasingly difficult to ignore. And then one afternoon I was photographing one of the town's most enchanting single women for a portrait series. The story was that her family could trace their roots back to a slave who was released by his master just before the Civil War. Now they owned huge acreage by the water and controlled one of the top law firms in the area. She had that self-confidence in her carriage. Pamela had just graduated with honors from a college in Ohio, and she was planning to go to law school, then join her father's firm. "Oh, I wish I were lucky like you and could just be an artist," she said as she strolled in with a self-confident smile. She came down the steps to my garage studio and stood at the landing to take it all in as if she had spent most of her life reviewing other people. As she sat on the stool and turned her upper torso sideways, her knee poked through a slit in her skirt. Maybe, I thought, maybe we should get better acquainted.

As I began to focus, I heard an abrupt bang outside. It was in the front of my garage door, right behind me. It was near my car, I thought, and still focusing I asked, "Pamela, did you hear that?"

No. The portable stereo box she had brought was on the table next to her, and the rhythm and blues was too loud for her to hear anything behind me. So I motioned to her that I would be right back and that she should stay there and relax.

Upstairs, I opened my front door. I saw them putting my car on their truck bed: A & J Towing, Norfolk, VA. My car! A short man with a vest and a cigar stood supervising the driver who was controlling the metal

ropes that pulled my white BMW. Its front was tilted upward as if it were
a plane about to take off. He looked at me as I stormed down the steps
and across the street. Then the conversation with Mr. Leserman came
back to me. He had warned me just the previous day that I had stretched
my late payments to the point where the bank was now close to
repossessing my vehicle. There was an amount—about four month's of
payments—that I needed to prevent what he termed "his dire event."

Harvey had advised me just a week earlier. "I could send you
something, man, but...if I were you, I would hide the sucker. I don't
know what keeps you going...all those setbacks. Have you contacted
Gahtsum? Put it in somebody's garage. Don't park it outside, whatever
you do. I guess you read about the little brother up here who was shot
outside the school. He was only twelve."

I slowed my steps as I stood in the middle of the street. Now Mr.
Leserman's whoever had turned and was facing me with his cigar
dancing in his mouth. And Pamela, where was Pamela? Was she
watching this ignominy? I turned my head slowly to the side to look back
to my unit. Thank God. I decided to go check on her, and then return to
speak to the cigar's owner.

I stuck up my hand as if to tell him to wait, as if we had been talking
for ages, and then turned to run up the steps to my front door. How would
I explain? Car going in for tune-up? Engine problems, wouldn't start this
morning, they just arrived? Then down to my studio. Pamela was sitting
on the stool, headphones on now, snapping her fingers as she listened to
her music. I told her that I would be right back, and ran out to the truck. A
& J was backing up, spitting and growling and hissing in a chant of
brakes, gears and exhausts. Leserman's man stood next to me, and for a
split second I thought we were partners as we both watched the truck
glide down the street ("nice car," he puffed) until I couldn't read the
license plates.

"This is a bank repossession; Mr. Leserman sent me." He
mispronounced my name. "You talk to him yesterday? Couldn't get the
money together? Well, you can get it back, just come up with the
money."

I walked back with the papers in my hands. And as I finished the
session with Pamela and thankfully took her deposit, I was vaguely
aware that the slit now exposed a circular tattoo on her thigh as she took
the stairs to my front door.

It was the Friday of Memorial Day weekend. I went out to sit on the
deck and looked at the other units straight ahead. I could hear the drone
of competing race cars on a dozen television sets. Once, pretending to be
a racer, balancing the bottom of the steering wheel with my palms, I had

pushed my sporty foreign car to ninety as I sped to Virginia Beach for a party. On many evenings I had slid in the driver's compartment, packed my photo gear and some jazz tapes, and dreamily sped toward the water to shake off the troubles burdening my shoulders. Now some truck was pulling it away at twenty.

In the unit across to the left, a couple lifted the top on their barbecue grill, releasing a circle of smoke. I was ready to try something else. I wasn't giving up, but taking a new direction, I told myself. I looked to my left at the empty beach and the setting sun.

Playing back the events, I felt a weakness in my stomach as if all the air had been kicked out of me. A few days earlier, I had sat on the bench with a group of fellow indigents whose telephone service—like mine— had been disconnected. The lady sitting on my left, with rollers in her hair, clutched a money order in one hand and the wrist of a leaning three-year-old in another.

I forced myself to suppress my gloomy mood so that I could capture that moment on film. Somehow the lady—who knows what hand of unkind circumstances had slapped her down—epitomized the plight of so many poor mothers scrambling daily to provide for their children. And the child, innocent yet bright, wore a shirt and slack set so stylish that he could have modeled for a magazine. So I pulled out my wide angle lens and shot them. The last was a close-up of him grabbing for my camera: "Jamal, come back here. You be working the rest of your life to pay for that man's camera."

To restore my service, the soft-spoken customer relations consultant explained, I needed to pay her in cash and give her the name and address of my nearest relative.

The next morning, the soothing warm spray pelting my body was interrupted by a shivering of the shower head. And then nothing. No water. Plumbing problem? Dripping, I stepped out to check the sink. Knobs turned, no water. I sprinted downstairs to examine the pipes. A yellow card had been slipped under the door and lay at the bottom of the stairway.

CHESAPEAKE SEWER AND WATER WORKS
Notice of Disconnection

Your account is in arrears and service
has been disconnected. To reconnect, you
must pay the amount in the box
below plus a $25.00 account reestablishment fee.
Payment may not be mailed.

Back upstairs, I sat on the toilet and held my forehead in my hands. I stood. I pushed the handle. I could not flush it. No water.

How much longer? I thought, looking at the barbecuing couple on their deck. Well, I could break down and call Gahtsum. He would understand as usual. I would need a short-term loan to get my car back.

"Now don't despair, son, things will get better," he said later that evening when he returned my call.

"I wish I could...just get a job and be paid regularly," I said, my voice so low I could hardly hear myself. "This freelance life is killing me."

"I'm sorry that things didn't work out at the magazine. But I heard that my buddy sold his interest just after you arrived and that the new editor has an entirely different approach." And that's when he arranged the interview at *Ontime* for me. "One of my clients knows the publisher. They're looking. I think it will do you well to be in a metropolis again. You need more variety, more exposure. You are a very talented young man."

And so now my editor at *Ontime* was sending me to Iowa on my first assignment out of town.

"This address to the..." Taney searched through the papers on his desk..."the National Council of Women of Color...thirty-second annual conference...building bridges for a powerful..."

I broke in. "NACWAC? Is that what you said? NACWAC?"

"You know them?" And kept reading: "Twelve hundred women from around the United States, the Caribbean and Africa..."

"You are right about Washington," I said, surprising myself with the upbeat in my voice. "We do need to try something different. I'm thinking of a brooding portrait, suggestive of inner power yet outward calm. And what a wonderful time to be in Iowa. Are the Hawkeyes playing?"

Now he really seemed to be in pain, and his forehead appeared to have added another uneven wrinkle line. Taney looked at me curiously. "Well...so you think you can handle it then?"

"Piece of cake," I said, smiling now. "If that's what they want upstairs, I guess I have to give it to them, right?"

"Right," he said, standing to shake my hand and smiling so that I almost saw his teeth. I walked quickly back to my office in a pleasant daze.

* * * * *

"I'm talking about thousands of sisters in one place, man—can you believe it?" I watched Harvey's expressionless face, his freckles pronounced as he sat drinking a beer in his kitchen later that evening.

"Yeah, well it makes a lot of sense," he replied. "You come to DC, the chocolate city to meet the woman of your dreams, and you start your search in Iowa. All the beautiful bright sisters in the world are here. Yeah, I think I understand your strategy, my brother." He rolled his eyes upward.

"Harvey, tell me where in DC can I meet thousands of intelligent, beautiful black women in one place *next Saturday?*"

"I heard about those NACWAC sisters anyway. Half of them are lesbians or divorced and carry so much baggage, they blame you for all the troubles they had with the men in their lives. You know what, I think Sandra was a member of that group. They had a skiing trip in Utah once. Maybe you'll go there next year. But then I forgot, you'll go anywhere if a pretty woman is involved."

"Why shouldn't I be?" We were sitting on the balcony of his apartment near downtown Washington and watching the dark clouds roll over the rooftops. "We weren't made to be alone."

A clap of thunder broke through the sky. "Sometimes I think you're in love with love," he chuckled. "Love your damn sister or brother or friend," he mumbled pensively, holding a bottle of beer in front of his face as if it were a telescope. "You put out everything, love somebody with all of your heart, and then what? They could walk out on your ass and leave you."

I turned in my chair to look at Harvey's profile. He fell silent staring at the sky. I knew he was talking about himself, about that evening he had come home to find Sandra standing at the door with her bags packed. I'm convinced that he would never forget it and never really understand it. He had tried, I know, and I watched him try. But he could never return to that moment when the heart surrenders itself with careless abandon— without caution, without reservation, without regard for emotional safety. Harvey was my age. He divorced just after we graduated from college and it had stunned him. And stunted him. On occasion he would venture forth to meet someone, to date (I thought Evelyn, the little nurse from northwest was just his type), but then he would pull back as if the prospect of happiness based on involvement was just too unappetizing. He preferred solitary detachment centering around no commitment at all. He was committed to the cause, he would say.

I have kept the scene in my mind exactly as he told me. He came home from his office on a Friday with a bunch of papers stuffed in his briefcase. Sandra was at the door stooped over a fully packed set of new luggage. She bent over and pushed the largest bag with her knee and suddenly looked up at him. She had often taken the liberty of surprising him by arranging for a weekend getaway, and perhaps, he reasoned, this was one of those trips. He asked, "Are we going somewhere?" Her hat fell, and they both bent over, reaching for it. He picked it up from the floor while kneeling and facing her. She looked *through* his eyes, not *at* them, he told me.

Then he stood up with her hat in his hands and searched her eyes, trying to find the horizon on which they were focused, waiting for the announcement that her answer was indeed a joke.

But she was serious: "No *we* aren't going anywhere. *I* am. I'm leaving."

In a sadistic way, he loved those lines. I can't count how many times he had repeated them, and how each time his calmness of delivery seemed even more passive than the previous. It would be in a restaurant, or in the living room of a friend or on a stool in a bar. And then, as if there had been no prior conversation or topic at all, Harvey would remind us that he had not told us about how Sandra had left him, had he? He would lean forward and quickly skip to the moment when he would say, as Sandra had, "*I* am." With this, he would stare into the eyes of the nearest listener as if to ask, can you believe that?

And sometimes the memory would be revived by another's story. If it had a character who was female, or a married man, or the word *leaving* in it, that was all the reference he would need to interrupt without warning the line of thought to ask if he or she or they had ever heard about...

I don't know if he will get over it. Once after we had gone out to take salsa lessons at a Latino club and he had drunk too many tequilas to drive home, he brought it up. I guided him to the elevator and up to his apartment door, and then he dropped his key chain. He couldn't get the key in the lock. The keys fell again. He picked them up and tried again...and again. Before I could take them from him and stick in the key myself, he grabbed me and started crying.

"Why'd she leave, man?"

"Oh, you'll be all right," I said, "you just need some sleep. A little too much tequila."

"I know, but I loved her. I loved her, man," and then he grabbed me around the shoulders. "I love you too, man. You're my best friend. You wouldn't leave me would you?"

"No, Harvey, I wouldn't; now here we are, good. Can you make it to your bedroom?" I opened the door.

"Wuv you, man," he whispered, waving, stepping backward and shutting 21F.

Yes, I was the diehard romantic. He, a trusted friend I met in my freshman year at college, was the radical realist, now directing a project that has breathtaking implications. He had stood as my best man (my first marriage to Atlanta) at the little church ceremony during my senior year in college. God, we were all just kids then. Out of law school, out of private practice, Harvey directs a street academy on the other side of the city. But his special project has consumed most of his energies just after he stopped practicing law.

Looking at the miles and miles of rectangles of land below, I remembered Harvey's biggest disappointment with Truman Washington. He had twice declined invitations by Harvey's group to address the youngsters at their commencement exercises.

"All he had to do was get in his limo and tell the driver to bring him to the other side of the nation's capital. Our kids are dying left and right. And we killing half of us ourselves," he told me at least once a week after I had arrived in the capital. "That little boy hadn't hurt anybody. Some teenagers just came up to his father's car and blasted him with dozens of shots. And Truman Washington and that jive HNIC ain't doing a thing."

I didn't know about all that, I thought, as I set my seat up straight for the landing into Cedar Rapids Airport. Yes, I myself had covered the deaths of several black men since coming to the chocolate city a couple of years ago. A teenager had been shot dead by two police officers who chased him to the end of an alley. His mother was a big, dark woman with a wide church hat and a diminutive voice that whined into her handkerchief. "Reaching for a gun?" She sniffed and looked skyward. "How could he be reaching for a gun in his sneakers? Oh lord...oh lord...my little Alfred. He wanted to be an astronaut, that's all. Just wanted to fly in space and now y'all done cut him down. Lordy, we ain' gon' have no more mens left the way y'all just killin' them. Just killin' them left and right. Oh Lord, he was on the honor roll too..."And then she swooned backward from the microphones and tape recorders. Three ministers with thin, trimmed mustaches stood behind her to prop up her swaying, and my favorite photograph shows their faces behind hers, the wide black hat with the stick-up feather covering most of the frame.

It was a sad moment. But to listen to Harvey, it was just another chapter of a recurring plot that was first written when we arrived on this land. I had to consider carefully all of his arguments before I could be as adamant as he. "It's been a consistent pattern," he argues, tilting his head diagonally and staring at me.

I smiled back at the attendants and the captain as I strode down the aisle and turned to get off the plane, walk past the assortment of metal news stand boxes, stroll past a bar, ignore the fast-food restaurants and pass the ticket counters. But as I turned the corner near the end of the counters, a huge pink and green banner hung from the ceiling:

WELCOME NACWAC
THIRTY-SECOND ANNUAL CONVENTION

So they were here all right. And so was I. I knew I had made the right move by leaving Virginia for the nation's capital. How else could I explain being at the NACWAC conference? How else could I have gotten here? And to think I was going to raise a stink about being sent to Iowa. I was smiling as I took the escalator down. And then my smile must have swallowed my face as I watched a dozen women in the baggage area below. One was holding a fancy red briefcase at her hip, and she turned to smile when someone said something like, "Girl, you go with that alligator!" Another couple was facing each other with hands on hips, engaged in what seemed like a deliberation on a matter of critical importance. One toe tapped like a woodpecker. Others were pulling bags with straps or pushing luggage carts. I almost went up the escalator again to get a better view of two cheeks pushing its owner's skirt to the splitting point as she bent over to tie her tennis shoes.

It was early afternoon. I had only a few hours to locate Washington and get my dinner tickets. My plan was to prepare for my sitting with the activist by observing his mannerisms as he spoke. At dinner, if I were lucky—and the prospects so far from my escalator surveillance suggested that indeed, NACWAC's finest would be in attendance. I would meet one or two ladies of startling presence and charm. And then we would dance the night away during the ball. If I were really lucky, I would meet somebody from DC—in Iowa, no less. It can happen, I told myself. "Things can change overnight," my Aunt Clara said, and then she would add, "you just never know."

* * * * *

I had showered and shaved and taken a nap and was adjusting my bowtie when a lady from Washington's officer confirmed that I was to meet him immediately after dinner in his suite for the photo session. "Maybe give him an hour to shower and rest, and then come on up," she said in a pleasant tone.

For now, I said to my mirror reflection, I should wander casually around the ballroom until I found a table that had the most promising ratio of earth angels. And like a spiritual escort, alight, offering my service for any assignment that might require engaging, witty conversation and a dedicated attentiveness. I practiced the introduction as I placed one hand in my pant's pockets to expose my cummerbund, and my right hand extended as if I were behind a podium: "Ladies, may I be allowed the opportunity to join your exquisite presence at this table?" And smile while standing there.

That is exactly what I did not say. As I got off from the elevator, crushed almost by several dozen heavily perfumed women, I was once again overjoyed by the magnitude of my good fortune. They squeezed in one-by-one. Each uttered either "excuse me" or "I'm sorry," as if the phrase were a password to occupying space that did not exist. Also: I could have sworn that one hand with an exceptionally strong thumb had clasped my thigh. And then the elevator's faint ceiling bell signaled our arrival at the ballroom level, the doors opened, and I saw hundreds, thousands, millions it seemed of beautiful women in the entrance hall.

Fashion this, Booby: they were wearing black mostly. Earrings and diamonds and gold and pearls. Thighs poking out of slits. Cleavages. Sequins. Short skirts covering lithe calves. Broad engaging smiles. Sparkles and murmurs and giggles and squeals. And maybe a third of them were men—fathers, boyfriends, some spouses.

No, it was far more than I had ever expected. This was truly seventh heaven. I was not prepared, Booby. So when I walked into the ballroom and identified a table that had an auspicious disproportion (there was only one other gentleman—an older fellow whose mustache shone when the light hit the gray areas), my mind fumbled with my script.

"May I...?" is all I could say. Did they hear my foot kick the chair? He and eight women looked up from their programs and nodded yes.

Smiling, shaking hands, quickly running my eyes from left to right to capture their faces in my mind, I began to study the dark lipstick of a woman directly in front of me who said that she had come from Chicago. But behind her...just behind her...

"Who is that?" I was talking to myself but the words came out. I watched Chinita preparing to take a seat at the table in front of ours.

"I don't recognize her," a voice responded.

I stared at the mirage in the pink dress, and I was bewitched first by the light bouncing off her sharp cheekbones. And when she turned her face, the light left a shadow that made them look like quarter moons. I was swallowed up in a whirl of excited incomprehension. Heart thumping, I saw, but did not see her exactly as she stood before me because her pink image kept telescoping and then fading away from me as she greeted her table mates. I needed to see more of her—unimpeded. I needed to be sure I was seeing what I thought I was looking at.

I needed to look at her directly. So I stood up with a frown as if I could not possibly imagine where the missing person I sought could be. And my eyes swept over the entire hotel ballroom, from tables to dais to tables. Finally I brought my view back to the table where she was now sitting with nine other heads that had continually bobbed like monkeys when I had been seated, foiling an unobstructed close-up of my not-yet-mine Chinita. For a second my gaze came down from the chandelier. Would they think I was checking for dust? My eyes went down directly and straight ahead to meet hers which (she told me later) had been following mine for the last histrionic half-minute as I searched for—"my cousin; I'm trying to find my cousin somewhere in here," would be my explanation. I settled on the crescents that were her cheekbones—crescents of strength and tenderness, I thought.

My legs dragged me to her table as if I were a repossessed car being towed away. Or a small dingy pulled over the waves by a smart cruiser. Except I was upside down. And then sideways. I know that I introduced myself, and that we talked. I don't have the foggiest idea of what she said. I know that the statement was animated and sensuous, and that we decided to meet again after dinner on the dance floor. For the moment, all I comprehended was a body wrapped in a hazy blur of pink, those cheekbones, and a head moving at the top.

At dinner, we stared at each other, bobbing our heads up and to the side as if we were playing optical hide and seek, trying to catch the other's eye in the spaces between their faces. I hardly touched my chicken.

A collective roar greeted him as he came to the stage. After his blue-suited frame was now in front of the microphone after a long introduction, adoring shrieks and sighs from the women followed. His personal magnetism was legendary, and it seemed that he brought a certain aura, a certain additional presence as he stood at the microphone basking in the standing ovation that welcomed him. His smile was bright and winning. Washington was a preacher too—and he loved to talk about growing up in Little Heaven, Alabama where he didn't have running water or a father. He had worked himself up to HNIC by hard, disciplined step after step after step. We had to do the same thing. And we didn't have to depend upon the government—those days were gone. We had enough strength ourselves to handle our problems. Nobody was giving anybody a break. Our grandparents didn't get a break. Our parents didn't either. We need to stop begging. Do it ourselves! Our salvation depended upon keeping the family together. And if our black men did not do their share—"Be a Man, You Can" was his best-known slogan—then we would capsize. He had outlined no concrete programs, I noted, to keep the family from disintegrating other than we must do everything in our power. But he instilled a feeling of chilling inspiration in us all. By the time he had finished, he was waving his handkerchief in the air left to right as if it were a baton. The entire room rocked left and right with him, chanting, "Be a Man, You Can."

A low undertone of residual humming still continued even after he left the dais and the stage was rotated for the dance band.

Did we dance! Chinita's pink dress was open at the back and had a bow, and we enjoyed every slow ballad. As my arm supported her, I pressed my fingers against her smooth back. She rested that lovely cheek against mine.

"And what are you wearing?—I love that aroma," I whispered. Two hours of knowing her suddenly felt like two days.

"My, you're quite a dancer. It's called Goddess."

"I should have known."

"Do you photograph at many conventions?" she asked.

"Not generally," I said. I'm here to shoot Truman Washington and go back to DC early tomorrow. When will you allow me to photograph you? I must come back and capture those cheekbones."

As if to confirm her assent, she snuggled her cheek contentedly against mine. I remember the tunes, big band sounds like "Don't Get Around Much Anymore" and "Satin Doll." We held on to each other and were the last on the floor for the closing piece, "Starlight." We talked when we didn't dance, and soon the hours of acquaintance that had seemed like days had turned into months.

We left the floor and walked through the hotel lobby, I at her side, my hand twitching to hold hers, my entire being alert to her steps as we moved side by side. Near the escalator was a man set up to take Instant Photo Memories—"Have Your Portrait in Seconds." We stopped to pose, she standing in front of me, my hand around her waist, my nose savoring the Goddess of my goddess.

"You two look very happy; how long you been married?" he asked. We both laughed, catching each other's eyes as we turned our heads, our fingers clasped together. Then we were watching him arrange the photograph into the small frame. He handed it to us. It was perfect: our smiles, her cheeks, the bright pink against my black tuxedo. That's the small color photograph that I removed from our album and took with me to every hospital visit during the last two months.

Steps later, we were squeezed together in an elevator, she standing in front of me so that my lips were this close to the back of her neck. Did I dare? No. We stopped at a room party, filled with people whose presence was obliterated by my concentration on her. We talked about everything, ravenously asking and answering each other, sometimes not even stopping to hear the other. And laughing as if everything and everybody were hilarious "You've got to be kidding me," she said. "You're not in your forties. You look so much younger."

"Who me?" We laughed again.

She responded to the unpleasant details of my two previous marriages with so much sympathy that I began to wonder if I had overexaggerated the woe in my tale. Chinita's replies: "Oh, you must have been crushed"; and "Oh, that happens so often. But you tried; that's important. Were there any kids?"

I sighed sadly and said yes, but I didn't want to talk about it yet.

As it neared the time to meet Washington, we were walking down the hallway toward her room. Have I told you all my fantasies?" she asked, stopping, her hands sliding inside my jacket and going down the middle of my back. "Have I told you that I've always wanted to be asleep on the bed when my lover entered my room? Did I tell you that I will be asleep when you come in tonight? Here, it's in your pocket, the extra key."

I stared at her in wonderment, reviewing what I had learned in the few hours (or had it been two months?): fourth-grade teacher, a Cherokee grandparent, ability to lift her left eyebrow into a V, and an auspicious list of unrealized fantasizes. Yes, I knew almost everything, I told myself. I was totally comfortable with her. So was she obviously, for she kissed me with a wide, inviting mouth. I skipped down the hall to the elevator. "Come back here," she whispered, laughing, that eyebrow up, and then wiped off the lipstick from my cheek. I pushed the button that would take me to the top floor.

When the door to the presidential suite opened, I entered a plush space accented in soft tones of wine and gray. Beyond the hotel busboy standing before me in a black suit and a tray balanced on his shoulder, I could see Truman Washington sitting on a large sofa. Above him was a chandelier. Papers and books were stacked on the table before him.

"Come on in, ain't nothing but a party!" his voice boomed as he waved his hand in the air. The busboy turned sideways to walk past me, then turned toward Washington. "Good-bye, Mr. Washington, it was a pleasure."

"Sure, my man, and remember, be a man now."

"Be a man, you can," said the busboy, smiling now and waving two fingers in a V as I closed the door behind him. Then I heard his muffled voice traveling down the hall in a sing-song rhythm, "Be a man, you can; be a man, you can."

As I moved closer, Washington stood up, and I almost gasped as I saw how short he was. A bright bow tie stood out against his white shirt.

His sideburns were exactly as one columnist had written, "the longest and widest in America."

"How are you sir?" I stretched out my hand as I balanced two camera straps on my shoulder. "Enjoyed your speech."

"White folks ahead, we still running," he said, throwing his head back in laughter. This time his words seemed to bounce off the walls and ceiling as he stood straddle-legged, hands on hips. "Boy you got some cameras there, don't you," holding out his hand. I gave him my business card. "Didn't forget the filim, did you?" and broke out in a big throaty laugh that sent his head back even farther than the first time, putting him, I thought, at the risk of falling backward. "Yeah..." he mispronounced my name..."you got any kin in Greenville? Oh okay...just thought I'd ask...sounds familiar. Where's your flash?"

"I'm using available light for mood," I said. "We want something really special here."

"Well, use all the light that is available, I don't want to look too dark," he said with short intakes of laughter. "They didn't do such a good job when I was in Miami two months ago before my nomination went through," Washington said, this time his voice lowered almost to a whine. "Had me looking like a damn fool. 'True Washington dancing on top of table.' Why not just say I'm undignified? Here I am on a table unscrewing a light bulb for the prom crew and a photographer comes in and takes my picture." He moved along the wall toward the kitchen, pointing his fingers at me. "You guys gave me a bad image."

"Well just keep talking and moving," I said, as I focused. "I'm here to get a new vision," and then caught myself as I stumbled over his shoes lying by the couch. They were brand new, but the black leather shone with a blazing brilliance. A designer's emblem had been sewn inside, and the soles were light, unsoiled. They seemed unusually heavy, I thought, before realizing that Truman Washington wore elevator shoes. The special heel made him appear two inches taller than he was.

"Had a hard time finding a bootblack in this hotel," he said, "and you know you can't look neat if your shoes are beat. I shined shoes as a kid in Little Heaven. 'Shoe shine, some time' was my slogan."

"I'm familiar," I said, remembering the photograph I treasured of my hometown bootblack, Roy.

Now, as he pointed at me, I looked at his short, stocky body, his pumpkin-colored skin, the red suspenders, and I thought that he looked like a very impressive nominee. "Hold that pose, right there," I said. Harvey would certainly accept this information about his platform shoes with glee. But I was still not certain why Harvey spoke so negatively of him.

"That handkerchief-head nigger is going to the top, can you believe that?" he weighed in one night. I was surprised at his derisive viewpoint toward a man who might soon be one of the highest-ranking blacks in the federal government. Washington had been director of HNIC, the Honorary National Interracial Commission, and had been its leader for more than five years now.

"He's just a sell-out." I heard him in the back of my mind as I focused. "Can you imagine," Harvey asked, "that little nappy-headed, high-yellow scoundrel going to the White House to represent us? I can't believe this is happening to us. And why doesn't he cut those damn sideburns?"

Now I was zooming in on Washington's face as he stood complaining, and I kept waiting for something to change as I shot. It seemed that behind the banter and bravura, there was a sad heaviness in his eyes. I kept waiting for it to leave. His mouth was smiling and his lips were moving, but the wrinkles under his eyes reflected something that contradicted his outward demeanor. I wanted to get a profile so that the famous sideburns would be in the center of the picture.

"Look straight at me," I said.

"Now who could that be," he said, leaning against a counter in the kitchen and facing me. "I'll get it," he said, moving toward the front door.

A loud greeting pushed open the door and behind it were a little boy and lady. "Hey, Uncle True."

"Hey, big guy," he said, and caught the six-year-older. I shot them as Washington gave him a kiss on the cheek and then threw him up in the air.

"Be a man," giggled the boy, pointing a finger at Washington's nose, then maneuvering to crawl down his back, where he was able to emit a muffled "you can."

I kept shooting as they moved inside. She was tall with round rosy cheeks and several gold rings on both hands, I noticed as we were introduced. I didn't want to stare, but she looked like someone I should recognize.

"Uncle True is taking some pictures. Do you want to take some with me, Champ? He's got plenty of filim." As I shot them moving around on the sofa, it suddenly occurred to me that she was the daughter of the great boxer who had dominated the sport back in the 1940s. No wonder the name Madison sounded so familiar. And was this her son? And what was the relationship? All I knew was that Washington was single, had never been married. I knew that the champ, Maddy Madison, had left two daughters when he died. But one had died in a swimming accident in the Bahamas. So this was the other. Maddy Madison's daughter. The great Maddy Madison's daughter. And his grandson. This was a photographer's treasure trove, I thought.

She excused herself and went into the bedroom. "I have to make a few calls, True. Champ, don't pull off his sideburns now. Don't be so rough."

I thought it would be a fitting end to my session to include these candids of Washington and his...whoever this young man was. He had a big smile accentuated by two teeth missing in the front, and a large head; perfectly photogenic. Taney would be impressed to know that I had caught Washington in a private moment that nobody else had captured on film.

For an instant, I telescoped back to when I was that age and I would jump all over Yo-Yo like that. Did Washington feel as warm and strong to the young man as Yo-Yo had to me? Did Washington pull him in a wagon as Yo-Yo had? Well, my time was running out, and I was further stimulated by the fact that I had a key in my jacket. Almost two hours ago (or was it two years?) I had left my earth angel. Soon I would be with her. She had surrendered. Had said that she wanted me to be her lover. That she was totally comfortable with me. Knew me, trusted me.

I left Truman Washington fifteen minutes before I actually left. For fifteen minutes I heard him talking, but my mind was with Chinita. I smiled and made gestures of intensity with my face, but I did not really comprehend. I wanted to be with my earth angel, my emerald, my mine. He was talking about poverty, and the government, and working hard, no giveaways, step by step. The way he did it. I was in a foggy land of half-listening, and then I awoke suddenly when jolted with the phrase "Call me if you have any questions," followed by a handshake.

I heard the door click, stepped closer and put my ear to it to make certain that Washington and Champ had walked away and back into the suite. I ran down the hall, cameras banging against my hip, nearly stumbling. I was on my way to Chinita. In the elevator, I considered how I would enter her room. Crawling on my knees? Easing the door open for a peek, then running into the bathroom? Dashing in, pulling off my clothes and diving on the bed? As I got off, three beautiful women in low-cut gowns entered. "Well hello, aren't you the photographer from Washington?" asked one with an inviting smile. I nodded, walking backward. I smiled and turned to look for 1244, where my lover dreamed. "Do you have a card?" I heard her ask as I turned the corner.

There was something both exciting and forbidden about Chinita's fantasy. And when I opened her door and saw that she was asleep (twice I whispered, "Chinita?" and held my breath each time), I tipped over to the bed. I thought as I stood over her that I was being somehow unfair, unsalvageably perverse. Her pink night gown lay across her back as if it were a scarf I had thrown. My eyes moved down her backside to the deep parting line separating two shapely lobes. From there, her thighs were spread in perfect symmetry. Then she sighed and raised her right knee in a climbing position, and I could no longer ignore the challenge of *midnitus interuptus* while she slept.

My lover must have been in a thicket of pillows, she seemed so tranquil, floating through an underworld of peace. My lover is what indeed I thought of her now. She represented something greater than mere bodily coupling. No, my lover was how I defined her as I glanced at the zigzagging belt of blue moonlight which came in through the window, spilled over the lamp and lace on the night stand, and then threw itself across her shoulder blades. The prospect of loving my sleeping lover to wakefulness and then maybe back to sleep became maddeningly intoxicating. My photographer's eye feasted on the visual repast of her sleeping form in climbing position on her stomach. I would title it, *Chinita on Mt. Everest.* Now the tangled band of nightgown clutched her around the waist. Her right thigh bent farther so that her knee was up to her breast. In a pool, she would be doing the breast stroke. As I spread myself over her body, *oh, the squeaking mattress, wouldn't you know it!* my lips finally rested on the indentation of her neck at the hairline. My nose swallowed the hot lust of her breathing.

I talked out my strategy, telling myself that under no circumstances must I awaken her. She lifted her neck. My heart hiccupped. "What are you doing?" she whispered in a soft daze, then dropped her face against the pillow and rejoined the movie that she was co-starring in. Soon I was sliding quietly but quickly into the beginning of a long sail through the night. I held myself to her as if she were a spaceship and I actually feared falling off into the stratospheric unknown. I stretched my arms up to slide my fingers between hers, and her hands locked me in. My lips brushed every hair on the side of her neck. I eased my thigh upward as if I were assisting her from behind to negotiate an incline that required extraordinary dexterity and balance. She need not worry. If she were to lose her place, she could only fall into my arms. Now I flexed as slow as humanely possible, and I moved my thigh over hers in the most meticulous, inch-by-inch manner...

We were soon past the stars, and as I held onto my *S.S. Chinita,* spaceship in the sky, as I held onto my clandestine bliss, I wondered if she were actually asleep. Somehow her drowsiness had a curious measure of discernment because she would moan or move an arm or leg at precisely the right place where I needed it to be as I roamed over and inside my sleeping little giantess. Once I had to stop frozen when she appeared to be close to awakening as she tossed and moved the way of sleepers who are between dreams. I felt even more like a true brigand, stealing pleasure from one who is not really conscious of what she is doing. If detected, I could be thrown off the deck to go sprawling, legs up, no doubt, into the unknown dark prison held for those so arrested by their lover's aura that they would do anything short of murder to experience the joy of that moment.

How stealthily I moved and didn't move. That I could not awaken her sparked surges of contentment within me. So I tried to lie motionless. If she turned her head, I lifted my lips from her neck. Filled with the fear of her waking, I stopped breathing if she moaned or expired. And it was in the slowest of slow motion that I flexed the muscles allowing me to squeeze out portions of unbearable pleasure from her.

What was she dreaming, I wondered in a moment when a spot of saliva dribbled out of the side of her mouth. Did she know we were sailing over the calmest, most compatible sky imaginable?

Once she lifted her head, looked at the clock, emitted a tiny snort and then lay her head back on the pillow. I panicked as if I were an undetected prowler in the closet watching her disrobe. But once more the sense of alarm filled me with a rush of splendor, and I lost control of myself and, trembling, emitted a final uncontrollable moan of intense relief.

Then in a drowse, I felt her squeeze my hands and lead me...into the woods, a deep dark comforting space that enveloped me entirely.

Chapter 3

When I awoke, the hour hand was pointing to the three. I didn't move for a
few seconds in order to enjoy the rise and fall of her perfumed shoulders.
Then I eased my thigh from between hers and pushed myself up to rest on my
knees, straddling her. I leaned forward to kiss her neck hairs and then got to my
feet. I was dressed, out the door and going down the hall toward the elevator in
minutes.

Nobody was around, thank goodness. The back of my head against
the elevator wall, I closed my eyes and enjoyed the soft fall downward.
Then I was stepping down the hall quickly, glad not to see a soul—or did
I? Was that a couple quickly ducking into a room near the end of the
hall? Did a smuggled outburst of laughter follow them, with a sound like,
"*Tru*...man"? Well, I was too tired to care as I put my hand on the
doorknob to my room. It was a mess—just like this traffic.

Look at this, Booby. It's crawling all of a sudden, just as we pass the
stretch of playing fields and riding stables. See that lady on horseback
over there—through the tree limbs where a convention of sparrows have
parked? Eventually we'll be going through the tunnel under the river, so
the radio station will be fading out. It'll be dark under here, so hold on,
Booby. I'll put in one of her favorite jazz tapes by Miles. She loved "My
Funny Valentine." But she also loved "Stella By Starlight." Maybe I'll
play both. Is that the kind of mourning you're talking about, Doctor
Phoenix?

The noonday traffic report by Brian Smart isn't saying anything
about this bottleneck. He's talking about "moderate to light congestion at
the National Airport exit, a car turned over on Pennsylvania Avenue near
the White House, and police working an accident just before the
Fourteenth Street Bridge, so better stay in the middle lane." But nothing
about this mess on the parkway.

He promises to have a special update on his talk show later about the black teenager who was shot 13 times by a police officer while running out of a store with a stolen wristwatch last month. The boy has been in a coma for 27 days, but doctors say today that he showed signs of consciousness, wiggling a finger. I want to turn the station, but I am morbidly reminded of how that kid's condition prompted me to make the decision about Chinita. They were both vegetables a month ago; but she is out of her misery; he is not.

I walked up to the doctor this morning and told him to stop the respirator unit. I had sat in the hospital garage for fifteen minutes with my face in my hands. She was a vegetable anyway—a shadow of her frail build. I didn't want to see her like that anymore. Let her die. Let her go on to something else, not this. There were papers that had to be signed. A special inquiry by the police. Then I was free to go.

Did I need help, some face wondered. "Watch your step," another one said. No, I said that I was fine.

Her tiny frame had gone to half its usual size. I couldn't help but recall how I had photographed a child grasping for life after an automobile accident last year. The jangle of tubes and plastic cords running from her body; gauges and meters; the scuttle of medical personnel shifting back and forth like a Greek tragedy—but here the actors and actresses had their mouths covered with white cloths, their eyes blinking.

It had been so quick. One moment we were enjoying the morning after we had met in Iowa, and the next, it was just two years later, and we were in a hospital. How could I possibly have had a clue as I awoke at three that night savoring her sleeping soul in Iowa? How could I, after leaving her and falling on my bed with my clothes on to awaken at seven? How, over the next fast-moving weeks, filled with our insanely intense communiqués, could I have envisioned such tragedy interrupting that exhilarating rush of elation? I knew that rush had not been a dream. It could not possibly have been. I had tried to wake myself up—to no avail, fortunately. I wasn't dreaming, so there was no waking up to be done.

I knew that Chinita would be preparing to leave early that morning, but I hoped with the hope that any lover would have at the moment that I would at least hear her voice. So by the time I had accepted the even still doubting resolution that I was awake, that I had without question been with her, that it was 7 A.M. in Iowa, I was dialing her room. She wasn't there. A dream after all? Then a voice—a nasal spokesperson for the hotel—announced that the party I had called had checked out that morning. She had been there. We had been together. I was not dreaming, the world was wonderful, full of possibilities, Booby! Full!

That realization sent my spirits soaring as I prepared to completed my assignment Sunday afternoon—photographing some buildings and political leaders for local color. Nothing was a problem. No challenge was overwhelming. The day would be simply an acknowledgement of how I could work without really paying attention to what I was doing. My mind was in my heart, in another world—adrift in the angelic sphere of my Chinita.

Then the ringing phone jarred me back to reality as I was dreamily loading my photo gear into my bags. "Taney here. How are you doing, kid?..."; and before I could answer—"We got a change. Forget about those corn-eating politicians."

"I got great shots of Washington," I said. "He's quite a character."

"He's a character all right, although I might use another word. Look, I don't know why we didn't think of this before, but we ought to get some coverage of the Plane while you are there."

"I didn't know we were doing anything about the airport. What's the angle?"

"Very funny, kid. I'm talking about Malcolm Williams, the basketball legend for the state university. Plane is up for player of the year out there, and I think we should get some shots for our stock library. There's an afternoon pickup game today, so we are in luck. Here's the number for the PR director who will arrange everything. See you tomorrow afternoon, kid. Safe trip back."

It came back to me slowly, the story I had seen in a television news clip about the college player whose tremendous acrobatic moves and shots had given him almost legendary status. My mind played out some of the details, but I hadn't remembered it all. Fortunately, the cab driver taking me to the university's field house filled me in with far more information than I could have recalled.

He was called the Plane because in one extraordinary moment in the early part of the season he seemed to have defied gravity like an airplane, according to the radio announcer covering the game. "He's like an airplane! My God, what elevation! I've never seen a player go that high in my life!" From that moment, he picked up the nickname the Plane, and various permutations, depending on who was describing. "Some kids call him Plane Man," said the driver. "Some call him Unplain. But I think we prefer the Plane."

The driver wore his cap backward. The yellow lettering of the school's name stood out smartly against the black background. I stared at the bobbing letters and the visor of the cap as if I were looking at his face. He told me that the Plane had come from the poorest background imaginable, that his mother had raised him, and that he had gotten no support from his father. "He's from the projects in New York, you know. That must be terrible, the way they live. You've been there, haven't you?" Then I was looking out the window at the cornfields that we rushed past as he spoke. They were one even column of stalks standing at attention. Those close to the road were blurred and yellow, pasted against a background of mackerel sky. Farther, they lay spread across the entire canvas of land until hitting the sky at the top of my window. I aimed my camera to capture the two horizontal bands of field and sky.

"Don't slow down," I said. "I want to keep the vagueness."

I could tell from his grunt followed by a quick movement of cap from left to right that he thought it an odd way to photograph a cornfield. "So the coach saw him playing in a summer league in New York and got him a scholarship here to the college. I think it's just great that the kid gets a chance for a decent education, you know? That's the only way to get ahead. And that guy...who's your leader?...that Truman Washington...he's got the right ideas. I saw him the other night on the news. What's he say, 'be a man.' Boy can he speak! He's a pistol!"

As we drove down the main road of the campus, the orange brick buildings on either side looking like a prison development, I could see the dome of an athletic structure squatting at the end. "Million-dollar center," he said, and with a chuckle, "they tell me that faculty wanted it more than the students. So how long will you be?"

"Just an hour or so," I said, lifting my camera bag to my shoulder and stepping to the sidewalk. Two giggling coeds excused themselves as they bumped into me and I turned just in time to miss having my bag knocked off. I pulled out my camera as I went up the wide steps to the entrance doors.

"Right on time," she said. She was tall, smiling, a clipboard in one hand at her hip, facing me as if she wanted me to go no farther. She put out her hand. Then pivoting as if she were in military formation, said, "They are just getting started, come on. I'm Loretta Billups, PR director, and you are from *Ontime* I gather. Did I pronounce your name correctly? So nice to have you with us"—now smiling, arms swinging forward as we looked sideways at each other's faces. "Malcolm almost fainted when I told him a photographer was going to cover today's scrimmage. God, is he psyched! He might even come up with a new move!—who knows?"

We turned to our left, down another hall. The doors to the gym were at the end, and I could hear the voices, the shoes squeaking, the ball bouncing. We pushed through the doors. It seemed as if we were late for the first act and had emerged from a dark dungeon. There on a brilliantly lit stage was the performance that had already begun. A figure floated in

the air. He had a ball in his hand. He was up near the ceiling, suspended.
He looked for a second as if he were riveted there, his arms like the wings
of a floating hawk. I dropped my bag and aimed my camera. I caught him
as he swooped down, shaking the walls with a thunderous explosion.
Players below him stumbled and danced out of the way. A surround of
yells and cheers filled the air. Some jumped from their seats and waved
their fists. And yes, as I looked up and to the right, there were two
students dressed in their yellow and black band uniforms. One stood,
sending a blast from his trumpet that was an alarum for more troops. Next
to him sat a collaborator whose *rat-tat-tat* drum roll echoed off the walls.
For some seconds, the gymnasium was an electrifying eruption of
feverish, reverberating acclamation. I felt a chill zip through my body as I
aimed my camera to capture as much as I could: his teammates embracing
him, the spectators waving signs (The Plane Lands Today!), a mouth-
agape janitor standing with his mop.

The PR woman, walking backward toward the basket now, was
signaling toward me, saying something like, "God, did you see that?"
But I had moved in the opposite direction, away from the center of the
gym and could only guess at her lip movement. I waved back at her. I
photographed the rest of the game mostly from my knees, planting
myself at different angles as I followed the Plane.

He did fly. He was more remarkable than I could imagine. He began
a jump shot from the foul line that looked as if he would just go high
enough over the defender to send the ball to the basket. But the jump
turned into a soar. He didn't just go up vertically. He went up—and
forward too. At one moment—and I caught it on film with the thrill that
comes from capturing that rare split second—his body was almost
horizontal. He was stretching as if swimming in the air. Was the
bewildered defender standing and looking up at the Plane's stomach?
Were we all looking up? Then he came down at a point so far ahead of
the foul line—and on the other side of the player trying to guard him—
that we all watched in disbelief. My ears rang from the pandemonium.

In another flash of unbelievable agility, he drove toward the basket
against a defender who must have been at least a foot taller. Again, in
that instant that can only be caught by the camera for posterity—an
instant that seemed to stretch for seconds—he averted the defender's
huge obstructing arms. He was there to block the Plane with such a
certainty of intimidating resolve and position that we were all waiting for
the inevitable swatting away of the ball. And perhaps an injurious
collision of bodies? As our eyes dissected that second into nanoseconds
of mini-moments, we saw the Plane on the right, facing the defender's
long high arms, the ominous terrible rejection impending. But then the

Plane spurted around his body, could have even tapped him on the back of the head as he wound up on the other side of the basket, making the shot. Again, the uproar was ear-shattering.

That is the shot that I hoped my editor would use, I told the Plane after the practice. The three of us—the Plane, the PR woman, and I—were sitting on the bench near half court. "I've got some good shots, I think you will like them," I said.

"Well, I hope he didn't shoot too well," said Loretta. She sat between us, so I had to lean forward to see Malcolm's face. "You do know the full story, don't you?" They both were smiling.

"You mean he may be player of the year? Everybody knows that," I said, recalling the reports I had just learned about.

"Yes...but the reason why he's getting so much attention isn't his scoring, you know. Maybe you should tell him, Malcolm."

He stood up, bouncing the ball. "I've never made a shot in a game," he said, looking down at his shoes. "Haven't scored a point yet."

How could that be? How could he be so agile as I had seen and not have scored—ever? And what did it mean? And if he hadn't, why hadn't he?

She stood next to him, was almost his height. "Our games are sold out, we have raised the ticket prices. Applications to the college have soared," she said, raising her arms upward. "The media is crazy about us. Everything is terrific—because of Malcolm. Why should he make a shot? Then the public won't give a hoot about him or the college. They don't care about performance, they want to be entertained. They want to see him fly. Anything after that doesn't matter. So coach and I—he's at afternoon Bible study today—decided that he shouldn't make a shot. Just go up and make those incredible moves."

I was dreaming, certainly. In fact, I hadn't really met Chinita and I wasn't really in Iowa. They weren't really standing there in front of me. I gazed at them both so long that I knew my mouth had been open for several seconds. But then a loud shot rang out from the far corner of the gym, and I knew once more that I was awake. We all stared to see the janitor pick up his mop.

"So...so..." I stuttered ..."nobody cares about him scoring..."

"He has an image, right Malcolm? And look, that's why *Ontime* has sent you here to photograph him, right? It's image that is selling tickets and getting us attention. And it's image that will make this young man a very valuable draft choice in a few years." He smiled hugely—in agreement, shuffling his feet. "It's not so much what he does, but who we think he is," she said.

"Yes, I understand," I said, my eyes blinking, lifting the strap of my camera bag over my shoulder. Booby, I must tell you that I was a confused brother as I digested their explanation.

I shook Malcolm's hand that was twice the size of mine and wished him well. I thanked the PR woman and walked out the gym, already cataloging in my mind the five rolls of film I had shot. I slowed momentarily to look at the newspaper page in the glass display box on the wall. "The Plane Drops Bomb on Central," it announced. When I walked out the front door and down the steps, I saw the cab preparing to make a U-turn from across the street.

"Get some good shots?" he asked, looking back at me, his arm spread across the seat top. The bill of his cap was still facing me.

"Yep," I answered, half-reliving a maneuver of Malcolm and half concentrating on a couple stumbling across a stretch of grass as he guided her with an arm around her waist. It was exactly the way I would have held Chinita. "He was incredible all right. The first shot he made was enough to convince me. Hey, what's his average, anyway?"

We were moving slowly down the long entrance road that led to the highway. "Average? What do you mean average? He hasn't made a shot that I know of." His eyes met mine in his rearview mirror. "What the heck is an average—that's just a number, right? We just want to see him fly, man...fly..." sending the fingers of one hand fluttering like a bird toward the window.

"So everybody out here knows he hasn't scored?"

"Out here? I thought the whole world knew it. Do you think he would be the sensation he is if he actually scored? Being the Plane is what entertains us. Darn," his brow frowning, "why would anybody care about how many points he makes?"

He blew his horn and drove around a huge, trudging tractor trailer that had slowed us down. Through the front window, I looked out at the spreading fields of yellow and green on both sides of the road. Every hundred yards, a red barn would pop up as if placed there by a landscape painter; then a pair of grazing horses, their tails swishing against the skyline; then some buzzards hovering in beautiful synchronization. "Gorgeous country," I said, as I moved from one side of the cab to the other with my camera.

As I sat back finally to enjoy the country's pure beauty without the necessity of worrying about exposure and shutter speed, I saw the inviting sign ahead. "Hey, can we stop please? Maybe I will take some corn back home."

We pulled off the road into the driveway. He wore blue overalls and was pulling on the straps when we both got out the car. He stood up from the bench, but the dog lying under his feet under it merely raised his head and put it back to rest on the ground. "First time anybody sent a cab to pick up corn," he smiled.

"Gentleman's from Washington," the cab driver explained.

"Oh, Seattle, I bet."

"No, Washington, DC, the capital. He's a photographer."

"Oh. How is the president?" He chuckled, then looked down at the dog for its reaction. It twitched its ears, eyes still closed.

"Doing okay," I said. "That sign—is it right? Is the price still the same...?"

"I didn't vote for that bastard, I'll tell you that. He don't give a damn about us farmers. And if you poor, he don't even know you. Make sure you tell him that. I can let you have even more if you want, huh Pluto?"—looking down at the dog. He turned to walk toward the mound of corn. "How much you want?"

"I'll take as much as I can, at these prices," I said. "I love corn. And Iowa corn is the best."

"You sure you like corn *that* much?" asked the cab driver. "How will you get it back?" He followed the farmer.

"He looks like a smart man to me," said the farmer. "He can figure it out."

"He's smart all right," I heard the cab driver agree, his back to me now as I marched behind him and the farmer toward the mound. "He knows Iowa corn is the best, I heard him say that."

"I could eat corn all day," I said, spellbound by the unbelievably low price. I would take some back for Taney. He would love me for being so thoughtful. And I could take some to Harvey. I'd have enough for everybody. Even some of the secretaries—especially Wilma, the receptionist.

"I can fill up the whole trunk for a few bucks," he said, walking closer to me, his hands now clasped together in earnestness. The three of us gathered around the stack as if it were a prized auction item. I calculated the value of that much corn if I bought it in DC. I hoped my lips did not reveal the enticing result.

"Oh yeah?" said the cab driver. "What are we going to do with all that corn in my trunk?"

So we decided to fill half the trunk, and I would give the cab driver whatever I didn't take with me back East. I couldn't resist the bargain—a trunkload of corn just for a few bucks! And from the corn capital of the world? Who would say no to such an opportunity?

He gave me some large brown burlap bags that read "Idaho Potatoes" in red letters. "You can probably check two of these on the plane." The airlines should be glad to see you helping the economy, right

Pluto? Well you wanna take a picture of me and Pluto before you go?"

I did. Pluto never moved, but the farmer went back to the bench and lifted his foot to it. He rested an elbow on the knee. It was a great pose— a smiling, hard-working Iowa farmer in overalls with his dog asleep under the bench. In a boat, he would have been Washington crossing the Delaware. And stuck in the ground, a big handwritten sign that offered a deal that I thought no one could resist: FEED CORN—and then the unbelievable price.

"I hope your friends appreciate your thoughtfulness," the cab driver told me as he left me at the airport. "It sure looks tasty, doesn't it? And what we see is what we get." He drove off, leaving me in the airport theater of a skycap's dragging my two burlap bags to the curbside, a loudspeaker paging someone to meet his party, a woman kneeling to reinsert silky items in her suitcase, a couple hugging in reunion.

As the plane ascended, I looked out from my window to see the remnants of the setting sun spread a golden-red blanket over the flat fields of Iowa. The countryside consisted of the usual patchwork of russet and chocolate rectangles that you see from any airplane, but on this pleasant fall evening their pattern seemed particularly charming. Booby, the man sitting next to me had fallen asleep and was leaning to the side just as you do. I wish you would sit up. I know now that my appreciation for those fields was a direct reflection of my newly inflated state of mind. Everything was beautiful. Just as this traffic in the midst of a devastating personal loss has made me sour and contentious, conversely on that flight back, my mind was perched on a limb of bliss.

Now they are phoning in like mad, as if they are stuck in traffic too and want to take advantage of the fact that they have nowhere to go.

One caller wants to know why our leaders aren't saying more about the killing of our black men. Why can't they take a stand? Why do they disappear when we need them?

Another caller—a woman—wants to know why a youngster that age was out so late at night. Where were his parents? she asks, insisting that our families need to take more responsibility for our children.

Well, when is the last time a white kid was out late at night because his parents weren't watching over him and he got shot down by the police? a caller from Maryland asks Brian, the host. Brian says that it's time for a break to hear from his sponsors. Booby, it's time for a break in this traffic—and look at this car trying to squeeze in front of us.

Looking out the airplane window was for me the first time since leaving Chinita that I was able to reflect without distraction on that enchanting evening capped by that wondrously magical moment. Yet I reasoned reluctantly that there were still those possibilities that it had been a dream, or that it was a fluke of some sort. Maybe she was mentally ill, and I just happened to be a ready accomplice for a spell of erratic behavior. I was tired but unable to fall asleep. I picked up a magazine—it was *Ontime*—but I couldn't concentrate on the stories.

Then I remembered that I had the photograph, and pulled it from my jacket pocket to cherish it. Staring at it, my mind kept flashing highlights as if it were a screen to the past. I would stop one and replay it. Then speed forward to another. Back and forth. For one second I was walking in the banquet hall, then in another I was holding her waist on the dance floor, then I was staring at the sharp narrow convexity of cheekbone, then I was inhaling the sleepy aroma of her neck. Ah, Booby, it was enough to make you almost ignore what was going on in the rest of the world. My mind, where was it? I must have dozed off while reliving some moment, and then I was groggily listening to the voice alerting us to the imminent landing.

Every airport couple holding hands, kissing in corners, and pecking each other on their cheeks were now the most arresting spectacle that I could imagine. I paused to stare at a pair sitting at the bar. He was running his lips down the side of her neck as his hand cradled a beer bottle. I watched. Was he using the same technique that I would have? Was he whispering in her ear? Where was her hand—did I see it rubbing the inside of his thigh? Her eyes were glassy and her giggle was other-worldly, as if she were transported by the moment into another realm of contentment. Then he turned to face the bar and put the bottle to his mouth—held it pointing toward the ceiling—when I must have shown up in his peripheral vision. Now he was looking at me looking at him, and I was standing there like an innocent bystander who had walked past their open bedroom window, glanced in, and unexpectedly found them in a precious embrace. Our eyes swept past each other's faces as we both tried to ignore the other while assessing if the other *might* be looking. Some speeding passenger, thank goodness, bumped into my shoulder, and as I turned toward his disappearing figure to apologize, I saw my opportunity to move my feet—to extract my body from the sudden magnetized posture of standing in the middle of the airport hallway while staring at this couple at the bar whose happiness had transfixed me. I hustled away, hoping that the pub romancer had identified me as just another passenger who stopped momentarily to look in his direction.

It was just turning dark when I sat in the cab and gave my address to the driver. The traffic going into the city had not quite gotten heavy. It was nothing like this, Booby. As I looked to my left at the famous buildings highlighted majestically against the dark sky, their lights illuminating their white marble facades, I wondered when I would hear from her again. She had taken my card, but I had nothing on her—not even an address, I thought—as the cab driver and I dragged my gear to lobby of the building and I loaded it all on the elevator.

Inside my apartment, I dropped my equipment on the table and ran to check my answering machine. Nothing from her. A wave filled with both disappointment and tiredness slapped me in the face, and I fell on my bed after undressing quickly. I tried like a struggling swimmer fighting against a heavy undertow to stay awake, to relive her scent, her smile, her touch. But the undertow manhandled me, tossing me about as if I were jetsam, and it seemed that the more I exerted myself to see, smell, touch Chinita, the stronger the undertow became. I didn't awaken until early the next morning.

Chapter 4

"Welcome back, you have a call already," the receptionist said, handing me a pink slip of paper. "How was Idaho? And what's in the bag—you finally brought me back a present? How nice." It was only 8 A.M., Booby, and Chinita had called just a few minutes before I arrived at the office!

"It was Iowa, and it was fine," I told her. "Wilma, I need these rolls processed, and send a set of prints to Taney," I said, taking the message and giving her my film. "I brought back two whole bushel bags of some real sweet Iowa corn. You can have some if you wish. Take some ears out for yourself and leave this bag for Taney." I rushed toward my office. "Let me know if anybody else wants some corn; I have plenty!" I yelled over my shoulder.

I closed my office door, put down my camera bag, sat in my chair and stared at the pink slip. Her name was on the message. It was already 8:30, and an hour earlier in Iowa. As usual, Wilma had misspelled my name. My heart raced as I picked up the phone and dialed. A squealing tone told me the number was not in service. My heart skipped. I had misdialed. I put back the phone receiver in its cradle. Perhaps she was not in her office yet, or had taken a break, or was in a meeting. I picked up the phone, dropped it, picked it up again. My elbow sent the paper with her number sailing off the desk toward the floor, and as I dove to catch it, I banged my forehead against the edge of the desk. Now I was on my knees, the paper in one hand, the other hand on the phone, ready to dial. One palm against my forehead, I heard her voice.

How coincidental, Booby, that her tone was so much like the woman who has just called in to admonish Brian Smart's listeners. Inez's is calm, measured, but lively, suffused with a sensual intelligence. She calls

37

to bring our attention to the young brother who committed suicide last week. He had been indicted for income tax evasion and fraud. The woman says that he had been an honest young man who had been a star athlete in a celebrated Philadelphia high school distinguished for its legendary track team. He had won a scholarship to a college in Ohio. He had a wife and three children, was making a decent living as a stockbroker. After they sentenced him to 40 years in prison at the courthouse in nearby Virginia, he walked out to his car and shot himself.

The caller says she cried when she heard it on the radio. She didn't even know him. Her voice starts shaking. She says that we have to be more vigilant of our brothers who may be under tremendous pressure. She says that many, many white men who have committed similar crimes have served just a few years. Then they are out, laughing. But that brother who shot himself probably knew this. They drove him to this, she asserts, and by not staying in touch with him, we allowed his despondency to send him down the dark path of hopelessness and despair. She starts crying and hangs up on a truncated sentence.

Brian Smart first admits that he knew nothing of the suicide. He agrees with her that we must talk to each other more, but what I heard also is that sensual, intelligent voice from the woman caller—so much like Chinita's who chuckled, "My goodness," when I greeted her with, "I'm on my knees."

"What are you doing down there?"

"Just being silly," I responded, wondering if the knot I felt on my forehead was actually growing. "I was excited to get your message."

"I tried early because I will be in class all day," she said. "Maybe you can call me tonight? Will you have time?"

"Of course I will have time," I said, and wrote down the wondrous digits that composed her phone number. I repeated them twice to be certain. She said some things—about the weather, how she hoped I had arrived safely—but I comprehended nothing really, only hung on to the tone of her voice as if her emissions were chirps from a mating robin calling out to an already identified suitor—who was no other than yours truly.

"Is that you?—is the reception bad?"

"Of course it's me," I said, breathing so hard into the phone that she must have thought it was static. "So I will call you tonight"—cutting off the conversation it seemed. Why? Was I just too overwhelmed by the moment, the actual fact of her having called me, the actual continuance of this dream become actual? And then she was gone, having assured me that she was looking forward to our talking later.

I sat in the chair and looked at the wall of photographs ahead of me, about to review the conversation when Wilma called. "Mister Taney wants to meet with you at eleven. In his office."

"Thanks," I said, and pulled out the small Polaroid of Chinita and me, set it on the desk, turned it sidewise, put...yes, Booby, I did put my nose to the shiny photograph to test for a whiff of Goddess perfume that may have lingered. And now I am almost close enough to this car in front of us to put my nose to its rear windshield. What happened?...an accident...construction...? Now we are standing still again and a caller is agreeing with the woman whose voice sounded so much like Chinita's.

The first hour of that morning was pretty much unproductive until I received a set of prints back from a messenger. Several were quite exceptional, I told myself, especially the shots of Truman looking quite ambassadorial and dignified, some light splashing against the side of his face perfectly, I thought. And one close-up of the Plane slamming the ball through the net with a face of scornful confidence was one of the best sports shots I had ever taken.

When I took the elevator to Taney's office, I was still shuffling through several dozen of what I considered my best photographs. He was sitting in front of his picture window, his head directly in the center of the Capitol, the dome sticking above it like a crown. A spread of prints lay on his desk, and holding one in his hands, "Come in, my boy," he said, lips smiling with forehead creased in a frown. "Have a sit-down." It was his smile-frown of deeper thought. It seemed that the deeper his deliberation, the thicker the creases in his brow went and the farther the edges of his mouth spread. I had seen him smile-frown when contemplating which messenger service we should use, where his secretary should make lunch reservations, and which elevator in the lobby should open its doors first.

"I always like coming into your office. You have a magnificent view of the Capitol," I said. "Why don't you turn your desk so you can see it directly? I bet you have some great pictures from this angle."

"Then I'd never get any work done," he laughed, and frowning too as if he were surprised himself at the answer. "And no, I'm not a photographer, lad. You let me know when you want to, and I will arrange for you to come in and shoot as long as you wish."

"That would be great, Mr. Taney," I said. "Well I'm very productive since I have no windows in my office," I chuckled.

"Yes I'm talking to upstairs about moving you upstairs. It takes time. Hey, mighty nice of you to bring back the corn; you remembered that Alice loves sweet white corn. And excuse me, I always mispronounce your name once a day. Now," picking up a photograph, he continued, "here is the kind of image we are looking for. I'm talking to upstairs about putting this on the cover. This is Truman Washington." Standing up, he dangled it in front of his chest with two fingers.

It was a photograph of Truman Washington looking directly into my camera while biting on a fried chicken leg. His smile was huge, his eyes bright and shiny. "He almost looks like a clown in that shot," I said. "I was just warming up, testing the lighting."

"He is a clown," Taney said. "He talks like one, dresses like one—and look at those ridiculous sideburns—even looks like one. So why not show him the way he is. Let the country see that this is the joker who may be getting a special government appointment. He may be"—he turned to point to the Capitol—"actually in there voting! And he's a leader in the black community...ha!" Now a cloud passed over, darkening the room and his face so that he was a silhouette against the Capitol for just that instant.

"I was thinking about these two," I said, handing him the prints.

He sat down and smile-frowned at them. "Nice lighting, my boy. But I don't think upstairs will go for them...a bit too benign. This one makes him look too thoughtful—and that's not Truman. And this other one isn't so bad, but don't you think he appears entirely too serious, as if he's trying to solve a problem or something? Lighten up, my young artist, you need to get more humor in your work...more relaxation. Anyway, we'll see what they say upstairs. I gave them my recommendations."

"Oh," I said, "you mean you decided on the basketball flicks too?"

"Well those had more energy, I must say...lots of action, real dynamism. But I think upstairs will have some problems, you know." He stood up and put his hands in his pockets, jiggled some coins.

"I really liked this one," I said, holding the photograph with my fingers in the middle just as he had. "Have you ever seen a dunk so decisive?"

He stared at it, squinted. "Well that's the problem, isn't it? We aren't looking for a shot where he makes the basket. We just want to see him flying in the air. He's the Plane, remember? All of your shots show him after or before he has scored. We don't want to see him scoring. The country is not crazy about him because of his scoring. They want to see him flying...entertaining us. Do you see?"

Booby, I was so struck with disappointment that I simply stared back at him dumbly. "Yes," I think I see," I said, and gathered my prints from his desk to leave.

"Well, as soon as I hear from them, I will contact you," Taney said. "You know we go to press tomorrow, so we need an answer tonight."

"Okay, I will check back tomorrow," I said, my temples burning with disappointment. For the first time in days, I sensed a heavy cloud hovering over what had been a splendid sunny sky. Walking down the hallway back to my office, I glanced at the walls where framed covers of *Ontime* issues that had won awards jeered at me. My photographs were as good as theirs, I thought, but when would one of mine make the cover? Almost all of my shots for *Week* had made the cover, so what if it had been 20 years ago just out of college. I slammed the door behind me and collapsed in the desk chair. I looked around the walls at my photographs. Two were of Ahmad Mazique in his cell. One showed his head bowed between his hands, and the other head shot showed him looking upward at nothing, his beady brown eyes strong and bright. The dim gray tones of inadequate light blended smoothly into the dark black shadows cast by the ceiling bulb. Taney didn't use any of those. He told me that one of the top executives upstairs had become sick on production day and delegated authority to another manager who decided to use photographs of the policemen's wives.

"It would be a thematic conflagration if we had that Mazique guy on the same page with the mourning wives of those poor assassinated officers," Taney had explained. "So we had to bounce your shots, kid—sorry."

I was tempted to tear them off the walls and walk out of there—forever. Never come back. Just go. Good-bye, Wilma. I swallowed hard to fight a surge of despondency. But as I looked at Mazique, I felt a little better. After all, I was free, he wasn't. So recount your blessings, as my Aunt Clara would say. And they *were* great shots. I knew that. Look at the one of the boy's mother—her torn face filling the frame. Well I certainly couldn't start crying just because I was being rejected. I pulled out the Polaroid and reminded myself that it would be only a few hours before she and I would be in auditory heaven. And isn't this a coincidence, Booby; somebody has called in about the Mazique case.

It's a man who used to live in Annapolis, where we are headed. He reminds us that the jury that convicted Mazique was all-white. How can that be constitutional, he wants to know? What happened to a jury of his peers? Has a white man ever faced an all-black jury?

Well if you ask me, declares Mary who calls right behind Annapolis, she would fault those young white lawyers. The lawyers should have worked to keep Mazique from ever being in a courtroom with accusers who are all white devils. That's not saying that all white people are devils, 'cause she has been working for them all her life and some have the nerve to be decent and act like they got some sense. But you don't expect them to get together, surround a black man like vultures, and allow him to escape. So she faults those young kid lawyers 'cause they should know better. "Did they just start practicing? You got to have some sharp lawyers when you fighting for your life," she advises. "These guys sound like that Calhoun fool who was on *Amos n' Andy*."

And then, staring at my photographs, I realized that it was lunchtime and that I had not talked with Harvey since my return from Iowa. I called him.

"Well how was the convention," he asked.

"I will show you at lunch," I answered.

"Let me guess, tons of pictures of young women in long gowns."

"No, I brought her back." And after the silence and my laughter, I said, "I brought back a picture of my angel to show you."

"Show me a chick who's an angel," he said, "and I'll show you a dead woman. Let's meet at the Grille."

I picked up my camera bag, locked my door, and took the elevator. Outside, I hailed a cab to go over to Harvey's favorite restaurant near the university. He liked it because it was near the black institution that had been founded after the Civil War to train colored ministers. It had gone beyond that mission in its 150 years, and had produced most of the leaders who had been in the vanguard of the black liberation movement in the middle of the century. Their graduates had gone to the South to march against segregation, many beaten and imprisoned, a few even killed. Later, they had become doctors, lawyers, elected officials and executives throughout the country. Its faculty composed the largest collection of black scholars in the world, and the school was nicknamed the Hill to symbolize what its leaders and alumni considered the epitome of higher education for black people. "I go to the Hill" was always said with the most flippant insouciance by students, the assumption being that if you didn't know what the reference was, it was your fault.

One reason I had liked meeting Harvey at the Grille after arriving two years ago was that I had found myself captivated continually by the display of photographs hanging on the walls. The handsome faces of the distinguished graduates and faculty evoked not only sober determination, but also a mood of invitation to the onlookers who might harbor, they seemed to understand, some hesitancy about whether they too could accomplish similar levels of attainment. The warmth displayed in the parted lips and the intensity of the eyes was almost palpable. So too was the attention to fashion seen in one woman's cocked beret or the handkerchief sticking out of a man's breast pocket. I wondered how each photographer was able to capture that mood. Was it the achievement of the photographers themselves, or was it a combination—a union of subjects possessing unique qualities with the sensitive photographer able to capture that inner spirit? I told Harvey once that they were "beckoning shots." They beckoned you the viewer to come closer, to imagine entering the world of the subject.

I had become familiar with their reputations through my own reading and also by listening to the conversations of some of the patrons. One of the more flamboyant alums had become a United States congressman just after the war. He introduced legislation arranging for poor children to receive free breakfasts in school. His portrait showed a face almost as white as his summer suit. Nicknamed the Cat, he smoked cigars from a Latin American country, went deep-sea fishing in Florida, and was married to a glamorous singer who dazzled patrons in New York nightclubs. Clyde the manager said that he often plotted his political moves in a back room of the Grille. A section of several photos showed him smiling from a yacht—one where he is holding a fat cigar and standing next to a huge marlin hanging by fishing cords. The Cat looked as if he were the cat that swallowed the mouse. His hair was straight and glossy, a strand falling over his forehead.

One of my favorites is of the physician who had invented a surgical procedure involving the heart that became the standard used by doctors all over the world. A dormitory at the Hill was named after him. I loved the story of his meeting a young teacher while traveling to a scientific meeting, becoming instantly and insanely enthralled by her, and asking for her hand a week later. They were married four months later and had three children. He died in an automobile accident at a young age.

When I walked through the door, Harvey was in a group staring at one of the photographs that hung above the tables along the left wall. He greeted me with a handshake, then invited me to stand with the other three. Most of the Grille's patrons were students, alumni and friends of the school, and they knew who their famed and honored were. But Clyde the manager would often throw out a simple extraordinary fact to see if a student was familiar with it. If the student's response was not definitive, then he would offer a seminarette on the subject, ending with "you got to know your history."

This time he had captured two prisoners of edification, and they were looking at the portrait of a bearded professor emeritus.

One student had turned to face Clyde and was asking, "You mean he never came back to live in this country?"

"No, he was too strong and too independent," Clyde answered. "He got tired of the government's harassing him so he emigrated to Ghana and became a citizen. He died there. The justice department wouldn't even let his wife go visit him. But he wrote fifteen books, including one of the greatest histories of the Civil War," Clyde said.

Harvey and I left the three to take a seat near the back of the restaurant. I couldn't wait to tell him about Chinita, and pulled out the

Polaroid photograph. "Hey, I brought back tons of sweet white corn from Iowa; I will bring some over for you later this week," I said. "Don't bend it please."

"She looks young," he said, holding the picture and smiling. We both ordered the fried chicken special when the waitress came. "Kinda cute. I like the cheekbones; she got Indian blood or something?"

"She's gorgeous, she's the one. I feel like Dr. Werd," I said referring to the famous surgeon. "She could be my soul mate."

"I just don't see how your heart gets so fluttery so soon," he said, sitting back in his chair to stare at me. His freckles, since I had first met him in college, always made him seem younger. "I'm not even sure if I could fall in love," he said. "I guess I had my fling. Maybe that's all we get."

"We get what we go after," my Aunt Clara used to say." If you don't go after it, you can't get it. If you give up, you aren't in the game. If you aren't in the game, how can you win?" I held out my hands to mimic the portrait of one professor's photograph standing in front of a class. "I don't know why you didn't like that nurse, Evelyn."

"Yeah, I guess I'm not in the game and don't want to play—not that one, anyway," he said. "I've been so involved in the game of liberation. Maybe that has dominated my heart. Don't forget that the national medical association wouldn't allow Werd to be a member because he was black. Can you have love under any circumstances—even when you aren't free? Doesn't love require supportive circumstances"

"That's when you need it more, I think," I said. "We need something to comfort us at night. What makes life worthwhile? What can you take with you when we leave the earth?"

The waitress was young enough to be a student, and placed our dishes on the table gently. She smiled and danced away after asking us if we needed anything else. I watched her as she walked away, her shapely posterior reminding me of that night with Chinita. And uhmm, Booby, you talk about some collard greens and potato salad that's out of sight— you need to taste the food at the Grille!

"I'm still working on the case; maybe one more year to go" he said, "and those two students have just volunteered to help. We have more than a dozen. They're in the law school."

"I wish I could do more," I said.

"You are a big help. Where would we store all that paper if you didn't give us the space down there on the beach in your garage? So tell me, how was Truman Washington—you get some good shots of that turkey? You know I wrote him again asking for his help and he hasn't answered."

"Yes, but my editor won't choose the shots that I like. They will make a decision later today. They want to use a photo of Truman holding a chicken leg in his mouth, looking like a damn fool."

"They the biggest news magazine in the country; what they show us is what it is, right?" he chuckled with his eyes wide and bright. "Actually, that's not a bad idea. Did you get a shot of him scratching his head? Why don't you ask them to name it *OffTime*?"

"Well I will be talking to Chinita tonight, and I will tell her you said hello. Let me get back to the office."

"Oh please do. And try not to run up your phone bill too large. Tell her I can't wait to meet her."

When I got outside, I had to squint from the bright sun. I jumped into a cab that took me past the main university buildings where young black men and women were walking along the sidewalk with determined elbows pumping, intense about reaching their destination without interruption. As usual, I glanced to my left to catch a glimpse of the gates through which the graduates marched at commencement. In a few minutes I was in the downtown commercial district of office buildings and hotels. The *Ontime* Building took up almost a block along the avenue, a large announcement carved in stone running across the entry façade: ONTIME MAGAZINE: THE WEEKLY IMAGE OF TRUTH. Looking farther down the avenue, you could see the majestic Capitol. Its two wings were spread out perfectly symmetrical, holding the dome in the center. Near the bank of elevators was a bronze plaque the size of a large envelope that read:

Ontime Magazine
Part of the Nash Publications Group
A Division of Stash Communications Ltd
A Falsworthy-Asahi-Linares Company, International

Two months earlier I had first looked at it as an impressive display of corporate status and style, but now as I saw the elevator doors close, I was less impressed with it all as I considered that not one of my photographs had yet been published.

Wilma smiled at me as usual. "Have some good shrimp fried rice?" she asked.

"The usual fried chicken and greens," I said. "Has Taney called for me yet?"

"Oh, I'm sorry, he said that there was an emergency and he had to leave early. He told me to tell you that another manager was in charge of next week's issue and not to worry. Your two stories have been pulled."

I stared at her sitting behind her desk and then turned without saying anything to go to my office. My temples were throbbing.

"Sorry," I heard from behind my back.

Inside my office, I plopped my body down in my chair. I pushed it up to the desk and rested my forehead in the palms of my hands. I heard the cheerful voices of some employees walking past my door. I hoped that they would not stop, knock, ask me how things were going, and then watch me break down like a baby as I described to them my disappointment. I heard one of them mention my name and I froze. "Is he in his office?" one asked. Then their voices dropped to whispers. I tipped to the door and put my ear to it. But their steps took them farther down the hall.

I sat down again, grateful that the office was in darkness. Then another voice went down the hall asking a question of someone obviously walking ahead of her. It was light, bright as spring, and reminded me of Chinita. The voice became Chinita, a nurse pulling off the heavy despondent covers of an exhausted patient. I felt strong enough to bend over, reach into my camera bag and pull out the Polaroid.

There was just enough light to see her shimmering pink dress and the two bright, expressive jewels above her cheeks. And then her image itself became the caretaker that I needed, the reliever of sadness. I felt better. I would soon be talking with my angel. Oh, it seemed an eternity rather than hours since I had first viewed those features. They say that the best face for an artist to draw is the oval. Well I must insist that Chinita's rounded oval is even more alluring than the perfect oval. I began to talk to her using the words that I would use when we talked on the telephone later. I smiled, turned the picture at different angles. The world outside of the office—Taney, *Ontime*, the people whispering— meant nothing now. It didn't matter that they would not publish my photographs. She was reminding me that I needed to recount my blessings. I had her. We had each other.

Hours later, before I knew it, the consistent pattern of footsteps and chatter marching down the hall told me that the workday was over. I had spent the afternoon gazing at the Polaroid in my semi-dark office, asking and answering questions. I felt my lips part in smiles. Sometimes I raised my eyebrows at a peculiar statement she made. Once being so tickled, I slapped my thigh, then took a deep breath for fear of being heard. But I had had the conversation that I was about to have. I had been soothed by my earth angel's memory. And now, I thought, as I rose to get myself together to leave the office, it would be only a short time before I would be home—with her.

Chapter 5

I heard the telephone ringing when I got off the elevator on my floor. I ran the few steps to my apartment, fumbled with the door key, dropped it, picked it up, finally pushed the door open and grabbed the phone off the table next to the couch.

"I couldn't wait."

Booby, I was speechless for seconds. Could this be magic? Was it a dream or was it for real? I stared at the gray twilight filtering through my living room window blinds. I heard the car horns outside. I sat on the edge of the couch and then stretched out on my back to look at the ceiling of my own seventh heaven.

"I just got in," I said, feeling my chest heaving, my breath in labor.

"I left school early," she said, then giggling, "a family emergency. I couldn't wait until tonight to talk to you. That seemed like an eternity."

"Me either," I said, my hand rummaging through my bag on the floor to pull out the Polaroid. "I was thinking of you all day." I lay back down and held it in my other hand. "I'm looking at your eyes."

"I guess I'm just impatient," she said. "I hope that doesn't scare you"—a slight titter.

Oh, Booby, I heard and didn't hear. The magnificent quickness of the unexpected reunion had sent me up to and even beyond the ceiling at which I was staring. Was I Doctor Werd at the dormitory of his beloved where he had gone to declare his intentions? Was I Pushkin confronting his beloved Natalia? Antar singing to his Abla? Napoleon at the knee of Cleopatra? Would I be able to rescue myself from the numbing that overtook me? In other words, would I be able to speak?

That night we began a trek down an avenue of revelation and declaration that lasted for a month. Timid sometimes, we stopped to

47

reassure ourselves that we were in the right direction. Sometimes we stopped to regain our energy spent on an exhaustingly intense topic. We hurried at some points, eager to spill out facts and attitudes. At other moments we slowed to almost a crawl—tentative, probing. Yes she had moved to Oklahoma after graduating from college. Her great-grandfather had been a slave in a Native American tribe—the Cherokee. They set him free, and instead of leaving, he stayed and married one of the chief's daughters. So Chinita had Cherokee blood in her. "I'll have to show you some of the herbal cures he handed down to us," she said.

We talked for hours. I ignored the groaning rumble in my stomach reminding me that I had not eaten since lunch at the Georgia Grille. I ignored the darkness that crept over the room still since I had not turned on a lamp. What fantasies did I have? Never mind. What were hers, I queried, stimulated totally by her admission that she had wanted to make love in the back seat of a car. And outside in a park while lying under a blanket. "Could we do that?" her voice going as high as a blue jay's screech. How very certain I was of fulfilling those needs; she could depend on me, I assured her, my voice dropping to the low baritone of the master of ceremonies at the fateful dinner that brought us together.

Her good-bye was the softest *adieu* imaginable—a sweet expiring whisper of two syllables, the last of which floated and soared to—who knows? It melted away like a vapor that I could almost touch. My hand went out for it—only to hit the wall behind the couch. We would talk again tomorrow night.

When I sat up to look out at the living room window, I saw only the reflections of streetlights hitting the buildings across the street. It was three again—the same hour that I had left her in Iowa. I was both exhausted and exhilarated as I almost crawled to my bedroom.

I awoke to an energetic feeling of weariness. Half dead, I was at the same time enlivened by my new life as I looked at a clock that said I had less than 30 minutes to get to my office. One part of me wanted to stay in bed, but some mysterious resuscitating force flowed through another part of my body, pushing me on. I bounded out of my apartment building like a soldier streaking toward the front lines, the strings of my heart going zoom, zoom, zoom. I dodged a truck, saw the bus load the last passenger before lumbering down the street, and dashed after it. After chasing it for a block, my camera banging against my thigh, I stopped, out of breath and hailed a cab.

It was a wonderful early fall day where you could see the upper part of the Monument with its white capstone puncturing the blue sky. Along one wide avenue, the grass was still green and the end-of-summer tourists were still in bright colors as they lined in front of vendors to buy t-shirts, hot dogs, and caps. I couldn't remember when I had seen such loveliness in the city: the grass, the sky, the people, the swirl of it all combining to increase the zoom in my heart. The gray-white cement structures of the government buildings seemed more stately. I even noticed the date on one cornerstone and studied it as if I might be quizzed later. When the cab driver rolled down his window, even the fresh stiff air was more invigorating than I had ever imagined. When he pulled up to the *Ontime* Building, I walked with bouncing steps to the elevator.

"Great day, huh?" Wilma greeted me, and before I could answer, said that Taney was back and wanted to meet with me.

Still on the cloud that I had been floating on since the beginning of my telephonic rendezvous talk with Chinita, I strolled in as if all were well in the world.

"Where the hell did you get that damn corn?" He was glaring at me and standing with hands on hips.

"Uh, well...Iowa. I got a fantastic deal from a farmer. What's wrong?"

"My wife is at the damn dentist," he shouted. "What kind of damn corn did you bring back? The damn kernels were as hard as marbles. No human could eat that crap. Did you taste any?"

"Well no," I said. "I haven't had a chance. But I brought back enough for—"

His arms shot out, his palms facing me as if he were afraid I would approach him. "Don't give that shit to anyone. It's no damn good for eating."

"It looked...they said..." My heart was beating so rapidly that I started to take a seat in the chair and then realized that I was already sitting. I searched for words that wouldn't come.

"Some damn farmers sold you that fucking corn?" They use that to feed cattle!" he yelled. "They should have paid you to take it. They must be laughing all over Iowa at you."

I stood, feeling the blood rush to my face, my temples pounding.

"I can't believe that someone who thinks he is a professional with images got fooled like that. You want to produce images but don't know how to examine them. Don't you know that everything is not what it appears to be? You have to go beyond the surface to get the truth. You must penetrate the image. That's all we at *Ontime* are about, my friend. We go beyond the surface to get the truth for our readers. The trumpet of truth."

He smacked a fist in his palm while contorting his face in the most pronounced smile-frown I had yet seen. I felt both chastised and forgiven, depending on which part of his face I focused on.

"If I were you, I'd tell all of my friends to throw away the corn you gave them with such kindness."

I didn't bother telling him that I hadn't time yet to distribute my unpalatable fare. He might think that I had deliberately targeted his wife.

"Fortunately for you, I had already talked with upstairs about this new assignment before I learned that you were trying to kill Vivian," he said, now sitting eye level with me and the Capitol visible again over his head. "Are you ready for something really challenging?" he asked, the smile-frown emphasizing the forehead part of his face.

"I can handle it, chief," I said, feeling that my lack of sophistication about corn farming was not as serious a blunder as it had appeared.

"Sorry they couldn't use those Iowa flicks for this issue," he said, but there's a chance we may do another piece on Washington—heck, he's always giving a press conference about something—and we might need some background material. Now upstairs wants to do a special on the other side," he said in a lowered voice. "We don't have a writer yet. We need somebody who really knows those people and can get them to open up and tell it like it is. No reason why we can't get started on the photos now, I thought, and that's where you come in, my boy. Can you handle it?"

"I can handle it, chief," I answered, realizing that I had lowered my voice almost to a whisper too. "What kind of people did you say?" Excited, I was thinking already of how I would describe it to Chinita that night. I noticed too that the sunlight was coming through his wall of glass on the left.

"You know, those people on the other side. Now I want you to be careful now. All kinds of things take place over there. Get the pictures and then get your ass out of there, okay?"

"Gotcha," I said, rising. Then turning toward him as I placed my hand on the door handle, I asked if I could use his office later in the week to shoot the Capitol with my telephoto lens.

"No problem," he answered, turning to look at it. "Wilma has my schedule."

In the two months that I had been in the capital, I had not been to the other side. I knew that Harvey did some work in a counseling center over there somewhere, but I just hadn't gotten the chance to see that part of the city. I was eager, Booby, and the tunnel going there is just a mile from us as we stand here in this mess. An hour later and still energized by my conversation, I was back home and easing my car packed with my camera equipment out of the building garage. I drove around a traffic circle that I miraculously navigated without going around a second time, and was flying down the street that led to the tunnel, my head bumping the roof of my car as it bounced in the air after hitting a pothole. When I reached the tunnel taking us under the river, the traffic crawled to a pace that was even slower than it is today, Booby; stop and go, stop and go. But from the other side, cars came out of the tunnel at a velocity near the speed of light, as if catapulted by an unseen force shooting them out like slingshots.

The tunnel sloped downward into one lane of darkness. The white walls were smudged with exhaust that was now billowing out from the car in front of me. Was I in a channel of fog, and were those red lights blinking ahead of me actually those of a lighthouse beckoning a lost dinghy? And the rushing sound; was it of cars pushing through the tunnel, or was it the wind rustling over the sea? It was a hypnotic voyage of red and gray that I would have captured with my camera if I could have taken my hands off the wheel.

When I came out of the tunnel, I kept blinking my eyes to adjust to the sudden change. Had night fallen? I looked at my watch to see that yes it was early afternoon—just after lunchtime. The cars ahead of me—I now saw one in front of the one in front—had melted into the blackness—gone. I drove slowly down the gray two-lane road that continued straight ahead until it met the black sky blocks away. On either side of me, gray buildings next to unlighted lamp posts rose upward into that same black sky. I was at a corner when a car sped in front of me from my right to left so quickly that I had to jam my foot down on the brakes. Shaken by the near accident, I pulled over to the curb, parked between two cars, took a deep breath.

Then suddenly the sky was filled with thunder. But it had a strangely familiar syncopation to its clamor. And it wasn't coming from the sky; it was coming from—the buildings. As I peered toward the shiny windows bursting with volume, I recognized the beat. It was the sound of the Kid, one of the most popular entertainers in the world. It was his latest release, "What Did I Do," and it was being played on all the radio stations almost nonstop. Somewhere in those buildings—no, it was everywhere, in all of them—the beat bellowed out with his high-pitched falsetto as if the entire neighborhood had decided to play it simultaneously. Booby, I even tapped the beat out with my fingers on the steering wheel. The buildings seemed to be leaning from the combustible audio exploding within them, and I was fearful that one was actually falling.

I got out of the car and almost lost my balance from the swaying ground. I slid into the back seat. I loaded two cameras with infrared film. As my eyes became familiar with the darkness, I could now see the gray

that moved against the black. Three gray figures came running down the
street. In front was a tall woman, her hands grasping for the sky, her
shrieks sounding like back-up for the Kid's falsetto lyrics asking what
did he do. As I focused, I could see even in the darkness that part of her
blouse had been ripped away and her bra was a lighter gray. The two
shorter women chasing her had broomsticks in their hands and were
running with them as if they were carrying oversized batons in a relay
race. They caught her in the middle of the street. One pulled her by her
hair while the other grabbed her arm. Their words too were high-pitched
but together had the cumulative effect of drowning out their victim's
wailing. They pushed her to the ground. I squinted at the thought of her
knees striking and scraping against the cement. The sticks went up over
their heads and then down with the rapidity of carpenters hammering
nails. Each strike produced a more resonant, distinctive wail from the
woman on the ground.

My brain was trying to recall where I had seen the movie before.
Had not civil rights workers in this country and black freedom fighters in
South Africa been struck like that? Had not our slaves been whipped
with the same rhythmic preciseness? But had it not been the authorities
usually who had brutalized *us* with those striking movements? The raised
arms with the stick came down, then up, then down. Had we picked it up
from them? And had it now reached the point that our women too were
comfortable with the flailing that prompted the wailing? I may have used
an entire roll of film before two large male figures jumped out of a
passing car and chased the attackers away. I was out of breath just
watching it all and feeling somewhat guilty that I could do nothing to
help. My heart pounded in near-fear as I reloaded my camera and
replayed the scene in my mind.

Then as if dropped from the sky, on that same side of the street, a
shiny gray vehicle crawled along the road behind another so slowly that
they both seemed to be stationary. They stopped. The car windows were
blacker than the sky. And from the same sky, gray figures fell from and
descended upon the automobiles. Some of the figures had come out of the
building entrance in front of which the cars had parked, walking with the
same brisk pace that I had seen the students at the Hill employ. (Were
they moving to the beat of the Kid's song? I tried to see their feet.) Some
suddenly appeared in front of a black tree as if they had been bark peeled
from the trunk. For a second I was looking through my high school
microscope at jelly-like amoeba. Another figure scared me as he appeared
suddenly in my peripheral vision to the right, racing from a building and
slapping my hood as he squeezed between my and another car to get
across the street. A line formed: five, six, seven figures converged on the

two cars, whose drivers rolled down the black windows so that the exchange could take place. They pulled away and another set of cars came behind them. It was too dark to tell for sure, but it seemed that tiny flashes of silver chrome belonged to a line of dark cars spread down to the next block.

Shooting it all from the safety of my parked car, I both applauded myself and cursed myself for my good timing. In a matter of minutes I had witnessed two electrifying scenes that would yield the most captivating photographic coverage. Taney could not possibly be anything but elated when he saw the results. But at the same time, I hated that the power of the photographs depended upon such violence and lawlessness in the community of the other side. I eased out of the back seat to the sidewalk. I crept toward the passenger door, got in, and like a drunken driver, leaned my forehead against the steering wheel and maneuvered out of my parking space. I drove down the street slowly, peering out for the first opportunity to make a U-turn. At an intersection, two cars zoomed in front of me from left to right this time, the beat of the Kid blasting from their windows. I prepared to turn at that corner, and as I did, my headlights caught the little figures frozen in the middle of the street. Booby, it looked like a caucus of Teddy bears. I braked, and they ran across, their bright eyes flashing in front of my headlights. I pulled over to the sidewalk.

"Hey mister, take our picture," one of the four shouted as I got out of the car.

"Jawan, you crazy. That man ain't studying you." He pretended to hit Jawan over the head with a lunch basket. They all laughed.

"Let me get a few shots, gentlemen," I said, kneeling to their level.

"Okay, get this," said one, imitating a dance step that I knew was called the ladder, made famous by the Kid. He raised his hands and knees as if he were climbing, his little hips twisting, his babyish voice blurting, "what did I do—ooh—ooh" to the beat that still encircled us like a musical tent.

"Bunsy, you can't sing. Hey, watch me do the stilt," said another chubbier figure, sliding his legs backward and jerking his arms as if they were made of wood sticks.

"What grade are you guys in?" I asked, shooting furiously as they danced and joked and hit each other playfully.

"We in the fourth, but Alex ain't gon' get promoted cause he not good in English," said one. They all laughed and turned toward Alex, who stood with his thumb in his mouth.

I patted him on the head. "He'll be all right," I said, standing now that I had put my cameras back in the bag.

"What kind of camera is that?" Jawan asked.

"It has a special lens for darkness," I said. I was in the car now, their faces framed in the passenger side window.

"Why you need that—is it dark out here?" one asked.

"Well..." I fumbled for an answer, realizing that to their eyes, all was perfectly visible.

"He uses a dark room to develop the film. Don't be dumb, Jawan," said the chubby one.

"Right, you guys are really smart," I said, thanking him silently for the answer.

"Where you from, mister? You live around here?"

I told them where my apartment was located, and their eyes bulged. "You rich," said one, expressing the feeling that they all seemed to share.

"Not at all. Just got a job guys. Hey, I have to go, now you all be good," I said, starting my engine. "Thanks for the photos."

They stepped back, and just as I was about to take off, Alex, standing farthest from them on the sidewalk, waved and shouted, "Hey mister, what's a gentlemen?"

The others laughed and hit him. "I told you he gon be in the fourth grade next year again," yelled one, waving at me.

I drove slowly past the line of cars being serviced with their eager street attendants. I eased to an intersection and stopped just in time as two gray vehicles zoomed past the black space, the thumping bass of the Kid's song vibrating from their roofs. Then beyond the next block I saw the tunnel entrance with a crescent of green lights at the top beckoning at me. I was so relieved I wanted to wave in thanks, but in my rear mirror saw a driver behind me impatiently speeding up. Inside the tunnel, it was all bright, with shiny white tile walls, gleaming divider lines in the middle of two lanes, sleek fluorescent lights in the ceiling. The ground was smooth as glass, and leaving the other side back to return to the capital was one of the fastest, smoothest rides I had ever had. All I heard was the comforting swish of our tires over the glass road.

The sunlight that we drove into at the end of the tunnel was almost too bright for my eyes. The exuberant mix of colors—the green grass, the sapphire sky, the gray buildings—almost shocked me. And the surround of sounds had a different timbre—a metallic jangling of car horns and police whistles. It looked, sounded like another country almost after the three hours I had spent within the bleak dreariness of the other side. Eager to see the shots, I hustled out of my car after garaging it in my assigned underground space and took the elevator straight to my floor.

I pulled out the rolls and placed them on my desk. Each was coded—seven in all. Two were of the kids. I stuffed the other rolls back in my bag and went out to see Wilma.

"I heard you had a dangerous assignment," she said, taking the film from me.

"It was okay," I said. "Get these done and send a set up to Taney for me please." I was already thinking ahead of my evening with Chinita.

"Were you scared?" she asked as I was walking out the doorway. "I hear it's like … uncivilized."

"Yes, I was scared," I answered. "When I came through the tunnel and saw all those traffic police with guns, I got really concerned about my safety." I looked straight at her before closing the door and walking swiftly down to my office. I nodded at two reporters coming toward me, ducked into my office and sat down. It seemed as if I were reliving a scene I had just left—the dark office, the sense of isolation, the shadows of footsteps outside my door. I hadn't had time to digest what had happened that afternoon; no time to reflect on how I had felt, what it had meant. I knew my heart had been racing most of the time while on the other side, that I had been overwhelmed with a mixture of fear and excitement. It had been frightening, yet I had been there and captured it with the creative bliss of some journalistic voyeur. The contrasting moods swirling inside me were confusing, especially since they were mixed with—well, disappointment.

I heard them whispering outside—this time in fast cadences about "danger" and the "other side" and "brave." I opened the door quickly, saw them almost bumping into each other like misdirected waiters. I nodded at them, saying "I'll tell you tomorrow" to their queries, and skirted down the hall. I was intent on releasing my tension in a few hours with the long-awaited talk with my angel.

Booby, it took almost an hour to get home. You think this is traffic! I had only to drive up Sixteenth Street for ten minutes usually, but I was in standstill traffic. And every other corner had a different hindrance. Fire trucks blared by one intersection, shaking the street with their red lumbering mass as a police officer in the middle of everything held up a white glove that warned us not to proceed. The blinking marquee lights on an ambulance announced that both the man on a stretcher and the one standing and holding a bandage against his bleeding forehead had starred in a tragedy of colliding cars. And just as I thought I was within minutes of my apartment, a snowstorm of feathers fell from the sky and landed on my windshield.

"It's a damn poultry truck up there!" a driver in the other lane shouted at me. "They ran into a light pole and chickens are all over the damn street. Jesus Christ!" As we crept up the street, I saw chicken wings flailing frantically as two men chased after them with a burlap bag the size of the ones I had brought back from Iowa. Their out-of-control truck was on the sidewalk and leaning against a tree now in danger of falling. Part of the sign on the panel could be seen—**Maryland Poultry Farm**. But the letters below it were obstructed and only said "**Since 19.**"

Easing very slowly around the mayhem of cackles and car horns blaring, I drove the final blocks to my apartment without incident and was finally sitting in my comfortable spot on the couch, my heart hammering against my chest.

We began with our laughing hilariously at my stupidity.

"You didn't actually buy all of that corn, did you?"—her voice squealing in delightful disbelief. I could visualize her lying on her bed in a white mesh gown, her knees up, her toes giggling in twitches. "We use that dried stuff only to feed the cattle." I heard for the first time the guttural weight of her tender voice—deep and more substantial than the tones of us from the East.

I was lying on the couch again, my eyes staring at the ceiling, and I reviewed the day with her. It was the same recline I had used as a teenager talking to girls I had just seen in school hours earlier and who were now captured in a private conversation that no one could interrupt. Each word, sentence, paragraph brought me closer to a binding connection between her and me. I told her about being on the other side, the women chasing that helpless girl, the drug dealing, and finally the fourth-grade boys. She wanted so badly to see those photographs of the boys.

"Oh, they sound so precious," she said, "just like the sweet little innocent kids in my classes. Well, most of them are sweet."

"Yes," and those are the only photographs that I will show Taney," I said. "I'm not showing him the shots I got of those women chasing that girl and then beating her almost to death. And I'm not showing him those shots of the cars rolling up from suburbs all around the district so that they can buy drugs."

"No, you shouldn't," she agreed. "Keep them."

We explored ourselves as if each were attached to the other in that and every successive conversation. Each time I felt that I was returning to a soothing and calming nest that was impervious to the clanging disruptive world beyond. I was eager, willing, trusting; not cautious, reluctant, suspicious. I thought of us as the robins and blue jays and cardinals that I had tracked as a boy in Oakbury. How they darted around each other, running up branches, preening, chirping in glee at the phenomenon of their togetherness. We too flitted gleefully in our own world, holding hands over the phone, thousands of miles apart.

On some evenings I held the telephone close enough to the radio so that she could hear the Tender Force. The lyrics were composed especially for me. I dismissed the fact that everybody in the city who thought he was in love and too needed a break from the hard-driving rhythms that dominated our airwaves was listening to the show. You didn't hear any of the Kid's dance tunes here. Instead, we heard the Penguins, the Dubs, the Flamingos, the Larks, the Wrens, the Orioles. But now *I* was a Penguin, a Dub, a Flamingo. They were my songs, for me, by me. I sang the lyrics with them, for Chinita.

"Oh, what a voice," she giggled.

Each song, in a continuous string of sentiments, expressed the rhapsody of my heart. One had me in my highest pitch calling her my earth angel and asking her to be mine. I would love her all the time, and yes I was a fool—a fool in love with her. Or I asked her why my heart was all aglow. Could this be magic? If so, then magic was love. My voice took on the young high school whine of the lead in a group featuring a thumping piano in the background when I asked if she was a dream, my long lost dream. Or are you real? With another group, I declared that love finally had walked in and said hello. And finally after all these years, my heart seemed to know and spoke back. I stood up holding the telephone as if it were a microphone, my shadow on the wall that was the back of the stage. I sang with intense conviction that she had flung her arms around me and brought me peace of mind. I dropped to my knees and sang with the group, my arms stretched out as the Spaniels had stretched out theirs to so many screaming women in orchestra seats throughout black America. I ended my concert with that expression of peace of mind, one knee on the floor as it would be were *I* the lead singer.

It was that peace of mind that hovered over me when Taney called me in to discuss the photographs of the boys. "Not enough energy," he fumed. "What else did you get?"

"Nothing," I said. "It was so dark I could hardly see."

"Upstairs wanted to show the real story. The despair. The gloom. These kids look joyful. The readers won't believe it."

"Why not?" I asked. I was amazed at how calm I was. I couldn't feel the blood coursing through my body as it had when he insisted on using the pictures of the police wives. My feet weren't tapping on the carpet, my fingers weren't twitching as they had when nothing about Ahmad Mazique's death-row shots pleased him. "They seemed pretty happy to me when I shot them."

"Well, we are trying to be patient," he said, the odd combination of facial features falling in a shadow as he leaned back in his chair. "But you haven't given us what we find to be the essence of our great mission here at *Ontime*." As I got up to leave, he looked at his watch as if signaling that time was running out.

For weeks I floated through the two worlds. One was a dreamscape that Chinita and I soared through as vacationers. The other was a world represented by anything that interrupted our journey, as if we had settled on a beachhead to picnic and were suddenly looking up to see washed-ashore fishermen who would not leave without burdening us with details of their ordeal. I was enjoying such peace of mind that I only half-listened to those from that other planet. I saw their hands gesturing, their eyes gazing, but I did not really comprehend. Half of my mind was occupied by a tenant far more enticing.

In this dazeland of half consciousness when I knew I was there but was not fully there, as in some cloud zone of pre-wakefulness, I had no firm grasp of my dislocation. I only enjoyed it as a harmless state of inebriation.

"She got your mind," Harvey said at lunch as I shared with him my luxurious yet confusing sense of languor. "I just don't see how you can get your nose bent out of shape so easily. Anyway, we are making progress on the project, I want you to know."

I hardly heard him, my mind drifting in half consciousness like a nomad through time and space. This time we were secreted in a half-lit booth in the back of the Grille. No one could enter without our seeing them walk through the glass entrance door. Several students with briefcases would march toward us and interrupt our conversation by placing a file folder of papers on our table, nod at Harvey, and leave. Alternating between dreamscape and reality, I saw them and didn't.

"Sweet as honey, don't you think?" I said as I unfolded the letter from Chinita. "These lines are classic. And how many women would take the time to pour out their heart like that?" I re-read in a low voice those entrancing lines from her first *billet doux* scented with Goddess that she must have dabbed on her ear lobes just before sending it off. My hands had shaken on the day that I pulled it—no, *ripped it* would be the better term—out of the envelope as if I had been expecting a message verifying my winning a lottery.

Her letter was a string of poetic sentences bequeathing her soul, her life, her undying commitment to me. An electric tingling went through me. I had never received such a letter before from an adult woman. Oh yes, Booby, there was that four-page missive of doubtful authorship from Grace who presented me with four beautifully handwritten pages (Miss Thump had always checked *commendable* for penmanship on the back of her report card) torn from her three-ring notebook. I say doubtful because her protestations and declarations sounded far too mature for the mind of a nine-year-old. But Chinita's avowals had that quality of unmistakable genuineness. When Grace had written, *I pledge my love with all my hart,* I began to perspire. She had drawn a tiny heart in red lipstick just above her signature.

"Very nice," Harvey replied. But he refused with a smile my offer to let him sniff the letter.

With no real assignment during one week of my dreamscape, and Taney out of town for several days, I decided to take advantage of his offer of using his office. And Wilma assured me of his plans. "I want to use my telephoto to shoot some pictures of the Capitol," I told her.

"Oh sure, he told me that you could do that," she said, exhibiting a smile that highlighted—had I been so oblivious before?—cheekbones even sharper than Chinita's. "Is there something wrong?"

"No, I was just wondering...nice earrings," I explained, redirecting my gape toward another part of her face.

"My grandmother's," she smiled, and then, moving around me to leave the office, "they are solid opal from South Dakota. She was Native American. And so am I," she said. "I'm not white." We stared at each other for a strange moment.

"Oh. I didn't know that. But we hardly have time to talk around here, everybody's so busy. And I'm trying to get transferred to an office with a window."

"Yes, I know. Sometimes I think they are all hiding or something," she giggled. "Funny, I thought all the offices had windows."

"Well you can stay if you wish. I won't be distracted." I adjusted my tripod and set my camera on it and started focusing my telephoto lens on the Capitol building.

"I'll just sit here quietly if you don't mind," she said, the large leather chair exhaling.

"Well I won't be long because I've got to get back. I've got an important phone call coming in."

"Oh, I bet she's really special."

"You remind me of Chinita, which is why I was staring at your cheeks earlier," I said. "Her grandfather was raised by the Cherokee."

"That's a beautiful name. I bet she's crazy about you."

Adjusting my lens to get a closer view of the Capitol building, I began to focus on the top of the dome. "You know, I never really looked all the way to the top of the dome," I said. "It's a beautiful bronze. And let me see what else...looks like a helmet on her head." I focused even closer. "A headdress maybe?"

As I shot at different angles, I heard her voice uplift, rising: "She's a Native American. It's the Statue of Freedom. On her crest are symbols of my people—an eagle's head, feathers, and talons."

"She's Native American?" I asked, focusing now on the strong features of a bronze face topped by a helmet.

"Of course; don't you know your history?" The direction of her voice told me that she was standing up. "It was built before the end of the Civil War. The Southern politicians didn't want to use any references to freed slaves as the statue designer wished, so they settled on the Indian woman. I thought everybody knew that. Doesn't she look Indian?"

"Well, she does have strong cheekbones," I said as the frame of my viewfinder covered the top of her helmet to her shoulders. "And I do see an eagle and talons."

"You sure have a thing about cheekbones," she said, and we both laughed. "I'd like to have some copies of the pictures of her face if you don't mind. They aren't easy to find. Actually, I've only seen a few in a history magazine. "

I used almost four rolls of film before I was satisfied with my coverage of the Capitol. I had started with the widest angle, catching the wings that stretched out from the center. Then I narrowed down to headshots of the woman herself. A stream of large cotton ovals passed over her at one point, but I had a mostly cloudless session. I sat in a chair to pack my gear and was putting the last roll of film in when Wilma rose.

"Shall I send them to the lab?" she said, standing over me with her hand extended, a silver ring on one finger. "You know, Taney always says that he loves being able to see the Capitol from this office because it reminds him of what this country stands for. I think it may be the best view in the building," she said.

"Well, I think I got some good shots."

"Is this for a story, or you just wanted to add to your own portfolio?" she asked.

"No story. I never pass up the opportunity to take advantage of a great perspective. When I first came in here and saw that view, I promised myself that I would capture it."

"Well have a great talk tonight, and don't worry about the pictures. I will take total care of them," she said as I went down the hall to my office. "Check with me when you come in tomorrow."

When was the next day? I continued to thrash about like a butterfly in a whirlwind, able at some moments, somehow, to inject levels of lucidity into my daily movements.

"Well, try not to get hit by a moving car. I know you are in a daze," Harvey told me one day.

When I photographed the woman that a team of large firefighters carried out of an apartment building on a stretcher, I narrowed my viewfinder on the sadness in her cheeks and puffed lips. I did shoot two hefty uniformed men perspiring, grunting, "Phew." Yet I barely heard the bystanders' sardonic queries about her predicament.

"Now that is just too fat. Couldn't even get out her own bathtub."

"Damn, I didn't know you could call the fire department for that."

"Who else could drag you out?—the Marines?"

And even when Taney expressed his disappointment, I saw him through a cloudy lens, feeling nothing like the crush of disappointment that I had experienced during other moments of criticism. "Nice if we were doing portraits," he said, eyebrows jumping. "But I don't see how you could give me four rolls of film of a woman who is so damn fat she got stuck in her own bathtub and you don't have any shots of her big-ass body for us. People want to see the whale woman, maybe the biggest female in the capital. That's the image *Ontime* owes its readers. But no, you do some headshot of her pretty little cheeks. And who cares about the damn firefighters unless they are struggling to carry the obese bitch. Upstairs is not happy with this. "

But the piece of mind hovering over me had reduced the impact of his disapproval. I sat, nodded, stood and left, walking down the hall and deliberately ignoring the prize-winning photographs draped along the walls, and merely nodding at the half-dozen staff members milling around the hall as I put my hand on the doorknob to my office.

No matter, Booby! Later that evening Chinita and I determined that we were soul mates. I was not the same, I could feel it. I was not alone. An expansion of self had occurred, obliterating the *me* and appending the *us*. I described the effect that sounding her name had on me—as if a chord had struck my insides; of how, thousands of miles away, I felt her vibratory warmth. She admitted that she too had been struggling with the same dreamscape, the same upended perspective on the world. She had floundered in the parking lot of a mall for half an hour because she had forgotten where she had left the car. "Oh, it was terrible," she moaned, "my feet were killing me." One morning she went to school without her wallet—left on the kitchen table—and "had to borrow money from the principal himself. How embarrassing, and it's all your fault." Giggling. "Look what you have done to me!" Yes, she had received my letter and loved my declaration of undying devotion (*You are the one I need; I am the one you need.*) "Oh, it was so sweet, I almost cried," Chinita said.

It was if, she said, we had known each other before. Maybe it was the time before anything. We could be reuniting, she offered. Yes, I agreed, separated some eons ago from you, I am now rescued from aimless floundering like flotsam discovered by a navy.

"I want to marry you," she said. "I told you I was impatient. I want to spend the rest of my life with you. Will you?"

"Yes," I said. "Yes." I screamed it out a third time, Booby. I stood and clenched my fist and gritted my teeth. "Yes, yes, yes."

I heard her voice far away, as far away as the eons that had separated us, asking if I was all right. It was a muffled set of metallic syllables way over there in the telephone receiver that I had thrown to a corner of the couch. I was jumping up and down, waving my arms like the cheerleaders in high school.

"Are you there?" crackled the little voice.

Chapter 6

We are making some serious headway here, Booby, if this traffic is really picking up as I think. We will soon be on the pike, and then maybe an hour to the beach. I can't believe it. Look, I'm actually pressing down on the pedal. Sit up so you can see. There's the motel and the car dealership, and now a young girl holds a bouquet of roses for sale while standing in the middle of the street.

I had done my own series one weekend on the young girls selling flowers in the downtown area of the capital. I didn't realize that they had come so far beyond the city to stand in the center islands of busy two- and four-lane highways like this artery to the pike. Looking at her shiny black hair and yellow face in my rearview mirror, I wonder if her parents fear for her safety. Suppose a driver wanted to make the light and didn't see her and couldn't stop in time? I don't think the parents fear. If they did, how could these little girls be out here?

Farther in the city that Saturday I had found them—all girls of color—brown, tan and yellow—on street corners and in parks. Their eyes had different compositions too—oval, wide, somewhat closed. They all seemed to smile, especially when a pedestrian exchanged cash for the small packet of roses or tulips or lilies. But the smile came from the mouth, not the eyes. The lips turned up to form the thank-you automatically, as if practiced. But the eyes themselves did not twinkle with the glow of genuine elation. They were sad innocent eyes, the eyes of the poor and hopeful. I stood with my shoulders against trees or buildings, in the shadows of their commercial exchanges, and used a telephoto lens that brought me close enough to put their eyes in the center of the picture.

It wasn't the mood that Taney sought. "We want to show

opportunity, success for all," he told me. "These poor things look almost desolate. Remember, my boy, that we are the biggest news magazine in the country. People consider us as *the source*. They depend upon us to know how to…to think about matters. We can't let them down by showing them contradictions to the values."

That last caller listens to Brian all the time and wants to congratulate him for an outstanding show. But he wants to know if they will let Washington get the special assignment. That other caller asked about where our leaders are. Hell, how can we have leaders if we have to wait for the white man to appoint us? "That's messed up with a capital *f*," his low-pitched voice asserts.

That Asian little girl reminds me of how excited Chinita was when she got the roses I sent to her at school. She said that she put them on her desk and wore a smile all day as the students kept asking her about the man who had sent them. And now a proposal! I didn't sleep at all that night as I reviewed our plans through a foggy lens of half-sleep. We would meet in the Windy City, go to the courthouse for the ceremony, and spend the weekend there. Then we would fly to her home in Oklahoma to meet her parents and stay for a week. From there? We'd decide on the rest from Oklahoma.

After I parked in the *Ontime* garage the next morning, I was hit with a strange combination of exhaustion and vigor. I felt as if I had barely enough energy to make it through the day, but at the same time I sensed a surging current of vitality that must have been sparked by adrenalin flowing through me. I even smiled at one of the staffers in the hallway who held up in front my face the cover of the recent *Ontime*. He had never spoken to me before. It featured his photograph of two politicians holding a shovel together to commemorate the groundbreaking of a new building. "Very nice work," I said as I ducked into my office. "Congressman Jones?" He whispered an assent with a broad smile.

The phone rang as soon as I opened the door. It was Taney's voice, not Wilma's, and he wanted to see me immediately.

She had a strange smile on her face when I walked by her desk to enter his office. I could see that his forehead was struggling with his mouth as I entered. "Good morning, young man, and I see you got in perfectly on time this morning. I like that. He lifted his gaze toward the ceiling, and the frown seemed to overshadow the erupting smile. He leaned back in his chair. "Got some good shots of the Capitol while I was away, I hear."

"Yes, Wilma was quite helpful. I haven't seen them yet. Thanks again for the opportunity."

"I saw them." He stared right at me, his eyebrows directing the upward movement of the rivulet of streaks in his forehead.

"I haven't seen them yet," I answered.

"So you didn't have any special plans for them; good. They aren't the kind of shots we need," he said, pushing some prints across his desk in my direction. "What do you think?"

They were all close-ups of the Statue of Freedom. "They look like the mood I was trying to capture," I said.

"Mood, hell. Look at the woman's face carefully," he fumed without a smile. "It's amazing. All this time." He looked out the window to my left as if he couldn't bear to watch my reaction.

"Nice shadows," I said, holding one in my hand.

"She's not an injun, you may have noticed. All these years I thought—the whole damn country thought—she was an Indian. Turns out she's a white woman."

"That's a problem?" I asked.

"It's a problem of image," he said. "A white woman doesn't show how open we are. How we adore freedom. How much we honor the Indians and their traditions. Thank God everybody won't be pointing a telephoto lens–or worse, binoculars—up there to see the truth. Let's hope they just continue to focus on the eagle and talons and stuff and connect it with those redskins." Now the forehead frown lines dissolved while the corners of his mouth pulled his lips into smiling crescents. I hadn't seen such a smile-frown in weeks from Taney. "I haven't told upstairs anything about this. I think we need to keep it quiet, don't you? I'm suggesting"—taking the photo gently out of my hand as if I might damage it with fingerprints—"that we lock these valuable photos in the archives. Since you have no special use for them, we can always get copies for you." Since the other part of my mind was actually calculating if I had received enough credit on that flight to Iowa to get a reduced rate for my imminent trip to the Windy City, I nodded my head in agreement when I heard him ask me, "Don't you agree?" And then: "Is everything all right?

"Oh yes, sorry. I was thinking of my trip to the Windy City. I was planning to put in for a short leave since I have been working on Saturdays."

"How much time do you need, my boy?" He stood with his hands in his pockets.

"Maybe a week," and before I could retract the word thinking that perhaps it was a few days too long for one who has only been employed for a few months, he had called in Wilma to instruct her to put in the paper work. "And oh"...the three of us walking out of his office and stopping at her desk..."I mentioned to them about getting an office with windows. Something might break soon for us on that matter." It was the softest of whispers, his hand on my shoulder as it would be on his closest confidant. He squeezed it too. "Take off early if you like, and have fun, my boy. I love that city."

I smiled, facing them both, my hand on the doorknob to the hallway. "Thanks, Mister Taney," I said, and closed the door. I walked briskly down the hall, for I had plans to make—airline, calling Harvey, packing. When I got to my door, I saw Wilma coming toward me on my right. I waited, then we went in.

"My goodness, there are no windows in here," she said, closing the door behind her. "Who's next door?"

"I don't know," I told her. "We have never met."

She held an envelope. "These are the negatives," she said.

I stared at her.

"Taney asked me to take the negatives back to the lab after he looked at the pictures. I thought you should have your own negatives, so I switched them. I gave the lab those negatives of some politician at a groundbreaking. I labeled them, *Statue of Freedom*. These are yours," handing them to me. She giggled.

I laughed too, taking the envelope and putting them in my camera bag.

She had covered her face with her fingers as she laughed with me. But she was still laughing after I had stopped. Wilma was wiping her fingers across her cheeks. They were wet. She moved backward and leaned against the door. "I thought that woman was one of me, a Native American. I wanted to see my people at the top of the dome. That's what they told us. All those years I thought she was my sister. She's just another American white woman—the kind you see everywhere. They didn't care about us when they built the Capitol."

Then she turned and left so fast she seemed a shadowy image that had disappeared. The last thing that I saw was her bent elbow.

I sat down and faced the closed door. There were no footsteps or voices in the hall. I was tired, in a swirl of confusion and elation as I picked up the telephone to call Harvey

"Going to the Windy City? Today. She proposed to you? And you said yes? Well I guess I have just about heard everything," he said. "I'll tell you one thing—you never give up on romance. How long you known her—a month?"

A few hours later I was at the airport preparing to board the plane to heaven. I had been staring absently at the loading and landing information when I saw the figure running toward me and waving his arms. I heard Harvey call my name. My mind leaped ahead to imagine the unimaginable—some event of catastrophic magnitude that he was about to report. Had I done something to cause my apartment to go up in flames? As I pondered another possibility, he spoke, now a foot away, almost out of breath: "You got everything?"

"My wallet? My film? My shoes?"

"You got a ring, dude?"

I had not thought of a ring, my thundering heart yelled at me. Harvey led me over to a seat and pulled out the little box from his jacket. A sparkle of light flew out from the diamond. "Here's the engagement ring I gave to Sandra. And this is the wedding band. I didn't hear you mention anything about a ring, so I thought I'd better check. Well I guess you can't think of everything in your condition." He had a huge smile on his face, the freckles glowing.

"Thanks man, you are a true friend" is all that I could say, and then the boarding announcement blared over our heads as we stood for a second looking at each other, our eyes locked. We hugged. Then I spurted to get to gate B7.

I sat looking out at the men loading luggage onto conveyer belts as the pilot's voice welcomed us and suggested that we keep our seatbelts buckled since slight turbulence was expected. But after laying my head against the window, I remember only a smiling flight attendant handing a can of juice to the man in the seat to my left. I was soon in the daze of sleep, barely able to appreciate the lights illuminating the Capitol and the Monument. When I awoke, the buzz of voices that had sent me to dreamland had dropped to a hush. I was thrown suddenly to my right as if I were lying on my arm. I was no longer in a plane but on a boat rocking and rolling over very rough waves. In the rear I heard an "ooh" from a woman, followed by the skitter of plastic glasses dropping to the floor. It was only a half minute of turbulence, but it brought me back to wakefulness as if I had rolled from a comfortable mattress to frozen floorboards.

It was a good time to put things in perspective since I was fighting through a fog and trying to answer the question of where was I. It was late Friday morning, I remembered, on my way to the Windy City, the largest metropolis in the Midwest to re-meet my angel for the first time since we had met weeks ago; it was meet that we meet, I chuckled to myself—perhaps audibly since my neighbor to the left turned toward me with a blank smile as if I had addressed him. "Oh my father will kill me...us..." she had said—was it just hours ago when she said that as we made our plans? "But he will understand. I always get my way. And he will love you," she assured me. I let my back relax into the soft comfort of my reclined seat and the consistent hum of the plane droning through the skies. She would be at the airport. She had made reservations at a large lakefront hotel that gave copious discounts to teachers. "Just remember that we are with the International Theosophical Society," she giggled. We could get our license at city hall and have the ceremony performed just a few doors away in that same building. We needed to get there Friday afternoon before they closed at 5 P.M. Then we would be man and wife. "I do," I practiced, visualizing the room as we were asked to buckle our seatbelts and prepare for landing.

"Did you say something?" asked my neighbor. He was pulling his bag from overhead, preparing to go down the aisle.

But it was her voice that was in my ears as I walked around the baggage area amid hundreds of arriving passengers. I looked for my Chinita, her eyes, her cheeks, her colors. I passed a young lady sitting at one of the baggage bins. I looked to the left, toward the doors and rental car booths. Then I focused my eyes straight ahead, searching each face that moved toward me. I was about to look to the right this time when the vision of the young lady whom I had just passed came back to me. I stopped and turned around. I stared and searched my memory. It had been weeks, and I had probably spent no more than a few hours in her presence. My Chinita? I walked toward her. Her eyes were searching the faces of hundreds. I walked closer. Her eyes brushed over my face and then turned away to look again in the distance. I had made a mistake. But then her eyes came back...to me...to stare. She jumped up, her face exploding in a bright sunshine of recognition. She ran toward me. I held her.

Both of us at once: "I didn't recognize you." Then giggling.

I squeezed her hand in mine—as tightly as I had when we walked toward the photographer in Iowa. We strolled out of the airport toward the shuttle bus. After weeks of telephonic encounters relying so much on imagination, I now craved as much physical contact with the corporeal Chinita as possible. I felt a charge through her fingers, sending electrical currents of happiness through me. On the bus, we squeezed our hips against each other while holding hands. She nestled her head in the crack of my neck as we looked out the window at the overcast sky. "Thank goodness for that National Neophysical Society convention," she sang. "I got us a great weekend deal. I wonder if we should dress like saints?" We held hands when we checked in at the desk ("Nice to have you, attending the formal ball tomorrow?"), as the elderly bell captain with the stooped back rolled our luggage to the elevator, as we got on the elevator, and as we patiently waited for him to unload our two bags, open the shades of the window, describe the location of the ice machine, point to the river and buildings of the Windy City beyond the large picture windows ("Looks like rain, you think?"), and finally close his palm on the dollar bills that I offered him. When the door slammed shut behind his back, we grabbed each other.

It was our first kiss since we had met. She was an earth angel who had to be held gently, but I was a famished seeker of her essence. I wanted to squeeze her physical soul into me and squeeze myself into her. When I placed my lips against hers she twisted her hips to readjust our togetherness. Our lips brushed against each other. Then she opened her mouth as wide as you would to scream for help, exposing a wet, luscious and warm passageway.

As we had on the phone, we traded turns directing and following. She breathed hard, short intakes, the anguished moaning of one in pain. She pressed herself against me, her hands behind my neck. Her tongue circled over mine in one direction, then in the opposite. She sent her tongue up to taste my palate, then brought it down to brush against my teeth, then took it to the side to explore the insides of my cheeks. She groaned playfully, as if she had been transformed from angel to mischievous tantalizer. She was different, powerful, almost demanding; and yet submissive, yielding.

And I? At first my tongue danced with hers, enjoying her sorties and following her lead as if we had reversed roles in a tango. But then I felt a rush of dynamism, a need to slow her down and reverse the momentum. I moved back one step, saw her open her eyes—they were weak and wild at the same time—and began my own foray. It was my tongue now that searched everywhere while I stared into her pupils. Oh, Booby, did I kiss her. We stumbled drunkenly, our feet with a mind of their own, knocking over a lamp, crashing into a wall, and finally falling on the bed with our clothes tossed to the floor. When she suddenly pushed her hands against my chest to look at the clock, it was: "Oh my goodness, we only have an hour before the marriage bureau closes!"

We jumped up to hear the thunder that we had not even noticed. Our window of the lake and downtown buildings was a speckled rectangle of raindrops against a mouse-colored sky. I was tempted to photograph the pattern but knew we didn't have time as we tripped and grabbed for our clothes—laughing at our ridiculous behavior. I wore a blue suit, she a white silk dress. Running ahead to the elevator, she whispered loudly, "Come on, silly, you will be late for our own wedding."

Downstairs, we accepted a hotel umbrella at the insistence of our new friend, who scurried along with us through the lobby. Breathing hard, he blurted out a melody: *"I'm gonna love you, come rain or come shine."*

"Very nice voice," said Chinita, pulling me toward the revolving door.

"Thank you, ma'am," and then in the next breath, his voice intoned deeper, *"Oh I wish it would rain..."* I placed some bills in his palm that he slid in his pocket with the practiced speed of a magician, never breaking stride while uttering "Thank you, sir."

We ran through the rain and traffic of the Windy City and reached city hall with thirty minutes to spare. One groom was dressed in a tuxedo, while his bride in white carried a bouquet of roses and never stopped smiling as we parked ourselves on a bench waiting to be called. On the other side of the room, another couple sat staring at the baby in their arms. They took turns tickling his toes sticking out of a blue blanket. In minutes we were standing in front of the magistrate (Chinita's new rings on her finger) and he was pronouncing us man and wife. We kissed and hurried down the hallway past the rooms and clerks who earlier had stamped various items of official minutiae: applications, certificates, licenses, followed by a looking behind us to utter: "Next please."

At the top of the broad steps of the municipal building we looked out at the rainy Windy City. Leading straight ahead from us was a wide avenue banked by buildings reaching up to the darkening sky. The avenue went straight from the city hall through the city. Cars and trucks, hampered by the weather, bobbed up and down the avenue in a slow consistent crawl. Immediately below on the sidewalk, people scurried in both directions, in some cases turned about by a wind that spun them and their umbrellas. I pulled out my camera to catch this panorama of rain, traffic, buildings and pedestrians when a voice from behind us asked, "Take your picture?" I turned to face a young man in a dark suit. He pointed at us. "Would you like me to take a picture of the two of you standing in front of city hall? I can stand here and not get your camera wet."

Booby, it's a shot I don't have anymore: smiling Chinita on my left in her white dress. In my blue suit I'm standing with my hand around her waist. The cavernous oak doors framed in glass and brass are behind us. Our wedding picture.

We had to hold on to each other going down the steps. The Windy City was now the Windy City indeed. Later we said that the wind had slapped us silly, because we couldn't stop laughing as we battled our way down the street. The unrelenting gusts became our opponent in a boxing match, jabbing and pushing and spinning us around. We found ourselves suddenly in the doorway of a jewelry store: the salesman beckoned us in with wildly waving hands. We grabbed onto a light pole at the corner with three others holding on for dear life. We reversed our direction twice because our umbrella had been turned inside out. Each episode prompted a new burst of laughter as if we had been thrust onstage in a comedy. At the same time the rain splashed our faces and formed puddles in the street that prompted a glee club shout from us and others as we stepped in it.

We were still laughing when we returned to our room. The thunder sounded like canons in a battlefield. As I sat by the window pulling off my wet socks, reciting a rain scenario and watching her on the other side of the room pulling off her dress—her head covered, her elbows pushing against the edges, the dark spot of her navel like a little camera lens—I suddenly stopped in mid-recital. She was an actress behind the curtains backstage. She was half in shadow, unseen by anyone but me. I became struck by a beauty that seemed more than beauty. It was a beauty on display for me. And we were each other's—for life. Then she had wrestled off the dress and thrown it on the bed. "This thing is all wet," she said, raising her eyes that locked into mine. We shared that burst of recognition, the abnormal reconnecting that we had talked about on the telephone. For a flash of time I was transported with her to some other sphere.

Without any clothing now, she walked toward me. The rainy Windy City had turned into the stormy Windy City. She sat on my lap, her back against my chest. We looked out at the rain andlightning, my lips against the hairs on her neck, my hands supporting two warm treasures. The window was perspiring with streaks of water. "Poor thing looks as if it is crying," she said, turning to kiss my cheek. Beyond its foggy pane was a landscape of purple, blue and gray sky. Intercepting it ahead were buildings poking through the dark like icebergs. On the left was a lake fogged over and surrounded by barely visible parks and trails. The buildings ahead and to the right were an architectural cafeteria. In some parts of the city we could see a plaza stuck between two towers. Atop one building were four huge silver antennas reaching toward outer space. Another tower was not a straight rectangle, but designed instead with curves as if the architect had wanted it to have lobes. Some windows were tinted with bronze. The columns on some were black aluminum. Only one had a band of white lights near its very top encircling the entire building. It was a marvelous view—the metropolis under attack by the elements. This wasn't the capital where it was decreed that no buildings could be larger than the Capitol itself. This was the big city, "a huge monster," in Chinita's words. The city, according to the poet, of big shoulders.

When the zigzagging streaks of lightning sliced through our canvas of night, Chinita rose to look out from the corner. She stood in blissful amazement. She was in shadow and sometimes not, her body striped by the bands of light. I rose to get my camera to capture her, the sky, the buildings. Each movement was a different pose. She leaned over to look downward. She stood bent with arms resting on knees to look ahead. She turned toward me, her back eased against the corner, her knees up. When she crawled along the narrow window ledge, I captured the tense beauty of the muscles in her thighs, the firmness of the lobes below her hips.

Eventually the swelling tension overtook us. We needed relief—like the confined pressure in a volcano releasing itself in an explosion. We had had no sleep for a day, had traveled, had staggered through a maze of offices, had trampled through the rain, and now had tingled sensual nerves on the verge of eruption. We were driven by a hot-blooded need to be together. We had created our own storm of thunder and lightning within us. We sensed our agreement on this instinctively with a look. We hugged, then held hands as we approached our wedding bed.

Chapter 7

We awoke in the morning to a light hazy sky, the sun half hidden. Her back to me, we were both facing the window, my nose relishing her new sensual fragrance—that of a woman who has loved, been loved, slept and awakened. It was an appealing tang of body flavors, of perfume worn off but still lingering. Its pull was not in its freshness or daintiness, but rather in its heavy, profound warmth. What an entrancing newness, our first night sleeping together, the electric moments radiating still in our hearts. With that thought, I gave her a quick tight hug, then freed my hand to roam down her hips.

"This is such a huge city; I don't think I could live here, could you?" She held my hand up in the air, making circles.

"Oh sure, I love the big city," I said.

"Only for a visit. I would get lost trying to drive. And so many people, goodness. I'm used to wide open spaces. What shall we do with the little time we have? We leave in the middle of the afternoon."

We decided on a museum. In the hotel lobby, I had picked up a flyer describing sights
and scenes in the city and saw that the work of "the region's pioneering new photographic talent" was being exhibited nearby.

"One day you will be bigger than all of them," she said. "You will be the most famous photographer in the world. I can't wait to see some of your pictures. You must be incredible."

I hadn't brought any of my portfolio with me. I hadn't thought about the fact that Chinita had never seen any of my work. "Well, you can see what I shoot this week. I'm sure the pictures of you will be splendid."

"I told my parents that you are a photographer, so be prepared to take plenty of pictures of them. Mom loves to pose. Dad does more than her," she giggled.

I watched her as we both dressed and talked as if we were old friends reunited after a long interlude. I was so intrigued by her movements. Her forearm made a V as she combed her hair. After she kneeled to pull up her panties, she snapped the elastic and winked at her attentive husband. While bending, her breasts swayed just enough to send a surge of joy through me. Oh I had seen it all before, Booby, but hers was a special concert, a command performance I could watch for hours.

Can you believe that we are finally on the pike? Well almost. There is the sign for the fork up ahead. To the right is "Beaches and Other Areas," and there are few cars indeed in that lane. Thank goodness. Come on now, sit up, it won't be long.

When Chinita and I got to the elevator, the door opened to a packed-together group sporting large plastic nametags on their chests. "Plenty of room," boomed a voice in the back, to which all giggled. Before I turned to face the buttons on the door and hold Chinita's hand, I saw that he was tall and the others were all women. "Going to the lunch session?" he asked. "Swami Vendaratha was great last year, I can't wait."

"We didn't like him," I said over my head when we reached the lobby. "Did we?"—turning to Chinita as we walked backward looking at their astonished faces. "We may hold off and just go to the workshops in the afternoon."

"Which one—is it Nanpreet?" The raised hand was from a wide woman in the back flank of the frozen-together Neophyscalists. "I love his workshops!" she said, pushing the others out of the elevator.

"Yes," we both answered at once, still holding hands. "We'll see you there maybe," and flew past the reception desk (our favorite doorman, back to us, was lifting a new arrival's bags onto a cart). "Have fun at lunch," waving to the throng.

Giggling through the revolving doors, we heard one of the female voices: "Which family are you with?"

We practically skipped down the wide avenue, our sweaters perfect for the autumn morning's soothing breeze. The streets were shiny and half dry from the night's storm. We stopped to look in some of the windows featuring the latest fashions, jewelry, furniture—all having price tags that made Chinita exclaim. From our left, rushing out the glass door of one famous department store was a woman in black cradling a white poodle. I had seen their ads in *Ontime*; in fact, she reminded me of one. Dark glasses covered her eyes. One hand went up in the air. Her fingers danced; two scintillating stones erupted like tiny pieces of fire. At her waist were three bags, the name of the store emblazoned on the side in their unique script. A man in a black suit and cap appeared at our right from nowhere and opened the door to a black limousine into which she melted behind black windows. "God, did you see those diamonds?" Chinita pinched my arm. "Don't look back, but did you *see* them?"

Then from the corner we spotted the tufted tails and short coats of two huge lions, their bronze turned greenish with age. Each stood—twice as tall as life—on either side of the stairway entrance. Two toddlers were trying to climb up a slippery foreleg of the nearest wildcat. Flags above the entrance announced the show of new pioneers and an upcoming exhibit of abstract revisionists. At the information booth a lady directed us to the second floor.

"Oh, it's absolutely stunning," was the first voice I heard as we got to the top of the steps. We moved behind her and her companion to look also. It was a-black-and white scene of …pipes? Yes, barely visible in the dark, I recognized two pipes rising out of the floor and curving to the base of a…sink.

"Ingenious," said her companion, bending his head to peer closely. "She's on to something spectacular." He read the title: "*Pipes Under Sink.*" He turned to look at us, his voice falling into an enraptured whisper: "Just marvelous; here, come closer."

I read the essay introduction to her work that hung on the wall next to the first print. She wrote that pipes were an integral part of our heritage and deserved to be viewed reverentially. We could not continue to restrict our vision to the practical, to plumbing and heating only, she insisted. Pipes were metal, but we not should fail to consider the reality of their spiritual mettle.

Immediately to the left was a photograph of several smaller pipes with the circumference of cigars lying in the bin of a hardware store. Above the bin was a sign:

Screwed Female Rods
Half price!

Continuing to our left, we stopped to view a photograph of a water pipe lying on the ground and covered with blood stains. Its title? *Murder Weapon.*

"They certainly are different," whispered Chinita.

"Quite," I answered. "Let's walk around them and look at the other photographers," I suggested, taking her hand. We went to the opposite wall where nobody was standing. From afar it looked like a blur, and when we got close enough I saw that, yes, absolutely it was a blur. It was called *Train 166,* but there was no discernible coach, locomotive, caboose or the like. It seemed as if a train had sped by the photographer as he was shooting and left a blur—some vaguely perceptible horizontal trail or ribbon of diaphanous gray. Just to the side of *Train 166* was the photographer's vision statement where he premised that understanding "how to see through, how to understand the nature of transparency was an issue of Himalayan importance in our optically challenged society." We looked at each other.

"What does he mean?" asked Chinita. And then she looked around the room. "I'm not used to this big city perspective. Is that how the great photographers think?"

"It's their way of looking at the world, I guess," I said.

"What a different world view they have. I don't like their attitudes," she said. "But I guess I don't know that much about photography—yet," she said, punching me in the stomach. I followed her as she began to walk along the wall, passing the other photographs of blurs. Stopping to turn in a circle, she said, "I mean, why aren't there any people in these photographs? How could I bring my fourth-graders here to teach them about the rhythms and spirit of nature?"

I was about to say that it would be a difficult task when we turned a corner to enter a smaller alcove. A family of three was looking at a wall of photographs—of people! We picked up our pace. The little girl was between them, holding their hands for support as she practiced various acrobatic maneuvers. When her legs went up in the air as if pumping on a swing, we went to their right to look at a photograph they had just passed. "Oh thank goodness," Chinita heaved, "I think I see a human being."

It was a human, and the photograph was part of a series. The camera man had traveled through three states to capture the images of these people. He employed similar compositions in each photograph. Explaining his special calling to produce these symbolic views, the photographer declared that only by asking his subjects to pose as they had could he dare think that he had produced a series that elucidated the modern dilemma. They were "metaphors for our society's current imbalance and uncertainty."

"Delfina, please!" begged the mother. Then she looked in our direction with a flushed face. Her young Olympic hopeful had turned herself upside down in a handstand and exposed her panties. Her shoes were in the air at Dad's stomach level.

"But Mommy, the man in the picture is upside down. I can't see his face unless I look from the floor."

Her mother made noises with her mouth and looked at us for sympathy, while the father folded Delfina up in his arms with soft sharp words, one of which I'm certain was *spanking*.

We smiled at the mother and walked past them to the end of the set. "I can't believe the only pictures of real people are these with them standing on their heads. He went all over the place asking people to stand on their heads?" She and I had walked past a half-dozen of the photographs symbolizing our lost society and were nearing a circular flight. "I think I know the problem," she said, holding my hands as our footsteps echoed down the wide marble steps. "Even when they put people in the pictures, there is something lacking," she maintained.

"What would you say it is?" I asked, excited by our first conversation about art.

"There is no soul," she said. "Mechanics and technique are splendid. But I don't feel any soul—no emotion." She shook her shoulders as if hit with a chilling breeze. "The heart, the feeling is missing. I'm your soul mate because you have my heart. Soul and heart are inextricable. Let me tell you one thing, my darling..." We were standing at the entrance looking down at the lions on either side. She turned and faced me. "Nobody has more soul than you." And pressed her lips against mine.

Well, Booby, I felt like Hannibal having crossed the Alps—a real hero. And that's how this guy passing me on the left is driving—as if he's going up a mountain. He really needs to slow down.

"I just want to say this to all the listeners," offers a woman caller from northwest. "I've been here a good little while and I know more stories than O' Henry and I tell you it just didn't start today. Y'all young folks may think this is new but it ain't new at all. Have you forgotten about those nine boys they say raped two white girls down there in the Sip? That was seventy-some years ago. Come to find out those lying skank hussies were whores with syphilis! Ruined those poor boys' lives; in jail for decades."

"She's right. That was a big case, I remember reading about it," confirms a male from southeast. "If I remember correctly, their attorney was a specialist in real estate who was drunk when he came to court. And the press...God, the newspapers had them guilty before the sun came up. It does seem to present a pattern, I must say. I have to agree with the other caller."

"Hotep," greets a new caller.

Brian returns the salutation, "Hotep my brother."

"I wish to remind those in the listening audience that even today beyond our local area there are incidents that don't receive widespread exposure in the oppressor's media. A brother was beheaded just the other day in the old confederacy. Then they tied his body to their truck and dragged him for miles. He was attacked for no reason other than he was by himself on a lonely road at night and was accosted by some hillbillies."

While Brian Smart takes a commercial break I see that the sign says 20 miles to the beach. Booby, we are almost there!

Almost there. Almost there. That's what I was thinking on the plane from the Windy City to Oklahoma later that Saturday afternoon. By the time we had left the museum to return to get our packed bags from the hotel, the sky had turned anthracite and getting darker. "Don't run into no tornadoes out there," our doorman friend had warned us with a raised eyebrow and a smile, pocketing the last dollars he would ever receive from me. I looked out from my window seat of the airplane just after the voice had announced moderate temperatures and overcast skies. It was all dark, and I was glad that we were almost there.

"It looks really messy out there," my new angel wife, my sweet Chinita said, leaning her head against my chest. She was wearing Goddess. "Don't you want to take some pictures of the blurred black sky?" We chuckled.

"No, I don't think I have enough metal for background," I answered.

"That was some show. I must admit that I have never been to a photography exhibit. Are they all like that?"

"Well, yes and no," I said. "Many are. Some photographers have no soul as you say. But as you can see, that doesn't stop one of the most important museums in the country from supporting them."

"Are you nervous? Your hands are rather moist."

"Somewhat," I said, reliving in my mind the picture of the short loving father and doting mother that she had described to me. I had a murky vision of how I would live up to my responsibility to announce that we were planning to get married when in fact we were already married secretly. Had we been man and wife for 24 hours yet? Then on Sunday before leaving we would pull out the ring and announce that, well…we were married secretly. If at dinner, should I be careful that neither was chewing food? Should I be certain that he was not using his knife? Or would we be facing them in the living room—they on one side, we sitting on the other? How would I begin—*I have an announcement*? I practiced clearing my voice. Did I have to tell them both at the same time?

"I will explain that we can plan a big official ceremony later—maybe around Christmas. But this is something I had to do," she rehearsed. "Look Daddy," she practiced, "you and Mom got married when she was only 16."

"But was it a secret?" She didn't answer me.

"You look great in that blue suit, darling—my mother's favorite color. Don't worry, they will love you, trust me. Here, hide the band in your pocket. Didn't I get us a great hotel room at the convention rate?

Trust me." She giggled. "The National Neophysical Society. I didn't even know they existed—did you?"

But I didn't look as good as we had thought, Booby. When they met us at the airport and Chinita introduced me, he asked, peering at my pants: "Is that the new style back there, wrinkled suits?"

"Oh, Daddy, we got caught in the rain and were having so much fun we didn't even notice our clothes were practically ruined. Look at my slacks—terrible."

"Is that the new style back there? I just love that navy blue,"—the voice was behind him. Her face stuck out from behind him like one playing peek-a-boo. She shook my hand with warm earnestness, then half-disappeared again. Chinita's mother was as tiny as a grade schooler, the top of her head reaching almost to his shoulder height. "Doesn't Nita look fresh and healthy, hon? The air out there must be good for her."

He had gotten a new pickup truck, and we would all have to squeeze in the cab together. He was as short as I had expected, but wider; skin the color of sand, lips that barely separated when he spoke. One hand stayed in the pocket of his overalls jingling coins. The hand that shook mine was hard as stone. We tumbled along shoulder-to-shoulder in his pickup truck, my angel holding my hand, my other shoulder against the door, my camera bag between my legs. "Some talk about a tornado coming through here," he said, peering ahead at the two-tone sky: The top band was a bright azure, while the bottom layer was as dark as the inside of our truck. I saw that the branches on the trees lining the road were bending over far enough to touch the ground. A low-pitched shrill sounded over us as we sped forward.

"The sky is practically black," Chinita said, looking ahead, squeezing my palm.

"We put some canned goods in the cellar, just in case," her mother told us. "And your brother called today. He's thinking of taking acting classes."

You think this is traffic, Booby, you should have seen the bare streets we were driving through that night in Oklahoma. I don't think I saw a total of four cars.

"The weather report didn't say anything about..."

"They never do," Daddy interrupted her. "Tell the truth, Rosalie. They either scare us too soon and it doesn't come, or they don't tell us in time. Or like the time they didn't say a wink and all white hell broke loose."

"They never do, that's true. Now, Norman, let's not go back to that again." She rubbed the back of his head. "Chinita and her handsome young friend are here for fun and relaxing, not to review the past with you. Keep your eye on the road and watch we don't get hit by a falling elm."

"There's one right there, sir!" I tapped him on the shoulder just in time as he swerved to the right and I looked back to see a tree crash down into the street behind us. It was tossed so violently by the wind that it crawled to the other side of the street as if its branches were arms and legs.

"We are just a few blocks from home, don't worry," he shouted as a squadron of tree limbs flew past the windshield of our swaying truck.

"We are just a few blocks away," her mother assured us again.

"Old Bessie will get us there in good shape," he said, patting the steering wheel. "You know I got this from one of my customers who couldn't pay his bill. Been the best truck I ever had. You can't beat a F100 Ranger. Except for a little rust on the pass and a door scratch on the right rear panel, perfect shape. Floor pans in excellent shape too. I rebuilt a roller 302 and then installed a speed pro cam and then changed the transmission to an automatic C6."

"Oh Norman, hush, we don't understand a word you're saying," said his wife, reaching up to pat the back of his head. "But didn't you have to coat that floor pan with naval jelly?"

"Daddy's the greatest mechanic," said Chinita, squeezing my hand.

"Next week I'm working on a beautiful Dodge Monaco. It's a four-door hardtop with a four-hundred cubic inch double-barrel. I don't know why he won't let me install a four-barrel carb, you know? Did I understand that you in the film business? I heard tell of some guys going out photographing tornadoes. You ever do that?"

"He's never seen a tornado, Daddy,"

"Well good. And, Chinita, you know what happened? Last week I worked on a Monte Carlo. Hadn't seen one in a while. It was in great shape, V8 engine, 350 horses. Remember when you were a little girl and went looking under the hood for those horses?"

"She sure did look for those horses," her mother chuckled.

He slowed down after turning onto a narrow road where the water seemed to have risen above ankle level. I saw the outlines of one-level homes on each side, shuttered and darkened. A telephone wire dangled from a pole in front of one.

Then Chinita's father was leaning to the right and turning his truck into their driveway with, "Here we are; made it. You two run inside while we bring in the bags. Go straight to the cellar."

"Oh Daddy, we only have two bags, Mom and I can take them." They looked like two sorority sisters returning from a night of drunken carousing as they held on to each other fighting the wind—one a foot taller and leading the older. They would take a few steps forward, be blown off balance, then make another advance until finally grabbing the handle and closing the storm door. From inside the entrance, they smiled and waved at us.

I was pulling my camera bag off the cabin floor when I felt his hand on my shoulder. "Get in; we'll come back."

As he reversed his truck out of the driveway, I looked up at the darkening sky. "Do you think it's coming soon?" I asked.

"Oh we could have a couple of hours, I think," he said. "Then it could pass right over us. That happens too."

"Let's hope so," I thought out loud, holding on to the door handle as the truck rocked side to side.

"I guess Chinita told you that my great-grandfather was Cherokee," he said, thank God keeping his eyes ahead as the tires sloshed back up the narrow road leading to the wider street. Each of the flat boxes of homes we passed now looked as if they had been long deserted. But I guessed that they were filled with families who had gone to their cellars with good supplies of canned tuna, bread, and Bibles. We curved uphill, then down. As the road flattened out, we were surrounded on both sides by open fields. The sky hovered over us like a giant black tent. "The troops chased my people off their land in the Southeast and forced us Westward, along the trail of tears. That's how we got here. Great-grandfather Sam was a black slave owned by the tribe. Although he was a slave, he was still allowed to mix in with the rest of the native culture. He fell in love with an Indian woman, Window Lemon. They got married, and so the chief made him free. She had long braids and a part down the middle of her head. I'll show you her picture when we get back.

"Then my grandfather became a partner in a bank in the city down there"—pointing to what I thought was the downtown area—"and was doing real well. The whole area was composed of blocks and blocks of black businesses. I have pictures of the post office, homes, stores, restaurants, offices, and churches we owned. Everything was just going great, just great." He stopped the truck and stared at me.

"What happened?" I asked.

"The white woman," he said, tapping his fingers on the steering wheel, his face forming a silhouette in the window. "She said that a black shoeshine boy hit her in the elevator. The police arrested him. Next thing you know, the newspaper runs an editorial saying he should be lynched. The white people went crazy, ran through the town and burned down everything that belonged to black people. Everything. Thousands. Homes, churches, businesses…my grandfather's business." He started up the engine. "Grandpop and hundreds were killed."

"I'm sorry to hear that," I said, fumbling awkwardly to straighten the handkerchief in my breast pocket and aware that it was a useless but necessary statement. I sensed that each recall simply mixed up and recirculated the bitterness within him.

"Just remember that if they hadn't burned down that section of town, I'd be in the banking business, and you and Chinita would have a great wedding present. But I'm not a rich man, young fellow."

"Married?" I said, looking straight ahead trying to suppress the thunderclap in my chest. I sat forward; maybe my suit jacket was getting wrinkled.

"I know my baby. She has never looked or sounded so happy in her life. Don't think I don't know what you two have gone and snuck off and done. You think you are the first to try to fool some parents?"

"Well...we..." I started

"I bet she was the one to propose. Girl ain't got no patience, always trying to be in charge. Not like her mom." The tires rattled over a short bridge, the curved arches disappearing into the sky. "Well, the important thing is whether you can take care of her," he said.

"I've been at the magazine for a few months," I said, "and they are considering moving me upstairs."

"I don't mean that," he said, and turned a corner that led us to another tunnel of darkness. It was a narrow two-lane. I heard the wind whistling and the loud scraping of tree branches smacking each other as if in battle. "The old tradition says that the man must prove to the father that he is worthy of the daughter. On the plains, that meant that the young man proved that he can hunt." We slowed down and he peered to the right like a driver looking for a house address on an unfamiliar street.

"Who me? I've never been hunting," I said, wondering if he meant tracking for live game in the nearby woods. "Well, I did have a BB gun as a kid," hoping this would corroborate my confession and disqualify me. "Maybe I should change out of my suit," I said, remembering that I had just bought it after my first salary check from *Ontime* and worn it exactly twice before—at a reception Harvey invited me to on campus, and at a dance club we visited and never went back to. Now I looked at my wrinkled pant legs and wondered what the rest of the jacket looked like.

"To hunt you must be courageous and fearless. That's more important than how many deer you bring down." He looked me in the eye. Then with a grunt that signaled his satisfaction with our location, pulled to the side of the road and brought the truck to a stop. The wind continued to shake us like passengers on a train snaking through an endless set of curves.

We left the truck to take a narrow path that was littered with kindling and brushwood, sometimes holding on to a tree trunk for balance. I followed the short trudging figure as he bore ahead resolutely. When he stopped, we had gone about 20 yards. He pointed down to a stream. His mouth was open wide enough to shout, but I couldn't hear him. Did he think that we could cross the stream? I tried to shout back that it was too deep, but he had started down. It would be up to our shoulders. But something kept me from turning back, something was pushing down the rush of fear flowing from my feet and rising to bang against the center of my heart. There was no path now, just some space, places to plant your feet one after the other. Then in some swift movement faster than the blink of an eye, he was on the other side leaning against a wide tree trunk. He looked over, waving at me with those short arms.

I took a deep breath and went down to the edge of the stream. I closed my eyes and raised my right foot, ceremoniously holding it for a second as if to memorialize my bravery, expecting to fall into cold dark enveloping water that he had magically sailed over and...I came down on hard ground. I kept walking. And walking. I opened my eyes. It was not a creek after all, just the optical illusion caused by the strange light from the sky that had turned a stretch of high grass into an undulating substitute for flowing water. I was walking on grass.

A few feet away, I saw him smile at me, cup his hands and shout, "Very good! What took you so long? Let's go." Then he spun to the left and was bending over to brush away the bushes in front of his face. I bent forward to avoid a low branch and followed him.

We had two more challenges before the tornado rose up in full force. The path he took led us to an open area—a desolate park except for some picnic tables turned over and a waste can rolling and spinning on its side. This time Norman walked up to the edge of a small pond, its dark surface surging and foaming. He went ahead of me and lifted his foot. But instead of sinking quickly to its depths, he walked across, once pausing to beckon me. So I took another deep breath and, with closed eyes, followed. It was not a pond, my feet told me, but a huge shiny tarpaulin that had been thrown over the ground to protect an athletic area. Again, instead of sinking to the bottom of depths I had only imagined, I was walking on level ground with a plastic covering.

"Not doing bad at all!" he yelled, although only a few feet away. Breathing hard, heart pumping, I nodded.

But the last challenge. On the other side of the pond was a brushy clearing that led to another road. This road just ahead and its sky was not quite as dark, perhaps because the wind had accelerated, sending my handkerchief out of my pocket and up like a kite, as if a hand had come and snatched it away. As it rose up against the background, the road had the appearance of something thrown against a landscape painting. It snaked through the center of the painting from the bottom of the frame to the top. On the sides of the painting were black telephone poles, the lines whipping up and down like jump ropes. From left to right, the sky was moving and alternating its color between violet and orange. Chinita's brave father began to run toward a couple of trees that appeared out of the blackness.

And then the foggy cumulus appeared at the very top of the painting that I was looking at (and was a part of too) and began to self-inflate rapidly. It was becoming as large as the sky itself, overtaking the entire landscape. And moving closer to us. Now he was climbing the tree over to the side and I knew that he expected me to follow his lead. One arm grabbed a branch, he pulled, his knee went up, and then he was almost standing on a limb. Almost. But the cumulus that had been miles away was now whirlpooling directly over us. I was knocked to the ground and grabbed—onto something, anything, like an infant crying out and wringing his arms in a fit of discomfort. But I wasn't wringing. My mind had sent me back to some dream where I was floating on my back in a raft charging down a river and was reaching out for something, anything to stop my drift. I was knocked to the ground and facing the sky. I held on to something with both hands and turned to my side to locate my father-in-law, who had wanted me to prove to him that I could take care of his daughter.

Did he want to tell me something? Could he tell me something? The cumulus became a funnel and sucked him out of the tree. I saw him go up as if he were in a swing, then come back down, so close to the ground that I thought he would come over and whisper something in my ear. Then, on a rollercoaster of wind, back into the sky, his four limbs forming an X, he flew away.

Was I delirious? I saw him reduced to a miniature, swimming in a small fish bowl. Then he was a single character in a television cartoon. Then he was in the window of a washing machine.

I kept hearing them ask me if I was all right and if I could hear them. "Can you hear our voice?" I kept telling them that I could hear them perfectly. When they asked me, "Are you all right, sir?" I kept answering, telling them that I felt fine and wondering if they had seen him and my handkerchief. And they kept asking me the same questions over and over. And I kept answering, kept repeating myself, wondering when they would stop asking me the same damn question.

"It's a good thing he held on to this for dear life. It was a miracle," one of them said.

Chapter 8

I was eight when I first discovered love's pain. Now understand me: love itself is an exhilarating bath that can cover your being in continuous, undulating waves of bliss. I have always believed that. But the pain comes from the separation, from the resulting chill that sweeps over you in love's absence. You stand shivering alone in this new circumstance of need, your knees knocking, teeth chattering as if stranded naked on a beach in winter. Where is the towel of comfort that will keep you warm in this new circumstance of painful need?

Maybe that is why I wouldn't stop laughing on that last ride with Yo-Yo. I could, but I wouldn't. I wouldn't stop laughing because I was afraid that the pain would catch up with both me and Yo-Yo. He might think that I wasn't having fun. So every time he turned around to look back at me, I sent forth another burst of deliriously loud squeals, throwing back my head. Yo-Yo pulled me down the potholed road, and I held on to the wagon's sides as if I were steering. Teddy hopped along the side, his head bobbing up and down as if he had only three legs. Yes, Booby, he was before you; a playful Airedale who loved to lick my face.

I threw back my head to look at the darkening summer sky. Yo-Yo grabbed at his cap while pulling the handle of the wagon and looking back at me with those bushy eyebrows. I laughed: ha ha ha ha ha. I laughed some more. Ha ha ha ha ha. How I wanted Yo-Yo to know that I so treasured these moments when he pulled me down bumpy Hudson Street in my wagon. I could hear the screeching of my voice in front of me, could feel my cheeks pushing up into my eyes as I just laughed...just laughed. No matter that I couldn't possibly keep laughing nonstop all the way to the end of the road and back—that didn't matter. No, I wouldn't stop laughing. I had been injected with nerve gas, and it had intoxicated me, lifting me into absolute rapture. I would never stop laughing.

There was too much pain, too much sadness within that exquisite moment of Yo-Yo's pulling me down the rocky red road, the tall columns of dark trees swaying on either side, faithful Teddy trotting at my side. I was so afraid that he might be disappointed. No thought was more frightening to me. Not my Yo-Yo. How could I disappoint him? And so I laughed...and laughed.

We zoomed down the road, over the red rocky plastic that I never really understood. It wasn't exactly rock, it wasn't exactly plastic, it wasn't exactly dirt. Somehow Yo-Yo had packed the material into the road until it had taken on the coloration of the plastic. And the plastic had taken on the constitution of rock. The mixture was a rocky red road, sometimes with rocky projections the size of a fist jutting out of the ground and sending the wagon rocking precariously side to side or leaping up and forward, coming down with a crash that burned my backside. I laughed at that too.

And the plastic had come from the plant where Yo-Yo worked. He took me there on some Saturdays. Everything in the long building—the walls, the floor, the ceiling—had a red, pinkish tint that glowed. The men standing with shovels would be coughing into handkerchiefs and looking up with wild eyes as if they were in a cold coal mine. Red dust covered their heavy pants and boots.

Then another room had jagged stalactites of plastic sticking down from the walls like huge icicles. This room, large as an indoor sports arena, was where the huge yellow trucks moved their metallic arms like insect tentacles over the floor to lift and throw the mounds of plastic balls and blocks that were set up by the workers.

I think Yo-Yo was in charge of something. Men in plastic cubed hats would come up to him with deference, then stand attentively while Yo-Yo talked to them with his hands on his hips. Sometimes he would drop his arms and shake his hands, which hung from his wrists as if rubber. They nodded their chins up and down, then raised an open palm upward in a salute, and then turned to march away snappily, resolutely.

Now thunder roared through the darkening skies and we were rushing back up the road in an attempt to beat the rain. And I was laughing, and Yo-Yo was pulling and running, and saying, "We don't want to be caught in the rain, do we? Teddy was prancing in a zigzag; and I kept laughing, accelerating the frequency of my squeals as Teddy barked and a team of blue jays shrilled over our heads. Every time Yo-Yo looked back at me—he was turned sideways and pulling—I laughed.

Suddenly, I started coughing. Out of breath, I could not laugh anymore. My throat tightened and a snake of air, more than I could swallow, rushed down to my stomach so fast that I gasped. What was the sound I was now making, I thought? It wasn't a laugh. It was a combination of a cough and gargle. I became afraid of myself as I reversed my position and looked at myself from Yo-Yo's eyes. I looked terrible: face red, eyes wildly bright, lips trembling. He stopped, and picked me up.

"What's the matter? Get down, Teddy, you know better," he said as he held me up and looked in my eyes. I started crying. Now we were walking back and I was in his arm, looking over his shoulder at the road and its column of trees, his stubble face scratching my cheeks, he pulling the wagon.

"Get away from my feet, Teddy," I tried to yell, but my voice tumbled down the road.

When we got to the front gate, I got down from his arms and parked my wagon under the porch. Aunt Iceland stood at the door as I held Yo-Yo's hand going up the steps. The drizzling started.

Toothpick hopping from shiny red lips, "I thought I was going to have to come out there with an umbrella." "How you like your last wagon ride?" she looked down at me, rubbing my head as I squeezed past her to get inside. "I know you gon' miss him," she said to Yo-Yo as I headed for the bathroom. I closed the door.

"That boy like a son to me," I heard him say as I looked in the mirror at my hands washing my face. I was transported back to that earlier day in the week when in the midst of the handful of white envelopes in Yo-Yo's hand was a small pink rectangle from which he had pulled a little sheet. In the center of the living room, Aunt Iceland and I waited in front of him to receive our designated portions of the newly delivered mail, while Yo-Yo stood balancing the envelope stack and reading the pink letter. He scratched his head, frowned, and then sat down as if he had been knocked over the head.

"Is it the electric?" Aunt Iceland had asked, standing over him now and pulling the other letters from his hands. "I thought we sent that money order."

"No, worse than that—it's the bus."

"Bus? What are you talking about?"

"They sending his fare next week. Clara got a job in the World's Playground. She ready for him."

"Oh...oh Jesus," she had said, sitting down with a heavy sigh, the other envelopes scattered in her lap.

I looked now in the mirror at my puffed-up eyes and listened to the drumbeat of rain on the roof. I could see him holding me as if the mirror framed a photograph of us, was a screen of the past, of rapidly changing scenes featuring Yo-Yo and me. I was tempted to reach out and touch Yo-Yo's beard in the glass. Like a collage, his bushy eyebrows stared back at me from different moments, one setting after another collapsing into each other—one moment after another where he was a warm cloak of affection around my shoulders. The collage began to rotate until the scenes went back into themselves and got smaller. Yo-Yo's beard, his bushy eyebrows, his suspenders melted down to the size of an apple, and then a coin, and then he disappeared out of the mirror and I was looking at my puffy eyes again. Yo-Yo was gone from the screen.

My knees felt weak, so I sat down on the toilet seat with my shoulders heaving. I didn't want to leave Yo-Yo. I didn't want to leave. They came in and pulled me by my arms, dragging me out of the bathroom as I screamed that I would not go.

In my mind I had just arrived. Now I had to go. A year earlier we had come in the night from Brotherly Love. Half awake, my body and mind in separate worlds, I lay on the back seat of the car while Aunt Clara talked to Anida, commander of the steering wheel and of a bouncing fedora hat.

Only portions of the conversation filtered through as I alternately fell back to sleep, awoke, fell back into sleep again.

"No telling what that crazy woman may do," Anida said. "Good thing to get him out of the city."

"I know," Aunt Clara said. "But I'm gonna miss my little boy so." I felt her body turn to see if I was awake.

"Well, Gahtsum ain't poor, that's for sure. But he is married."

"Never mind."

I fell back asleep for an eternity. And then in some hazy span of time that I could only describe as time itself, I was jarred again to wakefulness. "Well damn; is this damned road paved or what?" she had said, both hands holding the wheel as we came up Hudson Street for the first time. Beyond the windshield, I could see the headlamps throwing tunnels of light into black open space. Straight ahead and above—I leaned forward with my arms on the top of the seats—a brilliant sliver of silver moon etched itself against the black canvas of sky. Soon I was thrown against the door like a sack of rice, Anida exclaiming, "Damn, they ought to pave this damn road." We took a quick incline and pulled off to the right where the gate stood. She parked.

"God, it's dark as hell out here," she said, standing by the car door, hands on hips, looking up at the sky. "This Oakbury is really the country, I'll say that. I bet there ain't a bar within 15 miles." They both giggled as they pulled me behind them and Aunt Clara lifted the handle on the gate. The three of us began the steps.

Then suddenly at the top, on the porch, a muffled clatter of knocking sounds erupted into a quickly opened door, and out popped two dark figures silhouetted against the rectangular frame of yellow living-room light. Yo-Yo cascaded down the front steps as if he were water skiing and had lost his balance. His white pajamas were tight as a baseball uniform. Still on the porch, Aunt Iceland stood by the door with arms folded around a white robe that had the brightest flowers, I remember.

I loved Yo-Yo immediately, from the time he had danced down those steps. "There he is," he said, kneeling to pick me up. ("Well don't let me get in the damn way," mumbled Anida.) I was in the air, just as I was earlier that last day in the wagon when I had laughed so hard I started coughing.

Oh, Booby, from the beginning I was in my own paradise. It opened up for me on the next morning after we all stood waving good-bye to Anida. "That damn road's enough to ruin a car, Oscar; you gotta do something about that before you see me again. Here"—she walked back from the driver's side and leaned down –"give Aunt Anida a kiss. You be a good boy now. Clara, I'll see you when you get back to the city." Then she was looking out the back window of her car, one hand outstretched along the seat back as she maneuvered it in reverse, then turned it so it crouched on the road across from us as if it were about to take off. Anida, smiling face bordered by the shiny window, rolled it down, stuck out her hand to wave at us, and rambled down Hudson Street.

"Come on around the side and see Teddy," Yo-Yo said, and we followed him.

"Why is he tied?" asked Aunt Clara. "He's got a beautiful coat...look at the brown patches."

"Thing wild. Ain't had no training. I just got him last week from some white folks he was driving crazy. They crazier than him. Don't get too close."

But it was too late, and I was on the ground, my neck scratched. Teddy stood on two legs, barking and straining against the chain connected to a rod in front of his house. I jumped back up and brushed the grass and dirt off my legs. I tried to control my quivering lip.

"Oscar, don't let him get close to that wild thing," Aunt Iceland said, then turning to Aunt Clara, "he gon' need some long pants to keep the poison ivy off."

Yo-Yo said, "Boy, be careful now."

I took one step at a time, staying just out of reach. That curly tan and brown hair—I wanted to hug him so badly.

"Well, you think he gon' like it out here in the country?"

"Oh yes, Uncle Oscar, and I really appreciate your hospitality. It's so calm and quiet."

"Ain't no need in struggling by yourself if you can get help from family," he said.

"That's right," Aunt Iceland said, working her toothpick on something that had lodged itself in the back of her mouth. Her face was tilted to the side. Was it a piece of the thick bacon we had eaten for breakfast?

If I could get his paws on my shoulders, I thought, I could hold him around his waist and keep him from licking me. Then I could hug him. They were walking along the side of the house toward the back yard. Teddy was standing, looking at me as if I were there to entertain him, red dripping tongue hanging out of his mouth, little butt of a tail wagging.

"Well, Gahtsum said that he would help take care...take care of...." the rest of Aunt Clara's sentence trailed off into the air. "So I will ask you to keep him here until I save enough to get my own place," she said.

This time I took a step forward and let him jump toward me. But I grabbed the ankles of his forelegs so that we were dancing. Still, he wriggled away, moving backward on his hind feet. Then he shook and twisted his body until he slipped his legs away from my hands. He was free. And poised to jump. I turned, but barely took a step before finding myself thrust forward, hands out to cushion my fall. I felt his paws bang against my shoulder blades. I lay stretched out on the ground, on my stomach. They ran toward me.

"Oscar, we gon' have to kill that dog."

My lips quivered again, and as I turned over to sit, I looked up at my trio of relatives standing a few feet away looking down at me with mouths open. Now I was close to tears. I wished they wouldn't stare at me like that, as if I were a wounded wreck. And Teddy? He sat at attention smiling, head up, then leaned forward to stretch out his legs and lie down. Begging me to come back, his big brown eyes stared at mine.

"I went over to the school last week," said Yo-Yo, talking to Aunt Clara and leaning to help me brush off the grass from my shirt. "He won't lose any time, they said. He can start in the third grade."

"You gon' be in an all-white school," Aunt Iceland said.

"Well isn't that something," said Aunt Clara. "All-white, huh? Isn't that something."

"It's the only one in the heights," said Yo-Yo. "Ain't got no choice."

Aunt Clara looked at me sadly, as if I were leaving her for an extended trip.

She turned and moved along the side of the house again with Yo-Yo and Aunt Iceland. Now their voices were mumbled.

"You sure you don't want to come out here? I can get you a job with

United." Yo-Yo said. "I been there for years—how long Iceland? No trouble. And if you have any problems, you just ask anybody where Oscar Lawson is, and they come get me. We ain't gon' have no nonsense. But you will be in the accounting office with the key punchers; them people got some sense over there."

"Too much country for me," said Aunt Clara. "And what do you mean by no nonsense? Just read in the *Courier* about those wild white folks out in Illinois. You know they had to call out the National Guard. Just 'cause a family wanted to live in a decent neighborhood. It's a shame. Oh Lord"—she put the back of her hand to her forehead—"and to think of those bombings. You know, Oscar, in the South they lynch a nigger every week. And this boy's mother—"

Yo-Yo raised his voice, cutting her off. "Biggest plastics company in the country, girl," he said, taking off his cap to scratch his head. "You can smell it when you drive into the plant. "Now they doing manufacturing too. They doing bullet-proof vests, and gun parts, and working on some new thing of plastic surgery that replaces neck wrinkles."

"You see Oscar done put half the plant in the road," Aunt Iceland said. "He thinks the plastic gonna make the road smooth." Smiling, she rubbed the back of his shoulders, then put her arms around his waist.

"It sure seemed bumpy last night," Aunt Clara said. "When does it smooth out?"

"I have to fill up all the holes first to get the road level. Then it will be smoother than that new turnpike they building. I can only haul fifty pounds or so at a time. And then some weeks the waste people don't throw out any plastic in the rubbish dump, so I have to wait for the next time."

"It's so nice and quiet out here," Aunt Clara said, looking up at a plane, "and it smells wonderful. Oakbury."

"I gotta water those collards some later," Aunt Iceland said. "Come on around to the back so I can show you the chickens. Don't walk under that ladder, now. No time for bad luck."

They went toward the gate to the back yard. Teddy followed them until his chain was taut, a straight line. I went over to look into his house. He turned, saw me, and in an excited squeal, leaped toward me. He looked huge. And was approaching in accelerated bounds.

"Teddy!" Yo-Yo yelled.

But I knew he was coming too fast for me to get away, and for an instant I stood paralyzed, saw only his pink tongue moving at eye level toward me. A wave of fear charged down my back. Then, just as quickly, a message of salvation telegraphed itself to my legs, and I turned toward the dog house and climbed, burning my knees on the silvery shingles that Yo-Yo had nailed onto Teddy's roof. I stood, a foot on either side of the center hump, Teddy pawing at my legs, Yo-Yo yelling, Aunt Clara screaming, Aunt Iceland threatening to get a broom, and I trying to keep my balance. Then, as Yo-Yo jerked Teddy back by his leash and gave him a sharp smack on the nose, they were all watching me. And then bent over rolling in laughter—necks tilted, tears in their eyes, pointing at me on all fours on top of Teddy's dog house.

Yes, they got a kick out of me. How often I seemed to be the object of their laughter. I was really the object of their affection, I realized at some point, and I loved it, loved Yo-Yo standing with hands on hips laughing at "that boy." It was as if the phrase, by its odd expression of distance, was affirming an even greater kinship of the heart. It was, frankly, a cold term—as if the boy were, through some unexplainable force, paralyzed to a spot *over there*. Not *my nephew* or by my first name; no, "that boy." But it was Yo-Yo's expression, and I wallowed in it, just as I wallowed in their reviews of my antics.

It didn't matter that my bedroom door was close enough for me to hear everything the two of them said when they sat in the living room to play music, review the day's activities or look at television. Sometimes they lowered their voices—a practice that only led me to ease out of the bed and tip to the doorway in anticipation of hearing what obviously had not been meant for my ears. Here is how I learned almost everything— listening from a black bedroom cracked by a slit of light where the door was ajar. Sometimes a chair would creak and scrape, signaling that one of them was moving toward the bedroom, just seconds away from me. I would take two quick steps backward and dive arms first under the covers. Once in an unexpectedly quick surreptitious retreat, I slipped to the floor, banged my knee loudly, and then had to pretend that I had fallen out of the bed as Yo-Yo came in to check on me.

"Why you sleep on the edge of the bed, boy?" He lifted me and lay me down so carefully, I felt like an invalid. Then he stood watching me. I rubbed my eyes as if had been awakened from the deepest sleep imaginable, as I had on another near-discovery. In that other moment, I had leaned my weight too heavily against the door, causing it to close with a bang. Their chairs squeaked and scratched the linoleum floor. Footsteps. My heart thundered. Then, miraculously, I opened the door just as Aunt Iceland and Yo-Yo were about to enter. I held my forearm against my eyes as I stumbled out of the room like the sleepwalker I was imitating. "Oh, he's going to the bathroom," Yo-Yo deduced, as I leaned toward the entrance like a drunk out of control. I squinted up as if entirely baffled by this new world of consciousness I was suddenly thrust in, and they stepped aside to allow me to pass.

On several occasions I heard them laughing uproariously about—well, the more I listened, the more it seemed—yes, it was me. The earliest was their wondering if in fact I was reading. "His legs don't even touch the floor when he sitting in that kitchen chair," Aunt Iceland's voice pondered, and I imagined her with the toothpick riding out of the side of her mouth. "But I asked him what he was reading and he told me just about the whole story. You heard of some detective called Ellery Queen?"

"Of course he reading," said Yo-Yo. "That boy smart as a whippersnapper."

He never knew how his peculiar behavior had bedazzled me. On those cold February evenings when he sat in the big chair, an island of shiny magazines surrounding him, a book in his hand, I would sit entranced on the floor. He was always reading something—a glossy magazine, a thick volume from the book club, a mail order circular, a newspaper. I loved watching him prop the material up in his hands and follow the rise and fall of his eyebrows as they reacted to what—a phrase, a scene, a character?

Then his lips would curl up into a smile, and he would chuckle to himself about a world that to me was mysteriously enticing. He looked down at me sitting by his feet but not really seeing me, for his mind was held captive by the contemplative hiatus that the narrative had thrust him into. He was considering and amplifying the scene beyond what the writer had described, and my face was merely a screen upon which he could project his own retelling.

Who were those people in there? What fascinating activities captivated Yo-Yo's attention so? I wanted to crawl up into his lap and look into the window of those pages and see who they were, watch their magical movements. Could I talk to them? Would they recognize me if I opened the same pages? Were they his friends?

"He get more mail than Ralph Bunche," Yo-Yo said at one time.

Well yes, of course. Thanks to perusing the dozens of magazines that lay everywhere, I discovered that there was a huge world of connectedness beyond little Oakbury, and that I had immediate access to it by establishing contact. The conduit between the world and me was only the black mail box that stood on a post by the front gate. I tingled at some of the opportunities blaring across the pages. To think that one could become something of such stature by merely studying at home—wasn't it in the comfort of one's home that was written across the top? One man, in a suit, described how they laughed at him until he sat down to play the piano—flawlessly no doubt, as I imagined his fingers

prancing over the keys. Another, on a beach, sent a bully scurrying away
ignominiously after developing a body with muscles rolling all over it.
He had taken the training course guaranteed to change your life. How I
tore ravenously through the pages in search of that special contact with
the outside world that I could reach by way of a mere stamped
envelope—or a post card. Journalist, clock repairer, photographer, coin
collector—the choices were limitless.

How many times did I watch with high anticipation as Aunt Iceland
tramped up the front steps, her hands filled with white and brown
envelopes—responses to my entreaties—pulled from the black metal
mailbox. "Oops," said Aunt Iceland, "what's this I dropped?" Kneeling
to pick up what?—Christmas cards that could be personalized for your
customers if ordered in time? Hundreds of stamps from all over the
world for a mere penny?

I could write short paragraphs and make lots of money selling them
to magazines that desperately needed my talent. I could sell packets of
seeds for five cents and become the envy of all the students in my school.
Make millions! Yo-Yo's collection of magazines included countless
sure-fire tested secrets to bring you the riches you have always wanted
and deserve.

And I could win prizes too, like the fancy red walkie-talkie that
never quite worked—or did it? With a waving hand, I directed Yo-Yo as
far as the wire attached to the end of his unit would allow—maybe from
the front fence to the back fence, a distance of 15 yards. "Can you hear
me?" I shouted.

"What?" I heard his voice—not through my red plastic receiver, but
in the air above me, just as loud and as clearly as if the voice itself were
asking, Why do you need a walkie-talkie if you can hear me without it?

"Well," he said after a 30-minute test session, his eyebrows
furrowed, "it's a bright shiny red, just as they described it."

But it was Gahtsum's gift that made me especially grateful to Yo-Yo
for helping me appreciate books. It's right there on the table, Booby. He
brought the tome on that morning when he came to pick up Aunt Clara. I
remember turning my head in the direction of the dark hum to see the
crouched beaver crawling up the road toward the house. Even Teddy
turned his head in a curious nod before barking. The eyes of flashing
glass and the smiling mouth was filled with long vertical strips of shiny
steel teeth. It was so low to the ground it seemed not to be moving at all,
barely inching up and leaning side to side in a hypnotic advance until
suddenly I was pulled out of my stupor. It was not a mirage, it was not a
shark cruising through the blue. And then, as the humming and ticking
came closer, and Teddy ran to stand, paws on the front wire fence, I was

overtaken by a strip of fear and ran under the porch.

I heard their foot steps. First Aunt Clara's—light, skipping down as if she were flying, and then the combined clopping of Yo-Yo and Aunt Iceland following her, and then the screen door slamming.

"Oh Gahtsum got some car there, don't he?" Yo-Yo asked, as he reached the gate. "That's the new Burk, right?"

"Well, he got enough money, don't he?" I heard Aunt Iceland reply. "They sure named him right."

"Hello, John," I heard Aunt Clara say. "Bought the Buick out again I see." Through the cracks of the steps, I could see her green dress.

"John," said Yo-Yo and Aunt Iceland at the same time, as if they had one voice.

"Oscar, tell that dog to be quiet. What he see under the porch?"

"Good afternoon to you," he said, tipping his hat. "Where's the master of the house?" The motor was still ticking. He stood in a gray suit by the front door of his shiny gray car.

"Turn off the motor and save your gas," Yo-Yo said. Everybody laughed.

It was the one I had ridden in before, a few months earlier, I remembered.

"Girl," Anida had said, "you got a lot of nerve going out with that crazy white man after what happened." And now you have the nerve to take the poor little boy with you," she said, looking at me sitting in a kitchen chair. "And what are you going to do at a damn airport, anyway?"

"He said it was important to talk. There he is," Aunt Clara had said, her finger on the window as she looked down to the street. "He sure is looking good." A wave seemed to have poured through the glass and washed her entire face with a smile. Then she turned to me and grabbed my hand, and we went out the front door, down the stairway, and out to the street. The sun was falling behind the house roofs on the other side of the street, and the metal wheels of a yellow trolley rattled down the tracks. At the curb in front of the house, Gahtsum was swinging his arms from the driver's side of the gray sedan, his hand matting down his hair, his straw hat in his other hand.

"What beautiful cream slacks," he said, opening the doors and closing them with swift, efficient movements. He rubbed my head. I jumped in the back seat, and we sped off down the main street, past the theater where I had gone to the movies on Saturdays with a pack of kids, run-stumbling in the dark aisles. People were busy—walking and talking and laughing on every corner we passed in that huge city of Brotherly Love, and my eyes jumped from them to Gahtsum's sharp long nose in the rearview mirror as he and Aunt Clara talked.

"To the airport?" she asked

"Yes, I hope you don't mind," he answered.

"No," she moved closer, turning to look back at me, asking, "we like the airport, don't we?"

"Yes," I answered, remembering two other trips we had taken as I grabbed onto the door rest to keep my balance. We turned a corner sharply.

"Well it looks as if they have more information than we thought," he said, the sentence itself collapsing into a long expiration of breath.

"Oh no," Aunt Clara replied.

"Yes. But don't worry; we just have to make new plans." Now we were moving slower in traffic, and Gahtsum tilted his hat back and raised his head so that I knew he was talking to me: "This is the university area, remember? One of the finest in the world. This is the kind of college you will go to."

I nodded my head in agreement as I looked at the ivy-covered buildings, tall and stoic, brick, gothic, representing to me even at that early age a majesty and style that was beyond just the ordinary. How heavy the wide wooden doors looked, and for a brief second I saw through an arch what seemed like the loveliest grass courtyard. The men and women walked across the streets or stood talking on the steps with an entirely different rhythm than those in my neighborhood or those I had seen everywhere else. They possessed something, I could tell. They knew things, I felt. They were different somehow, I was convinced.

After we reached the downtown area, Gahtsum took the route that led to the outskirts past the oil companies' huge storage tanks. "Oh, that odor," Aunt Clara shook her head, turning to look out the window to her right. Soon we were on the entry road to the airport, next twisting around small roads dirt-covered and dusty, the planes droning over our heads. I stood forward on the edge of my seat to see the silver birds lifting themselves off the ground and into the air. With one hand on the wheel, Gahtsum steered us down the side road until we got to the parking area. We pulled up to a wire fence barrier. One by one they soared over us as if we were in the front seats of an auditorium, their jet streams spurting behind them like intermittent bursts of thunder. The sun was going down.

Between a burst, I heard him say, "Oakbury sounds like a good safe place. Things look okay there."

"Whatever is safe is what I want," Aunt Clara said, her head leaning against the window.

"Clara, it's the best thing ...the best thing."

"The best thing, huh? I guess that is important. I wonder what the best thing was eight years ago. Do you know what the best thing was then?" Then a sustained blast roared overhead and their voices were lost in the explosion. They turned moving closer so they could hear each other, but I caught only the last words that ended in something like "his mother."

We had two other trips to the airport, and each time it seemed like a replay of the previous outing. They sat in the front, talked, and I tried to hear as much as I could without redirecting my attention away from the game I had devised. I would guess whether the plane would have two or three engines, or whether it would first appear on the left of the dashboard or the right, or whether its markings would be in red or blue or black. So concentrating on my own amusement often left me with my eyes closed and huge gaps of the conversation lost on the wings of a departing jet. What did "he will have to know someday," and "they have some idea" mean? Who was this *he* whom they talked about with so much affection, and who was that *they* whom they seemed to despise jointly?

That day when Aunt Clara wore the cream slacks was the last time I had seen Gahtsum before moving to Oakbury with Yo-Yo; and the flashback of his other car, the university, and the planes roaring overhead swept through my mind in a series of instants as I watched him through the cracks of the porch steps.

So I stumbled out from under the porch. They were standing, now surrounding the gray Buick with its huge ticking chrome grille sparkling in the afternoon sun.

"Now what on earth were you doing under that dirty porch?" You done ruined those white pants," said Aunt Iceland.

"My, look at how he has grown," said Gahtsum, his thin lips barely separating. "Come here so I can look at you, son," and he put his white palm over the back of my neck. "Mister Gahtsum has brought you something," he said, turning back to the car to open the door. I looked in at the soft gray upholstery and the shiny dashboard with the dials. He lifted a large bag from the back seat.

"Look," breathed Aunt Iceland.

"Oh," said Aunt Clara.

"Here," he said, his voice rising, handing me the bag. It was heavy.

"Don't drop it now," warned Aunt Iceland.

I pulled out the huge book. A large white crane stood on the front.

"I never seen a book that large in my life," laughed Iceland. "Look, Oscar, it has nothing but birds in it. Gahtsum, where you get a book so big? He'll be the rest of his life reading it."

"Say thanks," urged Aunt Clara.

I did, walking backward to plop down on the steps to sit. *Birds of America* was the title, and inside was a magnificent heron standing in a lush marsh.

"Something I thought you could keep for the rest of your life," said Gahtsum. "You remind me of Audubon a bit," he said. "Same intense eyes."

"Oh he won't lose that book, I'll tell you that," said Aunt Iceland. "You coming in for something cold to drink, or you in a hurry?"

"I could use some iced tea," he said, his eyes twinkling, hand on top of his Panama hat.

"Well, go around to the side road there and have a seat at the table. Clara, act like you know what to do with a house guest."

Chapter 9

The walls were gray and shiny, and so was the floor. A tide of faces, all white and as shiny as the school walls themselves, flowed by me as I held on to Aunt Clara's hand. They giggled and stared, marching down the hall to an admonition: "No talking please, boys and girls."

Turning the corner, we found the entrance to the office. A tall woman in red smiled from behind the counter, then led us into another room. "She has just returned from the dentist," said the woman, head half turned to us, her hand pushing the door knob. The office was filled with sunlight, streaming in through the curtains from the left, painting the small plants lined up along the windowsill, along the principal's desk, along the side of her round face. We stood gazing at her, and I blinked from the bright rays.

She caressed the side of her mouth. "Please thick town," she said, frowning and smiling at the same time.

"Please sit down," her secretary offered, and she took the chair to the side of the desk. We sat facing them both. "Miss Thompson had an emergency dentist appointment this morning, but she insisted on coming in to meet with you."

"Tho happy to have you," she said, standing. She moved around her desk to shake Aunt Clara's hand. Her silver hair exploded in brightness. She tilted her head in her hand as if she were holding a telephone to her ear.

"Some more water, Miss Thompson?" asked her secretary, moving already toward the door.

"Yeath, please, Joyce. You must have had some..."—here she took a pause to work on each syllable—" re-ser-va-tions, some wor-ries ...of course, the way things are going town in...well the entire South." She was behind her desk again.

"Down in the South? Yes it is terrible. This is the closest school," Aunt Clara said, "and he can ride his bike. So we decided to try. We believe that people are people until they show their true colors—like those animals in the Sip that hanged the boy for arguing with a white man. They just aren't civilized," she maintained while I saw a huge wave of regret spread over the principal's face. "And the other school in the city isn't as good. But Miss Thompson, we don't have to talk that much, please. You look so uncomfortable."

"Oh that's a school with rubble," said Miss. Thompson, taking the glass of water from her secretary.

"Lots of trouble," Joyce explained, now back in her seat. "They fight every day, you know...a bunch of little hoodlums. I don't know what their parents teach them."

"No, rubble, pheasant," Miss Thompson said as she put the glass to her mouth, then fumbled it momentarily. The water trickled over her lips and down her chin. She pulled out a handkerchief to blot it. "Oh," she moaned in frustration. She nodded her head at Joyce as a signal for her to continue.

"Miss Thompson wants his experience to be pleasant, without trouble" was her interpretation. "Our kids are good kids here. We don't think you will have any trouble at all"—looking at me and then to Miss Thompson for approval. "And you are doing a wonderful job without...well we understand his dear mother...?"

"His father died in the war," Aunt Clara said, crossing her legs. "He was in the paratroopers."

"Thorry," said Miss Thompson.

"Yes, we are so sorry," continued the secretary. "And such a handsome young man . Now I hear you are going to school at night yourself. That is so admirable. Taking courses in keypunching."

"Tom see?"

"Some tea?" replied her secretary. "Well!" she said as if she had discovered something of great magnitude. "I don't know why we didn't think of that before. Let me boil some water and get you some tea." Rising and turning, Joyce scuttled out of the room The three of us sat smiling and fidgeting, waiting for the secretary to return with the hot elixir that might bring Miss Thompson's numbed mouth back to normal.

As we sat and I half-listened to them chat, I thought back to how many times after arriving I had stood by my bedroom door gap to listen to them. My game was to try to transpose some kernel of reference made to my father into some concrete description of an attribute—any attribute. Just who had he been? What did he do? How did he do it? But it was a losing cause. Rarely did they say anything about my father, and if they did, it was always in so low a whisper that I had to resign myself to never hearing even so much as a half sentence. They referred to him— like me—as "he," and it was always in a sentence that either expired immediately or dropped in volume to nothing if I were within hearing distance. A sentence here, a sentence there elicited some facts—from Aunt Clara, Yo-Yo, others. They had met in a dance club. He went to the war. He was killed. And there were no photographs of him—none.

In the early morning after Aunt Clara and I had arrived at Oakbury, I had heard them in the kitchen employing some concoction of secret exchange that was between a mumble and a whisper. They talked about my mother, but it was really about me. I was dumbstruck, they said. A cabinet door was slammed shut and two pots sounded, blurring the next sentence about my ignoring it as if it hadn't ever happened and she was still here. I heard this clearly: "Such a shame; he just went and put her out of his mind."

The secretary brought my mind back to the room, and now Miss Thompson was lifting the cup of tea to her lips without spilling it, and a huge smile spread across her face. Her features reminded me of the lady in the moon. Miss Thompson rose from her desk, walked around it to take a chair facing us. She folded her hands. "I just think it's terrible what's going on down there," she said, and then smiled broadly. "Well, I seem to be talking normally again. I just wish I could do something. We must take care of this young man. Why on earth do you think they behave like that?" She leaned forward now with arms stretched so that her face was out of the sunlight, and she stared at Aunt Clara with the most intense eyes for a long moment. "And even in our capital, next to the White House, they don't want you to sit in the restaurants! Oh, it's just terrible...terrible!" She put her hands to her temples as if struck with an unbearable headache. "Well," she stood and put her hand on my shoulder, "we are going to make it just fine for you here. Don't you worry."

"He doesn't seem too concerned," Aunt Clara said. "If they will just...let him be himself. It's simply another move for him. In Brotherly Love there were white kids in the class."

"Yes, of course," Miss Thompson responded. "But I don't know how I would feel if I were the only white student in a school of black people. And that's why we are going to do—nothing special. But we won't stand for any nonsense, I will tell you that."

And there was little if any nonsense from that first day beginning with the moment when I prepared to leave the house, throwing my leg over the bicycle's center rim, my metal lunch box bouncing in the basket attached to the front of the handle bars. Teddy was standing on two legs and barking as if he would never see me again. And Aunt Iceland and Yo-Yo stood on the porch and waved in unison. "Be sure," she said, raising as best as she could get her modest voice to a shout level, "you don't step on any cracks in the sidewalk."

At 8:30 I would pedal past the rear yard of apple trees and chickens, then to the left when I could pump while sitting and coast along the level yet craggy road toward the other part of the town. It could be no longer than three miles, and I arrived before nine unless it was raining or snowing. On those days, Yo-Yo and I would chug along in his unheated dilapidated pickup, the windshield wipers squeaking back and forth in an unsteady rhythm.

Tim and Gunther attached themselves to me immediately, leaving the rest of the school—in my memory as I think back—as just one large building of many youngsters, all of one color. They sat on the front steps on my first day. Tim: shorter, freckles and red hair. Gunther: dark hair, chubby, wild eyes. They waved, then started down the steps.

"Know where to put your bike?" Gunther asked.

The three of us then walked around the corner as if we were old friends. They talked and punched at each other and laughed and accused each of being silly and scared of everything.

"Gunther just learned how to ride a two-wheel," laughed Tim, then pushed Gunther. "You got a Monarch," he said to me, "that's nice."

"Well at least my sister isn't cross-eyed," Gunther replied, and at this he put his arm around my shoulder and leaned on me. I almost lost my grip on my bike handle, nearly falling. He pulled me back. But now Tim was in front of us walking backward, expanding on the erratic behavior of Gunther whose eyes flashed like bulbs. They were still arguing and giggling as I locked my bike. Then we were in a line, some students turning to wave at Tim and Gunther, who were near the rear with me.

And they became my friends, my confidants that one year at the school. They had adopted me, I guess, out of some natural inclination to befriend a stranger who just coincidentally fit into a category that they may have read about or heard about: a black person. But had they ever seen one, touched one, talked to one ever? No, from what Miss Thompson had told us that morning, no black child had ever been in the building, much less sat in a classroom with them. Somehow, their minds had not developed any attitudes yet. Yes, Tim and Gunther knew that I was different, they could see the visual proof immediately: my skin was not white. But they had not jumped to any conclusions about those differences. My features, my skin color, my voice did not suggest to them anything other than the fact that I looked differently from all the other children they saw every day.

"Oh it is just so awful why they hate the way they do," complained Miss Thompson that morning of our interview after her medication had loosened her mouth, allowing her to speak with so much more animation. "How can anyone hang another human being? What makes you so—detestable?" she asked, her hands cupped in front of her mouth as if she were praying, and the finger's width of sunlight crossing them.

"Lynching. I can only say that I don't know," Aunt Clara answered, softly—as if she were dreaming. "I just don't know."

After school on the first day, the three of us rode back to Gunther's house. It was on a wide side street covered with leaves. His front steps were guarded by two stone lions, and a spacious porch wrapped itself around the sides of the house. The streets on this side of Oakbury were paved and clean, unlike like the rag-tag combination of plastic and mud of our road merely a few miles away. Perfectly spaced oak trees rose from the sidewalks. Gunther's mother marched with heavy legs from the kitchen as we entered, and came toward me with the most pleasant manner—an apron tied around her waist, her eyeglasses large as she bent over to pat me on the head.

Once I discovered that they were so easily awestruck, I was determined to keep my schoolmates flabbergasted. The third-grade teacher, one of the few whose name I can't remember, applauded my first presentation during show-and-tell, where I kept the entire class in suspense as I slowly unveiled the events leading to my holding the very brown package in my hands that they were looking at. It had come from the Sure Growth Seed Company. It was the walkie-talkie that I had won by selling so many five-cent packets of seeds that would sprout to "a great flourish of colors in any yard." Whose yards? I must have sold most of my inventory to Aunt Iceland and our two neighbors on Hudson Street. Tim and Gunther's mothers had bought a handful, carefully looking at the pictures to help them decide which stunning variety would populate their gardens.

When I saw the eyes of Tim and Gunther widen with interest after I opened the pages of my book of birds that Mr. Gahtsum had given me, I became the angler who had hooked a large sport fish and under no circumstances would allow it to escape. I was determined to reel them in. The volume was larger than any they had ever seen, both admitted as we spread it out on the porch and kneeled over it. "Four hundred and thirty-five pictures," I said. And yes, I even knew the sounds that the birds made—a necessary attribute if you hunted them with a BB gun.

"A BB gun?" Gunther's eyes became wider than any game fish I had seen in the magazines. Buoyed by their queries, I disappeared through the front door to return like a magician with the air rifle. As we marched up the side road to look for our prey, I began my lecture on the different tones, sometimes pointing in the direction of an invisible warbler whose song came from a wooded area too thick for the human eye to penetrate.

"Bob White," I said, pointing to a movement of leaves along the ground that suddenly had wings that alighted on a fence. "And that's what he's singing—*Bob-White*. Hear it?" I sneaked a glance at them as we strode up the road. They were elbowing each other in awe. Then two squealing blue jays chased each other overhead just before I had named them. "They are so loud, they sometimes sound like crows, don't you think?"

With each outing, I felt myself advance higher in their esteem. "You're crazy," insisted Tim, "that's a bird lost in the woods."

"No, that's a catbird," I said.

"Gunther, can you believe it? He doesn't know a cat from a bird. Whoever heard of a bird meowing?" And at that very instant we noticed a rustle and flutter in some dense shrubbery followed by the landing of a gray catbird on a tree. I reveled in my victory as it flit its rusty-wine undertail on a branch and imitated the sound of a cat's meow.

From my giant bird book and my own individual excursions into the woods surrounding our Hudson Street abode, I had gained enough facts about our winged creatures that enabled me to throw out observations in my conversations with Tim and Gunther as casually as a medical student employing Latin to describe parts of the body. I told them about my spotting the woodpecker glued to a dead tree and religiously drilling its beak into the bark as if it had lost its mind. The banging rat-tat-tat reverberated throughout the woods with the same volume generated by construction workers nailing a floor. And when it hesitated for a few seconds between hammering—was it watching me watch it...? examining its accomplishment...?—I marveled at its striking black-and-red outfit and wondered if its beak ever dulled.

I had learned and shared with my third-grade intimates the distinctive songs of several birds: the three-syllable whippoorwill's extended soliloquy, the simple chirp of the robin, the owl hooting in the daylight—so near but yet invisible despite our bent necks—and the cardinal's long chirp followed by three shorter tweets. We were usually transfixed by the give-and-take of two mockingbirds. What?—courting, showing off? One began with *keep it, keep it*. The other responded with two syllables longer: *keep it, keep it, keep it*.

But I never told them that I had actually killed two birds with my rifle—one sparrow and a cardinal. They both fell over so quickly that I was startled. I had discovered the sparrow in the rear yard where the water pump and apple trees had fascinated my two comrades from the other side of Oakbury each time we set foot back there. I had to kneel to sneak up on the sparrow, its gray and brown feathers blending so neatly with the background of the tree. Then in a fatal moment of rest where its tap dancing was interrupted for six seconds, I pulled the trigger. It fell with a plop, and for an instant I feared that I had missed the prey and hit an apple instead (I had sent an apple swinging for its life in one missed shot earlier in that week). It lay without a twitch, its beady blue eyelids closed. Then my thumping heart that had pounded in keyed-up anticipation of the kill was now pounding with fear. I had killed a living thing. It lay there—tiny and innocent. I turned away, shrugging off my guilt and running up the steps and inside to see if Aunt Iceland had finished dinner.

"You out hunting with that BB gun?" she asked, rubbing her hand on her ubiquitous apron, lips bright red, toothpick waving.

"Yep, I just shot a bird," I said, looking for her response.

"You better leave those birds alone," she chuckled, turning to slide a pot over the stove. I think she thought the idea that I could kill a bird with a tiny pellet coming out of my air rifle was a mere fantasy. "You should be looking for a four-leaf clover while you in those woods, to give you some luck."

But Yo-Yo's response after dinner was more definitive: "That boy gon' be a hunter when he grow up," rubbing my head.

The second kill—of a cardinal—came just a day later as I lay on my stomach on the hammock side of the house. He had mesmerized me for some minutes as he skipped up and down our front steps with a live worm in its orange beak. It ascended one progressive step after another, his bright red plumage contrasting against the gray boards as if they were designed not only for the lift of the human foot, but also for the bird's enjoyment. Its hopping was both deliberate and carefree—as a child who finds some new toy like an empty can to kick or a tire to roll and therefore focuses its entire soul on the experience until exhausted by boredom. He stopped to shake the worm wildly, as if mocking it. Then he dropped it and pranced sideways, then up the steps, then back to pick it up. Did it jump up the steps one-by-one for the mere sake of amusement? And was its return to the worm a symbol of responsibility and commitment that could not be tainted by irresponsible skipping? At each step it paused, cocked its head toward me (*What? Does it know I'm watching!?*), then hopped. The worm was still struggling in the cardinal's beak, curling up its head to pray to the heavens when I pulled the trigger.

Here were the worm freed and its attacker dead on its back, its limbs tucked in. I kicked the bird off the steps and ran to the other side of the yard to play with Teddy. My guilt hung over me still as I stood at a distance safe enough to prevent Teddy's leaping paws from reaching me. I was trying to erase its image, the gorgeous brilliance of color that I had obliterated, the carefree movement, the small helplessness, the same dulled eyelids that the sparrow had showed me the day before. I laughed with Teddy, but inside I knew I was trying to fool myself and not succeeding. I was ashamed at what I had done and knew at that moment that I would never again shoot a living thing.

Each visit that Tim and Gunther made to Hudson Street offered me opportunities to keep them regaled. Only once did they come close to making me angry, demanding with red faces ballooning from laughter that I explain why I called my Aunt Ida with the name I thought I had heard all my life: Anida. "He says that's what it sounds like," roared Tim, punching Gunther who was already roaring on his back, legs kicking. We pumped water from the well and concluded that it was tastier than any we had drunk in school or in their homes. The apple trees in the back were similar to the ones in their neighborhood, but they didn't have a pear tree yielding such tasty firm samples as we did.

I kept them entertained continually with my vast store of new arrivals via the post office. A company in New Hampshire had promised to send me hundreds of stamps for my collection. I would become a numismatist, able perhaps to auction off my collection for millions of dollars, I announced one day as I shared with them my dollar's bag of stamps from around the world. An all-occasion assortment of greeting cards had been sent to me on approval. I could make the amazing amount of five dollars—"easily, quickly, in spare time." As I read the letter to them, I heard Tim's wondering (in a voice so low it must have been addressed to his shoe sole) if it wasn't something that he should look into. But I didn't allow him the liberty of contemplating that before I bombarded them with the catalog pictures of walkie-talkies, crystal radio kits, kites and other prizes that could be won if you sold...this...and that. What infinite potential, I emphasized as I swung before their bright eyes the pages—some having arrived just a day before in the mail. At the end of it—the sun floating down between the trees, and their eyes drooping— I would jump up cheerily and declare that I was going inside to get my big bird book.

My two good friends were usually gone by dinner time. And they never visited on the weekends, as if they knew that those were special times when Yo-Yo and Aunt Iceland might get the party spirit and dance and drink most of Friday or Saturday night. I liked seeing them together, especially on blues nights when they held each other closely and sang "Everything I have is yours" along with the husky baritone vibrato of a tall handsome singer featured in the magazines. In the front room, the

Philco record player sometimes squeaked out faster beats from high-spirited whining saxophones by men called Pres and the Hawk. They swung each other around in circles, her head back, laughing. I watched, holding a big vinyl record in my hands to play next. I practiced the hucklebuck with them—a dance that had me stumbling madly all over the living room, sometimes on my back kicking up my legs to their amusement.

"He's got it, look at him." Yo-Yo would smile down at me. "Be careful, son, don't bust your head against the table now." He placed his hands on her waist and spun her around.

"Oh, he's doing it, Oscar, look at him," Aunt Iceland would say, turning at his lead, her hand over her head. "Now don't turn so much you get dizzy, that's bad luck."

Or Aunt Hattie and Mister William might be visiting from the Apple. Impeccable, yes, especially standing in front of the hillock of a background, as if posing for their portrait. The orange bus would have just gone into the next world and left them standing: she with bent elbow to hold her hat against the onslaught of dust, he steadying her at the waist, one outspread hand in the air to restrain the wind, his mouth flashing gold as he smiled. His hat was black and cocked to the side, and her dress always had flowing lines that swayed with her movement. She was the essence of warmth and good cheer, always ready to chuckle at my stories or comments. And Mister William doted over her as if he were afraid that she might at any moment wish for something that he had not already arranged. He must have felt that his inattentiveness could be an event of catastrophic proportions. Stepping down before her, he had held her hand as she alighted from the bus. He was here pulling out her chair at a Sunday dinner, here opening the door to Yo-Yo's truck, here going to the front room to find her bag with the gift for Aunt Iceland—"I brought you a little something...William, where did I put it?"

He would jump up and go looking, alerting us with, "I got it."

When they were visiting, there could be five of us on the floor, I alternately watching and dancing and bumping into them. But this time, this last time that I saw them, they had come for more than just relaxation.

"William just helped a woman at Harlem Hospital," Aunt Hattie said as we drove the few miles back from the bus stop to the house.

"Prayer heals all wounds," he said with his huge glassy smile.

"That woman had a terrible case of the gout," Aunt Hattie said. "William helped her."

Yo-Yo only nodded. They waved at Teddy on his hind legs as they pulled their bags up the stairs to a waiting, smiling Aunt Iceland at the screen door. "Gotcha some cool lemonade," she said. "William, give me that hat to hang up before you go throwin' it on the bed and causing us bad luck."

Less than an hour later we were sitting in the side yard, Aunt Hattie looking up at the pear tree from the hammock, the others in chairs surrounding her. Sitting on the ground near them, I aimed my BB gun at the Pabst beer can placed on a pole.

"It didn't look like too much change," said Mister William. He was scratching his head and looking at Yo-Yo. "Let me see again."

Yo-Yo stood up and pulled up his pants legs. I turned to look. His ankles and shins were orange, like the rays of the setting sun. I had never seen the discoloration before. I turned my head away, facing the fence again, as if I had seen nothing.

"If you weren't so dark, you wouldn't notice it," laughed Aunt Iceland.

"Oh stop," said Aunt Hattie, "he's the same complexion as Billy Eckstine. He got nice carmel skin, just like his momma..." But her eyes were focused on me just as I turned my head to meet her stare. She breathed in quickly, seemingly caught having said something that I wasn't to hear. "Oh," she said, and turned sideways in the hammock.

"They asked me to sign some papers in the office," Yo-Yo said. Mister William was kneeling in front of him and looking at his legs.

"I wouldn't sign anything," Aunt Hattie said. "You may have to go to the hospital or see a specialist. William, honey what do you think?"

"Seems like it's spreading," he said, one knee on the ground, head turned sideways. "Most of my prayers were to stop the spreading. That's what I concentrated on." He bent his neck and put his forehead in his palm.

"Well that lady with the gout was cured in two weeks if I remember. William had to pray day and night to heal her. She gave us a little extra too."

"It's those chemicals, that's what it is," said Aunt Iceland, her cheeks bright from makeup. "And then all that dust. No tellin' what they playin' with over there. Who ever heard of somebody's skin turning orange. First it was just a spot on his shin. Then it was his whole calf. Now look...both legs. And going higher."

Mister William pulled his face out of his hand and stood in front of Yo-Yo. He was a few inches shorter than my Yo-Yo. "I can keep you in the treatment if you want," he said. "I can give you another week of deep prayer. Maybe I need to do mornings and evenings."

Yo-Yo sighed and sat down, introducing a moment where nobody moved, a moment where the only sound for seconds was the call of a crow very high above. "I sure appreciate your help, William. I know you did your best with your prayer program. Hattie told us you were on your knees at six in the morning one time. Maybe I *should* check in with a doctor," he said.

"Well I sure wouldn't sign no papers until I saw a doctor," said Aunt Hattie, walking past me and looking back at us as she went toward the steps. Then at the top: "Those chemicals he work with could eat you alive," followed by a hand over her mouth as she slid inside the door and closed it behind her with a soft "oh."

"Whatcha want, Hattie?" asked William.

"Just to pee, William," she said from the bathroom window, and Yo-Yo laughed heartily while taking a chair. William's gold tooth flashed as he himself chuckled.

At dinner, the sun splashed through the dining room windows onto Aunt Iceland's fried chicken, potato salad, and greens that she had grown in her garden on Teddy's side of the yard. "Now this is some potato salad," said Mister William. I kept watching Yo-Yo at the head of the table. He didn't display his usual spirited demeanor, passing the bowl of greens as if it were too heavy to hold. Even after dinner when Mister William told Aunt Iceland that he would teach her some steps nobody had ever seen before, Yo-Yo just smiled. I even tried to expand my Hucklebuck repertoire by standing on my head for a few seconds. But he just laughed the laugh of one whose mind was elsewhere.

When it was time for me to go to bed, he picked me up and swung me in a circle in my pajamas and then hugged me tightly. I was merely a half minute from dreamland, but I strained nevertheless to hear their talk now that I had been sent to bed. My head on the edge of the pillow, I heard the words about something in the plant that was on Yo-Yo's skin. He should see a doctor, a specialist. The plant was at fault. I had an overpowering sense of dread, of fear that somebody had wronged Yo-Yo and would not accept responsibility for it. Somebody had hurt Yo-Yo.

As I tossed in my bed listening to their cheering for the Cuban boxer named Kid Gavilan on the *Cavalcade of Sports* that night, I wondered. Next they were singing along with the commercial: "What'll you have— Pabst Blue Ribbon, Pabst Blue Ribbon Beer." Mister William's voice was the loudest, higher in tone than the others, yet mixing in nicely with the slurred and incoherent laughter-mixed contributions of his partners in almost rhyme. "Look Oscar, I got my own bolo punch too," he said, and I heard his feet scuffling on the linoleum floor as two voices laughed with his.

Had that been the reason for Uncle's leaving the office so somberly that day he had taken me for a tour of the plant? I had brought my huge

bird book. I was sitting on the bench in the hallway—against the wall—
and looking at the page of the three blue jays in various positions on a limb
when the two tall men came pushing, almost falling through the wide
swinging doors. They coughed in their handkerchiefs. For just a split
second I saw a flash of open space of smoky orange dust before the door
closed.

"Phew," said the taller one, coughing and stumbling and caught from
plunging forward on his face by his companion who, himself barely
steady, grabbed his arm. "Damn that's enough dust to kill you," said the
rescued man, coughing and standing in front of the door. "Who's this,
the new supervisor?"—looking at me.

The other sneezed, blowing dust and blinking, then waving his
handkerchief in front of his face. "Well look, it's Oscar Lawson, our
transportation man. Hey, Oscar, this here the little nephew you always
talking about? Damn, that's a big book you got there, little man. It's
bigger than you." They both laughed, but their voices quickly turned
from mirthful outburst to coughing and wheezing, and they bent over at
the waist as if that would ease their discomfort.

"Did you sign those papers for us Oscar?" asked the taller one whose
cheeks were smudged with dust. He was removing from his head a metal
football helmet with a light in the center and throwing it on the dirt floor.
The front of their white diver's outfits was a canvas of orange and brown
stains.

"No," said Yo-Yo, "and I think I'd better get some medical advice
about this. My skin is starting to itch bad."

"We need to go into the office and talk, my friend," said the taller
one, sneezing and facing Yo-Yo. "Come on, Jake." But just as he was
walking past me he stopped, bent over and began sneezing so
uncontrollably that I turned sideways to protect my book. Jake bumped
into him, and now they were both bent over sneezing in opposite
directions—one quick rhythmic expiration after another. "Come on," he
said, leading them, a sudden intake of breath suggesting that he might
sneeze again, and for a moment we all watched him as his mouth opened
to emit an outburst. His head went back, we waited. But it didn't come,
and he opened the door and led them inside.

They went into the door to my left. Yo-Yo said to me, "I'll be right
back, son," pinching me under the chin. "You keep reading."

I turned the page to show him that I was indeed concentrating,
looking at the full-page print called "Robin"—one bird sitting
contentedly while the other stood looking in the same direction.

When we had first driven through the wide security gate of the plant,
I could see the mountains sticking up in the background. The ground was

red-orange, almost the same shade as our road surface on Hudson Street. It went straight for the length of a football field before ending at the foot of the mountains. The buildings along the street were one story high, made of gray stone. Gigantic trucks hauling cubes of plastic rocks roared up and back between the mountains and the buildings. We had entered a bustling terrain of truck gears shifting, clouds of orange dust flying everywhere, and men in diver's outfits and shovels on their shoulders dancing between the trucks and the buildings.

"This is where Yo-Yo work," he had said, his comforting hand on my shoulder. They all seemed to know him. The drivers honked their horns as we drove through to the employee parking area. The hustling workers in smudged uniforms waved at him. Fascinated more now by the brilliant color spilling out of the pieces in their original form—not banged and crushed into the road and colorless as I had first known them—I stopped to pick up a few rocks that had fallen from trucks. They seemed unaccountably brilliant and strong—like something magical dropped from another planet.

I sat on the bench and turned the pages to the American Flamingo, a huge pink-orange thing with a neck that seemed to be several feet long. Would I ever see a bird so large and so unusual? Before I could resolve the possibility, I heard the muffled voices behind me in the office rise to a higher level.

"We think it's a fair deal," declared the voice of the taller one. "We won't report you for taking our property without authorization if you forget about this idea of seeing your own doctor and a lawyer. It can't be that serious. We just took a tour through the lower cave, and everybody seemed quite healthy."

I heard Jake sneeze and then say, "Very healthy."

Yo-Yo told them that the rocks had been in the garbage mound. " I didn't need authorization to take trash that nobody else wanted."

They continued to insist that he had done something wrong until the exchange took on a different tone. The voices ran into each other and I couldn't distinguish them. Then the voices were so low that I could hardly hear anything although I sat so that I could place my ear against the wall. It sounded as if they were pulling out chairs and sitting. Quiet. Then some rustling of chairs and movement, and Yo-Yo came leaning out of the door with the slowest gait I have ever seen him use. He was putting on his cap and grabbed my hand without saying anything. In his other hand was an envelope that he tapped against his hip as we went down the hallway to the exit.

It lay between us in the truck as we drove back to Hudson Street. Part of the bulging envelope said *To Whom*. What could I do or say? I wanted to do something, say something, even be something to Yo-Yo, who had pulled me in the wagon on so many journeys down Hudson Street and picked me from the bed to hold me tightly at night when I had fallen down a nightmare tunnel to awaken in a crying sweat. Just as I was afraid to stop laughing when he pulled me down Hudson Street for that last time, now I was afraid that I couldn't laugh. Despite my opposition to it, something pent up in me had grabbed my shoulders. I didn't want him to see me cry. But I couldn't fight it any longer, so I stared out the window and let my shoulders go, shaking as if I were an epileptic.

Chapter 10

I breathed it in deeply—the curiously intoxicating, the inviting freshness of the sea. It was curiously intoxicating because I wasn't sure about it. The composition of its tangy concoction must have been from several sources, as if it had picked up aromas in its roaring path and intermingled them like some nautical chemist. Yet its essence was indubitably the sea. But the sea—blue, green, and shades in between— had roared through many places, and its odor was an invigorating mix of those spaces. I loved its inhale; it was pungent yet fresh, thick yet light, deep yet on the edge. And as soon as I was sure my nostrils had captured its soul, it was gone and we were off the pike and in the world's playground itself, riding up the boulevard that was only a few blocks from the boardwalk and beach that ran parallel to it.

Booby, I forgot that while we were driving on the four-lane pike where the entire city loomed ahead of us as well as surrounding us on both sides, a car had passed. A dog was leaning his head out the side window. His black snout pointed to the sky, sniffing the sea with closed eyes as if it were a heavenly sent scent. And his tongue drooped out of his mouth, gathering the taste of the sea's moisture. I wondered if his tail was outstretched straight like the hunting dog Blue that Yo-Yo took with him to shoot rabbits. Booby, if you sat up you could smell the sea air we are about to enjoy. But no, you keep falling over. Now Brian Smart is fading out and we are finally on the narrow road to the house.

"That last lady is right in some respects," says a caller. His voice crackles and weakens and soon will be transformed into another station. "But she and so many of our people don't really know what the issue is. Don't make me no never mind, but still y'all don't seem to understand that you can't change nothing you complaining about without power.

And as long as you don't have somebody in Congress to fight for you, you ain't got no power. Ain't nobody listening to nobody with no power. Whoever heard of people living next door to the White House and can't even vote for a senator? That's ridiculous. But I haven't heard one caller complain about paying taxes to a government where we have no representative—and therefore no power. We need..." And he faded into classical music.

Just above the skyline of hotels crossing the horizon was a droning Piper Cub flanked by seagulls flying reconnaissance, swooping toward it and then floating away. Streaming from its tail was a sign identifying GEORGE HAMID'S STEEL PIER. Below that, supported by wooden beams was the biggest sign I had ever seen. On a billboard as large as the screen on a drive-in movie was the picture of a magnificent white stallion. The High-Diving Horse's jockey was a blonde sea goddess in a rhinestoned bikini and a tiara, directing its leap into the sky in the same arc that a horseman would take his charge over a fence in a fox hunt. And then the horse and rider were to splash bravely and safely into the Atlantic Ocean. It had to be one of the wonders of the world. It had to be stupendous. No wonder that they called this the world's playground, I mused, my bones tingling as the billboard disappeared to my right.

The world's playground was nothing like little bucolic Oakbury: no woodlands, no unpaved roads, no screech of birds. From my window on the passenger side, I saw a boulevard of bars, stores and churches. Above the stores were apartments with signs offering rooms for rent. The boulevard bustled with a colorful kaleidoscope: most marched with hurried determined bops that took them to whereabouts of inestimable importance. Others sauntered slowly, perhaps returning from a demanding regimen that had already sapped their energies. Still another group remained static, observing the flow while leaning against telephone poles, doorways and windows, awaiting the herald that would spark their movement.

I hoped that we would go far far past this neighborhood of hardship. But I was wrong. The address Anida located from her notepaper was above a candy store and a shoe repair shop. The apartment we sought was at the top of a dusty stairwell. At the landing was a door on either side. Anida turned to the apartment on the left and knocked.

"Who is it?" The tiny voice seemed to be at the height of the doorknob.

"It's us, who you think?" said Anida.

"Need any help with those bags?" Tiny Aunt Shirl stood rubbing her nose. A red bandana covered her little head, and a white apron draped her lower body. She turned in a half limp to lead us in and then took a quick turn into the kitchenette.

"No, I got both," Anida said. "Here, take one," she said to me. "Don't be so lazy," she said, smiling.

"Just leave them in the hallway," said Aunt Shirl. "Clara be home soon and show you upstairs." She sat at the kitchenette table. It was covered with little books and writing pads and the cartoon sections from newspapers. Anida sat in the chair to the side of me. We formed a triangle, with Aunt Shirl at the apex. I peeked to the right, into the living room where the furniture—a sofa and two chairs—was covered with plastic. I checked again...no television.

She peered over a newspaper and looked at me. "I was just finishing my workout. What you think will lead today? We at Pimlico you know." Before I could answer: "I see Archie with his mouth wide open"—she held up the page for me—"so I'm thinking an 'oh'," she said, and wrote something on a small pad.

"He don't know nothing about numbers," Anida said.

"Well at least he's mannerly," said Aunt Shirl. "Can he read? That book bigger than him. Clara got a job at Weinstein's. She get off at five."

"Is that a hotel?"

"Restaurant—she's at the soda fountain. Down in Ventnor. Them Jews love her; you know she keep them laughing. I used to work for them but my bones bothering me too much now." She thumbed through one of the tiny books and scratched her nose. "See, that three-nineteen played last year about this week, August 20. And Arthur told me he dreamed about a hurricane last night. "Let me see what hurricane is...yep, three-nineteen. And this is a current dream book," she said, smiling at me. "I'm playing three-nineteen straight, I like it. And I like a three to lead."

"What happened to the 'oh'?" asked Anida.

"I'll play that to lead too," she said, unfolding a balled-up handkerchief stuffed with bills and some quarters.

"Well put two dollars on three-nineteen for me then," Anida said, standing up and reaching in her pocketbook. "If I hit, give the money to your new boarder." She came over to stand in front of me. "You be a good boy now, you hear? Your Aunt Ida gonna get back to Brotherly Love."

"Thanks for bringing me," I said. I had just turned to the page on the golden-winged woodpecker. One was at the top of a branch flirting with the male whose beak pointed upward.

"You not gon' wait for Clara? She be sorry she missed you."

"I may stop around Daddy Lew's and see what's doing," Anida said, "since it's on the way to the pike."

"Well I hope it's too early for them niggers to start shooting at each other. I don't know why you wanna go to that low-life joint. Get you some class. Bad enough Clara go there and stay out all night gambling. Maybe this boy'll slow her down. Did you see Mister DC out there? His runner should have been here by now. You know I hit yesterday."

"No ma'am, didn't see him. I'll be all right, Aunt Shirl," she said, biting a nail. "Don't worry." She was backing out of the kitchenette and looking down into her pocketbook. Then her eyes met mine just as I looked up from the book. Could she read my inner throbbing? I wanted so badly to ask her not to leave me, not in this miniature apartment with old miniature Aunt Shirl who seemed to have something bad to say about everybody and everything, whose bones would be too old to pull me in a wagon, who was too short to lift me up at night, who knew nothing about hunting, and would probably never say "leave that boy alone," as Yo-Yo had whenever Aunt Iceland spoke to me in a stern tone. And it was obvious that she didn't read books, as Yo-Yo had, but fooled around instead with the funny papers. But I could not bring myself to blurt out that I didn't want to stay any sooner than I could have stopped laughing when Yo-Yo pulled me down the road in the wagon. I didn't want to make her feel bad. Maybe I could love Aunt Shirl.

"You want some pancakes?" she said when she came back. "I know that girl didn't feed you."

"Yes, I thank you," I said, surprised suddenly by a sound like the Piper Cub that had announced the high-diving horse.

"That your stomach? My goodness, let me hurry."

We both laughed. She watched me eat a stack of pancakes, bacon and the best cold milk I had drunk in a while. She continued looking through her dream books and newspaper comics, scratching her head through the red bandana, looking up at the ceiling, then jotting down things on a pad the size of a playing card. When she discovered some ideal combination of circumstances, she expired a little "humph" followed by a little smile from her little lips.

"How your Uncle Oscar?" she asked. I could see that she was studying a comic. "I bet them crackers in that plant are givin' him hell. Nicest man in the world. Nancy got her fingers crossed like a seven—see?"

I looked at the cartoon page and felt my eyes filling up at that image of those sheets covering Yo-Yo up to his neck.

"You tired, honey? You wanna take a nap?"

She sent me upstairs. At the top on the right was Aunt Clara's room. On the other side was my bedroom, and walking through that you reached Aunt Shirl's, separated by a doorway and an alcove. Ceramic miniatures sat on it. Through the alcove I could see her windows facing the boulevard. And through the window I could see the city hall clock. Lying on my back, I stared at its hands and wondered about Yo-Yo. He had been in bed when Anida and I waved good-bye earlier that day. Only his face was above the covers, and I could see that his lips were becoming discolored. "Just kiss him on his forehead," said Aunt Iceland, who was in the corner looking out the window. "Lawd, the devil is beating his wife—look at that sun shining in the rain."

I lay in bed looking at the hands of the clock and mourning about Yo-Yo for a long time. And then it was a short time. All of a sudden I had lain in that bed for weeks. And then I had lain in it for months. And I wasn't mourning anymore. I had adjusted to the beat of the world's playground. It was a fast-moving syncopation, a continual replay of the boulevard that Anida had first driven us on, populated with the fast movers, the exhausted and the watchers.

Prominent among the fast movers either as soloist or ensemble collaborator was Aunt Clara. Her favorite introductory riff was "and look." From there her performance would recall a scene or an attribute that elicited hilarious outbursts from her audience of one (usually Anida visiting) or several. Her narrative genius was in the verbal, using only a few well-timed gestures that might require her to stand rather than sit. She didn't dramatize by standing and gesturing, but rested rather on her ability to sit in a chair and stretch out the details until the denouement was far too powerful to acknowledge with anything less than a howl, followed by "Clara, you oughta stop," or "Clara, you something else."

Her mood changed only when she parried a question about my circumstances from an inquiring visitor or relative. Her eyeballs rolled upward as if the ceiling held the mystery, or they would shift quickly toward me to see if I were listening before she explained the block I had developed. It was a discussion best pursued under more private circumstances. I too looked up at the ceiling but then turned my attention quickly back to the page so that they would not think my concentration had been diverted to their adult exchanges.

In the back room of a candy store in the next block, she was the only woman who played poker with some fast movers after midnight or on Saturday afternoons. From those sessions she gathered material for her solos. They highlighted high-pitched descriptions of how Willy, too much bourbon in him and "high as a kite," had bluffed Julius; or when "that faggot" Clarence had threatened to smack Chink and then "switched on out of there." She stood to imitate the sway of his hips. "He switches better than me. I know Mister DC must be sick," referring to Clarence's father, the millionaire numbers backer. She acquainted us too with how Pete, one of two black attorneys in town, had lost a fortune only to return the next night with another bundle and in a suit that made him look "cleaner than the board of health."

I could hear her stories from my bedroom and followed the action with the familiarity of one who once had to rush a handkerchief of money to her after a frantic phone call. "You fast, take this down to Clara," Aunt Shirl instructed me as she counted out the bills and tied them up in a handkerchief. I rushed down the block, knocked on the door behind the candy counter and saw a dark room with one light in the ceiling with smoke circling it. Their faces popped out of caps turned backwards and hats cocked to cover half their cheeks. Their lips twisted cigars side to side, while their hands slapped down hard on the table or slid over its top with a smooth swishing sound. They held cards closer to their chest than a mother holds an infant. A few turned to look at me yet continued concentrating.

"I told you he was fast," she said. "And smart in school, too. Now what's trumps?" Before I left, two of the men whom I had seen on the boulevard earlier that day listening to a baseball game rewarded me with a quarter.

A number of her stories were about my doings and characteristics, suggesting to me that not only was my life known to all of her associates and friends, but that also I was much more often the source of amusement than I could ever have imagined. "And look," she said once, "Mo-Dear found him with a flashlight under the sheets trying to read because she had told him to go to bed. You know Mo-Dear says the book is bigger than him"

Now I was in the fourth grade and I had my Aunt Clara and her mother whom we all called Aunt Shirl and their swarm of friends and relatives who were as fascinated with me as Tim and Gunther ("Is he really reading?" so many asked Aunt Shirl), but who expressed their wonder by enveloping me with such thorough and genuine tenderness that Yo-Yo was eventually a distant image in my mind—a scene you cannot replay because time has eroded its features that slip away like the sand falling through your fingers.

The one duo who brought me closest to the memories I held of Yo-Yo and Aunt Iceland lived around the corner, above a barber shop. I only visited them on Sunday evenings to watch television since we didn't own a set yet. First Aunt Shirl would call to alert them to my coming. I would run around the corner and ring the bell. Then their stairway would shake as Mister Arthur lumbered down the stairway. Peering upward through the curtains, I heard his huge shoes sending off a detonating clap with every footfall. I actually ran away the first time I had visited, so loud were the steps and so wide was the body almost filling up the entire hallway, explaining to Aunt Shirl that nobody had answered the doorbell. She called them again and sent me back. A colossal dark shadow, a twisting of the doorknob, and he would appear with the friendliest smile beaming down from the ceiling. "Hey, come on up, just in time for Ed Sullivan," then turning to lead me. "Rachel, he's here."

She too was large—her head reaching the ceiling almost, with legs that seemed too thin to hold her. The floorboards creaked when she passed in front of the screen to walk toward the kitchen for the cookies and lemonade. We all sat together on the couch facing the TV, they together holding hands and smiling in each other's eyes with a murmur at each act that tickled them: a dog standing on his hind legs and barking out a tune; two men juggling while talking to the audience and even to each other, a man playing a harmonica while walking on stilts. His laugh was more like a chuckling hiccup that sent his head bobbing. They both would turn to me to see if I had thought the show was funny too, and recalling my wagon rides with Yo-Yo, I would chuckle with them. They never asked me about school, Aunt Shirl, Aunt Clara, or anything or anybody. They watched television and held hands, as if there were nothing outside of their living room that counted; the two of them existed for each other. This, I concluded, was their variation of the blues nights that Yo-Yo and Aunt Iceland enjoyed.

The school was only a ten-minute walk away and had a mixture of mostly black and some white students. I could read better than most, gaining a popularity that I basked in with modest acceptance despite Aunt Clara's boasting to everyone that I was on the honor roll, was on the safety patrol, and "could run faster than a cheetah at dinnertime." According to her, as a result of my academic accomplishments ("He's good in school" was Aunt Shirl's phrase), I was "in the paper more than Pete Lloyd," a well-known politician who was not at all publicity shy. It all happened—the adjustment to the whirl of the world's playground—within a few months. Then its beat became cacophonous and I found myself upside down and confused.

Why it took me a month to notice her is still a mystery to me. There were only two dozen students in the class and she was unquestionably the most lovely. But I saw them all as aliens of the other sex at first. I had not the slightest inclination toward any kind of relationship beyond the return of their smiles and giggles.

In fact they were interrupting my striving to perfect the angelic image that Aunt Clara and Aunt Shirl had branded me with: a smart little good thing who minded well, did well in school, and loved to read. The combined effect and constant image of the smiles of admiration were like one large cloud circling me and reminding me—if not threatening me—of the high expectations they had. And in the back of my mind was the reassuring prospect that this reputation would serve as the perfect defense if evidence ever surfaced about my having killed a cardinal and a robin.

Imagine my shock one day during my usual lunch of a mound of pancakes stacked as high as my large glass of milk. John Durham had come home with me and was sitting in the same chair that I had first sat in just a month earlier. He was waiting patiently so that we could dash back to school.

"The girls are crazy about you," he burst out in response to Aunt Shirl's asking him about school matters that had nothing to do with me at all. Before I could shoot him the threatening look I was generating, he continued. "Especially Grace. She's really crazy about you." I looked at him without speaking, hoping that the stare was enough to convince him not to mention her letter illustrated with the lipstick heart.

"I can't stand her," I said, almost slamming down my glass of milk and glancing upward at Aunt Shirl sitting across from me. Here was a defining moment, a critical juncture where I had to maintain my angelic innocence, my worthy separation from those little vixens of the other sex who could so easily drag me down into the gutter. I had not yet formed the features of the gutter yet, but it had been used by Aunt Shirl to define those without proper direction in life. To her, those who frequented bars and taverns like Daddy Lew's, Truxson's and Big B's Corner were wallowing in the gutter—and Anida's and Aunt Clara's crowd was dangerously close.

The girls inhabited a world that symbolized the other, the strangely different. My response to this mysterious group was not only to stay away from them but also to scowl disparagingly as I maintained the distance. No, I could never be the angel I was to be if I were to get involved with those—those girls.

So far my dutiful preoccupation with cementing in her mind my proximity to Saint Peter was making an impact on Aunt Shirl especially. I was on the safety patrol, proudly wearing my white belt as I stood on the corner to protect my classmates from their recklessness. My report card showed lots of A's and B's. I noticed in our Saturday evenings when we sat at the kitchenette table, sharing the pint box of Neapolitan ice cream (vanilla, chocolate and strawberry!) that had been cut in half with her butcher knife, that she was monitoring my extracurricular interests.

"You don't like girls, do you?" she asked one night, licking a spot of the strawberry from her lower lip.

"No, they too silly," I said, thinking this to be the most appropriate response for one of such virtuous standing. Later I heard her tell Aunt Clara and other visitors with great relish that I didn't like girls.

I didn't—until two separate events forced me to wonder. When walking home from school one day in one of the regiments of our groupings of two and three and four students, I saw Danny Bunn run past us, then turn to flash a devilish grin, use the word *pussy* and skirt around the corner. At the same time that my mind told me that it was a word I had never heard before, I also struggled with the contradiction of admitting that I nevertheless knew it as one of those terms you were to learn about later. But when *later* was to loom in time as *now*—this all depended upon one's individual growth and acculturation. What did it mean? Where was it? How could it happen? Why was it bad? That was a Friday.

I tried to dismiss it as another crazy moment of Danny Bunn, whom Aunt Shirl had termed a "little hoodlum" anyway after hearing of his fourth-grade exploits (playing hooky, talking back, pulling pigtails). Once in the cloakroom somebody whispered that he had tried to cop a feel—actually placing his hand on that part of a girl. Before falling asleep on Saturday night, I heard the downstairs front door squeak, the heavy footsteps trying to sound like feathers as they mounted the steps, and the closing of Aunt Clara's door. Very early the next morning, the door would creak, open and close; the feet would descend with a faster yet heavier rhythm as if invigorated and uncaring. I got up to look, and in her doorway was Aunt Clara. Her gown was too sheer for an angel like me to catch sight of, so I turned my head and heard her scamper down to the bathroom, a funky whiff of intimacy following her. The front door slammed behind Mister Bat, the married West Indian postman who was Aunt Clara's lover. On this weekend the sequence of steps and closing door had more significance than ever before. Is this what Danny Bunn was talking about? Of course it was. Was it bad or good? Or was it bad *and* good? Aunt Clara was good, so how could it be bad? But Mister Bat was married, so how could it be good? Yet they knew I knew, so how could they let me see bad?

From that moment my attitudes about the little irritants, the silly little things was transformed irretrievably. Now I paid more attention to the recess and fire drill conversations ("There is to be *no* talking, boys and girls!") detailing who liked whom, and who wanted to go with whom. I didn't acknowledge and turn my head to the other direction; no, I acknowledged and...and looked longer, with sincerity. Was that a note that Gene had slipped to Yvonne, and had she smiled before magically making it disappear? Maybe there was more I needed to know.

Without warning, a quiet, lovely sweet thing was assigned to go with me to the principal's office to pick up some materials for Miss Sontop. She was hardly more than a presence moving on my left side at first. Then a cumulus of fragrance fell upon me like a light fog and wrapped itself around me as if it were another wind itself. Where had she come from? How did her eyes sparkle so? What cosmetic concoction from the Egyptians whom we were studying had produced that sweet caramel skin? Look Booby, you know that at nine years old her body was as developed and flat as yours. But my eyes were those of a nine-year-old boy who had been smitten by the unexpected discovery of her as a being possessing a magnetic dimension. Even her red Buster Brown shoes were cleaner than any I had seen. "Are those new?" I wanted to ask as I had sequestered every impulse to open my mouth during that long, wonderful 45-second voyage to discovery—to the principal's office. I was completely off balance and regaining my footing as we entered.

Who knows what he said, what she said, what I said. Yes, my lips moved, my feet stirred, but my mind was elsewhere, struggling to place the set of details that had been so unimportant before. A side glance revealed that she was neatly dressed in a skirt and blouse. Her hair was shiny, exposing eyebrows and lips that reflected the most tender and humble demeanor. I decided then—as one waiting at a corner suddenly dashes across the street—that I liked her and wanted to go with her. Previously she had been the little girl with the name Florine, sitting in the other row over there. Now she was an indispensable part of my life. From afar, like a pickpocket mapping the route to steal her heart, I observed her every movement—what she wore each day, the route she took home, and most important, how her eyes returned my stares of endearment whenever I could lock our views. Oh I wanted her. I liked her. I wanted to go with her.

But there was competition—on two fronts as it were. An angel cannot be a thief. I could not steal her heart because I was too angelic, too shy. The other obstacle was Super.

How I lay in bed those nights listening to the Young Fellow for an hour before Aunt Shirl declared that it was time to go to sleep and turn off that radio. He was actually in his 60s and had a voice of gravel that reminded you every fifteen minutes that the show was sponsored by Snyder's Junk Yard. "Remember," he admonished, "they move trash, they don't talk it." The Young Fellow played the young music—for those fast-movers who were buying the new sound on the 45 rpm records with the wide holes in the center. When the rhythm was fast, the music set your feet flying and kicking to flashy patterns displayed at the dances at the YMCA, where I didn't frequent until I was a teenager. Some of the lyrics were "too grown" for me, according to Aunt Shirl, and she would tell me to turn off the *Young Fellow* when he played those songs declaring that Annie had a baby and she got it while the gettin' was good (*soo good, soo good*). The ballads were sung by whining falsettos that caught the very essence of my pining for Florine. In my bed, I placed the big bird book aside and turned over and rolled over and twisted and turned as I heard them mouth the very words I wanted so much to offer up to Florine. One night I hit my lip caressing my large bird book as I lay in bed listening to a luscious doo-wop ballad. Its voice was as falsetto as an oriole. How could they have known so precisely what I was feeling? Oh, if my vocal chords could just force out a few of the words from their melodies. "Only You," one group sang, with *only* stretched out to three syllables in exactly the same stutter I would use to emphasize my catatonic state. I played that song repeatedly on my record player.

Whenever I was close enough—those moments when Florine was a foot away and facing me, or two feet away walking ahead of me or about to leave the two friends she was standing with and looking so innocently in my direction—I panicked, transformed into a helpless mute. I could not muster the strength necessary to emit the words of endearment that on the tip of my tongue now carried far more weight than I had imagined at night when hearing on the *Young Fellow*. And so the fall and winter came and passed, each season bringing on a fresher Florine whose colorful coats and hats that battled the rain, the snow and the wind set off a new set of endearing thumps of my heart as I peeked at her—from the wings.

Soon it was spring, bringing the ritual of the Easter boardwalk parade. My second competitor arrived just at the time when I was managing to suppress my shy fears and erupt into a bold suitor determined to declare his intentions. Super was a year older. He attended another school several blocks away that was all black and considered to have a greater share of problem students. His dark complexion and muscular stature looked to me like a combination of a movie star and a gangster, and I was frankly intimidated by his white silk shirt. It reflected a nature that was beyond mine—advanced, seasoned, mischievously bordering on the devilish. Without warning—whenever he decided to go to school, I guess—he would stop on the corner where I was assigned— in the mornings and in the afternoons—push my arms out of the way and cross the street on the red light.

After a few weeks, this brazen flouting of my safety patrol authority—even if he was outside of my jurisdiction—became too obvious to ignore. My more amenable classmates looked at him and me in amazement as he snarled at me after reaching the other corner and continued hopping down the street. They giggled, but it was a nervous forced titter, as if aware that a showdown was imminent, one of those meetings of fisticuffs that was announced in the hallway by the phrase, "I'll see you after school." Oohs and Aahs always followed the threat, and by the end of the day, the entire school was alert to the upcoming bout.

At some point, I decided one night while listening to the *Young Fellow* that I would have to fight Super. I would have to stand up and insist that he stop pushing my arms out the way. When I visualized the encounter, I heard him say, "You wanna make something of it?" His bright wide eyes were threatening in their certainty that he would vanquish me. In the scene, I usually choked and felt my eyes water. Then the worst part of the picture shot across my mind: coming out of the candy store on the corner at just that moment would be Florine, astonished and disappointed at my tentativeness. Would she care that I was a self-ordained angel and unprepared to deal with devilish Super? Humiliated, I'd be crouched over fending off his blows while she and the entire school watched. But most important, *she* Florine would be watching.

The answer came crashing down on me like a huge wave from the ocean. It was a page that I had turned without interest on so many occasions. But now I stopped and studied the magazine advertisement with a curiosity that sent thrills through me. Here was the promise that I too could be subduing all of those well-endowed ruffians who were pointing with derisive laughter at the skinny man sitting in the sand and looking straight at me. I didn't have to be like him—weak, insulted, lacking confidence. By enrolling in the proven mail-order self-defense course designed by the Champions of America, I could learn in just a matter of weeks, in the privacy of my own home, all of the boxing skills that the champions themselves use. I could defeat any opponent with swift professional precision. Shrinking away like cowards, men would fear me. Women, amazed at my power, would line up to feel my biceps grown to the size of three bananas.

The very idea of possessing such power frightened me at first. Perhaps everyone would scatter as I walked down the boulevard. Would Mister Arthur the giant stop too in frozen fear? But the championship creed centered on building a healthy body that made us all better citizens for the country. We were disciplined athletes prepared to defend ourselves and all of America if necessary. I hurried, taking the admonition seriously—*Send your money now!*—*Don't wait!*—and watched daily for the package to arrive.

"I don't know what that boy will be sending away for next," Aunt

Clara said one night. "All of his allowance goes out in an envelope. Every day something is downstairs in the post box for him. And look, he gets more mail than Ed Sullivan."

"Well that's the least Gahtsum could do is send him that little piece of change of an allowance. He ought to come see the boy. He ain't no good. "

"Oh Mo-Dear," she replied.

I decided not to have the patch sewn on my shoulder declaring that I belonged to the Champions of America. They would find out soon enough. Each day after school I ran home, breaking away from the knots of three or four just in time to avoid Super's sashaying toward me. I practiced by the side of the bed facing a mirror, just as the instructions outlined. It was a simple basic sliding motion of your feet—up back, up back, one two, three four. That was it, a shuffle. And there were only four punches—a left jab, a left hook, a right cross and a right uppercut. Now I understood why Yo-Yo and Mister William imitated Kid Gavilan with such reverence. His bolo punch was an inventive variation of the uppercut. It was delivered like a windmill and was foreshadowed, then accompanied by spectacular footwork in white shoes.

You had to snap back the jab as quickly as you propelled it forward to enhance its stinging effect. It "opens up your opponent for other more deadly punches." The hook was an awkward sideways punch requiring a bending of the elbow; it was your most powerful left hand, "capable of knocking out your opponent." The big punch was the right cross, saved for the momentous opening, lying in wait like the queen in the end game of chess. Not the head, but the chin was the closest point to the brain. Hit him on the chin with enough power and you will knock him out. God, Booby, I was so fascinated by the art and science of it all and the straightforward need for discipline.

The Champions of America were right. In a few weeks I had become a different little boy, aware unexpectedly that not only was I a better reader than most, but also a better combatant. I realized by watching them "go to the body" or "light to the head"—their variations of street corner boxing matches—that they knew nothing of the real science, although they prefaced their challenges with "let me see what you know." They—Danny Bunn and his crew, and others too with reputations for being bullies who would beat you and take your money— depended on the power of intimidation and vaunted reputation. The combination was enough to scare away most of us. They hadn't the discipline to learn; they were good on the streets, leading with their rights and bobbing and weaving, looking good and making verbal sounds imitating a hard punch. A critical assessment of just what they knew came when I checked to see if they led with their left hand—like all professional boxers. They had no idea. I knew I could beat them all and didn't ever worry again. Maybe I was even afraid of hurting them, so I feigned my disinterest in sparring on the corners as if I were just too unskilled.

Now I was ready to demolish Super. I would wait willingly for his sauntering, his taunting, his coming toward me like a defensive back opening up a hole for a runner in a football game. Looking at the city hall clock from my bed as I set the scene in my mind, I would step back and pop him with a quick stinging jab. Then I'd take my stance, ready to shuffle left, right, forward or back. This time I'd be smirking, transformed into a "fully prepared human dynamo able to defeat any foe."

Before that fateful bout could be set, I was floored by a devastating setback. Now that my bashfulness had been transformed into a bold new resolve, enhanced by the makeover of my angel image, I decided that I would escort Florine on the boardwalk for the Easter parade. At recess in the schoolyard or before running home to practice the four-step shuffle, I had listened to the giggling banter about who was escorting whom for the colorful, ritualistic promenade along the famous boardwalk.

One night I heard Aunt Clara talking with Aunt Shirl about my insistence that I have a charcoal gray suit for Easter Sunday.

"And look, Mo-Dear," she said, "all the older kids started it—the ones in the sixth grade. They decided that charcoal gray was in this year. I took him up on the avenue to Goldblatts and he wouldn't look at nothing but charcoal."

"My legs too stiff, I can't take him on the boardwalk," Aunt Shirl mumbled.

"I think he's going with David and Freddy from around the corner. You know I picked out a cute little pink vest to go with that suit, just in case he takes a little girl with him. Some of the older kids got dates."

"What?" I heard her chair legs scrape against the linoleum as if she were pushing back from the table to breathe easier. "He ain't grown yet. And he don't like them hussies. What's-His-Name told me at lunch."

"Oh Mo-Dear, all they do is walk along the boardwalk and then spend the day at the Steel Pier. I think they look so cute all dressed up."

"Them little cute things will eat all his money up begging for salt water taffy and cotton candy. And a vest too? You must have gotten some money..."

"Yes, he sent something," Aunt Clara said in a lowered voice.

I fell asleep that night fighting to keep the image alive of participating in the stylish yearly procession with Florine at my side. I saw her in pink socks to match my vest. We would wave at Walt and Peggy from the sixth grade, and Gilbert and Nancy from the fifth. The grownups strolled in straw hats and parasols. Some cruised by in the push carts. Many had come from the Apple and from Brotherly Love.

The next morning after that conversation—it was maybe a week before Easter—I was determined to seal the deal in school that day. I thought that noontime—during the noisy crunch of speeding home to grab lunch—would be the moment. I would assert myself, a deep breath gulped down, a racing heart steadied. In the schoolyard, I leaned my shoulders against the fence and waited for her to come out of the side door where she usually tipped down the steps with those shiny red Buster Browns steadying her progress. I could walk over to her and then escort her out of the yard. When we got to the sidewalk, I could ask her.

From nowhere, Danny Bunn suddenly appeared on my left, his arms moving him toward me as if he were rowing. When he got to within two yards, his voice was louder and clearer, and I could hear his listing of couples he had heard about. In the list, in the inconsequential blabbering that I was hardly listening to, he now was a yard away and announcing an alliance of staggering relevance. In the sounds made by his mouth that I was now staring at, I heard and didn't hear, but really did hear: "...and Stuffy is taking Florine." Oddly, she too was coming toward me—from another direction. She was smiling, about to pivot through the gate and to the sidewalk. He pointed at her as if to dare me to inquire. "There she is," he said, running past me to continue his heraldry.

The thumping in my stomach was not from hunger. I had waited too long, was my first thought. And then: Stuffy? Ugly, overweight, silly Stuffy? Had he not been forced to stay after school for disrupting the class once? Had she no pride, no discretion? Would she go with anybody? She couldn't wait? Didn't she know I liked her?

Trudging down the boulevard toward home, I felt my stomach squirming. This time I walked on the side of the street where the poolrooms and candy stores and bars were situated. The others were walking on the other, safer side—according to their parents. Their cherry and jolly dispositions told me that their charcoal suits and white dresses had been purchased already, and they were certain who would be their partner on Easter Sunday. By the time I took my downcast shoulders up the staircase to our apartment and sat across from Aunt Shirl and the heap of pancakes, I was thoroughly dispirited. I chewed forever on one piece and hardly heard her talk about what Dick Tracy presaged in the day's comics. I had scarcely noticed the scurrying in of the numbesr runner, the diminutive Mister Eddie. After his rapid routine of picking up pieces of paper and counting bills, rushing past me to leave, he smiled:

"Got that charcoal suit all ready for Easter?"

While I had been running home to take my boxing lessons, the others had been scheduling their big day on the boardwalk. While I had been anticipating how to knock out somebody, they had been planning how to go out with somebody. Their concentration had been on romancing, mine had been on battling. John Durham was absent with a cold that day, and how I wished that he were sitting and watching me now, telling me about how the girls were crazy about me. Which one, what was her name? Did she have an escort? Was she as cute as Florine? Had Grace mentioned whom she was going with on the boardwalk?

I was subdued during that entire week before Easter, and tried to smile whenever Aunt Clara mentioned to anybody that I had a pink vest to go with my charcoal suit and that I had not revealed whom I was escorting on the boardwalk. "I know he's going with somebody," she told Mister Bat, who had made one of his unusual weekday visits, "but he won't tell us. The girls are crazy about him."

I didn't want to go with anybody else. My mind had fixated on Florine, just as it had fixated on Super. I had not seen him for several weeks and, in my dedication to my boxing lessons, had not really noticed his absence. And then at recess on Friday morning during a kickball game, I saw Danny Bunn huddled against the wall in a corner with three others. Waving his thick arms, he seemed to be sharing a great secret the way their eyes widened. As I waited for my turn to be the kicker, tall Gilbert came over to me with the report.

"You heard about Super?" he asked.

"No," I said, the very name sending my heart racing.

"His parents sent him away. He was getting into too much trouble. Danny's father is a janitor at the school. He heard them talking. Super brought a knife to school one day."

"Sent where?" I asked.

"Some reformatory, that's what Danny said."

"For kids?" I wondered.

"Kid hell, that nigger is almost twelve years old," announced Gilbert before running over to the other side of the schoolyard. He turned and, walking backward for a second, cupped his hands: "He got left back twice."

I could hardly kick the ball as I considered the change in events. Was I glad that he was sent away? Did I really regret that I would not be able to pummel him? Could he have pulled out a knife on me before I could jab him?

That evening as I looked through my bird book, focusing on the goldfinch described as being unusually wise and listening to the Young

Fellow spin the tunes that I had associated with Florine, I resolved that I would let Aunt Clara continue to think that I had a date. On Easter morning I would go around the corner and knock on David's door and the two of us would walk the three long blocks to the boardwalk together. Freddy had a date. Maybe I would suggest that we might meet a friend at the Steel Pier and she would think I was being secretive. David, tall and so awkward that he once fell twice during recess and endured the afternoon walking with his knee poking out of a torn pants leg, was the last friend I expected to be concerned about escorting anybody. When I knocked on their door, his mother's huge smile and compliment on my suit and vest raised my spirits as much as her confidence that we would have a fabulous time spending the day at the Steel Pier. As we turned to go out the door, I heard her pull him back and slip a few dollars in his hand with "Here, a little extra."

Our first fabulous encounter was with the boardwalk itself. Its herringbone planks made it almost four times wider than any sidewalk in the world's playground. Walking toward us, behind us and beside us in both directions was a stream of paraders sporting the most magnificent colors and styles you could imagine. It was a moving fashion show. The models wore elaborate hats that ranged in size from a small cap to a spreading sombrero. Some had canes in their hands; some had leashes with poodles on the end, prancing with collars that sparkled. I saw a man in a plaid vest pull out his watch on a chain. A woman stopped to cool her brow with a folded fan. Men pushing couples in the wheeled chairs warned us to move to the side. We were both speechless, both awed and not willing to admit that neither had ever been on the boardwalk during the Easter parade.

We gasped at the amusement piers on the ocean side. The other side toward the city featured a string of venues designed to take every penny that David and I had stuffed in our pockets.

Gifts and souvenirs were available as ashtrays, cups, flags, glasses, bookmarks, and a dizzying array of other products. A mile-long grilled hot dog was a necessity, covered with mustard, onions and relish, on a roll that was soft from the steam that warmed it. Then there were big soft pretzels covered with mustard. Boxes of salt water taffy were in the window of every other concession, but David's mother had convinced him that it would ruin our teeth. Through the restaurant panes, we saw waiters in bow ties standing at attention as they took orders.

Looming behind all of these shops were the splendid hotels looking out over the Atlantic.

And then we saw it: the huge marquee announcing the same GEORGE HAMID'S STEEL PIER that had welcomed me when Anida first brought me to the world's playground the previous summer. Breathless, we stopped and looked up. Then we looked ahead, imbibing the sumptuous odor of roasting peanuts filling the sky. Standing in front of the ticket booth was a huge talking peanut waving its arms to invite us to buy a bag of roasted treats. We entered the pier munching from our brown bags.

Where to start? A long bright noisy hall of electrifying delights invited us, beginning with the hypnotic combined whiff of roasted peanuts and barbecued hot dogs and hamburgers. Between snacks, we threw darts, we shot basketballs, we tried games of chance, we took the merry-go-round twice, we let the magician fascinate us, we lifted the hammer and banged it on the grail to show our strength, and we let the world's smartest speculator guess our weight.

Passing each concession brought us closer to the high-diving horse at the end of the pier. Moving toward this momentous event, we were tantalized further by a series of booths exhibiting various oddities of the world who attracted a gathering so large we had to stand on our toes to look over their shoulders. When the lady in a black skirt held a sword high over her head before inserting it slowly down her throat, David clutched his stomach and ran to the men's room. Stepping along, we watched and oohed with the fascinated throng at the Siamese twins joined together on a floor of sawdust and trying to move independently of the other. Two boxing kangaroos attracted so many that we had to ease around elbows and shoulders before glimpsing the tall, off-balance punchers.

At the next booth, a crowd was discharging a steady stream of giggles mixed with fearful gasps. They were throwing peanuts in the cage, then stepping back with an apprehensive pant as he moved closer to them. "Oh, he's ugly," said David, throwing some peanuts over the heads of the watchers and bouncing on his toes.

I looked up at the sign: ARTHUR, THE AFRICAN GIANT. DO NOT FEED. "Let me see," I said, pushing through the crowd. When I was close enough to grab the cage bars, he was on the other side bending down at a group of taunting kids. They were making faces at him and pointing at him. Bent over so that his head did not bang against the ceiling, his arms swinging at his sides, he moved back and forth looking both menacing and helpless. "Hey," I said so softly that I thought nobody heard.

"You know him?" David asked, pushing my back.

"No," I said, "let's go." I didn't want Mister Arthur to know that I had seen him.

Finally, the splashing sound of the waves and the strong whiff of the sea that I had inhaled on that first drive to the world's playground hit me.

We were entering the stadium at the end of the pier to see the greatest act in history. As we took our seats on the wooden boards, I had just a faint glimmer of remorse that I was sitting with David rather than with Florine. The pier's joyful surroundings featuring so many food and amusement stands had almost wiped away my disappointment. I waited for the magnificent white stallion and the gorgeous sea goddess. As the man in the candy-stripped suit holding a bullhorn put us on alert, I sat looking in the sky, estimating how high they would leap up, up, up to splash bravely into the Atlantic Ocean—which was now a very dark blue—almost black—this far from the beach. "And now ladies and gentlemen, the moment you've been waiting for…"

The horse was a roan as old as Methuselah, to use a phrase from Aunt Clara. Its color reminded me of the chestnuts that lay sprinkled on the sidewalk of Gunther's house in the fall.

"Ladies and gentlemen, please welcome your high-diving performer, *Bold I am*, sired by *Fair Play* and of *Lordamussy*, with former Miss America finalist Mary Lee Murphy on top." The nag looked as if it were dying and too weak to fall. It was piloted by a very former beauty queen whose thighs were thicker than Bold's neck. Atop her head was a faded silver dunce cap, and her bathing suit—pinching her—was of the same faded silver turned gray.

"And now, ladies and gentlemen, the moment you've been waiting for…"

And now, Booby, I tell you the truth that is a disappointment. The horse gave a

sideways glance (was he begging me to stop the show?) that told me he was a very reluctant partner, then stepped forward. Two men appeared suddenly as he nodded his head, and they pushed his rump down the sliding board into a large round tank. Water splashed up on the queen, who dabbed her forehead in a great histrionic flourish, then climbed off his back to take a bow. Encouraged by the announcer, everyone clapped, the recorded music from the top of the little stadium blasted louder—a march song from Sousa—and I stood to leave.

"Is it over?" Donald asked, looking at the horse being pulled out of its misery by four stable hands. He was throwing away another empty peanut bag.

"Yep, that was the high-diving horse leaping through the sky," I said, and was again glad that Florine had not come with me. I had bought into the image of its magnificence and had been duped. Suppose she had been with me to discover that I had not only been taken in, but also had taken her in to watch the taking in.

Chapter 11

Booby, I feel a bittersweet pang already riding into the familiar landscape of restaurants and shops dotting the expressway leading to the beach. A few minutes later we will be turning onto Sandpiper and then pulling into the garage. Chinita had always thought the name of the street was perfect since we could walk out to the beach and marvel at the little birds hopping ahead of the surf's threatening rush in their special syncopated skip, sometimes on one foot, propelling themselves just fast enough to escape. Then they turned to chase the receding waves, then stick their beaks in the sand until the surf returned to send them skipping again.

The townhouse was a wedding present from Gahtsum, and we used it as much as we could, relishing the views from the deck that looked down on the swimming pool below it. Beyond the pool is the gate that opens to the beach. Sitting on the small deck in the evenings, Chinita and I followed the movement of the flashing lights from the freighters with our fingers, drawing a line from the right corner of the horizon to the left. On a clear night we could see the lighthouse beacon and the bridge that spanned the bay.

Well, we won't be pulling right into the garage, not with all those boxes of papers that Harvey and his people have been storing for years. They are leaning against every wall and filling up every foot of open space. We will park at the foot of the garage opening. Before he explained the project, I didn't think that any case could generate so much paperwork.

Here we are near the sea, finally. I can smell it, the air deeper and thicker than that of the world's playground. The special ocean mixture of sand differs from beach to beach.

At the end of this street is the beach, and long is the row of townhouses. "Well, just who is Mister Gahtsum to you anyway?" Chinita had asked me one night as we sat on the beach with a bottle of wine. I turned to see her profile highlighted by the bright moon. She continued to look forward. After I explained that he had been a good friend of my Aunt Clara since I could remember, that he seemed to be wealthy, and that he would alight and leave in the most unexpected times, leaving with you with a foggy memory of his coming and going, I took her silent acknowledgment to suggest that she felt there was more that I had not told her.

Now turning left toward the townhouse, I see the usual crowd of beachcombers scattered along the beach's perimeter. And then we are here, turning right and stopping in front of the garage door. I feel a little better, my spirits not totally drained, but an ache of memory slices through me to bring back the melancholic heaviness within. Let's go up the steps, little guy. Okay, I carry you. I hug you as we go through the door. You must be tired. We can sit over here and look out the window at the sea. But you must sit up now.

Gahtsum told me that living by the sea would be a soothing experience. I hadn't had much contact with him for months. And then he called to say that Aunt Clara had told him that I had met the girl of my dreams. "I'm sending you something," he said, in his usual fashion. When I opened the thick envelope, the deed and pictures of the condominium made me take a deep breath, then turn to see if anyone had heard me. Once again I felt as if I were inhabiting a world that I wasn't really a part of. You didn't have to be rich to own a condominium on the beach located fewer than two hours from the capital. But still it seemed to me that it connoted something about my station that wasn't absolutely true. On our first visit, I tried to suppress my astonishment at its value as I stood at the foot of the living room and looked out of the sliding glass doors. I took the stairs to the upper level to find two bedrooms. The garage in the lowest level was like a bonus upon a bonus.

That was always how it was with Gahtsum—his alighting and leaving like some night bird, dropping off goodies, a pat on the head, a voice that came from the belly, softly roaring as if it hid unleashed power. His name and he himself surfaced regularly during those first years in the world's playground. A package would arrive unexpectedly— a record player, a watch, a model airplane kit. In a clipped phrase, moving as if she were late for an appointment, Aunt Clara would announce the arrival with "Gahtsum sent this to you." I opened it with glee while Aunt Shirl grunted, and David would insist, "You must be rich—look at all that stuff you got."

I was too busy to give more than a passing acknowledgment of his presence as I stayed abreast of the urgent rush of everybody to stay afloat in the thundering rushing demand of subsisting in the world's playground. My new world within that scuffle and scuttle was a new school and a new heartthrob—Atlanta. The Young Fellow had helped to usher in a fresh burst of excitement within me as his shows became a drumbeat for the rush that everybody was engaged in. The fast-beat music was as up tempo as the fastest numbers runner, the fastest waiter, the fastest hands at the blackjack tables Aunt Clara frequented. The slow ballads were as funky and warm and tender as any hug or embrace I had experienced, seen or imagined.

One song kept me glued to the bed whenever he played it. I lay looking out the window at the city hall clock, agitated yet soothed by the promise of the lyrics. They extracted from within me the deepest feelings—as if Yo-Yo were pulling me down Hudson Street again. Yet these lyrics seemed to foreshadow an even deeper attachment of the heart, as if there were a love even more profound and mysterious than that I had felt for Yo-Yo and was feeling now for Aunt Clara and Anida. It could be even more... electric...passionate, like the bond that Aunt Clara shared with Mister Bat on Saturday evenings. It was an awesome possibility—that one person could draw from you such an outpouring of emotion, could seem to be your *Earth Angel*. Their voices were so smooth, only a piano accompanying them as the lead asked if she would be his. He would love her all the time since she was the vision of his happiness.

> *I'm just a fool dear...*
> *A fool in love with you*

Right after that line, the thumping piano seemed to pound its beat straight through my body. I could hardly concentrate on the next song as the aftermath of *Earth Angel* distilled itself throughout me until I finally drifted off to sleep, my bird book on the other side of the pillow.

Now the new school brought me closer to the rhythms that the Young Fellow played and that surrounded the world's playground. It was all black. It was still within walking distance from our apartment—just in the opposite direction from the first school. She sat in a row to the side of me with a face shining from Vaseline, a ponytail that was just long enough to tie a red ribbon around it. What was it—the beady eyes, the innocent raised eyebrows whenever we made contact? In some romantic novel this would be the perfect encounter—meeting at age 12 the girl who would be your first wife ten years later.

She lived in a small house near the inlet, a few blocks from the boardwalk in an area that was barely a level up from the paucity of my neighborhood. Her mother served in the café at one of the large hotels, the Traymore. Her stepfather, whom she and her mother referred to by his last name—Lowe, or Mister Lowe—worked in a funeral home and wore a dark blue suit even on the weekends at home. He moved with a consistent need to catch up, peeking as he closed the door with "I got to work on a body. Won't be back 'til late."

I barely noticed her that first year. Adjusting to the new school took enough of my energy since it was twice as large as the first and offered a variety of personalities and activities. She was there; but so were others—rough and dark Yolanda with her bow legs yet alluring smile; Lenora revealing a snatch of a mustache and the most innocent of eyes; and puffy-cheeked Velma, who had made it clear that she liked me, but whom sadly I had to eliminate from consideration because of her height. She was at least an inch taller than I. So I saw Atlanta and didn't see her, as if I had pulled her from a crowd to photograph and then forgotten that she had been a subject until I looked at the prints after the film was developed later. Aha, now I remember her, is the phrase of rediscovery that is used in these circumstances.

But we were all listening to the *Young Fellow*, and we all knew the songs by heart and their singers by name, reputation and style. All of the men had processed wavy hair that could be thrown back in outbursts of emotion. It flew all over his face when the Soul Man swung himself in a circle, dropped to a split, rose to dance across the stage on one leg. It stuck up in a pompadour when the Little Racket pummeled the piano keys in his patented breakneck style, eyes aglitter below lined eyelashes. When Wicked Man twirled, dropped and hoisted his microphone around his body, his hair stood straight upward as if pulled by static electricity. All of the members of the male groups kept their curvy hair in an unbroken mop atop their heads so that when they crooned shoulder-to-shoulder they seemed the epitome of cool precision, while women in the audience fainted from their screaming crying frenzy.

We knew too that the songs were emblematic of something that was happening to us physically and emotionally. We were both scared and excited. The lyrics suggested that a magical world was being concealed behind a wall of adult goings-on. It could be better understood as we grew older, but who really wanted to wait? All of the lyrics seemed to be based on narratives that had taken place behind those doors—or could take place if the singer could get through the passageway that the door blocked. Wonderful, tender feelings were described. Rhythms that grabbed your foot and your hand and made you want to keep a beat and swing a partner and twist and shout would follow the soft slow ballads. While the scuttle and scuffle and the hustle and bustle kept Aunt Clara and Aunt Shirl moving like the rest, they were intent on keeping my angelic nature intact. Look, I was years away—until junior high school— from going to the Friday dances at the YMCA. So were most of my schoolmates. But we heard about it all, were prepared by the Young Fellow, and did know that the fabled YMCA was just around the corner from the school. Just around the corner.

We also had some idea that there was scuffle and scuttle elsewhere in the country. I had started here in a school that had blacks and whites. Now I was in a school that was all black. One day I heard the term *northside* used to describe where we lived. White people were in the other sections and in the surrounding little towns. There was no place that we were told we couldn't go. But there were enough places where we knew we would not be greeted with the widest outspread arms.

"They got a pool in their Y," David told me one day.

"Well, I wouldn't leave those magazines around," I heard Gahtsum tell Aunt Clara one Saturday morning. I had slept late and was worn out from listening most of the evening to the *Young Fellow* while imagining myself holding Atlanta tightly in a dance at the Y.

"That's what got him interested in photography anyway," she said. I stood at the top of the stairs, ready to retreat and leap back into the bed with two noiseless steps if Aunt Clara's voice moved from the living room. "You the one bought him that camera. Them kids already think he rich, and now you got us this television, and Poor Arthur and Rachel don't even see him anymore. That three-speed bike ain't cheap-looking either. Poor thing, all he can say is that his uncle gave it to him. They must wonder why he living along the boulevard if his uncle got so much money."

"Now you know"—it was a thunderous whisper coming from his midsection—"you know we don't have to let it all out; doesn't ask many questions"—his voice trailing as if facing the city hall clock. "I'm amazed that Aunt Shirl let him keep the bike in the kitchen."

"Where else can we put it? Mother love that boy too. One thing, he's smart in school, and he in the paper more than Pete Lloyd. He up for the American Legion award. Here's the clipping. I think he's got that block and certain things just don't get...his brain just don't worry about them. Mother say he in his own world. When he heard that Uncle Oscar died in the summer, he just went upstairs and got in the bed. Didn't even cry."

There was a silence that put me on my tiptoes, ready to leap back in bed in two steps. He must have taken the clipping with "Nice, very nice; I'm proud." And then: "That *Jet* has all those pictures of what's going on down there. I hate for him to see it."

"Well, it's not new, you know. Ain't nothing new under the sun."

"Yes, but that child is the same age; that's what got me thinking. They killed him, then threw him in a ditch for whistling at a white woman. I don't see why the magazine had to show the pictures of him in his casket. I arranged for the company to send a contribution to the family."

"And look, up here they can whistle at those white girls on the boardwalk," laughed Aunt Clara. "He been taking pictures of that beauty pageant. He don't miss a thing. That boy know what's going on and what's important."

I heard Gahtsum sigh. "Everywhere seems dangerous. That's what those pictures show. I wish he didn't see all of that peril. It's not good for young people. And there's been enough...you know, enough violence, Clara. I guess your mother will be back from the market soon." They were quiet...for moments. Were they staring at the clock? At each other? Were they holding hands as they had at the airport?

I started down, taking loud steps.

"Mister Gahtsum is here, sleepy head," she said, greeting me at the doorway to the living room. "I showed him the newspaper article about the American Legion award," holding up the page that had a one-inch story about the contestants circled by her in red crayon.

"I hear you've been going up to the boardwalk and taking pictures of the pageant. Who do you like to win?"

I hadn't thought of who would win. I had only gone to shoot the excitement surrounding these young beauties who had come from all over the country to represent their states. I wanted to capture this history of the prettiest women in the world as they waved from their floats, tiaras on their heads, their gowns glittering in the boardwalk spotlights. *Everybody* talked about them as if their lives depended upon it, as if they were intimately connected, as if the girls were like cousins from Brotherly Love who would sit right in your living room and eat your fried chicken and laugh and joke over a game of pinochle with you.

All of them—the bopping scufflers, the sauntering scufflers, the standing scufflers—had a favorite contestant who would be crowned. All scufflers survived on the tip—as waiters and waitresses, as bellhops, as busboys, as parking attendants, as doormen, as cabbies, as maids, as anything that would prompt a tourist to add an extra coin or bill to the regular tab. Even Roy the bootblack on the corner, whose motto "you can't look neat if your shoes are beat," I had heard way before meeting Truman Washington, guaranteed his gratuity by finishing with a flourish, snapping his rag over your instep with a resounding *pop!*

"It's the last weekend of the summer, and then all the tourists be gone. We got one last week to make it. Right, Miss Shirl? I mean, those tips got to last us 'til next summer," I had heard Mister Eddie say one day as he announced his preference for Miss Ohio because, for the talent portion, she had ventured onstage with her rendition of a tap dance routine made famous by a favorite vaudeville star of his. "Too bad she had to drop the cane," he said, running out with Aunt Shirl's numbers after placing a quarter in my palm.

"Oh you are growing. I can't believe you are twelve already. Been reading your book on birds I hear," Gahtsum said. You will see one day how important that is," leaning down with his hand on my shoulder and looking me straight in the eyes. "You can learn a lot from that book if you read it carefully."

"Yes," I said, looking straight in his eyes, emanating as best I could my sincerity, my angelic disposition that had no doubt helped me get nominated for the American Legion Award for citizenship.

"Tell him about the pictures you took of the Cat," Aunt Clara said as Gahtsum picked up his hat from the couch.

"Oh the Cat was in town?" Gatsuhm asked, his eyes widening as he stepped backward through the kitchen while looking at us. "Be sure to tell your mother I said hello."

"Yes indeed, had a big meeting at the Soldier's Home. They were celebrating the Supreme Court decision. All those big civil rights people were over there."

"I've always supported their work as best as I could," Gahtsum said, opening the door. In the dark hallway, he said, looking down at me: 'It's a shame that those people in Virginny have closed down their schools rather than obey the Supreme Court. Be thankful that you aren't down there with those ignorant Southerners."

"And look," chuckled Aunt Clara behind me, "I told you about my uncle who was in politics in the South."

"No," said Gahtsum, his hand on his hat.

"He ran for the border," she blurted out with a laugh, while Gahtsum went down the steps with the usual comment that she was crazy, she was just something else.

As soon as he closed the door at the end of the stairs I felt Aunt Clara's hand on my shoulder as she pushed by me to go up to her bedroom. "Aunt Clara gonna take a nap to get ready for tonight," she said, a familiar trace of perfume following her.

It was a sudden bouquet of Atlanta's as I watched Aunt Clara's black dress ascend the stairs, I was transported to the world of our sixth-grade cloakroom a day earlier where I had gotten close enough to absorb the fragrance of Atlanta. Tossing her pigtail, she had placed her red coat on the hanger and turned to look at me, then passed. That combination of the sudden aroma—some lotion that her mother had obtained probably from the hotel pharmacy where she was employed—and the beady eyes sweeping over me in the most innocent yet inviting flash, left its imprint. It was a page, a copyright of sorts that lay at the beginning of a novel of many chapters. And although each chapter took you through a different set of adventures, you were still under the control of that introductory moment that defined the entire book at the outset.

So it was. Oh, the succeeding chapters were riveting, filled with colorful characters and fast-paced plots and plot reversals and memorable scenes. But at the end, although you were faced with a completed story, you were branded nevertheless, hitched in a way, to the initial encounter that had sealed itself in your mind.

Of course there were moments when the seal's imprint became stuck even tighter. Look, during the celebration of the one-hundredth anniversary of the founding of the world's playground, *I held her hand*. I had stared intently—being the American Legion award candidate that I was—while others gaped blankly at Miss Dower's oration about the founding of the city a century ago. She went on and on, hands clasped in front of her waist, then turning to point at a chalked diagram on the board, about the first Indians, the Lenape who came from Delaware. Had we been to the lake with that name? I noticed a few nod their heads affirmatively. When a kid from the inlet asked, "Where are the Indians now, Miss Dower?" the scattered giggles upheld Miss Dower's decision to ignore the malcontent.

"And now, boys and girls, you will all have the opportunity to take part in the cavalcade of schools demonstration at the convention center. Every grade school in the city will be there with you, and I know that you will make your parents and Superintendent Harsh proud of you." She nodded in his direction: "And young John Durham will be playing the trombone in the all-city band."

We were to perform a series of exercises practiced during months of physical education classes that required us to raise our arms to the heavens, twisting them like helicopters, bending like weight lifters to touch our knees, and then placing hands on hips in the most precise fashion. The all-city school band would be on the stage to our right, blaring out a marching beat that seemed to lift your feet for you.

But striding in, wearing our white shirts and blue slacks or skirts— we were to hold hands to form an unbroken connection of grade school correctness. We had not practiced that entry in recess, had only been told about the arrangement. Suddenly, the thousands of eyes on us, the band's brass horns filling the hall; Atlanta, walking next to me, slid her palm into mine. Her glance of recognition was shorter than a nanosecond, but it too was as momentous as that Friday in the cloakroom. How long had we touched—a second...a minute? I dared not look. It was an out-of-this-world feeling, marching toward the spot that would separate us into our assigned line of exercisers. Her palm was a soft, moist, magical feeling, something that was related to every sensation that I had imagined when listening to the Young Fellow play "Why Do Fools Fall in Love?" Her fingers clasped mine. I was frightened for an instant by the seeming violation, then in seventh heaven at the unexpected award. It reminded me for some reason of Aunt Clara racing down the steps in her negligee on a Sunday morning after Mister Bat had left. It reminded me that I had never held Florine's hand. I thought back to Danny Bunn's boasts of how he had felt some girl in the cloakroom. Just as we were separated into our respective lines of students ready to salute the flag of the United States and begin the cavalcade, her sweet limb slipped out of mine like sand. Why, I had never held any girl's hand before, Booby.

Now I was a madman, imbued with a new force that I could neither explain nor contain. I had been recruited by Touissant L'Ouverture to charge ahead against the British, the Spanish, whoever—saber brandished high, eyes wild with resolve. Hannibal would have had no braver trooper than I climbing over the snowed summit of the Alps. Look out, you mountain tribes! Oh, talk about elation! I heard John Durham's clipped *alarums* from the stage fifty yards away as if he were standing next to me with the trombone in my ear. Talk about precision! I threw my arms in the air with a force that almost took me off my tiptoes. I twisted my body to the left and to the right as if it were possible to pivot along an axis more precise than ninety degrees. I became John Ferris testing his new wheel invention. When it was time to bring our hands to our chests and then throw out our arms to the ceiling, I seemed to float above the ground for a second and looked to the sides to be sure that the others were with me. And oh, I had never appreciated marching music so much. It ran through my new soul and lifted me up like the gospels that grabbed my insides when I went to church (on Easter) with David. I became fanfare itself, elevated in spirit and body, arms and legs moving with the certainty of never ending.

After the finale, the applause of a city's full of parents and relatives and teachers in our ears, the band members moving in circles to pack their instruments, we exercisers running toward the exits, I looked for one thing—one pigtail, one white blouse, one set of eyes. She was ahead, just in front of that Amazon Velma. And at the very moment that I thought her head would melt into the hoard, Atlanta turned as if she knew exactly where I was and smiled. Then she lifted that magical limb and waved.

Branded, yes, but still adventurous and exploring. In one chapter, I became infatuated for a moment with Yolanda when she told me that she needed my help with the spelling tests. But she caught on quickly and passed the next exam with ease. In another—was it just the natural consequence of seeing her every day?—Lenora's mustache radiated a spark that I had never seen before, and I invested some time in exploring her character at the expense of ignoring Atlanta, who must have seen us talking in the hallway. Still another: to eliminate Velma on the basis of her height did seem outlandish until, walking down the street together on some rainy day on my tiptoes to hold the umbrella high to cover her head, I heard snickers about a "midget and a giant" from at least two classmates behind us. I was too busy to talk with her after that. And then without notice, I was walking down the auditorium during an assembly to receive the American Legion award for citizenship. My fellow pupils applauded me ("Every pupil is not a student," Miss Dower reminded us), the principal smiled, Miss Dower beamed, Superintendent Harsh massaged my shoulder as he handed me the little brass medal with his other hand. It was the end of the school year, my last in grade school, and I was on my way to junior high school and, finally, Friday night dances at the YMCA. The Young Fellow kept playing the song that asked a question that we were all curious about: why do fools fall in love?

Chapter 12

Booby, you'd be surprised at how many people you can meet, how many places you can go with a camera in hand. I look out the window now and remember that when I first walked along this beach with camera over shoulder, people whom I asked to pose for me agreed quite readily. I began my practice of walking all over the city that summer before junior high school. If I pointed my camera, people stopped, smiled, turned their bodies, peered—did whatever I asked. They were in my control, eager to participate in an activity that would lead eventually to a small print likeness—a photograph of themselves. Was it the love that we all have for looking in the mirror? Was it the assumed compliment in being asked to stand in front of the lens? Was it curiosity? Most may never see the actual photograph, but remain contently associated nevertheless in the ritual of posing. They force a smile, fighting the sun in their eyes with a squint until ordered to relax with, "Got it, thanks."

I had exhausted Aunt Shirl and Mister Eddie and Aunt Clara as models in my dinette studio. I moved around the table as I knelt and bent and leaned to focus at all angles on her small oval head with the red bandana. "Oh Lord, he at it again." She patiently followed my directions to look over here and look over there with, "Like this?" I would catch Mister Eddie's smooth caramel skin as he scooted in with his wad of folded bills in one pocket and stash of numbers slips in the other. His smart thin mustache accentuated his easy smile, followed usually by a disclaimer: "Who me? I may break your camera." Then turning sideways, he would insist that I "get Miss Shirl in it too." She never objected to the compliment. And Aunt Clara was always relaxed, especially if I caught her in a new hat and earrings. She would sit smiling in my favorite yellow dinette chair, my reading spot near the living room. She smiled and talked to Aunt Shirl about the previous night's monkeyshines while turning her eyes from Aunt Shirl to me. I would stop her on her phrase "And look"—describing how Julius "had pulled out a switchblade from nowhere to warn Willy that he was messing with the wrong damn nigger. Oh honey, excuse Aunt Clara's language. "

"Hold it right there, Aunt Clara."

The first neighborhoods I discovered in my walks were like the boulevard on which I lived—of hardship. They were nothing like the wide avenues in Ventnor and Margate, these towns nudging the world's playground to the south. When they did visit these towns, the playground's strugglers went as delivery boys driving trucks, as maids, nannies and sleep-in housekeepers, as janitors in the apartment houses, as clerks and waitresses—like Aunt Clara and Atlanta's mother—in the small restaurants, pharmacies and shops. There was a section or two of the affluent where some homes were as dignified as those in Ventnor, and there were even a few dwellings stuck within the zones of hardship that were owned by teachers and owners of businesses, by the two doctors, the one lawyer and others who occupied a position far above the poverty line that identified most black people in the world's playground. But those sections were farther out, not easily reached during my casual 30-minute walks or more ambitious bike rides.

Just around the corner and over a few blocks I discovered Big Man standing by the ice cream store where I bought the Neapolitan that Aunt Shirl and I relished in the evenings. He was the shortest boy in the school and wore shoes that flapped because of the loose soles. Gigglers in the cloakrooms and in the schoolyard corners called him High Water because his pants bottoms rose above his ankles. "You live around here?" he asked, then turning to go up an alley that I had never even noticed before. Remarkably, after a few steps, at the end, as if we had been dropped on a movie set of a city within a city, I saw a lane of identically designed shacks stuck together in a sixsome that seemed to be falling forward. Each had a weather-beaten door in the center and a window on each side of the door. "Let me check," he whispered—limping; it was said in the schoolyard conversations from an injury caused by falling off a horse on the beach.

"On the boulevard," I said, shooting him with arms folded before he turned to open the front door. My eyes caught the moment to view a dark room, its walls illuminated by the red-yellow glow of kerosene lamps. A sofa was against the wall. A strong rich trace of seasonings flew at me, and I thought of the special meals that Aunt Iceland prepared for Mister William and Aunt Hattie. No electricity?

"Yes ma'am," I heard him say as he closed the door and faced me.

"My momma getting ready for the night shift, so I can't have any company. But wait here and I'll bring you back one of my mig fighters. I have a helicopter too."

"Big Man?" It came from inside.

"Yes ma'am."

"That the smart boy won that American Legion award?"

"Yes ma'am."

"Well you ought to ask him to help you with your home work. Put those model planes away for a minute and work on those fractions and decimals giving you all that trouble. First it was horses, now airplanes."

Farther back, as if there were an invisible room darker than the darkness of the room from which she spoke, I heard a voice: "He taking pictures?"—a stamping of boots, a clicking of belt buckle and a muffling of cough, and then a large shadow emerged from the darkness to become Big Man's father standing at the doorway. His white apron was tied to his waist. Above it were his black folded arms and his thin dark face. His flashing wild eyes blazed at something behind me as I moved backward to focus on his face in the doorway. His smile was generous and authentic when he said to me, "Big Man told me you shoot all over with that camera, even the Miss America Pageant."

"Yes." I didn't say "Yes sir," as I heard Big Man and a few others address men. It sounded too country to me, as if they had just come up from the South. But it was my angelic, innocent, respectful *yes*.

"Which one of them white women you like, Miss Arkansas?" His smile changed so that an eyebrow went up in an arch. I was glad I had the camera in front of my face because I didn't know what to say. "You probably like all of them, can't make a choice. How can you not? They parading all up and down the city like queens and goddesses, and my wife, your mamma, our grandmammas running around working their butts off and cheering for them. How can you not like them? Everything you see tells you how gorgeous they are. The whole world loves them. Right?"

I nodded and stepped back to get some full-length shots.

"At least up here you can look at them and take pictures of them. You see what they did to that poor boy down in the Sip. Talkin' about he whistled at her. Ever since the beginning of time they been trying to keep her—Miss Ann—away from you. I believe that's why those crackers don't want us to go to school with them. Scared you might touch one. And the craziest thing—" here he unfolded his arms and held them out toward me as if engaged in a debate—"is that these gigaboos are all running around here like Miss Ann is our friend for two weeks. Didn't you hear their favorite singer say that all we can do for him is buy his records and shine his shoes? You supposed to be smart, but I bet you can't tell me why we don't see through them—the real them. Can you? When you took their photographs, did you see the real them?" He had that smile again, as if he expected me to answer him. Heck, Booby, I hardly knew what he was talking about. And thank goodness at the moment when time had stopped for me and it felt as if the entire neighborhood were waiting for my answer, Big Man's mother appeared behind him. She wrapped her arms around her husband's neck in a playful choke, and it was the perfect time for me to unlock my lips.

"Hold it right there," I said.

"I got my Miss America right here," he smiled, leaning his head back so that their cheeks touched. "She the real Miss New Jersey."

Farther up the boulevard between our apartment and the first school I attended were a succession of storefronts, bars, poolrooms and other shops. On this route—which sometimes took me up, down and around the side streets—I encountered a picturesque assortment of characters who not only intrigued me with their photogenic qualities, but also with their spirited exchanges that proceeded without censure of language or topic until one would notice that I was just a child. Then the speaker would either apologize to me or cover his mouth dramatically with the palm of his hand, eyes up to the ceiling.

Their stories drew me closer to that mysterious wall that my friends and I were discovering because they so often featured the events that occurred behind that partition of unspoken adult sensuality. The Episcopalian priest whose parish sat around the corner from my last school and just a few doors from the YMCA had been uncovered in the bedroom of a teacher's wife. When I photographed the narrator holding a stick in Johnson's Billiard Academy, he was telling the entire poolroom how Father Matthew, in his underwear, had jumped out the window and climbed onto the roof. "Father Matthew running across the roofs in his shorts, poor Evelyn husband looking out the window, up and down the street trying to figure out where he went." Wally leaned over the pool table and placed his hand next to his forehead that turned first to the left and then to the right and back to the left to demonstrate the husband's searching. A huge roar of laughter and chuckles filled the pool hall. Encouraged, Wally the actor then circled the table on his toes to imitate Father Matthew's wobbly course over the rooftops.

Often the full narratives were cut off when they discovered that the person behind the camera focusing on them was I, a school boy, so that only the beginnings or the middles of the stories reached my ears. But even the truncated versions left enough scenic material to expand my vocabulary about the range of activities in which men and women might

engage. A fascinating, recurring set of possibilities emerged as I listened
to them. Men showed that they could lose their minds over a woman.
Women showed that they could lose their minds over a man. Men could
treat their women so cruelly. Women could be just as cruel with their
men. Wives like Evelyn would be untrue to their husbands, and husbands
like Father Matthew would be untrue to their wives. In no more than a
few memorably hushed exchanges was it made clear that some men, like
Clarence, loved men only, and that some women preferred to love other
women. A tall handsome wavy-haired man in one tavern described
Frances' homosexual leaning as a terrible loss to mankind: "That fine
yellow thing up at the inlet is a damn bull dike, can you believe it?"

In all, one undeniable fact emerged continually: men and women
could not live without the other. Was there a maddening irresistible need
to connect that drove them toward each other? Is that why there were so
many variations of plots, scenes, and characters while the underlying
theme in each story centered around one quintessential need—love?

Nay Booby, I know what you are asking as you sit comfortably on
the couch, your legs lying flat. They spoke of more than must men and
women. When they did, the characters and settings may have changed,
but never the theme. It remained the same. The characters may have been
the police officers outfitted in blue, the politicians smiling in their gray,
the mob in their fancy reds, the judges in their black, the teachers in their
brown, the employers in their white. Each was just another aspect of the
constant danger. Some consistent campaign had been launched that had
suppression and even extermination as its goal. No date of its beginning
had been mentioned—as if there had been no real time when it did not
exist. In the clubs farther out, near the pike or over by the inlet, these
exchanges were uttered in lowered tones. They were voiced by men and
women wearing suits and dresses, stepping out of new cars, using proper
language that needed no apology.

One photograph I took was of a tall dark man who coached the youth
basketball league at the YMCA. He directed a toothpick back and forth
and managed to keep his listeners entranced as much with his story as with
the possibility that his lips might lose control. I didn't understand
everything, but I knew that the scenes and landscapes they discussed were
of places far away, and that the implications were greater than those about
a recent infidelity. No, their themes were collective and universal—about
black people in general—all encompassing. When I left those locations I
often felt as if I had been exposed to yet another wall. But I wondered if
they were a bit too vehement, a bit too fearful that some plot was afoot
leading to extermination. And who was most in danger of this
annihilation? I kept hearing that it was I. I was in the most danger.

I saw no danger at all as I continued my expeditions during the spring and summers of my high school years. How did I lose touch with Atlanta and then Phyllis too I have asked myself so many times. How did the story—*their story*—take such a dramatic turn? Was it my preoccupation with uncovering the mysteries that lay behind that wall as I journeyed from junior high school to high school? Is that what displaced from my memory the thunderously fateful encounters with Atlanta and Phyllis? Just that quickly, from the innocent fourth-grader who couldn't stand girls, I had become one who was fanatically consumed by their existence. Before my descent from the top of the steps one morning, I heard a painful gasp from Aunt Shirl when told this by Aunt Clara: "Mo-Dear, He's a little Romeo."

"Oh Lord," she replied, and it was in the same tone she had used when I last saw her, lying on a cot with a blanket covering her from the waist down. "Them girls will ruin him." The "sugar" had taken its toll swiftly—causing a set of ailments that the doctors were optimistic about containing to a full-scale invasion of her body that left them pessimistically with few options. One leg had to be amputated. It was my first year in high school and I was fully wound up in the mad whirl of contact with the opposite sex. I forced myself to sit longer than I wished during my visits with her in the back room of Mister Arthur and Rachel, who had volunteered to watch over her. Her panting made me uneasy, and the fact that only one leg was under those covers sent a sadness through me that I hated to endure. "Oh Lord," she replied when I told her that David and I were going to Brenda's for our first house party. It was her birthday celebration and we would be dancing to some of the tunes that the Young Fellow played. I saw the one leg kick upward as if Aunt Shirl were trying to trip us up and keep us from reaching the dance floor. "You be careful now. Them girls ain't got no sense." She turned from staring at the ceiling to look at me. She held my hand. It had the rough, hard feel of a limb belonging to one who had scuffled all her life.

Romeo? I hadn't thought so. I was simply outrageously curious, naturally magnetized, swept up in the dash that had pulled us all toward the breaking down of the wall. I don't even remember enjoying that first fateful moment with Maureen. She was considered a scag who didn't have many friends, attended the dances because she lived in one of the second-floor apartments around the corner from the Y. Her soiled gray skirt was short, her hair was short, her words were short—clipped as if she were afraid to say the wrong thing. Several of my new high school friends, already successful in making the transition out of virginity status, had encouraged me to pursue her. "She'll give you some," they said with certainty. It was an almost inconsequential moment. Did I enjoy it? Did she? Afterward—was it in her dark living room one Saturday?—I remember a sad smile of disinterest on her face and my own disappointment that nothing spectacular had occurred.

At Brenda's party, I realized how many friends I had made by walking all over the town with my camera. So many knew me or had heard about me. I had actually taken some of their photographs and didn't remember them. For a few, like Big Man, I had stayed after school or met them in the library on Saturdays to help them with handling fractions and decimals—their biggest math challenge.

Like Atlanta, Brenda lived in the inlet section but farther toward the pike. Her eyes were bright and her lips were full and she was a great dancer. Her teeth took on a special radiance because they were set against her dark skin when she laughed or smiled. She tilted her head to the side when she laughed, introducing it with a chuckle that sounded like a gurgle. Her eyebrows would rise.

They were rising when she smiled at me from the kitchen. Her body was small and compact, swaying side to side. She wanted to know if I were enjoying myself. Did I study all the time? I told her that it was a great party. She said that her mother was working but that she agreed to Brenda's having a party. A tall thin guest wobbled in with a beer in his hand and yelled out a happy birthday greeting. He leaned over and kissed her on the check. She smiled at me while squeezing him around the neck. She was chuckling at what he was whispering to her while staring at me. Weeks later I was in her living room after school.

If Aunt Shirl had been alive, she would call Brenda one of those fast girls. It was known that she had gone with guys much older than she and that she was sexually active. She didn't come to school every day. She drank wine on the weekends and smoked cigarettes. It was said that she had been slapped by an older man. Her group of girlfriends was known to be in the high-speed lane also, moving at a pace that put them in tight sweaters and among those grinding-hips-in-the-dark-corner couples at the YMCA dances. I tried not to stare when I saw one, Alice in the corner with a partner who seemed to be bending her back into a C to *Can I Come Over Tonight*? My weakness for Brenda: her alluring, murmuring smile and those raised eyebrows.

No wonder I was bold enough to walk up the steps of 1407 Caspian Avenue without looking right or left, straight down the hallway to the door leading to their kitchen. Soon I was in her living room and kissing her lips, undressing her, having been already assured about the agenda with a "You coming over after school?" murmur between classes.

Then one summer day before I entered high school I took a side street going away from the beach and boardwalk. If you followed the street to the end, you would reach the very boulevard that Anida had driven on when we first arrived. The farther I went, the more things changed. Soon there were no apartments on top of stores, no snug little homes with porches that could hold no more than three rocking chairs, and no sixsome shacks glued together and leaning perilously. Now I saw grass and even lawns, wider cross streets. A robin hopped on a front lawn. Two wrens dove and darted near an oak tree. There was no hustle and bustle. The street was quiet except for a Shepherd rushing toward the wire fence that imprisoned him in a corner lot. He came with enough velocity to jump over it, but slid on his forelegs to a standstill at the last moment. He stuck his black snout through a hexagon of wire, snarling and growling. He lost his mind when I pointed my camera at him, jumping and twisting in a circle almost as perfectly as the fantastic dancing seal had done at the Steel Pier. He raised too much dust for me to take my shot.

"Come back, Killer!" Her shout was filled with anger but it lacked enough of something to seduce the would-be killer to a calm. He jumped with even more ferocity, spitting now and turning what had been a fairly rhythmic set of utterances into a gaggle of frustrating yelps. "Time to eat, Killer!" Suddenly he stopped and turned, his tail up and angled back toward me, his head facing the girl standing on the front doorway as if she had waved a magic wand. "Come," she ordered, bending down and stretching her arms out toward him. He murmured, turned to look at me and then trotted toward Phyllis, went up the steps and into the house. I heard his single bark echo inside. "He doesn't like cameras," she said to me. "Didn't you win the American Legion award? You should know how to be a better citizen, coming around causing disturbances."

"Yes," my voice low from a racing heartbeat.

"I thought so," she said, walking down the steps and toward the gate where I was standing and testing its lock. It was my first conversation with the girl who would become my second wife. "You live around here?" Before I could answer, she missed a step and barely caught her balance in time to keep from falling. "Oops, forgot there was a crack there."

"No, just taking a walk with my camera," I said. Oh we knew each other as schoolmates recognize each other. I had seen her walking to school in that clutch of westside girls who carried books dutifully and wore trendy clothes and sat together after school in the popular sandwich shop. We had spoken to each, waved to each other—but never really, really stopped to talk to each other. As she balanced herself to check the toe that she had stumped and then laugh at her clumsiness, her face—as smooth and as caramel as Mister Eddie's—was just inches from mine.

And I saw her lips. I didn't taste them, relish them until months later, but I knew at that moment that I so wanted to press my mouth against what I saw: smooth, moist, warm petals of unimaginable promise that now were glistening in the flash of sunlight suddenly breaking through the clouds. No it wasn't until I had walked her home from the high school bus one day and was standing in the vestibule that signaled the allowed and the forbidden that I was able finally to taste. Her parents had not yet arrived, Killer had greeted me coming through the gate as a reliable visitor ("Oh, he likes you; maybe you should feed him." *Uh, that's okay thanks.*). We had had a lovely walk from the avenue down to her neighborhood, and I had been captivated by her stinging sense of humor that featured wickedly disparaging remarks about our schoolmates. Now we stood as usual at the doorway where we would say good-bye and she would press her lips against my cheek and smile like sunshine.

But this time, she whispered, "Nobody's home," and smiled, licking her lips as if they could possibly be dry. She was facing me as she unlocked the door and leaned against it. I followed the course of her tongue as it glided horizontally. But she was falling, losing her footing, stumbling. I grabbed her. Next: books on floor, her hand behind my neck, her body against the wall, my body against hers, my leg between her thighs. She opened her mouth and introduced me to the kiss that I had not known about. It was the kiss that everybody on the Young Fellow's show sang about. It was the kiss that Evelyn had lured Father Matthew with and later tempted her boyfriend with. It was the kiss that I had fantasized about, had lain in bed thinking about, thought I knew something about, but had never really experienced.

Phyllis had a kisser's mouth and a kisser's mindset. You cannot really kiss a woman whose mouth does not open fully enough, whose lips don't part in a way that begs you to explore this gateway to her very soul. To touch the spirit of her soul, you must approach the opening as a tunnel of delectable offerings to be savored as if time were suspended and you were free as we are in our dreams to explore and enjoy. She begs you to give yourself up to her hypnotic power and accept the dissolving of both the past and the future. There is only the trance of now. A woman's appetite for the kiss is fueled by a passionate generosity that has contradictory moments. On the one hand she wants to give with a maddening readiness. But at the same time she also wants to be explored, wants to be mined so that the consummate moment of ecstasy is wildly reciprocal.

Oh yes, Phyllis knew how to expose herself to and encourage my exploratory beggings, the passionate importunings of my tongue, obsessed with capturing the nectar of her lips. Oh yes, her mouth was generous, parting at my pressing to open up a planet of sweet discovery. My tongue traveled over, under and around hers, and then hard against its firm wet muscles, exploring with increasing abandon. I was in league with Estevanico and Hannibal, searching for as much sweet softness that may lay ahead as they had searched for new lands to conquer.

My concentration would swing from two sensations. First was the charge from her lips. Then this charge was accelerated by the thrill coming from our thighs pushing into each other. I tried to experience the combined thrills and collect them into one sensation, but I could only go from one to the other. It was impossible to focus on both at once despite my giddy hope for that gormandish possibility.

Her fingers up and down the back of my neck and then massaging my scalp, her hips twisting into mine, who knew what would have happened had not Killer's barking warned us. Old Miss Randall was walking by and had stopped with hands on hips to check on her neighbor's front door that was ajar.

"Oh that girl never closes the door behind her," she chuckled. "I thought that was you. Y'all cute walking home from school together," she said with a broad smile. Her cane waved at Phyllis, who had pushed me down the steps with such force that my books were in the air and I was about to land on Miss Randall. "Watch it, young fellow," Miss Randall tittered, then moved out of my path and bent to study the lawn: "These grasses need to be pulled up here; let me see." I gathered up my books from the walkway and was beyond the gate, then up the street, safe, thrilled, waving at my new lover as I skipped backward.

Chapter 13

I was jolted by the realization that I knew so many students—or that they knew me. One day between classes it seemed that everybody called me by name—even pronouncing it correctly—and greeted me with big smiles. But how did the white students know me? I hadn't walked through their neighborhoods taking pictures or to help them with their homework. I couldn't have gone to their all-white junior high schools. Had Aunt Helen left copies of articles about me in the delicatessen? Had they read about the American Legion award and kept the clipping?

True, I had maintained my image as the innocent angel—ever vigilant about doing the right thing, as shy as I had been in Oakbury yet just as eager to gain attention by speaking up or reaching out whenever there was an opportunity. But this was high school, not junior high or elementary school, and there was no show-and-tell session in the mornings. So from the time I met Herman on the freshman cafeteria committee, I never stopped reaching.

"This shit is easy," he said, shaking my hand and introducing himself as naturally as if we had known each other since the third grade, and never considering the supposed obstacle of his being a Jewish boy whose parents owned a delicatessen and my being a black boy whose aunt may have worked in that delicatessen now forming an instant friendship. "All we have to do is stand here every day and we get credit," running his hand through his dark hair, dark eyes blazing, dark trousers so baggy that they seemed to be obeying an unseen wind. "What else are you on?"

I ransacked my memory for the list of clubs, teams and committees. "I'm looking at the chess team, wrestling team, photography club, and cross-country team," I said, afraid that I may have missed a possibility.

Eyes searching the ceiling, he wondered out loud, "Well are you going to do any studying?"

That first conversation with Herman and then the subsequent encounters with so many black friends had put me in a terrible bind during my first two years. They had already identified me as their representative in the school. After all, I had won the American Legion award, I could prove that I had read every book about birds in the library, and I had pummeled one theme constantly when asked about my plans after school. I was going to college. So they expected me to make the honor roll. Not just for myself—but for them—the black kids, many of whom hadn't one clue about what they could do with their lives.

It exhausted me, Booby. I couldn't stop reaching, trying to please both audiences. And I couldn't finish anything. On my first day with the cross country-team, I sprinted down the boardwalk as if I had been sent by Aunt Shirl for that pint of Neapolitan. I was far ahead, the nearest footsteps sounding miles away, the few fall visitors to the world's playground smiling at me in my sharp blue and white warm-ups as I passed them with an extra special lift in my knees. I pushed out my chest so that they could see World's Playground HS Cross Country on the front. Oh the fall sea breeze felt good against my face, the firm pound of my toes on the hard boards sounded so...good, like a special drumbeat I had composed. And then a small tornado of resistance hit me in the chest. The tornado had hands that clutched and shook both my heart and lungs of all its breath. My legs, just seconds earlier light as hair strands, now felt heavy as iron rods. One, two, three...and more passed me. The ones who had been behind me were way ahead, their elbows swinging so rhythmically that they could have been soldiers in a drill.

Gasping for breath, I dragged myself to a rail. I held on, looking at the ocean. My shirt lifted mightily in tempo with the surge of my heart. I hadn't run so far in my entire life. I looked ahead. Where were they? How far would they go—to the Steel Pier? From where did they get their stamina? Had they had more rest, a better breakfast? Were they cheating?

"Are you all right, young man?" He was in an apron with food stains all over it.

"Yes, just decided to rest," I said, my breath more level than I had anticipated. I looked behind him.

"Would you like to come in for a glass of water?" He had walked out of a restaurant in front of a hotel. I looked behind him and saw the name Traymore. I remembered it as the place where Atlanta's mother worked.

"Oh no thanks, I've got to get back to school...chess club meeting," I said, and pulled from within me the last ounce of energy to sprint away from him.

I hadn't pushed myself more than a few steps farther when I heard him say, "Keep up that discipline, young man!"

Yes indeed, I thought, I sure will. I will keep up enough discipline to keep me from having a heart attack. Who would want to run across the country anyway? Hadn't Aunt Clara said that I was faster than a cheetah at dinnertime? Had I not rescued her from losing countless poker games with my speedy delivery of funds? Had I not returned once with a pint of ice cream before Aunt Shirl had had time to pull out her knife? Hadn't I beat David and others in countless street races? No, this was some grueling variation of real running, and I was not buying into it. I was having none of it. There was one way to run, and that was full speed— like Jesse Owens and Jackie Robinson.

"I've got to get ready for the wrestling season." I explained to Herman, who had gone to the first cross-country meet of the year and wondered why he had not seen me. To the group of brothers who sat together regularly in the cafeteria, I made it clear that it would be impossible for me to make the honor roll and keep up the rigid cross-country travel schedule. After all, we were scheduled to trek all the way up to the New Ark. Their widened eyes convinced me that my explanation had generated the understanding and sympathy I sought.

With my superior knowledge of boxing, it was almost unfair of me to take advantage of wrestlers. They couldn't move as fast. They seemed to circle constantly, grabbing at their opponent's shoulders, smacking at their arms and legs, bending and squatting and grunting like cavemen. Shuffle up and down, moving with precision, bobbing and weaving? They didn't have a clue. I was looking at them practicing through the window of the weight room one afternoon with a measure of real condescension when I felt a hand massage my shoulder from behind. "Going in?" It was Herman.

"Huh?" I turned to see him with a stack of books in his hands, pants falling from his waist.

"Aren't you on the team?"

"I think I missed the darn tryout deadline," I said with as much sucking of my teeth and exhaling as I could muster. "I may have to wait until the spring. My studies just got the best of me and I forget all about the schedule."

"Shit, that shouldn't be a problem," he said, opening the door and pulling me by the arm. "Mister Brack, here's a great wrestler from the northside who wants to try out. Can't you give him a shot? My dad will be really grateful for the favor."

The practice room smelled as if they had been sweating for hours. One couple never looked up, locked like bulls in a struggle to throw the other by his shoulders to the mat. In a corner, two sparred with their hands out, feinting various movements in an attempt to trick the other. Coach Brack, in a bowtie, looked at me. I could feel others staring at me but going about their business nevertheless.

"You wanna wrestle, young man?"

"I'd love it," I said, wondering again where I was able to muster the response.

Booby, it was like this. During the few weeks of practice, I sparred with two others in the same weight category and beat them consistently. I became the starting wrestler for my weight. Then came the first match, and I faced the skinniest boy I had seen in my life, his ribs bulging from their cage as if no skin covered them. Was there a mistake? Didn't he belong in another weight class? I saw the referee move away, the miniature boy crouch. I saw his arms, thin as broom sticks, swinging back and forth. I saw his eyes. They were gray, unblinking. It was the same color gray of the ceiling that I was now watching from my back. He had thrown me down, pinned me, and was holding me for the count as I lay kicking and wondering what had happened. Just above me, just below the ceiling, I saw Superintendent Harsh—there unannounced to cheer me on. He was bending over and looking in my eyes, completing the nightmare that had started and ended in seconds. I saw him cup his hands to his mouth, and although the gym was filled now with screaming sounds—some begging me to get up and some begging Armon to keep me down—I could see his lips forming the words: *Get up.* I couldn't, and it was too late anyway. I had lost.

Thank God there wasn't a black face in the gym that evening, nor was there a white face belonging to Herman or any other who might report back to him. The next morning I told Coach Brack that practice was taking me away from my books and that I had to devote all of my time to making the honor roll.

"Well I understand," he said. "The honor roll, huh? I guess you will have time for the chess club," he said, adjusting his tie and walking away.

Yes it was the honor roll, and it was college, and it was not going to be photography. Aunt Clara and Gahtsum had made that clear on the day that I submitted my educational intentions form for her signature. I had already perused all of the college guides in the library and found the best option—photography at a large university in Beanton. From there I could get a job with a newspaper or magazine that would send me all over the world to shoot fires, wars, famous people, tall buildings, pretty women.

"Absolutely not." Gahtsum's voice came softly yet powerfully from his midsection, as if he were gasping. It was a Thanksgiving weekend

where he and Anida had joined us, and the first we had celebrated
without Aunt Shirl.

"Mister Gahtsum's going to help pay your way through college,"
Aunt Clara said, sitting next to him on the living room couch after we
had eaten. I sat on the other side of the room with Anida. Between their
heads I could see the city hall clock.

"Yes," and I want you to fulfill your potential," he said. "You've
done a great job—that award, the Legion…"

"It's the American Legion award for good citizenship," said Anida
from the kitchen where she was cleaning up.

"Yes, and you made the honor roll your first year. What was that,
Clara—freshman class representative? But young man, you should set
your sights on the highest you can obtain. Your potential is unlimited."

"You ain't gon' make no damn money taking pictures, boy"—her
voice again from the kitchen, this time fighting with the sound of a
banging pot. "You might as well be out there with them hoodlums who
won't have a pot to piss in."

I saw Gahtsum flinch. "Well, in fact the arts are an important source
of amusement for our society, but it's no way to make a living. It's so
risky…no guarantees. And what you people need…what we need…are
leaders. These are critical times that you may not understand. But I had
hoped that you would be contributing to the community uplift, being a
part of history. I feel that you have a special calling."

"He ain't paying your way if you insist on studying photography—
that's it. And your Aunt Clara ain't signing that damn paper." Anida had
gone and returned to the middle of the room. Her towel wrestled with a
dish that had held candied sweet potatoes. She faced me and kept drying
the dish without looking at it. Instead, her eye stared into mine.

"And look, Mister Gahtsum's going to help Aunt Clara buy a house
on the west side too." Aunt Clara reached over to touch his arm.

"You should be planning to go to law school," Gahtsum said,
uncrossing his legs and leaning toward me. "Then you can really
contribute. You got students down there in the Sip risking their lives just
to eat in a restaurant or enroll in a school, and you want to waste your
talent by taking pictures? I got that camera for you to have fun with, not
to try to make a silly artistic career out of. You go to college and take
pre-law courses and then go on to law school. That's where we need you.
I wish I had gone on from college to become a lawyer."

"You ain't done bad, Gahtsum. You probably got enough to buy a
college. Now you know Mister Gahtsum has never told you wrong,"
Anida said, her voice shouting over the running water in the kitchen. He
been helping you and us since you can remember…ever since your

mother…" Aunt Clara's eyes went up to the ceiling.

Looking out the window, I felt that I couldn't hold back the tears or the choking feeling in my chest anymore. I was swallowing and coughing. "You should be looking at those colleges in the group," Gahtsum advised, "They are the best we have. And I've got good connections with one or two. In fact, one in New England has an exciting new program that I think you should look at. We'll talk, young man," his fingers forming a cage.

"Oh we don't mean to upset you, honey," Aunt Clara said, her arms reaching out toward me. "We just want the best for you, that's all. Come sit over here. He's right about those colleges in the group. They are the tops. You probably don't remember driving by the one in Brotherly Love when you were this little. And ain't that many of us in them schools."

As I sat between her and Gahtsum, his soothing cologne winning its war against the food odors, the warm hug I received was more badly needed than she could imagine, I glanced at the city hall clock again. It was really Aunt Shirl's clock, and she wasn't here anymore. She had always darted around the week before Thanksgiving to prepare a cafeteria of offerings that I knew I might never savor again. Turnips, sweet potato pies, potato salad, greens—who could ever match her fare? All the while, scurrying from the tiny kitchen to the dining room (me reading my bird book and agreeing with nods), she would be complaining and criticizing—Aunt Clara's gambling, Mister Bat's mean West Indian personality, Anida's crawling in the gutter. And yet, these were the very people for whom she was lovingly and exhaustively preparing her spectacular cuisine. When I looked at the city hall clock and at the same time listened to them declare their opposition to my college plans, I was overcome by a more powerful disappointment. So I couldn't study photography in college. That I could handle, and it could even be challenged or modified later. But what couldn't be modified or challenged at all was the fact that Aunt Shirl, whom I last saw lying on a cot in Mister Arthur and Rachel's back room, would not be with us ever again at Thanksgiving.

Chapter 14

Herman told me that I should run for president. He was sitting on the other side of the cafeteria table with four others, eyes bright with intensity.

I recognized them immediately. We all knew that tall, short-haired Marie's parents were both doctors who could watch the seagulls cruising over the bay from their living room in Longport. And the shortest of them all—a brain in all the math courses—Evan was already looking blankly through me, his chin resting on his cupped fingers as if he were calculating the votes by neighborhood. Wasn't his father a partner with his brothers in a big law firm on Atlantic Avenue—named Evan Evan and Evan? Herman of course was the ring leader, pulling up his pants and finger-brushing-scratching-combing his hair as he declared that it was simple: I would get all of the Jewish votes and all of the black votes too. "Who can beat that?"

"Well, I think he'll get some Italian kids too," said Marie.

"Look," said Herman, his hand reaching over the table to rest on my shoulder. "You've done all these things—freshman class rep, student council..."

"Cross-country, wrestling..." Evan interrupted, counting on his fingers. "Don't forget the athletics."

"Well now, to tell the truth ...I didn't..." My voice was at whisper level.

"Shit, you were on the team, that's all," declared Herman. "Guys, I told you he gets emotional. Don't be so modest. That's why"—he turned to his campaign team—"that's why he needs us. The kid's too humble."

"We can have the first party at my place," Marie volunteered. "My parents will think it's great."

They didn't have to invest too much time in convincing me. I stared out the window day-dreaming on the jitney from school that afternoon. Should I start preparing my speeches—like the one that had captivated me, the one that Bill Wagenheim made when I had sat down in the auditorium as a scared freshman?

I thought back to his standing in front of the class as the jitney stopped at one corner, puffing and snorting as the driver changed gears. As we pulled off in the late fall dusk, to my right I saw a shadowy Swing in a hotel uniform coming down a street from the boardwalk. I recognized the determined sway of his arms, which is why we nicknamed him. He would have to catch the next jitney all the way to the inlet. I guessed that he was leaving work, but it was only an hour after school. Had he not gone to school that day? Had he thought being in class all day not worth it? Was it too rigorous? Did he need to work to help his family?

Now I started to worry. Black votes, what black votes? How many? How could they vote if they didn't come to school? I wasn't sure why so many were so disinterested in school. Is that what Aunt Shirl meant?: "Free schools and dumb niggers. They ain't goin' nowhere...just hoodlums."

In junior high school I had been barely friendly with two classmates who had been sent up to the Burg. I wasn't sure why they had spent time in the reformatory, although it had been rumored that James had raped a girl and that Ron had made some permanent imprints on a man's throat with a broken bottle. They both wore processed hair, removing their handkerchiefs just as the bell rang to start classes, revealing a perfectly styled head of waves as shiny as those who sang in the groups. Ron was tall, his voice barely rose, and he sat in class bothering nobody and turning no pages. The shorter James smiled with a turned-up lip that put you on guard about his earnestness. He was constantly whispering suggestions to the girls, and when he turned to see who was watching, you could see that smirk partially hidden by his palm.

Where were Ron and James now? And Super? They weren't in school. So where were they?—back in jail? Which? For how long? What happened to Durham, and Little Man? I remembered tall Gilbert's telling me in junior high school that he just couldn't understand fractions. As he sat on the ledge, I noticed the quarter-sized hole in his shoe sole and wondered: Could his parents help him?

That evening, Aunt Clara was telephoning Anida. "Now he's in politics," she said. "As soon as it's in the paper I'll let you know. Yeah he still using his camera, but he ain't got time for that now."

Oh, am I moving too fast, Booby? Do I need to slow down and orient you? Oh, I know I keep skipping around, moving you here and moving you there. You were in the capital just hours ago, and now you are at the waterfront. And who were those people calling in on that talk show? Were they for real? I know, Booby, it's confusing. Let's go back to my last year in high school.

By senior year we all pretty much had girlfriends. Ralph courted Eva, a heavyset girl who lived uptown and was in his car as often as he. Wayne was going with Dot—freckled, with a smile that warmed everybody. Me? I had spent much of the summer before senior year with Atlanta. We had been enjoying a reunion of sorts since we had not seen much of each other since the very beginning of high school. It was as if that summer we accidentally decided that we wanted to spend a great deal of time together—and we did. Her mother allowed her to drive the Chevrolet on the weekends, and we went to the seawall often to look out over the Atlantic from the spacious back seat. But now at the beginning of my senior year, for some reason we weren't glued to each other. We were floating in some fog that had temporarily obscured our views.

Maybe the fog had been brought by the return of Hurricane Phyllis in the fall, who frequently descended from some nether world of elsewhere for some forgotten period of time. Suddenly she had departed; a relative in Bop Bop—a town in Texas, she said—was on her deathbed and needed immediate personal service. Gone. Then suddenly she would be here—at the sub shop or at a cabaret dance—as if she had left neither you nor the very conversation that you are having with her now. It had all been so electrifying, so steeped in adventure, but she could never remember the names of the people involved in the scenes. "And whatchamacallit—you know who I'm talking about..." Of course we didn't, but laughed with her as if we actually should remember something that we never really knew because she had never really told us. At the same time, she would be apologizing for picking up and biting a sandwich that wasn't hers. "Oh honey, is this yours? Why didn't you tell me?" When she was around, I felt the excitement of confusion. What would she do next? Oh if I could just keep her in one spot and enjoy those lips!

Maybe the fog was prompted too by the intoxicating swirl of new activity that pulled me in other directions. Now that I was running for president, I observed more closely my white classmates observing me. Some observers had looks that extended beyond the glimpse and the peek. Some were simply staring, not averting their eyes at all, even when mine met theirs. And then one stare was more obvious than any of the others.

She was a pert little thing in a big blue sweater, a campaign volunteer who distributed leaflets during lunch hour. *That little grin of hers, that funny chin of hers.* Before I knew it, Booby, I had won the election. But in the excitement of all that had been occurring—beginning, I'm now sure, from the peek into that mysterious world of sensuality prompted by the *Young Fellow*—we had hurdled ourselves over a wall that none of the songs had foreshadowed. Wall? It was more like a barricade—forbidden and fortified. Whether it promised as much or more was not even a concern. It was there, like any wall. We had to explore it. Oh Booby, no stop us please!

Booby, next thing I know, I'm facing Bwana.

Bwana in slick gray suit. Big-time liberal principal, him and his daddy too had gone to New England colleges and him daddy had been a dean at one. Finally he faced me in his office. Crossed legs smiling, clasped hands smiling, even he might have been smiling but my eyes were blurred from the tears you could hear plopping on the rug. Big monsters booming down onto my pants.

First the lie—some teacher had told Bwana some things. You know how they convolute the facts of the matter.

What violation of rules, I wanted to say.

Bwana's gold swinging on fingers which direct the rising rhythm of official sentences. Bwana stern, say this serious matter here, boy. What he didn't say is that you fucking with white lady and white man darling daughters. You here to come sit read write go home. You student, you not like Mozelle who run track, zip faster around field than hell allows, bring athletic dimension to school. You student, you should know better. And now this, we find out. Judas had no stronger adherent.

Suddenly I heard no more although his lips were separating and banging against each other; I heard only the hollow vibrations of sounds as my mind took me back to the grin, the telephone calls, the rendezvous. This darling daughter with the blue sweater had arranged to meet me in the halls one day and, smiling, poked her nearly pretty face into my view.

"I've been looking all over for you," she had said, her voice screaming over the din of between-class greetings. The hallways were like cattle rushing for five minutes before the bell and another class. Stop the heart from thumbing away your good sense, your understanding of the encroachment you were engineering. This should not be, you know: white girl, black boy. But your heart took you away from your senses.

"Really?" Faces in a hurry stopped to turn, frown, flit on.

"Call me tonight. I gotta get to class." Gray slacks down the hall.

Well, it was the thing, Booby, you know. Ralph going with that gray girl was the talk in Spellman's Billiard Academy. Wayne supposed to be seeing Judy whose dad had the bread.

"Y'all keep messing with them white girls, see what happens," Spellman had said, his half smile flashing vibrantly in the dark corners of the pool room as he engaged in his perpetual motion of sweeping the floors. If not that, he was racking the balls or giving change for a five. "You know all they daddies is lawyers and judges; you be hanging."

"Them niggers don't know what they doin' or who they messin' with," offered one perpetual main stayer, whose name I never got. He was between the tables, a beacon that you take for granted, never really distinguishing him other than as a blurry humanoid figure. "You know that Bernstein girl father with the police department. I think he the captain. Keep messin' around, you'll find out."

Some cyclical influence had taken over and made us vulnerable to its demands. Now we—as if we were the very first ever—saw ourselves as irresistibly charming, popular young men whose mindset was focused on little more than exploring as much of our unseen world as possible. There had to be more, we were certain of that. We were helpless as a needle controlled by loadstone: bending and turning and moving as the magnet pulled us. Its tow swept us up and tossed us like lifeboats against a huge wave. We were able to assess it as nothing more than forbidden fruit. Nothing more than? Doesn't every fruit identified as forbidden become the most desirable? And isn't the very fruit that is forbidden fighting against the same magnetism that is animating its suitor?

Was it the boy they had eviscerated in the Sip that we were taunting them with? This was the North. They couldn't stop us from doing anything that was legal. What were we doing that was illegal? They weren't going to hang us or throw us in a river or shoot us. For what?

So we exchanged the most clandestine smiles and blinks of the eyes and even an actual squeeze of the hands—all within the dark craters of protection formed by various hallways, stairwells and cloakrooms. "Oh, I just helped her with her homework," I'd say when somebody asked me about the rumor that had a few of us were hanging out with gray girls. But I always smiled from the corner of my mouth, a giveaway to the untruth that I was supposedly hiding.

Then one evening we had organized a sortie, riding in the dark sedan of Ralph's father. We eased into Ventnor—maybe the only black people at that time of night not going to work—through the dark boulevard of fewer street lights, saw their flashing headlights on their car parked in the black lot. We pulled next to it. Doors opened, slammed, and we had switched. She was in the back seat with me. "Oh, don't squeeze me too hard," she whispered.

Now Bwana in slick gray suit pretending that it is all on account of the parents who have telephoned in their outrageousness. "Don't worry about your college applications," he says, "you'll still be listed as the senior class president."

I wasn't concerned about the college applications and the official records. I was concerned about the fact of the matter. Why can't I continue my presidency? I was the first black to be elected. Cut the crap about the rules. Which rule are you talking about?

Bwana's smile uneasy. Something prodding him uncomfortably. "The rules have been around for ages, you know that. You can't hold office and break the rules, you know that doesn't sound right, don't you?"

Me facing Bwana and twitching as if I were asleep and snatching at flies or mosquitoes. That answer so simple. Yet answer so complicated. Answer imbedded in dark chasm. Me can't pull it out, Booby. There was a penalty, but what was the rule? Bwana's hands spread before him, saying, that's it.

His assistant made it formal two days later. Belly sticking in my face, the stuffed arms swinging from the elbows. His eyes focused on the top of my head, not my eyes. His breathing was heavy, like a passing sneeze. The tie was brown.

I had asked him about speaking at the pep rally.

"You ain't president no more," he said, wheezing, "You can't speak in front of the class." His nostrils expired sibilant choruses as he spoke to someone behind my face. The senior class advisor told me that, in the hall between third and fourth periods.

The hall was suddenly a square of several feet on which he and I were standing. No swinging arms of passing students, no bells—*nothing* did I sense but that face way up there from the pillow of a stomach poking me almost. Short sleeves exposed splotches on his arms. I wouldn't be giving the class oration. Four years earlier as a freshman, listening to Bill Wagenheim talk from the podium of the school auditorium, I had visualized that I might stand in that same spot in this time. Well I couldn't stand there with my mouth wide open forever, so I stumbled away, fading into the dream movement of the lined troops marching to class, my feet carrying the rhythm of his sentence, my brain dumb, yet fire in my eyes.

Yes I know, Booby, that I should spend some time getting ready for Harvey's group coming over to pick up some of the papers.

Chapter 15

As I looked out at the glassy bay that the train was speeding over, I felt that there was hardly a facet about the college that I was unfamiliar with. Listening to the train horn's blare, I felt a rush of anticipation flowing through me again. From the time that Gahtsum had driven me past the university in Brotherly Love, I had become as fascinated with the idea of going to college as I had with connecting to the outside world through the mails. Hadn't I been impressed as far back as a child in that ride with Gahtsum when he took us past the campus situated on the west side of Brotherly Love? From the back seat I had glimpsed for the first time the magical demeanor of the university: its splendid imposing buildings hidden behind high cement walls and iron gates as if a fortress within the city; the perfectly nurtured yards of green within those walls, and the determined pace, the neat attire, the scholarly looks of the students who walked in and out of the gates.

"It's important that you keep a modesty about you," Gahtsum told me at the end of the summer as I was preparing to leave the world's playground. He had come for dinner that Sunday just after Labor Day when the playground had been transformed into the ghost town of a resort whose tourists had used up their summer vacation time and scuttled back to their East coast residences to prepare for the winter. The three of us were sitting in the living room, Anida and Aunt Clara holding a drink.

"That's right," Anida said, massaging a glass in her hands. Mister Gahtsum has helped us all these years, but nobody needs to know you ain't really poor. It's our business. And this house on the westside—Oh, John, it's just too much! I'm so sorry Aunt Shirl can't be here to enjoy it. She'd love to have her own room and a nice kitchen. Look at that damn refrigerator and that shiny linoleum floor." She stood up to point with her free hand. "Too bad the nearest bar, Hickory Dickory, is way over on the pike where those "five hundred" niggers sit around profiling."

"You are right," said Gahtsum. "It's our business. Nobody else's. I had some concerns about what people might say. But anybody can save up enough money to buy a house. And who's going to ask anyway?" He sat in a chair to my side, his legs crossed, we facing them on the couch.

"Right," repeated Anida in almost the same tone as if she were imitating Gahtsum. "Who's going to ask anyway, Mister Bat?" She looked at Aunt Clara.

"But I just wish I could have said something about that outrageous mess at the school. It just wasn't fair." He uncrossed his legs and stared at me intently, as if certifying his judgment.

"And look, when you want the press to cover something," said Aunt Clara, "they're nowhere around. Don't want to touch it."

"No, but when that boy got tired of that kitchen chef at the Claridge giving him hell and he hauled off and busted his lip with that ladle, it was all in the papers," Anida declared.

"When was that? I missed that," said Aunt Clara, her eyes large.

"It was in all the papers and on the radio in Brotherly Love. I think *Jet* covered it."

"Well, he did get a nice picture in the paper for the scholarship," said Aunt Clara. "Where did I put that clipping"—looking at me as if I had a clue.

"It just wasn't fair," said Gahtsum, and I began to feel a tinge of bitterness that I had suppressed for months through plain resignation. Yes, I had cried that day on the bus home. The impact hadn't reached me until Brenda, sitting just a few seats in front of me, turned to point me out to some freshmen.

"He's the senior class president," she announced with so much pride in her eyes that it stung. I pressed my face against the window and rubbed my eyes as if I had been caught in a dust storm.

"I could have gotten my lawyers in it," Gahtsum said.

"No, it's good you stayed out of it," said Anida. "And look, he done got a scholarship to that fancy college, so what's the point?"

"The point, my dear friend, is justice—doing the right thing. That's all I've ever cared about. It seems as if no amount of money can guarantee you that. But I want this young man to meet his mark with as few obstacles as possible. I made a promise..."

"John." Aunt Clara interrupted him.

"...To myself. That he wouldn't have to...well, look what's going on. They still acting crazy down there, keeping kids out of school just because of their skin color." Then he turned to me again. "I just don't want you to get involved with those freedom riders. You stay up North and be safe. Just promise me you will stay in school, young man. You have a bright future. Remember that photography is a hobby. You are up for bigger things."

"You won't have to worry about him," Aunt Clara said, passing by me to rub the back of my neck as she went toward the kitchen.

No, Booby, not to worry. The more familiarized I was with the college's features, the more intent I was on making my mark there, attaining the success that Gahtsum was speaking about. Although I wouldn't be allowed to concentrate in photography, I would be at one of the most prestigious colleges in the nation and practically on an unimpeded fast track to success. I was scared and hopeful. The train's whistle sounded like a screech owl as it passed over the bridge. I picked up my bird book and thumbed through it to find pictures of those that lived close to the shore—the gull, the sandpiper, the heron.

I knew that it sat on College Hill. It was part of the group of eight venerable and wealthy institutions ranked among the very best in the country. Getting accepted to one guaranteed your future, according to all that I had heard and read. Their graduates left to become captains of industry, leaders in government, accomplished educators and artists. "They may send graduates to the White House," I heard the dean say about the other schools at a sherry hour one evening, "but we send people into the world—to help dispense the offices of life with usefulness and distinction. They may send graduates to the White House, and you know of course that this country has had dozens of presidents. But how many of those have been great? To quote Cicero, 'Oh thy percentages are not encouraging.' "

I checked my watch. We were just an hour away. Like most of the group, the college was in a small New England town and just three hours from the Apple. The photos in the viewbook had first captivated me in junior high school before I became progressively awestruck by the magical paragraphs detailing its fabled history. It had been founded before the Declaration of Independence was written. When I first looked at the viewbook, I wanted to step inside it and lounge on the green with those students who seemed perfectly oblivious to the coveted positions they held as enrolled undergraduates. Yes, Evan was hoping he would get into Harvard, and Herman started wearing the tan cotton pants preferred at the Yale he was in love with. But I preferred the college on the hill because of its singular motto. It said that people went to those other schools for prestige, but came there for an education. I wanted to learn what they learned, wanted to wear the tweeds and flannels they wore, wanted to gaze too between classes at the seven majestic buildings that surrounded them on the college green. Who knows what kind of girls I would meet. Maybe one would have lips as luscious as Phyllis, seductive beady eyes like Atlanta, or hips that rolled with each step as Brenda's.

When the train pulled into the station and I got directions from a porter about retrieving my trunk, I looked around me. Only a few passengers had gotten off, and they all carried suitcases in their hands as they strode briskly to the front doors to arrange for transportation.

"Where you going, young fellow?" He held open the back door of a yellow cab. "Leave that trunk there—I'll get it for you."

"To First Arch, at the college," I said, remembering the instructions in the freshman orientation package and trying to sound as if I had taken the journey several times.

He stopped lifting my trunk and stared at me, his stomach heaving already at the expense of energy. "What you got in here, bricks? You said the college, right?" Then he turned and waved at another driver leaning against a black cab a few car lengths away. "Going to the college!" he yelled. But that cabbie shook his head to decline, so my new agent turned to his left and repeated his announcement. This time a driver responded by putting his cab in reverse and pulling up next to us. "Can you get to the college?" he asked his replacement.

"I did it once," the replacement driver replied, placing my luggage into his trunk.

"I'll keep these," I said, holding my camera bag, my bird book and the briefcase that Aunt Clara had given me. It contained her collection of clippings. I sat in the back and was peeking up at the statue of man on horse in the middle of the town's plaza when we pulled away. Above a traffic light was a street sign with an arrow directing us to College Hill. Within blocks everything in the taxi windows was turned topsy-turvy. The horse and rider who had been jumping so elegantly over its base of waterfall, pigeons, and a few citizens, were now flying toward the sky like a jet taking off. I fell against the seat and was lying on my back. The cab's motor sputtered and groaned. We stalled, sliding in reverse and lurching forward as if stuck in snow. Lying on my back, I could see only the tops of some buildings intersecting the sky.

The driver was in the ceiling talking down to me. "We are going up the steepest hill in the state," he said. "Most cars don't have motors strong enough to withstand the pull; that's why those other cabs couldn't take you. Come on, baby, come on." It was more than a steep incline, it was a curving incline too, throwing me around the back seat like a bag of groceries. The climb took no more than 10 minutes, but when I was finally able to sit up and see the street and buildings on a level plane, we came to a momentous halt that sent my chest hurtling toward the front seat. Then I saw the arch.

"Are you getting out?" I heard him banging my truck against the sidewalk.

I opened the door and stood at the arch and looked beyond it to see the college green and the buildings surrounding it just as they appeared in the viewbook. Two students marched toward my trunk and picked it up. The name cards pinned to the lapels of their tweed sport coats said Freshman Week Committee. "We'll take it to your room," one of them said, his tie blowing over his shoulder so neatly that it seemed to have been placed there. "He's in Hope College, Seymour," he yelled. "Do you need directions to the dean's office?"

No I didn't. Thanks to my devouring the viewbooks and catalogs before I arrived, I had already memorized the layout of the college green. I knew about the portraits and huge organ in Salem Hall, its stupendous twenty-foot-tall double entry doors with round brass handles, the oak appointments, the stained glass windows. On the other side facing it was University House, which wasn't in the photograph of students lounging on the green. But I had read that the president, top administrators and deans kept offices there. It had been a stopover by the commanding general during the Revolutionary War. They had burned candles in each window to commemorate the general's visit, and now, two hundred years later, the bulletin alerted me, it was a tradition to light candles at Christmas in each of the 36 windows of the hall I saw to my right. Yes, the campus that was now my life for four years was as I had imagined: ivy crawled up the buildings, slate covered their roofs, and cherry blossoms stood like sentinels.

I didn't take any photos because I had seen so many scenes of the green. But I didn't want to wait another moment for one experience. I wanted to enter Salem Hall. The advance of students about the college green reminded me of passengers at a train station—all preoccupied with one destination and fairly oblivious to others at their sides, in front or behind them. I skipped to the left of a duo moving toward me and went up the wide steps. I tried to pull the huge brass ring of a door handle to Salem. The door was too heavy. I had to put down my bird book, briefcase, and camera bag and heave with both hands. It creaked open.

I knew that huge oil portraits of former presidents were hung on the walls of Salem. As I walked in, the sobering odor of old oak greeting me, my eyes swept over the walls. Their lips were thin as a hyphen, as if they were capable of uttering only the most abbreviated clips of wisdom, advice, rebuttal, query, admonishment or encomium. Their firm eyes— gray or blue—buttressed their demeanor of solemn determination. Their pink skin contrasted sharply with their dark academic robes. A quick thrill shot through me as I considered that weeks later I would be sitting here with the other freshmen. I imagined looking back to the rafters where behind the organist would be a dedicated attendance taker who, aided by a seating chart the size of two clipboards, would be surveying the room for errant matriculates to be notified by campus mail of their infraction: ABSENT AT MONTHLY CONVOCATION.

I heard my steps echo as I walked down an aisle toward the entrance. Then my head went up as if pulled, and my eyes rested on the largest portrait of all hanging over the doorway. The founder. I almost gasped. The man who had first purchased the land on the hill more than two hundred years ago and given it to the college that had enrolled only a dozen students was looking down, welcoming me. I put down my things, setting my things on a wooden seat, and stood at attention and saluted. I murmured to myself that I would live up to my responsibility to dispense the offices of life with distinction. And as I looked directly into his eyes to demonstrate my sincerity, I examined the picture more closely. Was there something missing? I stood on my tiptoes. I turned around quickly to see if anybody might somehow be in the auditorium without my knowing. Not a sound. So I stepped up on a seat, balancing myself with arms spread out to get a better view. I was right. Unlike the other men on the walls, the founder was not wearing a robe. But why not? He had been both a successful merchant and educator himself, I knew. I got down from my chair and walked backward to get a different perspective. And then I came to the conclusion that indeed there was no robe in the portrait because his head took up all of the space. The painter could not capture it all—not the huge head and the huge ears and the space below his chin. So it was a portrait of a face with ears pushing against the margins of the frame. I had read about him, but had never seen him—or a face as large. I thought I heard a sound in the back, maybe a janitor, so I walked quickly toward the door and went out.

Standing on the front steps, I looked across to University House, then took the walk that circled the green and went inside to the dean's office. "Oh yes," said the secretary, urging me to call her Miss Alice, her small face overshadowed by a prominent nose, "Dean has been waiting for you, please come with me."

I learned later, listening to some upperclassmen at dinner, that Miss Alice had been nicknamed Miss Eagle Beak because of the noticeable curve of one feature. Following her up the stairway, I marveled at the spotless white walls and dark mahogany wood appointments at the top. Seated in the rotunda were Harvey and two other black students. They all smiled at me. I was shaking his hand and about to put down my things to take a seat when the door opened and Dean stepped out. A pipe in his hand, bushy eyebrows, he directed us inside.

We sat facing him as he settled himself behind his desk, the rich aroma from his pipe swirling around us. Behind him I saw the other side of the green, the library, and two tall buildings downtown that I had glimpsed from the cab. The dean put his legs up on the desk. He wiggled the slippers on his feet. From the corner of my eye I saw Harvey beam a quick grin at me.

"Gentlemen, welcome. Or as Cicero would say, *'All doors are flung open.'* "

We responded in one voice as if we were one of the groups played by the Young Fellow.

"Well," he said, uncrossing his legs on the desk.

We shifted in our seats and cleared our throat at the same time.

"Do you gentlemen know each other?" We looked at each other—again.

He introduced me first, explaining that I had been a stellar student since junior high school, that I had been president of my graduating class and that I had been a star on the cross-country team.

"Well not exactly," I started, my book on my lap.

"Did I miss something?"

"It's fine," waving my hand.

"That's a huge book you have there, young fellow; may I see it?"

I stood to hand it to him.

He had to sit back in his chair and place it on his desk. "My, so heavy—hundreds of pages. Ah yes, the great bird book. A valuable treasure indeed. And very expensive. I guess being on scholarship doesn't mean you can't own valuable things, does it?"

We all chuckled softly.

The short student near the wall was in a white African robe and cap. His eyes were bright, his smile filled with hope and friendliness. The musical sentences formed their own run-on staccato lilt, as if the periods would be erased if he were writing them. They ran into each other and pushed the next one out of the way. And after each sentence he would giggle, the voice rising and falling like a mocking bird's. Accents? They all sounded odd according to everything I had ever heard. Words that had emphasis at the beginning were now accented at the end. He was from Ife, a town in Nigeria.

But he wasn't one of those black Africans—a term we had used in grade school to heap the cruelest verbal attack on someone we didn't like, and a term Aunt Shirl had employed. After the no-good West Indian nigger, symbolized by Mister Bat, the black African was least deserving of respect. No, Kwame possessed a proud regality, and his smooth skin was almond, not black at all.

Darnel was taller and lighter skinned than all of us. Being just another shade lighter would allow him to pass for white. From a Virginia prep school, he reminded me of a Southern gentleman who interacted with you in a certain time-honored manner. He sat with an uncommitted yet cordial smile—listening, inviting, open, his long legs crossed, his hands folded on his lap. When we had walked in, I determined finally that the pleasant cologne that had just hit my nostrils did indeed come from his cheeks. His soft manner became even more obvious when speaking. He flexed his wrists and fingers as if they were in flight. They didn't jab or point. They fluttered like two sparrows chasing each other.

"I'm not sure what I'll major in," he said with a throw of his hands. He looked at us for a response. "I want to be a great actor on Broadway."

"Very good. Just remember what Cicero said," the dean added, " 'Acting is a form of confession.' And there are plenty of opportunities for you on this campus."

Harvey admitted that he wasn't sure what he would do. But like me, he had been encouraged to go to law school. He might concentrate in economics.

We spent almost a half hour chatting, but I was hardly paying attention. I was dazedly more interested in the rich ambience of it all—the dean's office overlooking the other side of the green and the downtown buildings; accented with mahogany and leather, a chandelier, and a colorful Oriental rug. On the tour of his office, consisting of our taking two steps there and two steps here, shuffling our shoulders to avoid bumping into each other (and stepping on Kwame's foot, I noticed that he was wearing sandals), we followed his finger point by point as he identified the framed pictures of distinguished graduates who had dispensed the offices of life with usefulness and distinction according to the university's charter. "Never forget," he said, pointing to a photo of an alumnus who owned the country's biggest airline company, "that you are gentlemen. And as Cicero said, 'A gentleman is a man of truth.' "

When we left his office and stood outside talking, I was filled with a satisfied sense of belonging. All that I had read as history and myth and folklore was now real, and I was part of it. I pulled out my camera to take a picture of them—my three male classmates. Kwame had the biggest smile, Darnel was in the middle. Then I wanted someone to hold the camera to photograph all four of us. I stood in the walkway to interrupt one of the many strollers, marchers or joggers. I held out my hand to beckon. I tried to step in front of one. I said "Excuse me" in my most gentlemanly tone. But nobody stopped.

Chapter 16

Those four years passed in a flash. I seemed to have moved through a rapidly transforming zone where I was alive for more than 60 minutes each hour and for more than 24 hours each day. As soon as I left the dormitory, a series of cascading developments hurtled at me and kept me thrashing and fending as if caught up in a floodtide before I could stumble back out of breath, up the steps and to my room.

I dragged myself to breakfast after a shower, ran to class, met with a university officer or professor, hustled to dinner, spurted to a committee meeting, danced over to the women's campus to search for that elusive heart tug who would hypnotize me into a catatonic spell of my loving her wildly, and finally hauled myself back to my desk to study through the night.

How deeply curious I was during that first year about going beyond yet another wall, another divider separating what I had known and experienced and what I thought lay ahead. Once on the other side, I expected to see a wide array of routes lying ahead. The wall too was a mountaintop from which you looked down. You saw an unbelievable number of enchanting possibilities—far beyond the disclosures that the Young Fellow had alerted us to. But here these unexplored possibilities were not simply the sensual. No, there were other facets that stretched far beyond the sensual. I directed my efforts at passing through, around or over this wall—or down this mountain.

Yes, I had accepted with unrelenting dedication that, unlike those who went to the other two nearby universities in the group, we were committed first to the book ("they to the look") and then to the proposition that from here we would go out into the world and lead lives of purpose, lives that were useful and distinctive. The dean, in one small gathering of freshmen council members who were invited to dinner at his home, urged us to remember Cicero: *"Thy role is to be useful,"* he quoted, holding a glass of sherry up in the air and in front of the fireplace, sending a warm chill down my bones as I viewed his silhouette. He reminded us (I wondered why he looked at me) that we were not to walk around as if we were merely sons and daughters of the elite being trained to run the country—and maybe the world too. No, others—his hand flew in the directions of certain schools—had already commandeered that mission. His hand stayed a few seconds longer as he pointed in the direction of Beanton. We instead on the hill were to be useful. That word was a dramatic whisper—so low that it hung in the air before expiring, and we seemed to be momentarily dumbstruck while a long second of silence enveloped us.

That dinner meeting had come long after I had eliminated myself from the cross-country team. I had agreed with them from the time that we had moved to the new home on the west side that there was no reason to reveal that Gahtsum had been the source of all of our good fortune since we had arrived in the world's playground. No one knew—not David, not Atlanta, not Phyllis, no one. Aunt Clara was still working at Weinstein's, and Anida, who had joined us from Brotherly Love to stay in the guest bedroom, worked for various Jewish families as a housekeeper. "That camera and bike and those nice clothes you wear make people think you rich," David had told me as far back as our Easter day adventure. "But your aunts work like the rest of our parents." By the time I got to high school, we had moved from the neighborhood of hardship. But it didn't matter to others. My official school records showed that I had lost my paratrooper father in the war, and that I lived with my only two living relatives, who themselves were scuffling and hustling like so many on our side of the playground just to survive to the next paycheck. In their eyes, I was as poor as most of the black students. "You'll have to apply for a scholarship and you should get it," the counselor had told me at our first meeting—one of three with him during my entire high school career. "Did I pronounce your last name right?"

"No, it's tricky; don't worry," I said.

"The more indigent your circumstances, the better your chances." He was licking his thumb and turning the pages over in my portfolio. "Oh and look at this: cross-country team. Excellent. Being an athlete is definitely in your favor," he declared.

"Really? Where does it say that?" I leaned forward to look at the sheets that were lined and charted and boxed. Some handwritten sentences in blue ink went from one side of the page to the other. He picked the sheets up as if they formed a book and held them in front of his face.

"It's here—your complete record," he announced with an intake of breath. "Quite impressive. You've done well."

But doing well wasn't the basis for the scholarship, according to the letter from the office of admission. They were suitably impressed with my overall qualities, it said, and my athletic achievement had buttressed their hope that I could come there to help them win a championship in the group.

"Go ahead and take it," Gahtsum and his two disciples insisted in another living room advice session. "They don't need to know the truth. As far as anybody is concerned, you're struggling like the rest of the black kids in college. You're poor, raised by your beloved aunts who didn't have the opportunities for education that you have. Just remember to be modest, as if every penny counts."

And so following the directions in the letter from the coach, I took the shuttle bus at mid-semester to the practice field. It wasn't a practice field but a landing by the river on the east side of the hill. It was a space by the boathouse where the crew team's sleek rowing shells were stored. They were doing jumping jacks when I arrived; and nodding to the coach whose white eyebrows acknowledged me with two twitches upward before his attention went back to his clipboard, I jumped in with the runners. Then he clapped his hands—"Let's go, boys"—and we were off, down a path running parallel with the dark river. On the other side, smokestacks were coughing out streams of smoke. I sprinted ahead and led the horde of pounding feet through some bushes, then upward over a rock-strewn section that narrowed so that we were in a single lane. Raising my knees high, I felt a growing wave of heaviness swing through my legs. A tugboat was chugging along in the middle of the river, and I looked to see if the captain was really smoking a pipe since I could see the silhouette of his face in the cabin. As I slowed my pace, I felt a dozen elbows bang into my ribs followed by the sound of deer rumbling ahead. I slowed down now that I was perfectly beside the tugboat to see if he was smoking a pipe.

By now I was painfully out of breath. I bent over to quiet the sting in my stomach. Then a jolt that struck from one side to another like a worm sent me down to one knee. My shoulders heaved up and down as I gasped for air. I admitted to myself that I hadn't really cared about the tugboat captain. They could say that they saw me stop to examine some activity on the river when they returned to the landing. I couldn't go any farther. I got up, my mouth dry, listened, and looked around. Not a sound. Which way? Could I get back to Elmgrove by navigating around the tall thick elms that stared at me? Their shadows were blocking the rapidly fading sunlight. Could I get through the thicket before it got dark? Half panicked, I fought through the brush, the sticky briars, the thin branches smacking back at my arms, stumbling and weaving like a drunk until—yes, I saw light, traffic, civilization.

I wobbled to the sidewalk and looked at the football field across the street. A man in a suit and carrying a briefcase was closing the door of a bright yellow taxicab. I yelled, but my voice was muffled, too weak, and I saw the driver begin to turn his steering wheel. I pushed myself to one final sprint and yelled for him to stop.

"Wow, you got that new uniform all spotted up, huh? You must have been looking for that puppy that run away."

I fell into the back seat. "Yeah, I give up," I said, "take me back to the campus please. I have…classes…a meeting."

"Oh don't worry, I'm sure they will find her. They should never have left her in the car by herself."

When I got out of the cab and walked through the arch, I moved with a casual wave at several throngs of students trekking in the twilight toward the refectory. I was starving, and rushed up the dormitory steps to my room to change and shower and select a repp tie to go with my green tweed when Harvey knocked on my door and then rushed in, almost falling in a lump in my desk chair.

"I'm going to the Sip," he said. "I can't stand it."

Sitting on the edge of my bed, I didn't know what to say, and picked up the freshmen girls book to stare at Sharon's picture without really concentrating on the text below listing her hometown, high school, and dormitory. From the time of our being introduced in the dean's office, Harvey had become my main confidant, coming frequently to my room to walk with me to dinner and return afterward to listen to music and talk—especially on the weekends. He had had several conversations with the dean because he had been summoned to University House to explain his having missed three convocations. The tradition, the responsibility— it hadn't meant that much to him. Instead of wearing the mandatory tie and jacket to dinner, he lashed a tie around his neck so that it hung like a kerchief pushed inside his jacket (that wasn't tweed). And as I dutifully accepted the student waiter's portioning at dinner, Harvey often demanded a larger allotment of meat or vegetables, loudly addressing the server with "hey." While I luxuriated privately in the maid service, he said that he made his own bed rather than wait for the elderly Portuguese women to change the sheets and tuck in the blankets—just as Atlanta's mother did so expertly at the Traymore. When he said that he was going to the Sip, I knew that his sense of displacement had become unbearable.

Had it started with our discovery that Darnel had practically vanished right before our eyes? He had talked with Harvey and me over coffee in the Blue Room one morning a week earlier about his tryout with the Jabberrocks, a theatrical troupe that entertained trustee members when they converged on the campus twice yearly. He had plans to revise their version of a skit about the Civil War and shocked us by blurting out a few lines of the title song with a voice that was controlled yet animated. And then he was gone—not instantly, but certainly within the following few days. Harvey and I knocked on his door in the west quadrangle and then pushed it open after an alarming silence had met our taps. Where could he be but in his room during a weekday evening? We turned on the light. Had he been robbed? The room was neat as a wallet: the curtains blowing, the bed made, the lamp in the center of the dresser. Folded notebook pages lay folded in the center of the bed. He had listed the tryouts he had engaged in fruitlessly. Under each was his handwritten assessment. The Buskin Players had said no, apparently because of their predilection toward Greek and Roman drama. So had the Stepbrokers, who performed original musicals written by students themselves who, of course, had their own partiality. The Glee Club that presented a concert in the Apple every year and took an extensive spring tour did not have a spot for him either. At the top of the page, in his handwriting, was the heading "Tired, just tired."

"They didn't give him a chance," Harvey had said, dropping to sit on Darnel's bed with a long sigh. "All that talent. He was probably a better singer and actor than all of them. Didn't he study Shakespeare in London for a summer?"

I hadn't known what to say as I considered that there were now only three black men and a few black women left. Exactly how many black women? I wasn't so sure since every time I went to that side of the campus and walked up the steps to Chapper or Anderson or Miller, the directory in my hands, camera hanging from my shoulder, I encountered a matron at a desk who would stare at a sheet after listening to my inquiry. She would look up over her eyeglasses at me with a bewildered frown and report, "The young lady's not listed here. Maybe she's moved and her new residence isn't recorded yet." From the lounge on the side I heard a squeaky titter from two women who were sitting on a loveseat and entertaining two male visitors who must have delivered the funniest punch line ever.

"What are you doing?" asked Harvey. "Oh, that directory again."

"I was checking on that sister Sharon who's in my comp class. I could have sworn that she told me she was staying in Miller, but they told me she didn't live there. So then I went over to housing, and they told me she was definitely in Miller."

"I've got to go back and help," he said. "They won't give us freedom, we have to fight for it. They don't want us to vote, they don't want us to have good jobs, they don't want us educated, they don't want us to have good housing, they don't want us to use their restrooms. They don't want us to have anything, do they? Now what—this. You saw on the news who they killed, didn't you?"

"Yes, it was terrible," I said softly.

"A sniper shot him in front of his house with a rifle. And trust me, the jury will let him go. You can kill a black man in the Sip anytime you want."

"Are you coming back, Harvey?"

"Oh yeah, I've got to go to law school. But I need to help the movement right now, and I can't help by staying here with these people. They don't want us here anyway, you know. At least down there they tell you. You were born and raised in the North, so you don't see the difference. And I can see that you like it here, don't you?"

Yes I did. We had had that discussion before. If this wasn't the place for us, then where were we to go? Who really wanted us? Here there was tradition, distinction, excellence. These qualities lay over the hill like an invisible mist and instilled itself in your consciousness as one central notion. The concept had its own mood, and you could feel it, see it— especially in the manner in which everyone moved about—whether as students marching across the green, as professors gesticulating with a hand, or as deans making quips at sherry hours. Even a visiting lecturer from a nearby college was found stopped in awe once on the green and had to be tapped on the shoulder to bring him out of his daze. "So that's the Salem Hall?" he was saying as his student host waited patiently for him to turn and proceed toward his lecture location. The college was almost 200 years old—older than the country itself. You bought into the venerableness that it represented. I certainly had—since junior high school when I first began reading the catalogs after Aunt Clara told me that I could not major in photography.

And Aunt Shirl had already convinced her that I should not consider any of our own colleges. "They ain't no good," she said maybe twice, and that was that. "All their graduates work in the post office," she said in one expansive moment, twitching her nose and patting the top of her scarf. I never considered attending a black college after that, thinking that my friends who were fascinated by them just didn't know any better. Although she uttered, "Oh Mo-Dear," Aunt Clara sided with her unknowingly since Gahtsum had convinced us both that I should try to gain admission to one of the eight in the group—one like the renowned university I had seen that morning in Brotherly Love.

Booby, was it not the removal from and obliteration of reduced circumstances that I sought? Had I not wanted to escape from the idea of being part of the strugglers and hustlers in the world's playground? I couldn't do anything about it but observe and appreciate their exotic adventurism, first as I listened to Aunt Clara's recital of gambler shenanigans, and then as photographer of those in the neighborhoods of hardship. Many of those who became my classmates would not be going anywhere, even if I had helped them with their schoolwork. I wanted to help and wanted to get away too. I wanted to help Big Man, but what could I do? I wanted to get away from his neighborhood too. Finally, it seemed clear that getting away was the best way to help—by ensuring my ability to rise above the kitchen, the counter, the front of the hotel. So when Gahtsum bought the house for Aunt Clara on the west side, I felt a wave of relief, as if I had obtained a new status. "You don't want to be working like Aunt Clara," she had said so many times.

"Well if they don't want us here, why did they let us in? And why did they give me a scholarship?" My stomach was beginning to rumble.

"It's for appearances," he answered. "They want to give the impression that they care, that they are different from those crackers in the South. If they really wanted us, then they would have done all they could to keep Darnel, make him feel comfortable. Scholarship? Rich as this school is, what does that little bit of chump change that you aren't paying mean to them?" His tie hanging, he stared at me.

"But some of them care." I heard the words come out, surprising me since I was formulating them in my head. "Professor Gut cares," I said, referring to the disabled tectonics professor who skirted around in a wheelchair. He had invited Darnel and me to his home one Saturday and served a spicy cheese with grapes and crackers to accompany the sherry. "And Canon Peddy goes out of his way to be accessible, always inviting me to the parish if I want to talk."

"Well, that's two," Harvey replied. "The problem is that there aren't enough, not two hundred, two thousand—not yet anyway. There aren't enough willing to stand up and behave properly when it isn't popular. Canon Peddy? I thought you was a Baptist man, boy." He exaggerated the widening of his eyes.

"I am Baptist. But the nearest Baptist church is way over on the south side of town. I can't go through all of that bus activity just to get to church on Sunday morning. But you are coming back, aren't you?"

"Of course. This is part of the system, the establishment. From here I can get into any elite law school. Then I have the opportunity, the possibility to walk side by side with those who make the rules. And then I can talk to them about changing the rules. Aren't you hungry?"

He pushed the chair under the desk, I turned out the light, and we stepped into the hall where three students turned momentarily to interrupt their chuckling about a professor before waving at us as they took the steps. Their voices echoed against the cement walls and metal banister.

"How much do we have to give up to reap the benefits," he asked. "And what are the benefits anyway?"

"Well, we always have to give up something to get ahead, to make some progress," I replied. "Do you know some colleges that are much better than this?" I asked. "How can you get into the best law school if you don't go to the best college?"

"Better at what?" he wondered as we stepped in with a group who were singing and shouting. "Taking all the money in the world and using it to train their boys and girls how to continue to dominate the world? Supporting a curriculum that nixes the contributions of everybody who isn't white?"

One in the group ahead turned as if he had wanted to stop and dispute Harvey's words. Instead, he asked for a match, then caught up with his group, his blonde head bouncing.

"He's never said anything to me before," Harvey said from the side of his mouth.

In the trio of words I caught from the group, I heard a mention of Lauren. Was she that redhead from horse country? Had she not said on the steps of Salem one afternoon that I could take her out for coffee in the Blue Room? The thought began to germinate within me, growing in interrupted stages as Harvey and I talked during dinner. By the time we had finished dessert, the proposition had mushroomed into an insatiable craving.

"Are you listening?" Harvey asked me before berating the waiter for a slice of roast beef that he thought far too thin. "You seem to be daydreaming."

I needed to know. I needed to know more about this particular divider. When I returned to my room, my hand trembled as I dialed her number, my heart banging at the prospect of once again pushing against a wall that I had peeked beyond before with demoralizing results.

Chapter 17

Yes, she would be happy to go to the Blue Room with me, Lauren said from a phone in her hallway, where the background of high-pitched giggling voices seemed to get louder by the second. Her sentences had the shivering rhythm of one who had just alighted from the shower, and I listened carefully to detect any tone of insecurity or indecision. "Well great," she said, "I'll meet you in the lobby. Gotta go."

I picked up the freshman women's book again. She sat in riding gear on a horse. She had gone to Miss Emily's. Her address? It had two lines. One was in Maryland, the other was in Rome. She would major in religious studies. I thought I had heard somebody say that her father was an attorney. I can't lie, Booby, I thought about the upcoming date constantly, walking around in a fog for that week, almost unable to concentrate on my classes.

What did I want? I wanted to see what the wall was about. What would going beyond it reveal? What had I missed? Maybe a phenomenon of dubious value lay stretched ahead, existing to be explored but then perhaps leaving you with the attitude that it had been highly overrated from the outset. But something was going on. Otherwise, why did inquiring lead to such ominous consequences?

As I showered that evening after classes and a meeting of the council where I casually mentioned to one of the few students who had ever engaged me in a conversation that I would be in the Blue Room later, I thought back to Ranida's assurance that I would meet my soul mate here.

"Oh, you will find a different kind of woman up there; trust me, honey."

"Well you know he's a Romeo," Aunt Clara had said earlier that Sunday morning when we were sitting around after breakfast.

"Oh really?" Ranida's eyes were large as she made the same exaggerated motions with her face as she always did when Aunt Clara joked with me. "I bet them little white girls like him too."

"Well, Gahtsum says they won't try to hang him if goes out with a white girl up there," said Aunt Clara.

"Well, Gahtsum ought to know, shouldn't he?" whined Anida. "But then he might not even be interested in pale skins and no asses"—this said as she, eyes toward the ceiling, shook her hips into another room.

I splashed the popular cologne that was being advertised in the men's fashion magazines on my chest, tightened the knot on my tie, looked in the mirror and saw not myself but Lauren herself, sitting in the lounge of Andrews with her legs crossed, her tiny lips pursed to greet me. I would ignore those triumvirates clustered in the corners and staring at us. We would walk out casually as if we were doing nothing extraordinary, as if this scene of a black man and a white woman walking together in pursuit of social intercourse had been witnessed thousands of times since the university's start almost 200 years earlier.

But in fact, it probably had not been seen a dozen times. Or maybe a half dozen times? I knew this as I reached the crescent of steps leading to the walkway of the women's housing quad. The walkway forked to the left and right stairways. Andrews was to my left. And I also knew that I had just been rebuked for initiating encounters that gravely threatened the sanctity of the decree prohibiting us from...touching...from behaving as if we were none other than man and woman. Had I not had enough, Booby? No. My hand patting the brass railing that lined the pavement ahead of me, I walked with a cocky jaunt that expressed my disregard for this stricture—especially when it blocked a channel to the wall that I was obsessed with knocking down. When I took the steps up to the green doors of Andrews, a coed came dashing out with a phrase thrown backward over her shoulder, "Tell him to call me after eight." She was down the steps before she stopped to apologize and ask if she could help. "Lauren?" Her lips trembled at my announcement. Then she ran back up the steps and pulled the handle of the door she had just exited. I stopped the closing door's movement and walked in to the lobby.

It wasn't until I had been waiting in the lobby for a half hour before I realized that I was the only person there. I had taken a seat on the west side of the hallway just as the house mother had directed me. "I have paged Lauren, she should be down shortly." Several knots of women came in and out of the front door and then went either to the hallway straight ahead to the elevators or turned into one of the lounges on either side of the hallway. Within minutes, a wind had come and swept up the six, eight or ten people whom I had noticed in the background of the scene I had joined. I was the sole survivor, sitting with hands clasped and legs crossed, shoes brilliant from the shine I had labored on, looking from a seat in the corner, looking out to the entry hallway.

Yes, the house mother was still at her desk. She rose swiftly, patted the top of her head, glanced at me, then twirled in the direction of the elevators to my left. I noticed for the first time the huge wooden clock near the window I faced. It started with a rumbling of gears winding before blaring out the two notes of the cuckoo bird over and over until the time was eight. Two students in tennis outfits, breathing hard and laughing hysterically came in, stopped to look at me and then proceeded down the hall. When the house mother returned with a cup of hot tea, I went over to ask her to page Lauren again.

"Oh she should be down shortly," looking up at me, the cup on the tip of her lips. This time when I sat back down I fell into a large upholstered chair and was that close to resting my foot on its arm when I remembered where I was. I leaned to pick up a magazine about decorating. A student wearing short pants and carrying a pipe came in, checked with the house mother, and then smiled broadly as his date waltzed down the hall to greet him and they went out chatting. I found a magazine on Southern living and skimmed through its pages. There was a story about a meditative garden and its soothing effects. I stretched out my legs and leaned my head back. My chin hit against my chest and I fell underwater into a fog of traffic where students came and went, a man with a broom busied himself in a corner, a couple sat in chairs near me and engaged in spirited dialogue about a restaurant for the coming weekend, and the house mother's footsteps echoed in some muffled tunnel. Finally, I felt myself being pulled upward to the room I had left. The cuckoo clock was singing again, and the hour was ten. Someone had turned out the table lamps and only a single floor reading light behind me was lit. I looked down the dark hall. The house mother had left. I stood up. Above, through the ceiling I could hear muffled titters and the patter of feet. My shoes hardly made a sound as I walked across the carpeted lounge and out the door.

Looking across the lawn at the other dormitory, I noticed some movement under a hedge. A white tail scuttled out of it, its ears flaring as if expecting somebody to notice it, and then leaped over nothing to get around the corner. I didn't realize it at the time, Booby, but that rabbit was a symbol of how the search for my new earth angel had gone during my years in college. Just as Lauren had never appeared—and seemed somehow to have been transferred to a totally different part of the campus, because I never saw her ever again—that is exactly how the others either vanished or just never appeared when they said they would.

No, I did not find Sharon, but that did not deter me from visiting one dormitory after another over the four years I spent to search for Melanie or Yvonne or Marquita—the other black women students. Yvonne had moved off campus in her second year, and Marquita, I was told by a house mother, had decided to take off a year because of "family circumstances." Hadn't I just seen her head rising with a group of others going down the steps to the post office?

And I know I saw Melanie go up the entrance to the Pembroke library where students sat either at the large old mahogany tables or in the stuffed chairs along the walls. I skipped up the steps and entered the main reading room and swept my eyes from one corner to the other. I didn't see her, so I strolled slowly along the stalls as if I were looking for a book. I kept walking until I reached the last row and strode along the window sill. The brass locks at the top were secure. So she hadn't jumped out the window after all. Ladies' room? I went down the hall to check. Across from it was a bulletin board that I studied for fifteen minutes, alert for any movement behind me. Nobody came out of the ladies' room.

Leaving the library, I lifted up my spirits by considering the check Gahtsum had sent—some extra money that had come from a legal case he had just settled—and how I would use much of it for the upcoming spring weekend festivities. I had already bought my tuxedo outfit and tickets that guaranteed us a table near the stage, and was visualizing the entry Heather and I would make as two coeds skipped ahead of me, swinging their book bags over their shoulders and talking in low voices as if sharing some intimate details. The one on the left had hair like Heather's—short, dark, neat. We were going to the formal ball at the alumnae center, and the announcements had promised a band that would keep us dancing all night. Leaving there, we would stop by the many fraternity parties.

She stayed in Spanish House, one of the small Victorian residences for twelve or fourteen women who were committed to speaking only Spanish to each other. They didn't have a house mother, so you could walk right into the living room and pick up the phone to announce yourself—which is what I did that night. On the wall over the phone was a gold-framed mirror, perfectly oblong, offering enough of a view that young male visitors would have a chance to comb their hair and straighten their ties. Some details needed attention, so I brushed some lint off a collar and picked at my carnation. Every few moments a lovely young coed would pass, and I'd turn to stop her. Each one seemed to have her own aura, as if she and the others who had chosen to live in this special dormitory were selected for more than their academic qualities.

Yet each, in her special ballet movement of turning and placing her body in certain positions, was able to do no more than spread her arms wide in astonishing surprise and regret. They spoke only Spanish—in the most tender and elaborate tone you can imagine, Booby—and therefore were of no use to me in answering my question about where was she?

Again, it seemed as if a wind had swept through—this time it was Spanish House—and left no one but me. This time the clock was in the corner and was almost two feet taller than I. Its bell tongue sent off thundering announcements—far more dramatic than the cuckoo clock in Andrews. This time I heard nobody's feet scampering over my head en route from a shower. And nobody had turned out a lamp. It was bright and empty. I realized from the clock that I had been adjusting my bowtie, my handkerchief, my carnation, my cumberbund for two hours. All that time I had been alternately standing in front of the mirror, then sitting with my legs crossed, rising to greet a pirouetting resident, walking again to the mirror, and picking up the phone. The line was always busy. By the time I had stepped down the wooden steps of Spanish House and looked up at the front windows, it was as quiet as a funeral home.

When I turned toward the street leading to the main campus, I saw the group of three couples coming in my direction holding hands and laughing. "Aren't you going the wrong way?" one of them joked, pointing over my head to the women's dormitory. It was short Frank from the end of the hall who was planning to go to medical school and who thought it nothing extraordinary to study all night for his biology course. "Hey, you look great in that tux." They all murmured in agreement.

I thanked them with a smile and kept walking, claiming that I had left my wallet and tickets in my room.

"Well hurry up," he said. "They are supposed to start on time. Did you say you were going to the Beta Psi party afterward? I'll buy you a drink."

"Okay, I'll look for you," I said as I skipped across the street and, landing safely on the other side, reached into my pocket to find the joint that .

Walking through the arch, I picked up my pace so that I could get back to my room without another encounter. I breathed deeply when I got to the front door of Hope College. I heard my shoes echo as I went up to the second floor. I stopped to listen. Nobody, nothing. Everybody had left. Good. Nobody would know, I thought as I closed my door without a sound.

I threw my jacket on the chair and lay on my back. What was I feeling? Anything? Was I angry or sad? Was I both? Was I more angry or more sad? I kept playing with my bowtie and looking up at the ceiling. The pillow had never seemed so relieving as I dug the back of my head into its soft comfort. I wasn't sure what to feel. Maybe that was my problem, that I wasn't sure. But Harvey was sure. He didn't think that we belonged here, that I was wasting my time "trying to date those white girls."

"But I can't find Sharon, I can't find Yvonne, I can't find Melanie," I insisted. "They keep disappearing—gone."

"Well check out some of the other campuses in the area," he said. "And besides, Romeo, don't you have a couple of girlfriends back in the playground? At least you keep telling me they all crazy about you down there." In our junior year he had gone back for another trip to the Sip and returned even more cantankerous and outspoken, holding up the newspaper in front of his face. "Can you believe it," he had thundered. "Look at this. I'm almost ready to take some more time off and go back down there. But I have to graduate." He read aloud the story about the student, Charles, he had marched with. Charles had continued to protest the rules that said he couldn't use their bathrooms, couldn't eat in their restaurants, couldn't shop in their stores, couldn't go to their libraries or schools. No wonder Aunt Clara said that her uncle had run for the border. Charles had disappeared. They said that he had gone to Louisiana to visit relatives. The relatives reported that they hadn't seen him. Two months later he was found. Harvey pointed to the photograph on the front page of a black newspaper from the Windy City: federal agents paddling in boats, searching in a river. They found his headless body with ankles tied. Two men confessed. A justice of the peace dismissed the charges.

He had just shown it to me the previous week, just after I told him that I was going to the spring fest with Lauren. Harvey instead was going to Brotherly Love for a weekend of partying and begged me to come too. "I'm not staying around here with those animals acting crazy, throwing beer bottles out the window and screaming at the top of their lungs. Why do you want to be a part of it?"

Well wasn't it something to be a part of? Weren't we here to be components of the larger mission? What had happened between Oakbury, where I was the only black student in the school, to here, where I was one of a half dozen? Why had it been so simple for Tom and Gunther to accept me as—as just me, a boy who talked a lot in show-and-tell, who owned a BB gun, and whose skin just happened to be a different color? I was still just another student to them. Had they been too young to have formed other ideas? Had Oakbury been just an exceptional circumstance?

Or maybe Oakbury was the norm and not the exception. Maybe everywhere else—here, the Sip, wherever they didn't want us, maybe all those places where acceptance was not practiced—maybe they were really the exception. And maybe the exception was just more formidable, more dominant, and more determined? Is that why Super had been able to intimidate us? He was the exception, but he had been able to dominate the innocent, the norm.

What were we supposed to do, hide, stay in our rooms, not audition for the Buskin Players? Go to the Sip and have our ankles tied and our heads chopped off? What was wrong with being a gentleman, dispensing the offices of life with usefulness. Maybe we were involved in the movement in our own way—by persevering. But no—I corrected myself in that long meditation on my bed that festive spring evening— persevering could hardly be as dangerous as putting your life on the line. So maybe they down there were the real heroes, the real men dispensing (literally) their lives with usefulness. I was lying on my bed feeling sorry for myself, wondering about something that I couldn't even identify. And they were going out—maybe at that very moment—against mobs of barbaric, bestial intent. And Harvey during that junior year went down to help while I sashayed over to the dormitories in my tweed jacket as if I deserved some special dispensation, as if I should be hailed as the colored messiah, the new chocolate dispenser of that usefulness of life.

Oh, finally it was funny, Booby. I must have fallen into a daze and then awakened, because I was stirred by the bombastic sonorous tones of so many parties that it sounded like a battle of the bands distilled into one cloud floating over the campus. Even that was funny, as I detected the flat melody of a song about a hound dog that we had danced to at the Y when it had been recorded by Big Mamma. But this version I heard— screechy and metallic—sounded like the one that had been recorded by a hugely popular white singer called the King. I wanted to close my window. But there was something strangely refreshing or invigorating about the sense of disappointment that I was feeling from the music. I was the joke really, I considered, thinking that I could come here and be a part, one of them, penetrating their inner sanctum and proceeding to gain admission.

No, Charles, the student who had protested with Harvey—and even Harvey himself—were the real heroes. Oh God, it was so funny, I thought, as I looked out the window at the closed main library. I had lit the joint that Frank had slipped in my hand and was feeling as if I had total control over the thinking process that just minutes earlier had thrown me into a whirlwind of confusion.

Hey, maybe my buddy Lamar—no not maybe, *absolutely*—was a

hero too. I went over to the closet where I kept my camera bag and briefcase that Aunt Clara had given me. At the top of the clippings file was the latest envelope from her. I pulled out the obituary page of Lamar in his cocked hat, the military rope draped across his shoulder. He had been killed in the battle against that tiny Asian country that we were fighting for a reason that I still did not understand. God, it was almost too funny. Here I was depressed because I was alone on a warm Saturday night without a date. But I was alive. I should have been depressed because of Lamar, and Charles. Lamar had been a drummer in the high school band—handsome, quick witted, one whom I admired immediately after our meeting in junior high. I liked him, but never really knew him or spent the time that I wish now I had. They were both dead. And they hadn't harmed anybody. I started chuckling loudly. Maybe I should go out to the green and just laugh and point at them as they trouped to the fraternity bashes. What could I lose? They probably thought I was crazy anyway. Why not prove it? Yes! I pulled the ends of my bowtie and put on my jacket.

I opened the door and stumbled down the hall and gave out a full-throated laugh as if I had heard the most uproarious joke. I went down the steps holding on to the railing, looking out the window of the first landing and seeing the throng of gowns and tuxedos floating over the green. I started singing—well, sounding out the first four notes really— of *Tenderly*. My voice ricocheted through the stairwell and almost frightened me. Damn, was that me? When I reached the first floor I had to lift my feet consciously, exerting myself as if I had taken on a great heaviness, as if my body had picked up extra pounds. I stopped to gain my composure. And then I heard it.

It was a voice. On the first floor. Singing. Down the hall. I turned to open the door to the corridor. Now it was clear, mellifluous, soaring down the walkway. Darn, it sounded so familiar. I walked down slowly until I reached the open door. It was Kwame. He sat on his bed, eyes wide, cap tilted, surprised.

We stared at each other speechless, then uttered the same words: "What are you…"

"I had no place to go," he said, "so I'm here."

"Me too," I answered. "Well I had a place," realizing that I was in my tux, "but I'm here now."

"Come in, have a seat," he giggled. "Have you been drinking?"

"Worse than that, I'm afraid," I answered.

He let out a roar, clapping his hands. "You look quite splendid in your tuxedo. I should take your picture."

"Don't bother," I said. "You don't have a date?"

"Oh the wenches are so unpredictable, I can't be bothered," he said, throwing his arms up. "I'd rather stay here by myself and write letters and work. History is the true story finally. Do you know it?"

"Know what?" I answered.

"The history."

"Of course, I had it in grade school. And all through high school."

"And do you know about the tree?"

"The tree? Which tree? Have you been drinking?"

This time he chuckled, as if my ignorance had catapulted him to a new level of excitement. He stood to move past me and close his door. He turned to kneel and pull out a box of papers from under his bed. He started chuckling again as he pulled out one sheet after another, spreading them over his bed. "They were involved in the slave trade. Ship building, molasses, rum, spices. They made more money than your Southerners whom you despise."

"Excuse me? Who are you talking about?"

"The founders, who else?" Now his eyes were flashing. "The brothers who started this school. They were dishonest men, let me tell you that. At least the younger one quit and went to England to live. That's why he's never mentioned. They built this school on money made from the degradation of black people. I have read about them in their own collections"—pointing to the main library. "They don't even have the decency to hide it. But then again, as I say, history is the true story. It's not the history, but the historian himself that we must trust."

"Did you tear out those pages from books in the library?"

His eyes went wild. "Will you tell? You are the proctor, aren't you?"

"Well, no, I won't tell; but you must be sure to keep them hidden. Let me see."

I sat on the other edge of the bed and faced him. The yellowed torn pages, the brownish pamphlets with their musty archival odor lay between us. We spent hours reading them.

Chapter 18

Well, my search for my soul mate had not been limited to those on campus. My raptorial instincts were as keen as the hawk's; and when I flew back to my nesting ground during holidays and summer vacations, I relished in the certainty that the comely young things there would have to possess almost magical qualities to disappear as easily as those evanescent figures I chased after in college.

We were on trains moving in opposite directions during those last two summers when I worked as a busboy in Herman's Delicatessen, owned by his father. I saw her and heard about her, but we never connected long enough to extend our relationship. One weekend (when everybody went to the beach), I caught her in a striking yellow bikini, sitting under an umbrella with a group from Brotherly Love who were listening to a portable radio. She waved me over and introduced me to Vincent, who had a well-developed mustache and was planning to go to medical school the next year. "His father is a doctor," she announced, and his smile broadened immediately. "Oh I hate this sand," she complained, brushing it off her legs, causing me to reflect that her shapely calves would be carefully examined (or maybe had been already!) by Doctor Vincent.

Walking back to my blanket where Ralph and Wayne lay laughing with some girls from the inlet they had met, it occurred to me that time had put some space between whatever tie Phyllis and I had shared. We weren't the same couple who had walked home holding hands during freshman year in high school. We definitely weren't the same couple who had taken advantage twice during one of those walks when we learned that her parents were coming home late. As we lay on her couch on those two wonderful occasions, she allowed my hand a freedom that

sent it under her blouse and up her back where I unsnapped her bra. By
the time Killer had started barking—it was just a passerby, but we
jumped up in heart-banging fear—I had slid my fingers inside her panties
where they located a magical spot that, when rubbed, sent her into a
gasping, thrashing fit. I had heard too that she had gone to Texas to train
as a flight stewardess and was living with a dentist. But Dot, who was no
longer attached to David and was attending college in Pennsylvania,
insisted that this story was not true because her cousin in that town in
Texas was engaged to the very dentist with whom Phyllis was
supposedly living.

But Atlanta. Oh yes, she was there for me during those months
before my senior year. In the evenings we were all free from our summer
jobs in the hotels and restaurants to explore the boundaries beyond yet
another fabled wall—the endless nightlife that had been restricted to us.
My neighborhood excursions as a youngster could not have taken me
into this nocturnal world of revelry. Yes, during my tours my with
camera I had heard the stories in the taverns and poolrooms. Yes, I had
caught the muffled voice references to Aunt Clara's gambling and
Anida's frolicking. But now we were young adults no longer limited to
the cheap wine that we imbibed secretly on the weekends as high
schoolers. Now we could drink whiskey and beer—like the adults. We
could sit on those same bar stools that Aunt Shirl had told Anida to shun.
And we could now see and almost touch those musicians whom the
Young Fellow played near the end of his show—those who produced the
raunchy, upbeat rhythm and blues tunes that blared out from the clubs
into Sunday morning.

The taverns were all over the city. Clarence's father became
fascinated with the term, and first opened the Hi Hat on the boulevard
near City Hall, followed by the Silk Hat near the inlet, to be
complemented by the Top Hat just below the strip. Ike's Corner, The
Wonder Gardens, and the American Legion commandeered those who
strolled down the boulevard. Scattered in other areas and sitting by
themselves to be discovered by the adventurous were the Yacht Club,
Hickory Dickory, Big C's and the Late Night ("Where It's Smart to be
Seen").

But one block vibrated with such an explosive, cacophonous outburst
of horns, organs, and guitars that it was given two nicknames by us
natives. We didn't refer to it as the vacationers did who read the sign—
Kentucky Avenue. To us it was either KY or the strip.

One block, and a spillover of clubs on its four corners. A blaring,
thumping dance of reverberation. The notes from the different clubs
stirred themselves together somewhere above the roofs and then fell over

you. It was like going through a tunnel. The sounds hit you as if you were proceeding too fast. Then the sounds feinted and jabbed, dove down and sailed upward, circling you again. To handle them, you moved your neck and your shoulders and your hips in whatever order that inspired you.

One block of clubs, each with its own distinctive donation, bunched against each other so that you could step out of the Cat Club where you sat at a table with a cocktail and listened to Our King as he swung his guitar from one side of his body to the other while the most regimented horn accompaniment filled in the spaces; step out to turn just a few steps to step into Shirley's Lounge ("Watch your step, step up please"), who could always be depended upon to feature Wild Bill, an organist whose theater in the round was surrounded by the circular bar. Inside it were Wild Bill, his drummer and bassist. Some mistakenly thought that the bartender was one of the group, he was so close to them. Wild Bill could draw out a piercing fire alarm of a note for as long as a minute, sending the room into hysterical "yeahs!"

Oh, Booby, don't expect to be lucky enough to sit at the bar that only had 24 seats. You stood around it in the shoulder-to-shoulder din, in the resounding vibrating roar of music, conversation and laughter, in the red fog of smoke and bulbs. You tapped your foot, you yelled for another gin and tonic, you smiled at a pretty brown thing who sat at the bar and turned to look for the ladies' room, the slit of thigh flashing for only the most attentive as she eased off her stool. All eyes were gleaming, all mouths were shiny, all foreheads were moist.

I think it was the strip that pulled Atlanta and me closer that summer before my senior year, as Phyllis and I seemed to drift. Maybe it was her hand that continued to leave its imprint on me. It was still a deft, thrill-provoking touch that I held on to so many nights of that summer. Or maybe it was her mother. Or the combination?

If anyone had latched on to my strategy set in grade school of establishing an angelic reputation, it was her mother. When I visited them for dinner on Sundays, Mrs. Baker exclaimed with unrestrained enthusiasm about how proud she was of my academic achievements. Atlanta had told her about my Legion award and my scholarship. I would almost be embarrassed at her detailed encomiums of my success in school. "Lowe, get the class president some more ice tea," she would say to her husband, her broad smile highlighted by slivers of collard greens stuck between her teeth. Now that I was set for my last year in college and then law school, it was "Lowe, get the judge some champagne." She trusted me implicitly, thanking me in a drowsy voice when I would call to say that I had experienced car trouble and that I would be bringing

Atlanta home an hour or two later than planned. In the late evenings or early mornings after a movie or night of clubbing, Atlanta and I would cuddle up on the downstairs sofa without fear of her mother coming downstairs to "get a cup of tea." She always asked from the top of the creaking stairs for Atlanta to deliver it.

So thanks to my saintly repute, coupled with my obviously being the only student Mrs. Baker knew who had ever won a scholarship, I was given *carte blanche.* I could have only the most virtuous intentions, the kind you would expect from one visiting from the hereafter. Atlanta and I knew exactly what I was here after, wherever the locale. I was after it on the couch downstairs by the stairway that always creaked in time if in fact Mrs. Baker might decide to boil her own cup of tea. I was after it in the back seat of the parked Oldsmobile I borrowed from Aunt Clara whether I turned the motor off by the sea wall at the inlet or in a narrow path found between trees in the woods ten miles along the pike. We had known each almost half of hour lives and were becoming better acquainted by the minute.

Whenever we were together, like a recurring dream, her hand was prominent—leading me, steadying me, directing me. If it wasn't the tactile thrill of her five fingers and palm, it was the stare of her beady eyes that churned up my insides and pulled me toward her presence that promised so much. One night as she stood at my side in Shirley's, squeezing my hand that lay against her waist, her sharp eyes glancing up, I was struck with the realization that she was entirely at ease with this bluesy, soulful realm that Shirley's embodied. How did I know? Because she moved her neck and shoulders and hips with the rhythm of the room itself, as if it had massaged her spirit and chased away all concerns of the commonplace world. She had soul, and that quality too captured my mind that summer. Phyllis seemed taut, even uneasy sometimes when I took her to the same dark loud smoky rooms. It wasn't just an unease about the surroundings themselves. No, it was a nervousness about her body itself. She knew that she could not direct it to respond in a certain way. And she wasn't even sure what that mode should even be.

All of those scenes flashed across the wall over my closet when Atlanta had called to tell me that she was pregnant. Her voice was softer than I had ever remembered it, and I could see her eyes looking into mine. Was she sure? How? When? Why? The typhoon in my stomach threw me out of my desk chair to the bed. Could she hear my voice over the choking? Was she sure? How many months? I lay there panicked, watching the movie that had moved from the wall up to the ceiling. I was staring at a film that I was starring in myself. There I was standing in a robe but not marching with the others. Crying and surrounding me were

Aunt Clara in a large pink hat, Anida in a larger hat and sexy dress, Gahtsum looking out from his sedan parked to the side. A crying baby was in my arms staring at me, its tiny feet wiggling. Then I heard Atlanta whimper, "I love you." Immediately after that she was a little girl tiptoeing across the screen, her little beady eyes bright, her hair in a pigtail, her magical finger pointing at me.

"I love you," I said, almost choking, "don't worry" and hung up the phone. My heart was hammering against my chest as I stumbled off the bed to look out the window. It was a windy, rainy gray spring afternoon. A coed on the steps of the library was wrestling with her umbrella, while others were holding their hats and leaning forward to make it up to the revolving doors. Was that all she had to worry about, I wondered—a broken umbrella? Was she pregnant? Did she have a boyfriend? Did I love Atlanta? Of course. She was pregnant, so I had to love her. We would be married and live happily ever after—just like Yo-Yo and Aunt Iceland. And Mister Arthur and Miss Rachel? Would we? Did I? Why did I think I would find the answer looking out that window? Maybe I needed to talk to somebody, I was thinking, when they knocked on my door.

When they came in I could tell by their faces that something was wrong. They fought to keep their lips from trembling, but the words kept pouring out in stuttering rushes. I wanted to ask them to take a seat, but it seemed that there was no time. So Larry and Ian, reporting, stood in the doorway.

"He's been making a lot of long distance calls to Africa; I've heard him, early in the morning," Ian said. 'I knocked on his door, and he wouldn't answer."

Larry, the calmer who kept a snazzy red convertible stored in a nearby garage: "Well you know the guy's always happy-go-lucky, but I just thought it strange that he kept laughing—giggling—all night. I couldn't sleep. And I didn't want to bang on the wall."

Unstated was, what should we do? What should I do? After all, I was the dorm proctor, a senior, responsible for guidance, orderly conduct and adherence to rules. So far my most memorable counseling session had been with a redheaded sophomore whose freckles, once you were close enough to see his complete face, were actually runaway adolescent pimples over which he nor the boxes of medications on top of his dresser had any control. He had reached the end of a long and onerous road of ignominy, he explained, and saw no relief in the pain he had absorbed. What was he to do? His eyes were as red as his hair as he complained about the mockery he had endured because of the name of his prep school. Yes he had gone to Admiral Dull Academy, in the western part of the state just two hours from Beanton. I assured him that he should simply ignore the taunts, that from what I had heard, he was positively not a dullard, not obtuse, not sluggish. Not at all.

"What do you think?" Larry asked.

"When it rains, it pours," I said from the side of my mouth. "I'd better go down and check."

Ian and Larry jumped out the way as I walked toward them without a word. I sped down the flight without holding on to the railings, and before I got to the first floor door, I heard him. It was a mellow moaning flute that could be used to attract wild animals in the veldt. Within minutes I was standing in his doorway. He was sitting on his bed, eyes bright, cap to the side, a beautiful oversized white caftan with gold trim covering his small frame.

"I have been talking to my friends," he sang, raising his hands. "They were very very happy to hear from me. You know I have only a few acquaintances here. Do you have any?"

"Oh I have a few," I said, trying not to look too conspicuously at the mess: clothing, shoes, candy wrappers, papers strewn everywhere. His phone receiver lay off the hook clicking on the floor.

"Do you like my friends?" he asked. "Do you hear them?" He looked around the room.

"Well no," I said, still standing.

"I think they like you," he chuckled again.

I didn't know what to do or say. They didn't mention anything in orientation about a student's losing his mind. That wasn't supposed to happen.

"Well come in, sit down," he beckoned. I heard Ian slip by and close his door. "Here, I'll make room for you."

"Been reading, I see," I said, sitting on the edge of the bed. I looked at a shoe box of pamphlets.

"Yes, all the information you need is in there. Have you noticed that the founder had the biggest head in the world? It was the size of a statue."

I turned to face him and couldn't help but break out in a laugh.

"Well you know why of course."

"No, I don't have the slightest," I said, thinking that talking to him calmly might help settle him down. The high pitch of his voice had subsided somewhat.

"Only an insatiably greedy human could have such a gigantic skull. His greed filled him up and spilled out of his ears. His face got bigger every year, you know. It's all here." He stood and then kneeled to look under the bed and pull out another box of pamphlets. "Oh I have it all," looking up at me as I imagined I must have looked at Gahtsum that Christmas as I opened the box that contained my first camera.

"And I will tell you one other thing about these devils," he said, still on his knees and waving his finger at me. "They do no understand the tree."

"The tree?"

"The white man sees the tree only as a connection to commerce. We see it as a link to the universe. To us, the tree is connected to the earth, the sky, the birds. The white man sees it as a precursor to chairs, tables, construction. They do not understand that the tree is a part of nature to be revered. No, my good friend, they see the tree only as a source of wood to make things. That is because they are greedy. And that greed made them enslave us. Do you not see, my brother?"

"Well of course I do, Kwame."

His eyes became brighter. "I have shared this with my friends and they are absolutely thrilled. They had no idea that I would find this information right in the basement of the devils' own library. Where are you going, my brother?"

"Well, I have to get back and check on some things," I said, rising and stepping backward.

"You won't reveal that I have taken these materials, will you?"

"Not at all," I answered. We both laughed, and I tried to lift my volume to the gusto that his voice projected. Soon we were laughing together, shaking hands, and I was easing out of his room.

The heads of Ian and Larry peeked out from next door. I know that they were thinking that I was the dorm proctor, so do something. I waved to them to go back inside and I went down the hall. It was supposed to look good on my application to law school, along with being on the dormitory council. So by the time I reached my room, I realized that there was nothing for me to do but what I usually did whenever a matter about dormitory behavior came up: report it to the dean.

Standing by the window as I dialed, I stared at the huge iron gates surrounding the rear part of the green below me. Usually I sat at my desk when looking out and focused on the downtown buildings backdropped against the main library. Now I could see more of the wet green spreading out from my dormitory and extending to the gates. Those gates were only open once a year—at graduation—when we would march through it in just a few months. I heard a deep intake of breath from Miss Alice, telling me that I should come right over. "Don't worry about a tie," she said softly, "come as you are."

Dean had the same thought as I when I relayed the details. His face was between his slippers that knocked against each other. "Oh it's a shame, a shame," his lips creating the *tsk* sound that Aunt Shirl had made when she talked about schoolboy hoodlums or Mister Bat's supreme indiscretion. Dean made a tent with his fingers, so from my seat his face seemed framed within geometrical patterns: his slippers, his folded hands, the buildings behind him. "This close to graduation. As Cicero said, '*Unhappiness is always a coincidence.*' And he never missed a convocation, from what I know, unlike your good friend Harvey."

He stood up, picked up his pipe, exhaled a small cirrus of fleecy smoke, and declared, "We'll have to send him home—immediately. He's going to need special medical attention. There is nothing we can do for him here. If you can pack his things for us—maybe this evening—we'll ship them back to Ghana."

"I think he's from Nigeria," I said.

"Yes of course. Well you've done a commendable job as proctor. And I hear you've been accepted to the law school with a scholarship. Be careful up there in Beanton, my boy, and don't forget the book. Professor Gut says that your work in tectonics has been exceptional. Well, we just have to concentrate on the positive sometimes. I know it's hard, but remember Cicero: '*The good man remains positive through suffering.*' Did you know him well?"

"No, thanks to Aunt Shirl," I blurted out.

"Who? Is that a French novelist I missed? I hated French lit you know."

"No, she was more of an orator," I said, rising from my chair. "She gave a number of speeches on folklore and myth. Did you ever hear her address about if it ain't one thing it's another?"

"I'm afraid not," he replied, walking me to the rotunda where Miss Alice seemed to be spreading her arms as wings as she moved a paper from her typewriter to her desk. "But I will certainly remember it." He gave her instructions about sending security to Kwame's room, shook my hand, and returned to his office. I sat in front of her to give my proctor's report.

"We'll certainly miss you, young man, and I know you will be a success in law school," she said. "And I hear that you have a scholarship too; I know your parents will be relieved."

"Thank you very much, Miss Alice," I said. And then a thought bounced around in my head, one that had been on my mind since my arrival on campus. "Say, do you know which book of Cicero the dean reads? I'd like to get a copy for myself since I'm leaving. He was a great thinker."

She looked up from her paperwork in surprise; in my mind her nose suddenly transformed into an eagle's beak waving in admonishment.

"Book? Oh, don't be silly," she clucked. "Everybody knows Dean just makes up those quotes. They aren't really from Cicero, he just says they are." Her eyes dropped back to the papers.

Was my mouth wide open? I can't wait until I tell Harvey, I thought, remembering all of those moments when it seemed that Dean was dispersing the most profound instances of philosophy and advice. Had I not jotted down some special jewels from Cicero in my journal? Had I not used them and found people to be impressed and thankful too at my recitation? And now...and now, it wasn't Cicero at all, I was told. It just seemed to be Cicero because I believed it was Cicero. Did the other undergraduates know too? How many?

Two students were coming out of the registrar's office when I reached the first floor where I stopped to button my raincoat. One directed a question at me. "Did anybody get into Yale Law?" He was holding the door for me. "Do you know?"

I looked at him blankly. His friend was already outside on the green and raising his umbrella. Neither had said more than a sentence to me during my entire four years in college. Now they wanted information that would soothe their own anxiety. "Oh at least six," I said, adding, "and two in Hope College." I beckoned toward my dorm. "I'm going up to Beanton myself."

They stood as if electrocuted, like two swimmers at the edge of the diving board who had decided at the last moment in fact not to jump, their mouths open as wide as the cartoon character Aunt Shirl used to corroborate her certainty of an 0 leading. In fact, she might play a double 0 if she had been there to see their faces. While they regrouped to disentangle their umbrellas and keep from stepping on each other's toes, I whistled as loudly as I could while walking toward the dorm.

I stopped as I opened the door to look back at the tinted sky that I had grown to love during those years. In the spring, the sunset always seemed to hover over the west quad just before dinner. I wondered how many painters and photographers had stopped to capture the darkening trees and buildings highlighted by the orange-yellow background. The pace of things for four years had left me with little time to use my camera. But I would take some time off between final exams and commencement, I promised myself, to shoot some of the scenes that had etched themselves in my mind.

Would any of this leave a positive impression with Kwame? Had the sunsets seemed glorious at all to him, or had he had time enough to appreciate it? At that moment I decided not to go in. I didn't want to be there when security came to take him away. I pushed the door back and stood on the steps. The clock over Salem rang four.

As the rain's fall slowed to a light shower, I felt an aching need again to talk to somebody. Despite my whistling exit from my two classmates, my insides were still in a jumble. The steps seemed grayer than I had ever noticed as I pretended that I was wiping rain from my eyes. Were those little brown stones in the cement? Funny, never noticed before. Walking up the lane toward me was a coed whose bright smile radiated under her rain bonnet. I was prepared to explain how I didn't really feel as bad as I looked, but she put her head down to pick up speed. Wasn't it bad enough that my life was now in total upheaval? No, that wasn't enough; I was accountable for some student-gone-mad from Africa. My whole life had been turned upside down, and now I was on my back looking up, reaching for a hand. Instead of a hand, I was getting a directive to go help somebody else.

I should run over to the quad to see Harvey. No, he would be in French lab—a requirement he had put off as long as possible. But wait, Professor Gut had asked me to come by for dinner whenever I didn't want to eat the refectory food that I thought was perfectly tasty but which most students squawked about. Maybe now that the rain had stopped, I would just walk down the hill a few blocks toward the private Victorian homes. As I passed University Hall I twirled my umbrella in my hand as I had seen that actor do in the movies. I went through the west gates. On the other side was the block of tall wrought iron fencing bordering the fraternity houses. Between the fence and the brick walls was a narrow ditch for drainage. It was filled with beer cans that had been thrown out the windows during the weekend parties. They would be picked up the next day by the maintenance crew. I never went to any of their festivities, but I knew that they had live bands and plenty of raucous shouting that reached all the way to the other side of the campus where I stayed. When I turned again, I saw a long white fence stretching for almost a block. They said that inside it was the estate of one of the old families that had been here for centuries.

Across the street, almost a block away, I saw Gut's large wooden frame house with the American flag sticking out from its post on the porch. I crossed, thinking of what I would say. Perhaps just admit that I was afraid and confused. Maybe say that I was just taking a walk now that the rain had ended. On the second floor, a window was lit. I saw a figure walking toward the yellow rectangle, then pulling down the shade. It couldn't be Professor Gut in his wheelchair. I hoped he was home.

Chapter 19

"It's the Negro student, honey—the one who goes to classes." Tiny Mrs. Gut, her blank face at my chest level, opened the door for me. She turned to lead me into the living room, her clogs clanging on the oak foyer, adding, "Oh, it's stopped raining."

"Oh marvelous." Professor Gut had rolled his chair to greet me and was now turning around so that I looked at the back of his head. "Hello, young fellow, so nice to see you. And Ann, my dear love, that isn't his name, please." He pronounced it for her. "Did I say that correctly, my dear man?" He was smiling proudly, facing me, his thumbs hooked into a red sweater vest. "Perhaps you've come for some dinner?"

"Close enough," I said, feeling suddenly exhausted and falling into the stuffed chair that his hand pointed me toward. "Well, I thought I'd come by to see how you were doing," I said, taking in the distinct odor of pipe tobacco. I glanced around quickly without staring to see that the living room led to a spacious dining room on the left with a chandelier. Beyond that was a kitchen I couldn't see. On the wall facing me were a fireplace and framed photographs of Professor Gut in his military uniform. Two Persian rugs covered the living room. I felt exhausted but calmer.

Mrs. Gut had gone into the kitchen and returned to stand at the beginning of the dining room. A circle of smoke floated out of her face. She held a pipe in her hands.

"Marvelous; and Ann, do put on another plate. This is the young man I told you about who's going to the law school with a scholarship. He'll be up the road in Beanton in the fall."

She stood for a second to inhale, then withdrew her pipe to ask, "I hope you like pasta." She turned to retreat to the kitchen with "Tell him about it, Hampton."

Professor Gut sat to my left, his fingers tapping the arms of his wheelchair. His wavy white hair, trimmed neatly around his ears, gave him one of the most distinctive looks on the campus. I heard a coed say that he was handsome enough to be an actor. He had been one of the few faculty members to stop me on campus to chat, and the only one who ever invited me to visit him at home. As I sank farther back into the chair, I enjoyed a wave of reassurance, a sense that I was in the right place to receive the sympathetic assessment of my predicament that I sorely needed.

"My dear boy, I'm so sorry that we aren't in our best mood. And how are you doing? All set for the procession?"

"Well, I did have some things on my mind..."

"He's lost his job," Mrs. Gut's voice sailed from the kitchen and struck us both in our midsections. He looked as if he had just discovered the fact. His eyes went blank. He tapped his fingers on his knees.

"Who?" We both said it at the same time.

"Me, I'm afraid," he said as if remembering. "They won't be renewing my contract. I just got the letter this morning." He whirled his chair around so that his back was to me, and I saw his right hand pulling out a handkerchief from his pants. "Excuse me...my sinuses."

"Here you are darling," Mrs. Gut rushed toward him with another handkerchief.

"Darn, that's terrible," I said. "I have had some bad luck also." The words came out in a voice lower than I had expected.

"Those people at the Rock Foundation don't want to continue," Mrs. Gut said, the pipe in her mouth, turning the professor around so that he faced me again. "We may"—she held the pipe to inhale—"we may have to go back to Ohio. And teach geography."

I looked at them stare at each other as if a tragedy far far worse than mine had befallen them. I looked up at the ceiling and thought back. On some Sundays Harvey and I had gone to the Little Derby for breakfast. It was a popular spot in back of the quad where you sat at large round oak tables and watched a chef who shouted out the orders and then brought the steaming plates of eggs, biscuits and hash browns to your table. The thick Sunday papers from three or four cities were spread all over, and it was not unusual for students to spend several hours eating, drinking coffee, reading the paper and discussing affairs of state as well as the state of affairs. Harvey and I got there as early as possible to get a prized seat by the window. It was one of those Sundays when he was examining the editorials about the killings of black men in the Sip and the releases about the black soldiers killed in the tiny Asian nation where we had

launched a war. I was distracted by two blondes bantering about
Professor Gut. They knew that he had started the unique program in
tectonics and that the Rock Foundation had funded him with "millions":
Her voice went up with her eyes. "It's an entirely weird concentration,
you know, April. Something about bringing us all together again. I think
it's utterly fascinating—even if I don't understand a word." They
giggled, their foreheads almost touching. "What about Josh...I heard you
two are getting closer. And they have very small classes—I like that,
don't you? I mean, look, for all the money my parents are shelling out,
come on, give us small classes, right?" They toasted with glasses of
orange juice.

It was Professor Gut who persuaded me to major in tectonics. I had
no idea what it was about, but I had read in the viewbook that the college
was the only one in the nation with a concentration in that field. Then
one day during my sophomore year I saw him being wheeled across the
green. One student pushed his chair while five others, panting and
jockeying for position, followed along the side, listening to every word
of his, taking notes. They were graduate student assistants and
researchers helping the professor work out the details of the new
discipline. Some undergraduates—and even faculty—referred to them as
Gut's army, Gut's flunkies (they were said to clean his house on the
weekends), and Gut's guts.

A few days later I saw him on the corner outside of Wilson Hall,
where he was waiting for his wife to drive him home. It was just a hello.
I expected to speak and continue walking. But we began a conversation.
Had I declared my major? Was I aware of the exciting new discipline
that he had pioneered? Did I know how my application to law school
would be enhanced?

By the second semester of that year I had registered for the
introductory course. Seven of us sat listening to him explain how we had
to come together in order to survive. He drew a globe on the blackboard
and then explained that it was not a globe as Seth, sitting in the back of
the room, had defined it, but merely a representation of a globe. We had
to penetrate beyond the obvious surface of things. The real globe had no
divisions into water and land. The idea was to bring the water and land
back together again. If we could just grasp that basic certainty about
things coming together, we would be on our way to understanding
tectonics.

I was fascinated by the simplicity yet confused by the complexity
behind it. We had no texts because Professor Gut had not completed his
manuscript, and nobody had published a book about the subject. We
didn't grasp the full meaning of his lectures because we couldn't hear

him most of the time. That spring semester they were building the new
main library across the street, and with the windows up, his voice was
overwhelmed by the banging and pounding of the construction work. Oh,
Booby, I forget to mention that Professor Gut had a hearing defect, so he
didn't know about the commotion that bombarded our ears. But I
received high grades on the exams and essays, and I was a major
contributor during the class discussions (carried out with the windows
closed). Sitting in a circle facing him, we pontificated about the most
complex ideological positions, usually precipitated by Gut's statement
followed by, "What do you think?"

"And look," Aunt Clara had said, "I can't even pronounce it. But it
makes far more sense than photography. That boy is too smart for the
average major. Is that what they call them? And what's a concentration
again?"

"Perfectly acceptable" was Gahtsum's response. "I have full
confidence in the Rock Foundation. In fact, one of my classmates from
college is running a division there. This puts you in the vanguard, young
fellow, of the new thinking. I heartily approve."

I didn't know what to say. Professor Gut sat there with his hands
cradling his face. His wife, pipe in mouth, stood next to him. Their heads
were at the same level. They looked at me. "Well..." I began.

"Yes?" He lifted up his head, eyes intense. She held the pipe in her
hand, waiting for me.

I thought about Atlanta's being pregnant and just started rambling.
"It could be a mistake."

"You think so?"

"Certainly. It could just be a mistake. Maybe you aren't the person. I
mean, maybe you aren't the one. Maybe the letter was meant for
somebody else."

He turned to look at Mrs. Gut. She nodded her head, looking at me
intently, as if I had miraculously pulled an elixir from the air.

"It happens all the time," I continued, encouraged by their response
and my ability to relate my situation to theirs. "You will have to inquire,
get more information. Make certain that it's really you, professor."

"Well of course!" he smiled, raking his fingers through his hair and
throwing it to the side with a neck movement he used when presenting a
particularly striking point in class. She lay her hand over his, patting it.
"Maybe it's not for me. Well, my dear man, you have certainly brought
us good cheer. Hasn't he, Ann?"

"Yes, Hampton, let me go check on the water." She said that while
turning and skirting back to the kitchen.

"But suppose they didn't make a mistake?" He had rolled his chair within a foot of my ankle. "Then what?"

At that moment, the shadow of Mrs. Gut, her face hidden by a fresh gust of tobacco smoke, appeared in the dining room. She had turned off the lights in the back rooms. "They didn't make a mistake?" She coughed, holding her pipe in front of her face. Then she entered to stand behind the innovative professor, peeking over his head at me. "Well, Hampton, we'll have to turn out all the lights to save on electricity." She went to a far corner and reached under a shade to turn the first-floor rooms into near darkness. "I may have to stop smoking," turning, exhaling so deeply it could have been her last. "Come, let's sit down and think this out." She rolled him over to the sofa to my left where they looked at me with faces that suggested the bleakest of possibilities.

Professor Gut, who lectured by propelling his wheelchair back and forth in front of the blackboard, suddenly stopping or starting before spinning in a 360-degree turn, who emphasized his points with hands that drew designs in the air as if they were birds in a mating dance, now seemed the most inanimate of orators. His face drooped, his arms hung at his sides. He began talking in eulogistic terms, as if Professor Gut had died. He talked about Professor Gut's dreams, his genius, his hard work, his commitment to the tectonic dilemma, his interview with the Rock Foundation, his love for his students, his fascination with the book tradition of the college...

I stood up slowly and walked on tiptoes to the foyer (his eyes were closed, his head back as if his eulogy had turned into a prayer) where my coat and umbrella hung on a rack. Mrs. Gut had rested the back of her head against the sofa and closed her eyes too, I noticed as I waved at her from the doorway. Just as I opened the door, a charcoal tabby cat came running from the other side of the kitchen. I pushed my shoe against its chest to keep it from slipping through. Outside, I felt even more confused and tired.

The streets were wet but drying as I headed toward campus. Two crows seemed to be laughing at me, and for an instant I thought of stopping to relish the contrast they formed as they tipped along the white fence. But I couldn't bring myself to appreciate anything that would lift my spirits ordinarily. The little man with the bent back walking ahead of me with his cane and poodle would make a good photograph. But not this time. The visit or interlude with Professor Gut had drained me more than it had soothed me. My spirits were sagging.

This time I went a block farther in the other direction so that I would walk up to the main campus on the front side and enter through the arch. It was the same hill that I had taken in the cab for the first time four years earlier. Good thing I had my umbrella, I thought, as I aimed its point in the sidewalk to help me up the rise. I heard the poodle's high-pitched yelp behind me and turned to see it pulling on its leash, the old man having stopped to get his breath.

It was still an hour or so before dinner, and the twilight was spraying the brick homes along the hill with a golden tint. Just as I was about to turn into the arch, I had to step back. A wave of blue was coming through with precise movements of arms and legs. I recognized the president of the interfraternity council in the front, his uniform pressed stiff. He acknowledged me with a glance but kept looking ahead. Their shoes gave off a brilliant sheen. They were planning to enlist in the military after graduation. Maybe I should have joined that officers training corps, I thought. But no, Harvey had convinced me that I would be shipped immediately to the tiny Asian nation. And what was happening there? Well, look at Lamar. Look at Stuffy. Ralph. The clips were in my room, thanks to Aunt Clara. They all had been killed. I didn't want to join the war in that tiny Asian nation or anywhere else. I was still harboring the guilt of having shot those helpless birds. How would I handle having shot to death a human being?

As I watched them march past me to prepare for the theater of military engagement, I was now hit with an unexpected sense of guilt. I had done something wrong in my own theater, let's face it. I had created a theater to feature yours truly as the angelic main character—one who would counter the negativity of that disapproving starlet Aunt Shirl—and it had collapsed, flopped. It was not an uplifting drama but a depressing tragedy. Atlanta was pregnant, and there was no doubt in my mind, despite the idea that I had proposed to Professor Gut—that there was a blunder about identity—I was certain that there was no inaccuracy at all.

When the dozen student officers-to-be marched across the street, I was standing at the foot of the arch looking up the street and noticed the building. The Episcopalian church seemed to have popped into my vision. And so did the soft, endearing face of Canon Peddy, the priest who had invited me to the parish if I ever needed to talk. "Just come on in, don't worry about making an appointment," he had offered, a soothing whiff of cologne hovering over the statement. He appeared at many of the lectures and sherry hours, and often stood by me as if we had arrived together and we were old friends. Sometimes he filled my sherry glass before I had even noticed it was almost empty. He had inquired about my progress with the sincerest blue eyes, staring with a tilted head to see if my face registered any discomfort. His small thin frame was always covered in black—except for the white collar.

I started up the street, staring at the huge Gothic edifice of brick and limestone that was now more imposing than I had ever imagined. I had passed by many times, barely glancing, never noticing its tower reaching through the clouds. The carved stone archway was twice as high as the arch at the college. When I stepped over the slate entranceway to the door, that too appeared to be larger and heavier than the entrance at Salem Hall. Inside, it was filled with the odor of incense and burning candles. I looked down at the terrazzo floors that suggested centuries, not decades, of existence. The walls were marble, and the banks of oak wood pews spread out from where I stood to the sanctuary itself—far enough to be a football field. The space was twice as large as Salem, which could hold all of the freshmen for convocation.

"Hello." A child's voice, from the ceiling. No, it was just an echo of a voice. The figure was in the far right corner, in the chancel, the hand waving like a child watching the Miss America parade. At first it was an apparition in a white gown, but as its steps brought it closer, the details of its gorgeous face and blonde hair became more distinct.

"Hi," I said, astonished at how my voice ricocheted from one wall to the other.

"May I help you?"

"I was looking for Canon Peddy," I said.

"A student?"

"Yes, I'm graduating and wanted to see him about some things."

"From high school?"

"Oh no, I'm much older than that," I said, smiling, and pointing my thumb in the direction of the college.

"Well, will you follow me please," the figure said turning, swinging an incense holder.

I picked up my pace to catch up. I looked over now that we were walking shoulder-to-shoulder. The figure was a boy. But I had thought at first that it could have been a girl; his features were so feminine: the wavy mop of hair falling over his ears, the soft voice, the angled rhythm in the walk. We went through a door and up a brick circular staircase to Canon Peddy's office. Two boys not quite old as teenagers were leaving his office. They too were exceptionally handsome, like models you saw in the department store catalogs. Over the door was a brass sign with Canon's name over it. My young guide opened it for me and then vanished.

"Well come on in. Hello, hello. Mario, Peter, give our graduating senior a chair please. And oh, get the sherry. Well, never mind." He rose from his desk and extended his hand while tilting his head to the side as if I were a visiting relative he hadn't seen in ages. He squeezed my palm and looked deeply into my eyes. "What is it, my son? Something wrong?" His expression of compassion sent a queer tide of both despondency and uplift through me, and I felt myself squinting to keep the tears from flooding out. I could hardly breathe. I congratulated myself for coming to see this man of the cloth, this compassionate gentleman of the spirit who could boost my lowly disposition and lead me in the right direction. The angle that he titled his head—as if fingering his ear canal—gave him an enhanced air of caring. We formed a silent quartet for an instant as the three of them stared at me before "Please boys, check to see that the vestments are ready. To the sacristy, go...go!" As the two acolytes scurried away, Canon Peddy sent a promise over my head to them: "We'll go to the ice cream shop later." And to me: "Will it please you, sit?"

"He didn't say anything about wrestling!" I heard one of the boys complain in the hallway.

It was so comforting; a dark calming silence. One reading lamp sat on his desk. Behind it was a wall of books. He sat in a chair next to mine and we both faced the other wall where a gold framed oil painting was hung. Two chubby cherubs sat on a hillock hugging each other.

"Marvelous work by Brother Pandolf—oh, those nineteenth-century masters," he remarked, throwing up a hand toward the scene. I felt as if I had all the time in the world to tell Canon everything. I wanted to tell him everything. It was time finally to confess, to admit that the angel image that I had promoted of myself was bogus.

"I shot the cardinal," I blurted out.

I heard him choke and saw his hands go up to his face. His wide eyes peeked over his fingertips. He stood up, and blocking the light from his desk, turned the room into almost total darkness. "Oh my God, child, you don't mean Cardinal Mahoney!"

"I don't think it had a name," I said. "And"—taking a deep intake of breath—"I killed a robin too, Canon. Two innocent creatures of God. They weren't harming anybody. I was eight years old." My voice was cracking.

"Oh, you mean birds." He sat down again with a great sigh and faced the painting. His cheeks had turned as ruddy as the cherub's. "Oh Jesus, thank God. I thought you meant you had killed a high-ranking member of the church."

"And my girlfriend just called me. She's pregnant. And Kwame. I failed him. I never talked to him. I was as bad as the others. Now he's gone."

"Oh, my son, you didn't shoot him too, did you?"

"No, they are sending him back to his country—Nigeria. He had a breakdown."

He placed his hand on my forearm and gave me his profile again as he continued looking at the painting. "My son, you have experienced a day of cataclysmic emotional turbulence. It's good that you came to see me. Rest your spirit. And what is the young lady's name? What are your plans?"

"I guess I will marry her," I said. "Atlanta."

"Well, do you love her?"

Did I? Did I love her? Yes, I thought, I have always loved her. I was just afraid. We hadn't talked about having a baby. Maybe I didn't love her and felt pressured. But if I didn't marry her I would be leaving her. How could I leave her? What did it feel like to love? Was it love that I was feeling? Was it the same as being in love? How would Canon Peddy feel if I said that I don't love her? If I didn't, why had I gotten her pregnant? "Yes," I said.

"Well my boy," he said, leaning his head back as if sitting in a dentist's chair, "I think it's quite decent of you to make that decision. I can perform the ceremony if you wish." He was looking at the ceiling.

Why did I feel that I had just slipped and fallen into a tunnel? Now my heart thumps took on an acceleration that I was certain would cut my breathing.

"And about the cardinal. And did you say a robin too? His infinite grace and sense of forgiveness will prevail and release you from your sins. As long as you have confessed in good faith, you can be forgiven. As for that Kwame fellow, you were not wise enough to understand the uniqueness of each individual." He stood in front of me. "Now go get some rest, my young friend. Have you had dinner?"

"No, I guess I should get something to eat," I said, collecting my raincoat and umbrella and walking slowly toward the door. Before pulling it shut, I turned to see him standing in front of his desk, his head tilted to the side, his wrist bent as if dispensing holy water.

Outside the sky was darkening and students were hustling toward the first meal sitting in the refectory. I turned onto the green and made a beeline toward Hope College. It would be a good time to pack his things—while most of the dorm residents would be heading for early dinner. I went down to Kwame's room. The door was wide open. Clothes, books, pictures, papers were strewn everywhere. I turned, a sinking feeling winding through me, and went up to my room to get my tan leather suitcase that Aunt Clara had bought with great fanfare on the avenue. "He needs this for college," she had said to a Blatt's salesperson who I was sure wasn't listening. But she did nod affirmatively when asked if she had seen my picture in the paper.

"I think I do remember seeing that," she replied, ringing up the transaction on the cash register.

I wasn't sure where to start as I looked around. The dean wanted him to have enough to travel with; the rest would be shipped to him. So I went to the closet to pull out two pairs of pants and two shirts. In the dresser were a sweater and socks and underwear. On top was a framed photograph of him and three African men in robes, one with a staff. The other was of Kwame sitting in a fancy German convertible parked in front of a palace. I packed those also, and was about to leave when I kicked the shoebox under the bed. Kneeling, I saw three little dusty books stacked behind it. I grabbed those and the shoebox, and with both hands full, closed the door with my foot and went back to my room.

The bell at Salem told me that it was too late to take the suitcase to the dean. I placed the items on the floor—the suitcase, the shoebox and the three books—and sat looking at them. Now Kwame is gone, and only two of us would be graduating, I mused. Had it been only four years ago when we all had arrived, each thinking of how distinguished our contribution would be as we learned to focus on the book rather than the look, of how we would dispense the offices of life with distinction? Now…what? I was dispensing life all right, but with distinction?

I stood to stick my suitcase with Kwame's belongings in my closet. On the floor was the large envelope of Aunt Clara's clippings I had taken out to empty the suitcase. I picked it up, and while kneeling, grabbed Kwame's shoebox and the dusty books. I set them all on the bed. A hunger pang ripped through my stomach but it was dissolved by the sadness I felt. I would sit on the bed that evening and read through the clippings. They would lift my spirits. Or would they? Just as I shook them out, I heard the familiar footsteps and the knock on the door. I knew it was Harvey. I sat still. He knocked again and called my name. I didn't move. Had I locked the door? He turned the knob. Thank goodness. He knocked again, asking, "You going to dinner?" He left, and I felt relieved. I didn't want to tell him that Atlanta was pregnant. I was already wiping my eyes. I'd probably fall apart if I had to face him trying to comfort me. Professor Gut and Canon Peddy hadn't been any help at all. But Harvey would have said everything to console me, and I couldn't stand that now. Just leave me alone—everybody.

Chapter 20

After I left my suitcase with the dean the next morning, I decided to take a walk. "Are you all right?" Miss Alice had asked, her head bobbing. "Did you sleep much last night" It was a bright spring day, the green still moist from the rain. A student playing touch football laughed uproariously as he slipped and fell. A dog romped in a circle around a baby whose carriage was being pushed by a professor's wife. They didn't have a care in the world.

No, I wasn't all right. I had spent the evening looking through the clippings that Aunt Clara had saved all those years. Then I pulled out some of the documents from Kwame's shoebox. After that I skimmed through the little books he had stolen. Each clipping, each document, each page led to a discovery that drove me deeper into an inconsolable funk.

Aunt Clara had written notes on the corners of the yellowing newspaper clips. Some were the size of a napkin, others were smaller like a postcard or a candy wrapper. I read for the hundredth time about my American Legion award. Above the text was a photograph of me standing to receive the little ribbon from Superintendent Harsh. Aunt Clara had identified me by drawing a circle around my face. I had shared the makeshift album with Harvey on a few occasions and we laughed at the old dress styles.

There was the newest article and picture about Lamar: how he had been cut down by enemy fire in a drive-by attack, the bullet going through his left cheek and exiting through his right arm. He died from his wounds a day later in the hospital. I flinched at the pain he must have Endured, as my imagination took me to his hospital bed to see his handsome face writhing in pain. How did he look in the casket? What happened to his cute older sister? Now I wished I had gone to his sixteenth birthday party.

And Kwame was so right, it was frightening. I would keep the books and papers for a few days before returning them to the library in the night drop-off slot. One was an old biography of the founder, written almost a century ago by a local historian who had never earned a degree but had done independent research. Yes, and his six brothers were among the great mercantile families before the thirteen colonies had become one under the same George Washington who had slept in University Hall. And for a half century they had operated one of the biggest slave-trading enterprises in the region. I thought about that number: fifty years. Fifty years of sending their ships to the Caribbean and Africa. One was called *Mercy*, another named *Hope*. They were filled with hogsheads of rum to return with valuable human cargo: black men and women to be enslaved laborers, enslaved domestics, even enslaved craftsmen. Yes, they were involved, profiting grotesquely. I hated to read about it and my fingers trembled at the details: the bodies stacked spoon fashion, the cadavers frozen by disease, the despaired leaping into the Atlantic rather than bear so terrible a fate; the selling of daughter and wife in front of helpless husband; the taking of nubile defenseless hips (*there was one they called the Guinea Rose, and they cast lots and fought to lie with her*) the lashes of whip against the back. It was all there collected by Kwame—in the dusty books, the pamphlets, the broadsides.

Before you knew it, a pamphlet revealed, one out of eight people in the colony was a slave. Men and women of good will and heart struggled to stop the trafficking. The authorities declared that the founder—whose head was said to be so huge that he frightened his opponents simply by standing in front of them—was guilty of violating the slave trade act. The court acquitted him, and he continued his enterprise undeterred.

Was this the beginning of the university's rich endowment, providing us with the sumptuousness that I prized?—the weekly maid service, the waiter-aided dinners, the perfect edging of the grass? Is this how those mansions on the hill were built a century ago? Oh it was more than that, according to the material. The entire region had benefited, controlling most of the slave trade in the country. They had outdone the Southerners whom we were ostracizing as the supreme racists. The same people in the Sip who would do anything to keep us from voting or attending their schools had taken nowhere near as much income from the slave trade. Is this why the transition from here to *the* law school or to *the* medical school was so smooth? No wonder the buildings were so old and stately. No wonder the tradition was so engrained. They had been establishing their institutions for centuries, supported by the riches generated by black capital.

So Harvey was right after all about our being here. Did they want us here? Should we be here? We had argued continually, almost every weekend over the years. He always said that the answer was no. What were the advantages? Did they outweigh the disadvantages? But how did we get here anyway? Was it because somebody among them, a minority voice, saw the justice, the fairness of it? Well, where were the rest of those voices?

But there was another envelope that I had never seen before. It had fallen out of an inside compartment of the suitcase when I emptied it for Kwame. Aunt Clara must have forgotten to remove it. Inside were three long browned clippings, torn at the edges. The wife of a wealthy mainliner had poisoned her housekeeper. I wondered why my aunt was interested. Maybe she knew the housekeeper? Another article published a few days later featured a headline, "Mainline Scion Alleges Infidelity." I read it casually, just following the sequence of events until I came upon his name. Gahtsum was the husband. His wife had killed the housekeeper. Why? The third story said that the wife had been characterized as mentally unbalanced. She alleged that Gahtsum had been having an affair with the housekeeper for years. She suspected that he had fathered a baby with the housekeeper and that the child had been taken away to an undisclosed location. The last paragraphs of the story were torn off.

My temples began to throb. I felt a familiar flood of vibrations circling inside my head that I had always been able to block. I wanted to stop it, thwart the spinning of my consciousness into identifying some relationship between Gahtsum and the housekeeper. It was like an echo from the past that I had already discounted as needless. I had anesthetized myself against the bombardment of scenes, facts, revelations. I would not let them reach my consciousness. So I decided to close down my thinking and go to sleep, hoping the painful headache would dissolve. At the cloudy periphery between wakefulness and falling into a deep sleep, I heard Aunt Clara say something about "that boy done just blocked it out. Nothin' else we can do."

Before I knew it, I had fallen asleep, awakened, left my suitcase with Miss Alice and started on my walk. I still had no appetite, so I skipped breakfast. The wind beat the romping dog to a flyer that sailed in the air and came across to my side of the green before falling in front of my feet. I stooped to pick it up, and just as I was about to tear it in half, stopped to read it further. The modern art gallery was featuring an exhibit of young photographers. I would stop in before continuing my walk. After looking at their work, I might get my camera and take those photographs of the campus that I had promised myself. I turned at the end of University Hall and walked down the path through the iron gates and over to the gallery. It was across the street from the main library on the crest of the hill. I remembered that an internationally famous architect had been commissioned to design its jagged roofline that looked like triangles of glass. Parked outside facing downtown was a black limousine.

I heard the footsteps and voices of a small knot of visitors who were at the far end of the exhibit room as I pushed through the heavy glass doors. On the information board was a description of the exhibit—"The President in *Week*—Outstanding Portraits of the President by Young *Week* Photographers." It was a mixed collection of mostly mediocre portraits of the president that had appeared in the news magazine based in the Apple. A few were of outstanding vision. I recognized many of the shots—having seen them when they were first published. And I recognized the same repeated examples of their uninventive approach. They did not know how to explore creatively the president's liability of being photographically challenging. He had no attractive physical features to boast of, and if you listened to the people around you—from the students to the cab drivers to the waiters to the professors—you might say that he was ugly. The photographs showed exactly how the deep, shifty eyes might be seen as devious and crafty if sprayed with the wrong combinations of light and shadow. The photographs revealed exactly how the firm yet thin lips might be seen as those of the tenuous and weak-minded. I would move the light source to a lower angle where shifty baggy eyes can be accentuated to reflect a man who is intensely thoughtful. Further, he should never be photographed in any other suit colors but black and blue. The contrast between those dark hues and his graying hair could be used to underline one dedicated to tidy stylishness. Of course they faced a challenge, but it could certainly be met by shooting from angles that did not have as its major focus to capture every pixel of a hairstyle that one columnist termed the "disheveled mop of thick spaghetti." By letting the forehead cover more than half of the frame, there leaves little room for the president's hair to show. These were simple matters of using light and composition creatively. Perhaps there is something about the creative process that cannot be taught. Perhaps the attitude cannot be taught—the special way that the artist looks at his world. In photographs of the president, he is the world. Your attitude toward him will shape your photographs. So you must change your attitude about him and enforce that new attitude onto your creation. You can't think of a person's being ugly and expect to produce photographs that don't show him to be ugly.

"Absolutely not. I agree wholeheartedly." I turned to my right, jolted to find him standing with his hands up to applaud me. He stepped forward to shake, "I'm Grantford Wiles. I'm a trustee. I was listening to your critique—quite impressive."

I had been talking out loud and he had heard every word. I moved my lips, but nothing came out.

"Oh do forgive me for listening. But I must tell you that I'm the chairman of Week Inc. Your thoughts were of real importance to me. In fact, I like them very much." When I turned I was staring at a dark blue suit with a gold chain across the vest and three fingers of handkerchief sticking out of the breast pocket. I looked up to see the sincerest eyes looking down at me. Suddenly the parked limousine made sense.

"Well, thank you. I guess I was just thinking like a senior who needs a job." I replied, wondering why I had said that.

"You're a senior?" He took off his eyeglasses and peered at me without them. "Do you have a job?"

"No, I'm going to…"

Before I could finish my sentence, he asked me if I would like to work for *Week* as a photographer starting after graduation in the Apple. In a sequence of moments that I kept trying to interrupt to be sure that I was not still a character in a dream that I thought had ended that morning, we were sitting in the back seat of his limousine like old friends. He told his chauffeur to drive me around the corner to the campus arch. He talked about his satisfaction with the college's efforts to recruit more Negro students and now that commitment had to be continued beyond the campus. "We in corporate America must do our share too," he said, turning to me with a cigarette in his mouth, the eyes still sincere. "And by the way, young man, I was on the committee that pushed for more of your people here," he said, tapping the ashtray. "I understand that we are enriched by the presence of several gentlemen like you." Before I could ask if he knew about Kwame and Darnel, he offered me a salary, gave me his card, and was leaning forward to wave good-bye as I closed the door.

I looked around, standing at the arch where you could always be certain of seeing dozens of students moving through. This time? Not a soul was there to witness my association with Grantford Wiles, one of the country's premier capitalists. He had given millions to the school, I remembered suddenly. But the long black automobile eased away, its engine ticking smoothly, and I skipped back to my room without one student observing me.

So it's good news and bad news for Aunt Clara, I thought as I ran up the steps. I could feel the smile on my face. In one day I had solved the problem of what to do. I could marry Atlanta, move to the Apple with a job after graduation, and not go to law school. Everybody would be almost totally happy.

Yes, I was in love with Atlanta. How could I have doubted it? Her fingers, her eyes, her soulful mysterious presence were necessary ingredients of my life. I was all of a sudden fascinated by the joys of fatherhood. I could teach a son how to box, fly a kite, ride a swing. And I would be a professional photographer. These are the themes I would pursue in my conversations with Harvey and Aunt Clara.

But Harvey was unusually quiet at our lunch, looking at me carefully, chewing slowly as I chronicled the unexpected chain of events that had occurred over the last two days.

"We didn't do anything to help him," Harvey said. "We never invited him to go with us anywhere. We laughed at him. We were as bad as the rest of them. And now look, just the two of us graduating. And that trustee—Wiles did you say? He has the nerve to talk about the school's commitment."

"But there may be some sisters walking. What about Sharon?"

"I checked with the registrar," he replied, banging his fork on his plate. "They all punched out. I keep telling you, it's just two little spooks—you and me."

What was the real root of Harvey's sadness? Kwame's losing his mind? My becoming a father? Not going to law school? Taking a job? Our being the only black students in the commencement proceeding?

It was all of that. It all had overwhelmed him listening to me just as it all had weighed me down. When was it—yesterday...the day before? "I never knew you were that interested in photography," he said. "And you getting married. That's a big leap. You sure you are ready? What about all those other girls in the world's playground you told me about?" We stared at each other and looked away, commenting on how some student needed a haircut. I swirled my fork around the remaining lump of mashed potatoes and nodded a thanks with my head down when one came over to congratulate me for getting into the law school. "I'd like to see some of those articles Kwame collected. Save them for me," Harvey said as he rose to leave.

I went back to my room to call Atlanta. Then I called Aunt Clara. I looked out the window at the downtown lights. And just as I had first gazed out the window over Aunt Shirl's ceramics to see the city hall clock and woke up weeks later, it seemed that here too time had changed while

I was looking out the window. Before I knew it, I was looking out the window during the week of graduation. Just a month earlier, Aunt Clara and Anida and Gahtsum had brought Atlanta and her mother for the wedding. "Mister Lowe had a body, he couldn't make it," smiled her mother, wedding cake icing dotting her lips. Harvey stood as my best man, while Canon Peddy performed a short ceremony in the downtown hotel suite that Gahtsum had reserved. Then they all went back to the world's playground (Gahtsum laying an arm around my shoulder for a long time, sighing without a word), and I was looking out the window at the downtown lights again—this time with Harvey on the night before graduation.

Each of us held a bottle of wine in our hands. We had not been invited to any of the fraternity or private graduation parties so we decided to make our own. We could hear the blaring of dance bands and the screams and laughter that flowed over the campus. We shouted back at them. We fenced with the canes we would use to walk down the hill. We practiced with the canes we were given to help us get down the steep hill. We laughed at almost everything—how we might fall down the hill, even the sad examples of our not being wanted. But we fell silent again when Harvey toasted me with "Old Romeo is going to be a father." I looked him in the eye and wondered what that meant as I clicked my bottle of wine against his.

I couldn't locate Aunt Clara and Gahtsum in the crowd. Each side of the street was crammed with waving, shouting delirious spectators straining against the ropes with cameras. We held onto our canes and started the steep fall-sprint down the hill to the Meeting House. Behind me a few graduates had fallen already, lying on their backs with legs in the air, a line of their fellow graduates stepping around them. One bumped into me, but before I could grab his robe to break his fall, he went sprawling against the rope, his cane flying in the air. A student with red hair falling over his face, whom I recognized as a refectory waiter, suddenly grabbed my shoulder to keep his footing, and as I turned to balance him (this time I was successful), I noticed a dozen black students in the line behind us. Who were they? Where did they come from? I couldn't turn because I would lose my balance and go tumbling...who knows in what direction? One of them, a tall coed, did look familiar. And so did two others. I had seen them in the theater school where Darnel had given a talk and I accompanied him. I wondered if all of them were from the theater school and planned to be actors.

At that moment, two elderly women cooling themselves with delicate fans were talking until one interrupted her. "Oh look," she said, "at the number of Negro students. Isn't that a huge increase from last year?"

"Oh my goodness yes. Why there must be more than a dozen total."

"Dorothy, it's simply marvelous how the school is recruiting all over the country to get more Negroes in school here. I may even make a sizable donation next year."

"Absolutely," was the reply. "You certainly should. I'll ask Herbert if we are liquid."

Chapter 21

It lasted seven years, Booby. That's how long it took for me to conclude that I had made a terrible mistake and that I would never be happy with the soulful miniature with the spongy palms and beady eyes. It didn't take me seven years to discover our lack of compatibility. It took me that long to make the decision to leave, to accept my responsibility for changing my unhappy state. We had started out innocently enough on a lovely, heavenly path. But that way began to turn and twist and rise and fall until the heavenly road became a passageway filled with unnerving, dislodging bumps and potholes.

At first we were swallowed up in our new freedom. Living at home for those first summer months after college with Aunt Clara and Anida, we no longer had to sneak as we had as teenagers to find the privacy that gave us access to furtive treasures. Now we were a legitimate couple and could actually snuggle together in bed—something we had experienced on just a few occasions when we had driven out to the pike to stay in a motel right after a dinner. Here was a new world, walls and barriers totally collapsed, everything bared. Now I could touch, fondle, those same previously forbidden areas and not be afraid of creaking steps, calls for a cup of tea, a telephone jangling, a wild animal in the woods, a drunk at the sea wall. On an evening: from the other side of the dinner table, in a skirt and sweater, she would move to our bedroom, her arms going up, her head covered by the sweater that she was pulling off, the bra that had been the first obstacle now there for me to remove without fear, without resistance. Then I would unsnap it and let it fall to the floor, then slide her skirt down over her hips to bare that wonderful triangle of fluorescence: her white panties in the dark. Now there was nothing to hide. Everything that the doo-woppers had sung about on the Young

Fellow's show was there for us. All of the routines that Aunt Clara and Mister Bat had practiced on Saturdays were now ours to duplicate. We need not fear. We were actors on that very stage that the lyrics had described: *Sincerely*; *Close Your Eyes*; *I Only Have Eyes for You*; *The Closer You Are, The Glory of Love*.

How magical it all seemed now that it was not forbidden. Each moment was like another page being turned, a curtain pulled aside. It wasn't merely the fact of her being unclothed that sparked the sense of magic. No, it was more; it was the discovery that her unclothed body revealed so many separate flashes of beauty. These snapshots could be appreciated now with a relaxed unhurried going over. There was no need anymore for those furtive, frantic glances necessitated by the limitations of time. We could take our time now and I could be far more conscious of her full frontal fullness, standing like a magnificent African fertility doll with bright adoring eyes. Or she might be in the bed bending over to pull back the sheets, the arch of her buttocks widened, the crisscross of her spine so prominent. Or she might be turning to reach the lamp, her breast swinging between her arms. How many pages, how many moments, I wondered as I relished each unfolding source of gratification.

Undressing itself even heralded a new wardrobe. Two gossamer flaps lay over her breasts and a snatch of sheer silk hung between her thighs—her stomach barely extended enough to disclose her pregnancy. One favorite piece was a negligee that barely hung below her hips. Another was a diaphanous vest without buttons—open, alluring.

In the mornings we seemed to awaken at the same time, automatically reaching out to the other. In a fog I would encircle her plump but small protuberance and then run my hand upward to her breasts, Then my touring hand would travel down over her hips and inside her thighs, again marveling as my lips brushed against the back of her neck. The marvel was that we were entitled to be here, beginning a morning by exploring each other. We did not have to sneak. We were allowed. Or I would feel her hand on my chest, cupping to form fingers that pulled and plucked and pinched my nipples before running it down and over my stomach to the inside of my thighs.

How wonderful, fresh and young everything seemed. How could there be so much bliss? Is this why Mister Bat visited still on Saturday nights? Did Aunt Clara own similarly revealing outfits? Did he venerate similar instants of revelation?

I told myself that I was happy. I told Aunt Clara and Anida whenever they found me alone and could turn the conversation quickly to how I felt about having a wife—and in a few months, a child. They liked Atlanta, but for some reason I felt they would have preferred that I not be married. "So young, that's all," Gahtsum had said one Sunday afternoon at dinner. Actually he had said that after a minute of silence when I had first called to tell him. "Your Aunt Clara told me the news. It's a surprising revelation," he had assessed. "I guess you must be confused about what to do next."

"No," I had lied. "We want to get married. I love her." I could hear him thinking.

"What about law school?"

"What about it?" I said, for the first time sensing the petulance in my voice directed at an adult and not caring. "I can delay it for a year."

"Well we can talk about it. I'll call you when I get back from New York. Need any extra change?"

No, I was between cloud nine and seventh heaven during those summer months before moving to the Apple. In my conversations I used phrases that described the most blissful state imaginable. It was my last summer stint at the delicatessen (Herman was going to the business school in Beanton and lamented that we wouldn't be on the same campus: "Shit, we would have a blast"). Was I convincing myself too? Is that why, out on the strip at nights with David and Ralph, I searched over and between the heads and shoulders at Grace's Little Belmont or Ike's Corner to reassess details of Yolanda or Velma or Lenora? I found myself staring at Lenora at a concert of the Wicked when she accepted his invitation to step up on the stage and dance with him. I strained to see, as she gyrated in the spotlight, if maybe her mustache that had seemed unsightly as a twelve-year-old was actually a deliciously inviting feature after all. What would it have been like to feel its fur against your lips? At the Timbuktu Tavern, Velma didn't seem as tall as she had been in the sixth grade. She was downright striking, her head only an inch taller than mine at the bar where she sat holding the hand of Mozelle, winner of two state high school championships, looking at himself in the mirror and now, according to Velma, "working in city hall." She smiled with sincerity when she congratulated me, while Ralph, elbowing me secretly, expressed surprise that Mozelle was not trying out for the Olympics. And Yolanda? I watched her bowlegged dark body swerve between the tables as she returned from the ladies' room at the Wonder Gardens. For just an instant, as she sat waving at us from her table of five women, it seemed as if she had gained a lifetime of sophistication. Maybe it was the flicker of the diamond ring and the new hairstyle.

By the time we got to the Apple I was flying even higher. Just after our son had been born on the hottest day in July, I had gone up and found an apartment on the upper west side, just a block from the subway. After giving the landlord a deposit and holding my lease as if it were a valuable bond, I stood on the corner at Broadway and observed with a tingling sensation the rhythms that were more rapid than any of those in the world's playground. I couldn't believe my luck. A new wife, a new baby, a new job, and in the greatest city in the world. To keep from being knocked over by the rush of men in suits carrying briefcases, elderly ladies with dogs, elderly men in wheelchairs, blind men with canes, and beggars with signs describing the most horrific personal tribulations ("Wife left, took shoes and parakeet, help please"), I leaned against the glass wall of the pharmacy and looked west down to the Hudson River where high-rise buildings sprouted upward on the other side in New Jersey. Looking north up Broadway, I could see a convention of twelve yellow cabs lined up to make U-turns around the grassy median where a crowd had gathered to watch two chess players sitting on wooden crates. Next to them on a bench, a man's knees stuck out from an opened newspaper covering his body from waist to forehead. Turning east, I saw the huge conical spire of a church that was almost one hundred years old. I recognized its Gothic features from the slides that Professor Gut had shown in class. He had described it as the epitome of tectonic progress because it was to be "a mighty symbol of coming together," in his words. "But, alas." He had spun in his chair and stared at the blackboard, his back to us. We waited in silence for him to face us again, and no one dared ask what had happened to cause that emission of despair. A bus hissed, sending three pigeons scurrying, the subway train under my feet shook mightily, a white ambulance blinked its red alarm. Booby, I was transfixed by it all, and was about to step down finally into the subway when I was interrupted by his standing in front of me.

"They'll never finish, you know."

I looked at him blankly. His long trench coat and white unshaved face told me that he might be a beggar. I tried to move around him.

"Do you think they will?" He had touched me lightly on the arm—just enough to slow me.

"Will what?" I asked, giving the impression that I was intent on not stopping.

"That church down there. They stopped construction after the war. That was thirty years ago. I don't think they will finish."

"It's not finished?" I asked, now stopped.

"No, and they won't finish. And you know why, of course." But then a horde of six came from nowhere to sweep me down the steps, through the turnstile and into the train.

After I squeezed between an elderly woman and a bearded man whose knees poked out from his tattered pants, I stared straight ahead. Looking across at two men reading their newspapers, I was reminded of the conversations that summer in the barber shop about my former school mates. I was lucky. Many of them weren't. Poor John Durham wasn't the only one killed in the war we were fighting against the tiny Asian nation. I had learned that Danny Bunn, who had given me the news in grade school about Florine, had passed the test to become a paratrooper and was shot down by helicopter fire. I imagined him jumping out of a plane with a wild smile on his face. At the bus stop across from Herman's restaurant one morning, his father told me that Big Man had been paralyzed in a mortar attack. "He won't go out the house and doesn't want any visitors," his father said, almost choking. And Ron...and James—from junior high school? Nobody knew anything. Maybe they were back in jail. Plus, Mister Bat had placed a veil of sadness over Aunt Clara when he told her that he needed to spend more time with his son. The boy was in a coma after a truck crashed headlong into the side of his sedan. I was one with no complaints, I thought, as I looked across at the full row of passengers and wondered if they were happy, and if so, what were they happy about? Did they have somebody to love? Did somebody they had loved gone on to leave them to survive on memories? Well, I had somebody to love— and a little son to prove it.

I opened my notebook portfolio to look at the portraits I would show the editor at *Week*. Most had been shot before college, since I had taken little time during my undergraduate years to spend on photography. I flipped the pages and felt a proud sense of accomplishment as I looked at the faces I had captured. Light was the key, was the paintbrush the cameraman used to wash his canvas, I would say in the interview. There was the afternoon shot of Roy, turning to say "You can't look neat if your shoes are beat," his hands holding the white soiled rag he used to buff loafers, brogues, oxfords and others. And the slash of light from the living room put a sheen on the left side of Mister Eddie's face that gave him the air of a movie star. I was smiling inside, even more contented with my work as I looked at Big Man's father standing in the doorway, the white apron highlighting his dark features. Suddenly the train lurched and jerked, the lights flickered, and then it slowed as it entered the station. The poor traveler with the holes in his knees stood shakily, holding on to the metal support as he stepped toward the door. His thin mustache reminded me of Mister Eddie. I wondered if he had a place to go or if he would just ride on the trains all day until it was time to find a safe haven in an alley or park to lay his head down for the night. He was leaning over me but I looked straight ahead, hoping that he would not start a conversation. I remembered Aunt Shirl's saying, "The best thing to do with riff-raff is to ignore them." The train stopped. Then, in an instant that was far too short for me to assess its significance or even respond, he said, "Very nice work. Reminds me of Rodchenko." And then he dissolved into the other bodies pushing through the door. Stunned, I opened my mouth to thank him, tried to stand, thought of waving, but the train was easing forward. He had liked my work. He knew of Rodchenko, an artist I admired, and I had done my best to ignore the traveler's existence. So much for understanding Aunt Clara's saying that you don't always see what you think you see.

I was still half-scolding myself when I came up to ground level. Their offices were in the downtown financial district of dark cavernous narrow streets, long black sedans and piercing car horns. Everyone walked with quick determined steps, as if 10 minutes late. But with my camera bag and portfolio on my side and plenty of time, I stepped with a steady yet deliberately calm pace. A security guard nodded his approval when I walked toward the bank of elevators that took me to the 35th floor.

When the doors slid open, a booming voice met me. "There you are! Right on time. Fantastic." He grabbed me by the shoulder and led me, "This way, I have a map for you." He led me toward the receptionist's desk and then turned down an aisle of desks and cubicles of smiling men and women. "Put your things down," he pointed to a chair in his office. "I'm Davis, chief of assignments, heard all about you. What's that, your portfolio? I'll look at it later. We need you to go up...to Harlem. Big rally. Here's a map." It seemed as if I had not really gotten off the elevator because I was standing in the same spot again. Now we were going down, my camera bag over my shoulder, Davis, shorter than Little Man, talking rapidly, his arms spreading out the paper atlas in front of us. "It's the Pumas. Be careful." Then we were in the lobby where the security guard waved him over. I stood there wondering what I should do. Davis said something that sent the guard's head back in a big laugh followed by a punch on Davis' shoulder. They both looked at me, standing there, wondering what I should do next, and the three of us were in a suspended moment of silently staring at each other before he said finally, waving, "Get going, guy! Don't forget to call in a progress report." And he turned to face the security guard again.

"Okay," I said, waving back and turning in a circle trying to remember which of the plaza entries I should go through to get back to the subway. A man swinging a briefcase went through the revolving door so I took a chance and followed him down a long marble hallway that led to a dark tunnel that spilled out into the subway platform. He set his case at his feet and pulled out a folded tabloid newspaper. I was going back uptown, past my new apartment, I told myself, searching the overhead signs for the right train number. Looking up, my eyes caught the headline on the front page of his newspaper: "Pumas Rally for Justice!"

Booby, that was the beginning of my success. When I emerged from the subway in Harlem that fall afternoon, I was hit by the exhilarating distinctions that you find only in that northern section of the Apple. The conversations seemed to be in shorthand, the sentences never finished but rather truncated into a special code. *Yo. Right on. Solid. Catcha later. I can dig it.* Everybody wanted to know *what it look like?* and *what's goin' on?* The cries of the peddlers seemed magnetic, as if you had a mandatory duty to buy the women's stockings, or batteries they held high in the air. The tempo in the swinging arms, the colors in the clothing, even the smiles on the faces reflected an energy that was irrepressibly ingrained.

What a treasure trove, I thought. I knew this was the fall, and winter was approaching, but spring seemed not far behind at all. Leaning against a display window, I pulled out my camera and felt like a child in a toy store before I remembered that I had a special assignment. "Yo dude, you sure is clean for a photographer," a broadly smiling man with a gap in his tooth told me as he hustled past, and "Scu' me man" as he bumped into an onwalker. Here I was in the hip capital of the world and wearing my navy blue interview suit. Well I was stuck with it, I considered and looked around for a street sign.

Almost a block away on the other side was the legendary theater that I had heard about. All of the most popular groups on the *Young Fellow* had performed there. Oh I couldn't miss getting a shot of its famous marquee. I sprinted to the middle of the street to join the knot of pedestrians who dodged the cars coming in both directions before reaching the sidewalk safely. As I approached, I looked for an announcement of maybe the Wicked or the Little Racquet performing. Instead, the letters declared in bold black capitals, PUMAS CHILDRENS RALLY. And then, if by magic, several buses began pulling up in front of the theater to unload a bounty of squealing jumping children. They fell down the steps and formed a crowd now chanting:

Umgawa, blackpower! Umgawa, blackpower!

I jumped ahead and knelt quickly to shoot their bright eyes and busy mouths running inside the theater. I followed them and braced myself to focus when I saw the dozen members of the Pumas standing to the side at attention. They all wore iridescent berets cocked to the side of their heads. Their iridescent shirts and iridescent pants fit them tightly, and they wore iridescent boots. The gleam from all of this made me blink rapidly. They held something across their chests that looked like rifles. I could hardly focus as I stood with legs spread to get in my viewfinder the three of them knitted together in the middle. But then a heavy-set man on the end came shouting and lunging toward me. He didn't have a rifle but he had swung back his arm and his fist was coming fast. In one motion I secured my camera on my shoulder and stepped back in time to sting his chin with a swift jab. His eyes glared with the hazy fog that one sees before losing consciousness. He fell to his knees and looked up. But now I wanted him to get up. He had roused who knows how much pent-up anger inside me that needed releasing. I wanted to pummel him.

Without warning, from the theater doors, "Hold it! Who is that?" He spurted toward me with arms swinging, his lieutenants walking in double file behind him. He kept right at me and then pulled up as if putting on breaks. That is how I met Sylvester Wade, founder of the revolutionary Puma Party.

In their weekly newspaper sold by members who were street vendors throughout the Apple——*Puma Pounce*——they published regularly a list of demands that included exempting black soldiers from serving in the military that was fighting against the tiny Asian nation; building decent housing for our people; ending police brutality against black people, and "saving our children." On the front page of each issue was a photograph of Sylvester in his iridescent outfit holding a rifle. They had established a free weekly program where children could come to the Puma office in their neighborhood to get free breakfasts before school started. On this afternoon, an after-school rally featuring boxed lunches for the kids had been planned inside the famed theater.

He was amazed but impressed too that, dressed in my business suit and looking like "a college student from one of the group," I had knocked down one of their captains. "Did they teach you how to hold your hands like that?" he asked with a snicker.

"No, I learned that in the world's playground," I answered, repressing the impulse to mention the Champions of America. "But I never got in a fight," I said, wondering if that is why I had felt such a vicious impulse to hit his man again and again. We talked and walked all that afternoon as he guided me around the theater, while various speakers rose from the table with waving fists to talk about a menace, a danger, a lie that had to be addressed. Immediately after the speech——especially by a tall, striking light-skinned woman with the new Afro hairstyle that rose four inches from her scalp——the students erupted chanting in front of the stage and dancing with a furious spontaneity before returning to sit with crossed legs and folded hands.

"Umgawa, black power; umgawa, black power!"

By the time I left the activities, the bulbs in the street lights and in the stores had come on and I had used dozens of rolls of film. Sylvester had introduced me to nearly all of the leaders in the movement since the Pumas had used the children's rally as an opportunity to arrange a strategy session behind the curtains. "He majored in tectonics at one of those fancy group schools," he said, throwing his thumb Northward. I had seen or heard about several of them, but only knew them as pictures or names in a magazine or newspaper. The short fiery bearded poet-playwright who recited his poems with screaming intensity wore a colorful dashiki. The balding entrepreneur whose black newspaper had an office just a block away wagged his finger to make a point, sleek in his dark pinstriped suit and goatee. And I saw the handsome young light-skinned man from the South (sometimes referred to as "Smooth") who had protested against the war and had therefore been removed from his elected position. They had no reservations about my moving around them and aiming my camera at their faces—the faces that formed the revolutionary leadership. They were from different organizations and groups, but they were united in their resolve.

"So what was it like up there?" he asked after introducing me to a soft-spoken gentleman whose face I recognized but whose name I could not recall. Somehow I thought he was connected with the United Nations, but would he be here? "Was it worth it?" asked Sylvester, still leading me around and looking ahead. "Well, you sure learned their dress code."

How many times had Harvey and I debated that question. How many times had he insisted that I was too enchanted with the school's image and tradition. But a university trustee offered me the job at *Week.* Where would I be otherwise—sitting in a law school class in Beanton? Or teaching high school history? Was what I learned worth what I had given up? God knows I had given up a lot, I remembered. But how would I have met Sylvester otherwise?

"It was okay," I answered, thanking him for showing me around and introducing me to the prominent. "My Aunt Clara always said that what you hope for is always better than what you have," I told him with a smile. Thanks to that spontaneous friendship with Sylvester Wade I had *carte blanche* with those leaders—access to the men and women who were directing the new liberation movement for black people. My photographs of them, seen by people all over the world on the covers and in the pages of *Week,* put my photography in the spotlight. They were usually candid shots of those who were spearheading the protest movement, the revolutionary movement, the freedom movement—each used a different phrase that expressed her special orientation. The photographs appeared on the front covers and throughout the inside spreads regularly, and I stared sometimes at my credit line (my name spelled correctly!) even longer than I did at the photographs. My reputation as the leading photographer of the black movement was spiraling upward.

No wonder I dragged myself off the elevator and trudged down the hall when I got home in the evenings, always playing out in my mind the scene that I hoped would change magically. I would kiss and hug Atlanta as she met me at the door and proceed down the hall past the bedroom to our one large room that was a combination living and dining space. I would get on my knees and put out my hands to my son. He always smiled at me and crawled backward—farther and farther away until banging into a wall or chair and bursting into a frightful cry. Then I would pick him up and hold him tightly, kissing his forehead and patting his back.

The pediatrician, whose office was on the top floor of a brownstone, had told us not to worry. "There's time, I wouldn't get too excited," he told us, sitting behind his desk where he had placed our son who sat between papers and a stethoscope and stared at him. "All the tests are positive. Not too unusual for six months. He's got time." He leaned back with his hands behind his neck. "Having fun on Doctor Livingston's desk there, young fellow?"

"Even when happy, he crawls backward." Atlanta reported.

"Well of course," the doctor replied. "The young fellow has to move around whether he's happy or sad; don't you, young fellow?"

"What shall we do?" I asked.

"Be patient," he counseled. "Let's give it some time."

But Aunt Clara and Anida had different perspectives. "And look, Mo-Dear always said that doctors were just practicing," Aunt Clara reminded me on the telephone. It's time for that boy to be doing something close to normal, I don't care what they say. And he's still crawling—and crawling backwards at that. Better see another doctor. And get a white one. Mo-Dear would die if she knew you fooling around with some Negro podiatrists. Too bad we don't know what happened to William and Hattie. Just up and moved to Georgia they say. I bet he could have the boy chasing rabbits with just one prayer."

"Oh my Lord, that don't make no sense," Anida said, visiting us on a December Saturday as part of a women's group who had organized a bus trip to the Apple for early Christmas shopping. "You got to do something about that. Girl, if I had known you were this close to Small's Paradise I would have been up here every weekend babysitting for you," she told Atlanta as we watched her wait for the elevator.

We did take Aunt Clara's advice and went to a specialist whom Gahtsum had recommended. It was a freezing day in January when we walked into the downtown hospital to see him. He welcomed us warmly. "Oh, and how is my old friend, Gahtsum? Still making money I suppose?" Soon he was opening and examining a series of file folders, shifting them from one hand to the other, peering over them at our son in Atlanta's lap, then looking at us, then studying the files again. He frowned, looked at us, looked at our son, then frowned again. "I'd like to call in my two associates to get their advice. Do you mind?" he asked, rising. "Leave your coats here."

We followed him out to where a half dozen nurses and orderlies and residents met him immediately and marched along as if he had summoned them for an inspection. We fell in behind them. "Did you get Overby and Saxton?" he asked a nurse. She nodded a reply, still in step at his side. At the end of the hall we turned and stopped suddenly. The nurse jangled her ring of keys and then found the one to unlock the door. "Our assessment room," explained Dr. Kurz, waving good-bye to his entourage and leading us inside to face a huge glass wall. The floor was white and shiny. The white walls seemed freshly painted, and the ceiling was white too with cones of spotlights in it.

It lasted about 30 minutes after his two associates knocked and introduced themselves. Atlanta and I sat in the chairs facing the window. Dr. Kurz placed our son in the room on the arena floor, and the three of them, standing shoulder-to-shoulder at the glass window, watched him. They took notes on their clipboards, looked at each other, stared at our son, looked at each other, stared at our son, took notes. Finally we all went back to Dr. Kurz's office, and they admitted, standing together with arms folded, that they didn't have an answer. They needed to study the results some more and would contact us.

When we got home we stared at the wall in the living room. That became our frequent pattern during our son's first two years—after he had fallen asleep at night and we could talk about it. During the day he had crawled backward, she reported, bumping into the walls and chair legs and continuing to move rearward around these obstacles as if they were part of a game. But his face did not reflect the gleeful mood of the playing child; instead, it was dead serious, as if he were embarked on the most solemn mission. When I returned in the evenings from a mentally and physically exhausting day of shooting, I would fall to my knees and clap my hands, inviting him to come to Daddy. No, he would scurry away, intent on the mission that pulled him in the opposite direction. When Atlanta and I lay talking in bed on those evenings, I found myself oddly disconnected from her, as if the spongy softness in her hands that had been so magnetic was now pushing me away.

The disconnection gathered momentum one evening when I returned from a midtown shoot. A wealthy socialite on the east side had sponsored a fundraiser in her penthouse suite for the Pumas. I aimed my camera when she exhaled, "It's so exciting, what they are doing." She waved a champagne glass across her face as she stood in the center of her dining room—the Empire State Building in the background. Sylvester and two lieutenants had given a presentation about the breakfast program and had received a spirited round of approval from the guests.

"We just have to do something," declared one guest who was bent over writing a check on the kitchen counter. "Should I make it out to your tailor? I just love those outfits you wear." The feather in her hat fluttered as she smiled with the two dozen others who laughed nervously—a good shot of sincere community activism, I thought.

I was thinking of how my photos of the snazzily dressed contributor might add to the *Week* feature story when I came out of the subway and saw the ambulances outside of our apartment building. Perhaps the friendly Polish lady with asthma had had another attack, I mused as I walked into the lobby. But when I got off the elevator upstairs, I saw that they were all standing outside my apartment door.

"I'm sorry," said a short gentleman in a suit whom I had seen in the lobby some evenings when I returned from a late assignment. He tipped his hat and squeezed my arm and skipped to run into the elevator I had just walked out of. Ahead, Atlanta was in our doorway talking to a trio of police officers whose heads bobbed up and down between their notepads and her face. One of them caught her at the shoulders just as she looked to see me coming and fell forward in a faint.

Our son had been crawling backward in the living room while Atlanta was cooking dinner. But he had disappeared. "She thought at first that subject—your son—had crawled under furniture items like the couch or a table," the officer with the unevenly shaved mustache explained to me. "But." He turned his head toward the group of officers congregated by the living room window. "But."

"He's not here, not a trace," stepped in a wide-bodied sergeant whose waist walkie-talkie kept sending squeaking voice commands and queries to him. "Negative that. Our data shows subject is possibly part of going back scenario. He may have gone back into history. We have no evidence of the contrary."

There was no other place to look, we finally decided some hours later after she had gained consciousness from the medication and had calmed her tearful shaking. We had two bedrooms, a kitchen, living room, and two closets. He wasn't there. For several weeks we moved around the apartment as if it were possible that we had missed some little cranny. But I began to accept the fact that we were hoping against hope, refusing to acknowledge the bitter reality that Gahtsum seemed to embrace.

For Gahtsum, it was a condition that he had heard about in Brotherly Love "sometime ago, before you were born," he told me one day at the airport where we met for lunch before he caught a plane to the West Coast—something about crude oil opportunities. "It's unfortunate, but one can develop a desire not to become a participant," he concluded. "Imagine being so discouraged at the possibility of it's ever working out, of it's ever coming together. So you choose to leave the present rather than be bothered with it. I can certainly understand how one can be fearful of the present, lose faith in it and return to history. Poor little guy. He came, he saw, he left." We both looked out at the planes lined up on the runway.

Harvey? He was struggling with his private law practice and not yet the true militant he is now. Yet he was consoling in a biting way. Sorry, yes. At least I had experienced fatherhood, although briefly. And maybe my son was smarter than all of us. Maybe he had seen what he was getting into and decided that it was far too formidable. "Maybe he didn't want to go to college in the group and endure all the crap we did." His telephone voice slurred, the way it did after too much vodka. "Makes sense to me," he snorted. "Sometimes my clients make me wish I could crawl back into history."

With just the two of us alone now, the disconnect between Atlanta and me escalated in my mind. The erotic injection that had traveled from her hand to mine and that had sent those tantalizing vibrations through me had turned into a serum that nurtured my disinterest. In fact, her touch was becoming unwelcome. Those formerly magical fingers seemed stringy and thin, the palms were coarse, I told the therapist whom Gahtsum had recommended. "You have a lot of things going on that you don't know about. Give it a try," he suggested.

I found one whose office was in an old building with a small marble lobby just three subway stops from the *Week* office: Dr. Fisher. He was his own receptionist and greeted me with a warm smile when I came through the door. "Well, there's nothing wrong with her," he said, looking at Atlanta's photograph that he had requested. "It's in the mind. All sex is in the mind, you know. You have a block. Something in your mind is telling you that you won't like having sex with her anymore. That's why you aren't enjoying her." He outlined a number of exercises for me that would get us "back in touch." One required that we hold hands after dinner, while looking at television to "sense the tactile vibrations." Another would have us holding each other around the waist—hugging—just as I entered the apartment in the evening.

Oh Booby, none of that worked. What did work is my seeing the Real Atlanta, the person, the being with a personality that I hadn't really apprehended before. I began to watch her closely, listen to her attentively, and think about what I had seen and heard. Soon I was in year six of my reconnaissance, and I became convinced that she was a character who had no real interests, no ideas to express. Did she have a personality? Was she all soul and sensuality—without much regard for any challenges of the intellect? Had she read anything, I asked one day when she had gone shopping and I looked around for a book or magazine she might have put down.

Let's face it. I had married her because I had made her pregnant. I had been too proud to admit that I had made a mistake. I could have told her seven years ago in my last year of college that I didn't want to spend the rest of my life with her, although I had been responsible for making a life with her. But no, I did what I thought I should do rather than what I wanted to do. I did what I thought would look good——making the honorable, principled decision——and refused to probe my heart deeply enough to see if I really, really loved her.

One Friday night she had prepared a wonderful meal (oh she was a great cook!) because I had come home early from a shoot. She flitted back and forth between the kitchen and the dishes of baked chicken, macaroni and greens. We talked. We looked at television. We went to bed.

The next morning I awoke not in her arms but on the other side of the bed, having lain awake most of the morning looking at the ceiling and refereeing the two voices that were battling within. One had called me a fool and bungler, while the other had insisted that I had done the best I could. But I knew I had to make a decision, so I turned to Atlanta when she came back from the bathroom and was standing at the bed, about to slide under the sheets.

"I'm not happy," I began.

"Was there something wrong with the chicken?" she asked.

Chapter 22

It had three great advantages, so I signed the lease on the spot. The living room faced the park, it was only four subway stops from the *Week* office, and it was partly furnished. On the southern side of the bridge to the Apple, the new residence was less expensive than the apartment Atlanta and I shared in the uptown area. Plus it sat on a street lined with stately old brownstones that were being broken up into two and three large apartments. After I watched the movers bring in my new sofa and chairs that spring afternoon, I opened the shutters to find the source of the guitar music. Across the street in front of the park entrance, two Latinos were serenading their girlfriends sitting on a bench. Looking at the lovers, I felt a bittersweet flutter go through me. I turned and sat down on the new sofa that was still wrapped in plastic and faced the boxes stacked against the wall. In one of the boxes was my bird book. I pulled it out and sat back down, turning the pages without concentrating. Each bird reminded me of a scene from the past, of a time when I had picked up the same heavy guide as a means of reorienting myself. But the memories of Atlanta all had a somber tinge as I stopped and stared at two swallows flying, picking at each other with their beaks. One was above the other as if it had just swooped down. I was almost thirty years old and felt as if I were starting my life all over again.

"You make a mistake, you learn from it, you go on," Gahtsum had told me a week earlier at lunch, in town for a few days before traveling overseas on business. We were in a dining room of a private club on the east side. The floor-length oil portraits lining the oak walls, and the glittering chandelier reminded me of my first walk into Salem Hall. All the men were white, wore dark suits and white shirts and struck one of two poses. Either they were huddled, leaning toward each other and speaking in tones so low that the entire room vibrated with one huge whisper, or they sat back in their chairs grinning at each other while holding the stem of a wine glass. "You are being recognized as a very talented photographer, so you should concentrate on the positive," he told me, his thin lips barely parting. "Don't let it get you down, my boy. I've heard from her lawyer and everything is settled. Aunt Clara and Anida are so proud of you. Well, we're all proud of you. I just want you to be happy in what you are doing. And you know your aunt has saved every issue of *Week* that has your photographs. When I chuckled at the thought of Aunt Clara's saving the magazines, it resounded throughout the room like a shout, and heads turned toward us as if we had released a great secret.

A tall handsome gentleman with a silver head of hair came over to our table. He bent down with a hand on his shoulder to whisper in Gahtsum's ear. Gahtsum nodded, then turned to introduce me.

"Oh yes, I've seen the young man's work," he said, looking into my eyes as he shook my hand. "Benson Tiff, class of forty-nine, nice to see you. And Brantford Wiles has spoken very highly of him. Have you been back up on the hill since graduation, my good man?"

Overcoming my impulse to say no, what for? I shook my head as if apologizing.

"Well nice to meet you," he said, voice almost too low to hear, and then in an even lower tone, "So stay in oil you say, right Gahtsum?"

I had assured Gahtsum at lunch that day that I was keeping up my spirits, knowing that it was easier said than done. But as I looked up at the blank white wall in my new apartment, freshly painted, I felt far less buoyant than I thought I should, as if some weight were pulling me back as I tried to stride ahead. In fact, I wasn't greatly driven about marching ahead, and I wasn't as excited about my work anymore.

Maybe I would be able to serenade somebody soon. But on that first day in my new apartment, it seemed like a far-off prospect. "Not to worry, Romeo," Harvey reasoned a few days earlier. "With your drive, it will be only a matter of seconds before you find somebody with whom you can fall madly in love again. I bet the women at *Week* are chasing you like crazy."

Sure, it was easy for him to joke. Everything was going fine with him and Sandra, whom he had met in law school. "Oh yes, the first couple of years took some adjusting to, but we are doing fine," he told me after the wedding. "I wish you could have been best man, but we decided on the spot one day just to go to city hall. We can't wait for her to get pregnant," he had said. "We want to have two or three kids."

Now the serenaders had launched into an upbeat tune, and I lay back my head to enjoy them. Listening to their mellifluous stringing, I was falling into a hazy zone of relaxation when I heard the doorbell ring. I jumped up quickly from my near sleep and turned in a circle before orientating myself, then almost stumbled down the steps to the door. His back was to me as he too listened to the lovers. He turned when I opened the door. "Telegram, sign here please" and "Hey, those guys can sing." Then, pouch hanging over his shoulder, he was skipping down the steps of the brownstone and off to his next delivery.

I'd forgotten that my telephone would not be connected until the following Monday, and here was the message from my assignment editor. He wanted me to go up to Harlem over the weekend because he had heard that the Pumas might be planning a demonstration.

During the last two years of my marriage to Atlanta, while I was tackling my own personal crisis with her, the Apple and the country itself were being confronted by accelerated protest activities. All of the tension that had built up during my years in college was now exploding into more frequent, more strident expressions. Some were protesting the war we were waging against the tiny Asian nation, some were combating the civil rights violations that Harvey had fought for during the semester he took a leave, and some were college students rebelling against the very governance of the universities themselves.

Brantford Wiles had not only been the trustee responsible for hiring me, but he was also the publisher of *Week* who charged his editors with covering the firestorm of protests taking place in the country. I often thought about how lucky I was to be in the right place at the right time— first meeting Wiles in the college art gallery and then getting the opportunity to shoot the turmoil erupting in the Apple.

"It's important that we cover these historic times," he told me one late afternoon during one of those chats he would initiate after summoning me to his office. "The country is going through a transformation that is unprecedented. Values are changing, all aspects of society are being questioned and challenged. But the center"—here he hesitated and whirled around to look out. "The center cannot fold." I loved looking out at the magnificent view from his wall of glass. The sun was close to setting and already had left the downtown financial district cloaked in semi-darkness. Just below was the gilded cross of the famous church that was centuries old, and I could make out a few granite tombs in its graveyard. To the left, a half mile away was the parklet of walkways and trees spreading out from the city hall, its copper roof and white marble now illuminated by street lamps. To the right and on its own island where the ferry stopped was the majestic statue given to the country by the French to celebrate our Civil War that emancipated the slaves.

"Two great leaders killed," he said, pulling on his suspenders. "It's disheartening to see men who stand for something glorious slain for their beliefs. They killed your dreamer, the man who did so much for your people's civil rights. And then they killed the young idealist attorney who was planning to run for president. These are trying times, don't you think?" He turned to look at me, and I looked back at the near silhouette of dark pants, white shirt, suspenders, his face. Was the millionaire publisher really asking me for my opinion about the state of things? Before I could answer, he walked back to the window and looked out at the statue. "I've got some resistance from the chairman about our coverage. He thinks we should cut back, but I don't agree. I think we have a responsibility to document what is happening."

I had nodded in agreement. "It's important," I said, wondering why I couldn't think of anything else. Maybe I needed a refreshing of my spirit that paging through my bird book or talking with Harvey, Gahtsum and Aunt Clara couldn't bring to me. When I first shot the rebelling students at the university near Harlem, I didn't feel the same sustained excitement that I usually had when covering an event of such electricity. My photographs were striking nevertheless, and Davis and several of the editors responded enthusiastically. "This shot of those students climbing up the walls to take over the administration building is outstanding!" he yelled, running down the hall to show it to an editor. "Their parents ought to be ashamed, paying all that money for their kids to act like that." He was especially upset with the attitude expressed by a sign held by one white student:

The People Will Run the College or the People Will Burn it Down

"I saw those shots of the black students taking over the building," Harvey told me by phone. "It's about time those brothers and sisters stood up and asked for a change. Do you think anything will happen? Will the college enroll more black students?"

I wasn't sure. I was too involved with keeping up my spirits and completing my assignments to connect myself psychologically with my subjects and their goals. My focus was on capturing the moments within the rectangle that I framed them in. I saw them raising their fists, I saw their mouths opened wide in shrieks, but I wasn't really concentrating on what they were saying. Not until I saw the texts connected to my photographs did the real impact register with me. By then I was off to a new assignment, almost oblivious to what I had caught previously with my lens.

But the resurrection of my waning enthusiasm and inattention began when I got off the subway that Saturday after receiving Davis' telegram. An air raid of sirens and red flashes hit me as I came up to the sidewalk.

The main street was roped off, a parking lot of confused drivers going nowhere. People were moving toward or pointing to the end of the block where Harlem's only hotel was located across from the theater. As I made my way with them, trying to elbow gently to squeeze through and around them to get ahead, I pieced together the snatches of nearly hysterical questions and statements—in strident, angry tones—to determine what had happened. The Pumas had paraded down the avenue that runs into the main street.

"The police told them they ain't got no permit; that's bull! You know they always get a permit. Then hundreds of them pigs with guns blocked their way, holding up their rifles like this."

"Was Sylvester there? Has anybody seen him?" I asked, but nobody could tell me.

A scuffle, pushing, and before anyone knew it, the police were arresting the Pumas, grabbing them by the backs of their necks and handcuffing them.

"They threw them boys in the paddy wagon like they were sacks of cotton. Oh Lordy, one of them look like my little nephew Jason. Hold me up, I'm too weak."

Outnumbered, a few of the Pumas reversed themselves to run back down the avenue, then sprinted through an alley and up the steps of an apartment building. The police surrounded the entrance.

"You shoulda saw them brothas run—moving like fifty—look like the Olympics!"

The police cars blocked the street from both ends. A short commander jumped out of one, demanding with a bullhorn pointed in the sky that all the residents leave the building—with their hands on top of their heads: couples holding hands, babies on father's shoulders, babies in carriages, old men with canes. Not one was dressed in iridescence. The commander then addressed the Pumas directly and told them that they had fifteen minutes to come out…or else.

"They didn't even wait five minutes before they started shooting like crazy and charging up them steps and in the building. All we heard was shots—shooting like crazy, sounded like a shooting gallery. *Rat-a-tat-a-tat-tat*. Smoke everywhere."

When I got to the corner and looked down the street, I saw a dozen blue-and-white police sedans with their sirens flashing. Police knelt behind and to the side with rifles and guns pointed at the entrance. It was quiet then, only the soar of a faraway jet splicing the air; and when the officer told me to "hold it right there, bub," his voice seemed the only other sound on the street. I shot everything—the police kneeling, the frightened and confused faces of the Harlemnites on both sides of the street, even the scared young face of one of the officers who could have been a rookie not quite prepared for this event as he kept asking people to step back. As if jolted, I was now in a new zone of artistic fascination, truly involved in the drama that I was covering as well as the capturing of the black-and-white rectangles of proof. I was back to my old self, of being excited about the challenge of my work that required me to capture the moment with as much artistry as I could.

As if they were heads of state, I focused on the four bodies that they took out on stretchers. I wanted every angle. I went in close, isolating the tiny white beds as if they were works of art themselves; I pulled back and placed them against the background of the police, the neighbors, the police cars, the sky, the pole lamps. I focused only on the strap that holds the body around the waist. I got a shot of the feet that stuck out at the end. And, of course, I caught the faces of so many standing by—so many torn, bewildered, angry expressions.

Two officers with twangy voices and hats covering their eyes tried to stop me from going up to the apartment. I showed them my *Week* identification. One took it, turned his back on us, stepped away and pulled out his walkie-talkie. Then he came back with a big sigh. "Chief says let him through."

The air at the top of the landing smelled as if something hard and metallic had burned and was still simmering. The door to the apartment was wide open. I walked inside. A couch and chairs and a table were all upside down, their legs almost the same width, like part of a suite. On the wall hanging at an angle were pictures of two soldiers and Jesus on the Cross—spotted with bullet holes. Ribbons draped the room like a birthday party, except these were yellow and had *Police* written in black. Bending under them, I stepped carefully so that I would not slip on the rings of blood to position myself to shoot. What was I shooting—the past, something that had happened already and had left historic remnants? What did it show—these items, these things? It registered that death had occurred, and it was my first time being so close to it. I was shooting death without the dead. My hand shook as I aimed.

My heart was thumping as I backed out to get a larger perspective. When I walked around to shoot the door, focusing in and out to get different views, it was a while before I was struck with what I saw. All of the bullet holes in the door had come from outside. Well wait. I stepped back into the doorway to look around the room again. All of those holes must have come from outside the apartment also. I was standing in a half daze when the feet of the two policemen echoed up the steps.

"Chief says you have to leave. We need to collect evidence."

Chapter 23

Harvey was right, a few of the women did become especially friendly after my divorce was finalized. From nowhere, it seemed, two whose presence had been just noticeable, women whom I usually greeted with a few trite expressions and a smile as I passed their desks, now seemed to blossom and shine with a previously unacknowledged radiance.

First the thin young secretary of Brantford Wiles himself began to extend our casual two-sentence greetings to more extended conversations. Her parents in Scandinavia had loved my portraits of the Dreamer, she told me in her thick accent, where *loved* sounded like *luft* and *the* sounded like *zee*. Of course she could never pronounce my name correctly, invariably following the verbal slaying with "Did I say it correctly? Oh you probably want to kill me. I should know by now." A deep smile cut across her mouth to brighten her blue eyes. On the very night that Brantford Wiles had assured me again of his commitment to *Week's* covering the revolution and allowing the challenging voices to have an audience, she was at her desk when I walked in, the lamp spraying a golden hue over her fur coat draped over a chair.

"Oh everybody thinks your work is just so splendid," she breathed out one afternoon as we chatted near the elevator. "They all talk about it." She was indeed a valuable source of information—usually imparted with a whisper and tender grasp of my arm—about who thought what in all areas of the magazine. She told me that Brantford Wiles was engaged in some tense discussions with the chairman about the coverage of the protesters. I rarely talked with more than two or three other writers and editors on our floor, and those conversations lasted only a few minutes since we were all scurrying up and down aisles trying to meet deadlines. We were caught up in the tumult: the black thrust for liberation, the students—mostly white it seemed—who wanted control over university governance, and others—black and white—who wanted us to withdraw our armed forces from the tiny Asian nation.

And then one early winter evening after meeting at an art exhibit that she had mentioned she might be attending ("Oh, I thought you might be here.") I was following her up the steps to her apartment on the lower east side. Her décor was accentuated with sleek modern touches of teak woods and blond colors and shiny metals. And her small living space with the starkly dark metal fire escape steps outside her bedroom window would have been immaculate had her cat not managed to upset everything that could not stand the paw swipe of a bored, inquisitive feline. Potting soil from turned-over plants lay on various parts of the living room floor—and on the living room cocktail table. In those first minutes looking around I knew immediately who was the culprit responsible for two vases lying on their sides, roses wilted. Without warning on that first night, the cat alighted from somewhere—the ceiling? I'm not sure. It ran between my legs, slowing to brush against my calf, then jumped on the cocktail table before scurrying toward the kitchen. It stopped almost in midair, one paw not quite touching the floor when Sonja called, "Noor, come meet our guest." It wagged its tail, licked its paw, and looked back at us before flying under the beige couch to pursue an invisible intruder. I never saw Noor again.

"This must cost a fortune," I said, looking around.

"Well, I'm a hard-working executive secretary," she said over her head, going toward the kitchen. "And my ex-boyfriend had lots of money but not too much time to spend with me."

She was delicate and thin with the smallest of breasts and had closets filled with stylish expensive clothes. I only took a few photographs of her because we always seemed to be going somewhere in a hurry. We thought that we were beyond the point of being concerned about her being white and I black. It didn't matter to us, but what did that matter? She was not raised in this country, so no systematic drumming of racist attitudes had altered her perspective. She thought that the black students who were clamoring around the country that the universities should hire more black faculty, recruit more black students and set up black studies curricula "were perfectly within their rights. After all," she told me with a giggle, "there are more colored people in the world than whites."

So Sonja and I went from the passing of comments in the office to the passing of compliments across various tables at coffee shops and restaurants for several weeks. But sometimes while walking together we were jolted into recognizing that others had not changed their attitudes. If the elderly couple had opened their mouths any wider when they spotted us skipping across the street while sharing an umbrella they would have choked. And once, had we not ducked in time, we would have been wet with egg yolk that evening we were strolling along the drive and staring across the river at the lights in New Jersey. The car's wheels screeched, two screaming passengers stuck their heads out the window, hurling the white missiles that whizzed over our heads and splattered against a tree trunk.

No, we told ourselves over glasses of wine in small restaurants or cuddling on her couch where tiny paws pattered under us, we couldn't behave like other couples. No, there was too much going on for us to relax completely in the outside world. She could lie in my lap and talk with her eyes on the ceiling about Swedish kings whose names always seemed to have a *K* in them. But the times would not allow us to escalate our relationship—into what? They would not allow us to be ourselves. There was too much friction afoot, too many raucous voices insisting on separation, differences, distinctions. You saw a few couples here and there and tried not to stare or behave as if it were so unusual. How had they met? What must they endure? Would they have children, and how would their multiracial lives be different? How would the children be classified—*half this and half that*? I wondered if somehow this was all related to Professor Gut and his theories about coming together. Was he watching all of it from afar with disappointment? Was he even teaching somewhere? I hadn't seen anything in the alumni magazine about him.

Our favorite spot was Luigi's, an Italian restaurant stuck in one of the little corners on the lower eastside where many of the artists, musicians, actors and supporters of all radical causes could be found. It was quite the thing in that part of the Apple to be different in any way and every way. Seeing an interracial couple was as common as not. I loved roaming the streets with my telephoto lens, especially during the spring and summer when the women wore tops without bras, their breasts freely and uncaringly bouncing as they strutted across the narrow streets with Great Danes and boxers on the leash, skirts as short as underwear, tattoos on calves, bright tie-dyed colors in their shirts, and dark glasses on their noses. Marijuana was passed around in shoe boxes at all the parties, usually in a back room from which guests stumbled out with blurry eyes and renewed spirit. "Hey, who wants to dance, I feel good!"

Often in a corner with his friend would be Brim, the jazz musician who always wore a hat while playing. He had magnetized and confounded everyone in the musical world with his compositions. His keystrokes would jump ahead of the rhythm and then come back like a boomerang, as if he had forgotten something, stopped, and then remembered that he hadn't forgotten anything and needed to catch up for lost time. A finger would hold a note longer than it seemed possible; it jangled and echoed and stuck in your ear before dissolving. His fingers hit the keys as if he were punishing them on the one hand, and on the other hand he could touch them so delicately that you wanted to lean forward to see if it were an illusion. Was he behind the rhythm or ahead of it—in slow motion or up tempo? He was all of that, and the public— musicians included—lined up eagerly outside the clubs to hear his "explorations into the future," according to the sign.

I heard one musician in the dressing room swear that Brim's magical rhythmic alterations had sent two admirers stumbling, having lost their sense of equilibrium. One man, walking up to the men's room, suddenly had to grab on to the handrail to keep from falling back down the steps. And another—"a big cat with an overcoat"—had been stopped outside the club by a police officer who thought he was too drunk to drive. "The cat didn't even know where he was," chuckled the witness.

For the magazine piece, I shot him and his wife in his tiny apartment that seemed even tinier when I saw the piano filling up most of the kitchen. I focused on his wife—tall, wearing an apron and hair bonnet— as she described to the reporter how Brim had been beaten so badly by the Atlanta police twenty years ago that a metal plate had been placed in his head. And everybody knew that the friend who sat with him in the restaurant was a wealthy baroness whose chauffeur transported the two of them around town in her English brougham.

He too was part of the revolution, insisted Sylvester, because Brim was reforming the tired approaches that had characterized the music. He was breaking the boundaries, forging ahead with new techniques and attitudes. "He hasn't sold out like so many others reaching for success," Sylvester told me before the police shootout. I hadn't heard from him since and didn't know how to contact him. "You know this country only likes jazz that's watered down. They don't want the real visionaries, the innovators to get any play. They only want the public to hear what they think they should hear—unoriginal crappy commercial shit that popular culture can relate to and will buy like crazy." But Brim, according to Sylvester, was not only modifying the stylistic vocabulary, he was also challenging black musicians to make a statement about the upheaval going on. One of his compositions was *The Sip*, filled with eerie portentous echoes of peril and danger. Another was *A Love Supper,* an almost religious expression of adoration. He even wrote a piece called *Benin*, filled with bells and cymbals and African instruments, reminding me especially of how we had ignored Kwame in college but now were realizing that the division between us—Africans and black Americans—is exactly what had been hoped for and planned. We weren't even using the term *Negro* anymore. We were black people—like those around the world with African heritage.

Later that evening, after handing in my film about Brim, I found myself in the doorway of Sonja's bedroom where she was bending over to turn back the blanket on her bed. We were both probably about to explode from the tension that had built up from those weeks of getting to know each other. We had held hands and kissed and cuddled, and I once squeezed her so tightly in her soft fur coat that I felt her knees tremble. She had often seemed to lose control as soon as I kissed her ("Stop, I'm getting goose pimples") and would push me back.

But on this night we grabbed and tore at each other's clothes like wrestlers. Did I need to rip off her blouse? Would it be better to tear off my shirt first? No, she was on her back pulling and pushing and grunting at blouse, skirt, me. I know she told me later that my eyes had the ravenous gleam of one who would do anything to end the starvation he had been subjected to. By the time I had slid under the blanket next to her, I saw that her eyes were closed and her body was limp. She had fallen asleep that quickly? She didn't move. But then she opened her eyes and shut them instantly, smiling. I realized that she was giving it all that she could, that her entire soul was in it. In her semi-consciousness, her body was tingling with excitement and her soul was a wind sailing through erotic splendor. But it seemed to me that she was almost comatose and I might have been holding on to a dead woman.

She lay next to me sighing. "You were wonderful. Did you like it?" Of course I brushed away the strands of hair to kiss her wide forehead and tell her how much I enjoyed it. She had no idea, I considered a few minutes later as I looked in her bathroom mirror at my tie. I shot a glance out at her from the open door: a smile on her sleeping face framed by the triangle of her arms. I wished I had my camera. An adorable, sweet little thing, Sonja didn't seem capable of bringing her physical response up to the level of her emotional investment. She became lost in some foggy world of her own incalculably immense pleasure. So hypnotized by her own enjoyment, she was unable to translate that into the need to reciprocate with her body. Ah, she lay there in a swoon, oblivious to the need of her partner.

I dropped my tie clip. Bending over to pick it up, I noticed something shiny in the corner behind the toilet. I picked up the cufflink. It had an initial: *W*. I put it back, getting on my knees to be sure I placed it in the exact spot behind the toilet. Then I banged my head against the sink and suppressed my ouch as I peeked out at sleeping beauty to be sure that she wasn't awake. Maybe it was hers, I thought as I rubbed my forehead. If not, it was none of my business anyway. She certainly had a life before we became friends just weeks ago.

I left thinking that we now had a second obstacle. Oh perhaps I could work with Sonja, show her what she needed to do. But how long would that take, and would it work and would she understand? How would she react? And suppose it did work? Where would that leave us? We would still be an odd couple in America.

We smiled at each other at the office with a secretive wink for the next several days. And then on that Friday I was sitting for the presentation for the next issue when I began to get an uneasy feeling. A man who was not Davis was introducing himself at the end of the conference table. He wore a suit. Davis never did. He was passing around my photographs that had been selected for the Brim story, and the editors were exclaiming as usual about the great quality. "Wow, look at that lighting," effused one who had been hired just a year earlier.

"Where's Davis?" a young reported on my left asked.

"Gone on to bigger and better opportunities," answered the new assignment editor, still shuffling photos. "Things are changing."

I really didn't like the selection of photographs although I had taken them. One showed Brim at the kitchen table as if he regularly wore his hat while eating breakfast. I had shot him and his wife standing next to the baroness and her luxury car, but the photo being passed around had cropped out his wife, as if he and the baroness were engaged in a secret liaison. I stood up to argue that those photographs were not the most relevant when I was attacked.

Booby, I never had to think so fast in my life. I was on my feet near the end of the conference table. I'm not sure what I had said that not only stopped the new assignment editor's presentation but also turned all eyes toward me. I looked at them looking at me and waiting for me to make my argument. I was frozen momentarily. Then I was trying to subdue the involuntary jerking of my lower body as if it alone were seized by epilepsy. I couldn't tell them that it felt as if a hundred little biting insects had been set loose inside my underwear.

"I'll be right back, I just remembered I left some film in the laboratory," I said, hoping that my lunging, almost falling ("Sorry, JoAnn, was that your foot?") into the door knob wasn't really happening and was the last scene from a dream soon to end. I ran down the hall to the men's room. Oh, thank God it was empty. I found a stall, locked it and unbuttoned my pants. God, they were all over me down there, like ants on a dead carcass. Some had burrowed themselves into my skin. Was I going to die? Would they crawl up and invade my whole body? I could try picking and brushing them off, but I'd have to touch them. Why was I about to cry?

The door squeaked. Footsteps. I jumped on the toilet seat and tried to calm myself. I needed to determine who, what, how, when as I balanced my feet and listened to the water running over his hands. What had I eaten? Chemicals from the dark room? I heard the door close and jumped down, then spurted toward it and stopped as my hand held the handle. How would I describe it to the doctor in Health, and what would he say? I would have to portray them as tiny crabs digging into me. I looked in the mirror at myself. I looked in the mirror at myself again. This time I saw myself in high school listening to a regular in the pool room talking about "some skank" from uptown who had given him the crabs. "I shoulda known the bitch was bad news, but hey, you can't always tell, you know what I mean? I shoulda made her pay for the salve."

Oh God, Booby, as I stared in the mirror and planned my escape out of the building to find a doctor who would treat me for lice, I saw a sweet Scandinavian looking back at me with the most innocent smile. As the elevator went down and I scratched and rubbed as much as I could until a passenger finally joined me, I decided that it was a perfect opportunity for me to take that week's vacation I had been thinking about.

Chapter 24

I did say two, right? Despite being infested with pubic lice from my first sexual encounter after divorcing Atlanta, I was still no less reluctant about being lured into another liaison. But before I was able to grab the lure that Lorene, a well-endowed clerk in the accounting office, threw out, the situation at *Week* took on some unexpected twists.

The new assignment editor was perfectly sympathetic when I told him that the real reason I had left the Friday meeting was related to an intense headache that my doctor was certain had been caused by extreme stress. Instead of taking a health leave, I thought it would be a good idea to just use a vacation week and relax a bit.

"Fantastic planning, where are you going?" His voice had an upbeat expectancy as if he were joining me.

"Well...I've always thought about...my dream has always been to visit...Montana." I tried to think of the name of a city.

"Wonderful place," he replied. "Where in Montana?"

"Oh...I...oh...darn, my headache," I moaned, hoping that he could hear me holding my forehead.

"Hey, don't talk, get some rest. Send us a postcard."

I didn't leave the Apple, of course, and was warned by Harvey's phone call in the middle of the week about the article. "I can't believe that they did this to you," he fumed. "Have you seen the story? Did they ask you about it?"

"No why?" I asked. By the time he had explained it to me, his words were all a jumbled blur in my head as I started down my apartment steps. Minutes later I can recall the shock that I felt when at the corner I paid for the magazine and turned the pages, reading them by the light of the newspaper stand during the rush-hour parade of bodies banging into me.

244

The captions under the photographs all distorted the wrong scenes, describing Brim in terms that my images had not meant to express. In the center of the page was the portrait of him thinking pensively about a question. But the caption suggested that he had been stultified by a mental block and was lost in a trance that took him to another dimension of crazed incommunicado. As my eyes traveled over the columns, I read that he always wore his hat while eating breakfast. Who was responsible? A surge of rage went through me. Each paragraph was a progressive misrepresentation. I resolved that, as soon as I got back to the office the following week, I would make an appointment to see Wiles. I couldn't imagine that he had approved a presentation so flawed.

Before the week ended, snow began to fall. "Feeling great, the salve worked marvelously," I told Harvey. "I'm a new man," I announced, watching the kids throwing snowballs and pushing their sleds in the park at the end of the school day. Maybe I would go out and shoot on the weekend.

"Try to take your time, Romeo. You don't have to start dating immediately, you know. Wait until you are fully recovered. Hey, did you tell that chick what she did to you?"

I wasn't planning on telling her anything. I thought I would just let the relationship between Sonja and me dissolve gradually. I would limit our conversations to just walking past her with a cordial smile. We wouldn't date and I wouldn't visit her. I would be busy, preoccupied, distracted as it were. She would get the message.

So when I got off the elevator that cold Monday I was rehearsing how I would walk past her with a cordial smile and what I would say to Wiles. The receptionist was new—a dark-haired woman who looked young enough to have just graduated from college. She smiled and told me that the new assignment editor wanted to see me immediately. At that moment a man and woman I had never seen before passed while chatting, their hands flying in front of them. They stopped, looked at me curiously and then continued down the hall.

"Come in," he said, not raising his eyes from his desk. "I'm sorry, did I pronounce that right?" I told him not to worry about my name. "Have a good time in Montana? How was it?"

"It was cold," I said, averting his eyes.

"You may have heard that there have been some changes here." He pushed back his desk chair, crossed his legs and looked at me. And before I could answer—"We have a new publisher, some new people, a new direction. New opportunities."

"No, I hadn't heard a thing. I left the last staff meeting, and now I see we have a new receptionist," I said.

"You are a young talented photographer who has established a solid reputation in a short period of time. And Davis, Wiles and that crew certainly gave you many opportunities. I don't think you will have difficulty finding another position."

"Pardon me?" I said. "Who me?" I could almost feel the frown developing on my forehead.

He sighed deeply. "New directions. We aren't doing the same old stories anymore. We aren't covering the movement. We're tired of it. The country's tired of it. All these weirdos protesting about nothing. Wiles is gone. So are Davis and his team. They're out, we're in. You weren't here last week so I'm just able to tell you now. I didn't want to write a letter, that wouldn't be decent."

The whole country? You talked to the whole country? They don't want to know about the most important changes in this nation since the World War? Well, who was reading the magazine before last week? What about the millions of subscribers? I was thinking this, Booby, but swept up by a typhoon; I could only sit there looking at the new assignment editor as his lips kept moving and I kept trying to interpret the sounds from his mouth while being tossed and thrown in my chair by a storm of bewilderment. I was much too restrained in those days to tell him what I really thought. Bwana him mad. Him not like marches and rallies and protests by students and blacks and radicals and militants. Bwana say him magazine not show them any more. Bwana say he fix them.

I heard his voice somewhere in the office. "What those guys didn't understand is that we determine what is seen and heard and what is important. That's our responsibility. We can't afford to let people make their own decisions. We have to lead them."

As the blurred movement dissolved and the dry taste in my mouth settled, I realized that I was in the office by myself. Had that been he holding the telephone receiver, then moving from around his desk and shaking my hand and closing the door softly? I rose like the ill-fated storm victim I was and stumbled slowly down the hall, past the cubicles of editors and writers who seemed elated about everything. Two were especially high-pitched, so I slowed down to hear. I thought I heard Wiles in one of the sentences.

"And his little blonde nymphet is gone too," one of them said.

"Well maybe he'll buy her another condo in Europe," snickered another; and they both broke out in a jeer.

I kept moving my feet, walking past the receptionist with just a nod of my head, still a little disoriented as I got on the elevator and moved to the rear behind a few others.

So Wiles was no longer the publisher of *Week*. And Sonja had been his mistress at one time? And now I was the last to know and the last to be fired? When I got off the elevator and walked down the hall to payroll, the woman at the counter almost a mile away was smiling at me and gesturing with her finger, guiding me toward her.

"I thought you weren't going to make it, you seem so tired," Lorene said when I was a few feet away. I had seen her so many times when I had submitted a travel voucher or cashed a check. We would exchange pleasantries at the counter while trading papers and funds, then smiling and thankful, I would walk away. Yes, I had noticed on more than one occasion that when she turned away to go to her desk or to a file cabinet that she seemed to glide, and that her skirt rose above her knees to reveal a pleasingly stretched calf as she reached up to pull down a folder from the top of the cabinet. Once I did lean forward to observe just how high the skirt would rise, and stared a second too long. She had turned and met my eyes and then we both looked away.

But from afar Lorene had seemed like the rescue worker who would lead me out of the rubble of the momentous storm. Seeing her, I saw my shelter. In one body she represented the helicopters and light aircraft that would ferry me to safety, allowing me to escape the typhoon's wrath. She would dig with spades and bare hands to pull me out of the mudslide, away from the collapsed bridges and roads buried by landslides. She was the supervisor of the government evacuation center. She was delivering relief goods. Dare I look back at the wreckage I had just left?

"Hi Lorene," my voice cracked as the upper part of my body fell against the counter.

"What's the matter, honey? You look a mess. Did they fire you too? Seems like everybody in editorial is gone."

From that moment I was wrapped up in her caring embrace. I looked like I needed a good meal, some good taking care of. Why not meet her downstairs at the subway and go home with her for some fried chicken. Yes, she knew that I had gotten a divorce; and there was some talk about my going out with that blonde, but she didn't pay it no mind. People have to do what they do. And they have their ups and downs.

"But people are just people, don't you think?" she asked as we stood next to each other holding our straps for balance on the swaying subway. I nodded at her, looking into her seductive gray eyes that reminded me of that high-yellow fine thing from the westside—Frances, who many thought preferred women over men. But Lorene's build was stockier— robust and solid yet just under the line of what would be called overweight. She was a few years older. "You have to accept people for what they are."

She held my arm as we were pushed backward momentarily by the wind surging down the exit tunnel of the subway station, dirty strewn newspaper pages flying past our faces. A warm reassurance poured through me as I felt her hips pressing against mine as we took the steps together. I waved away some snowflakes. We had gone past the main station in Harlem to reach her stop in the northern part of the Apple. Her apartment was in a stately Romanesque building with a granite façade that seemed to be made of individual rocks that you could pull out. The spacious courtyard led to the set of wide entry doors. Our footsteps echoed against the marble squares when we walked through the lobby.

"I'm on the second floor. Elevator or steps?" she asked, pointing to the circular stairway against the wall to our right.

"Let's walk up," I said, squeezing her arm in return.

Booby, she was my resurrecting angel for several months as I stumbled like an infant to gain my composure again. She became my night, my day, my planet. How I loved to embrace her and lose myself in the encirclement of her shelter, a buttress against the jangling discord of the outside world. With her, I was able to ignore that world as our enfolding isolated us from their clutches. We cuddled with her knees and shoulders against me. My lips tickled her ears. I breathed in and bathed my senses in her flowing essence as if she had willed every nasally detectable ounce to flow upward. What I imbibed was the combination of shampoo, bubble bath, and perfume dabbed behind her ears, over her breasts and across her wrists.

Her capacity for giving was endless. Where had she learned it? What drove her? Her exploratory nature led her all over my body, usually with interrupted moments introduced by "Do you like this?" YES, OF COURSE! I wanted to shout. How she could nibble, her lips kneading the side of my neck or the softer part of my underarm as if she were sampling a flavorsome delicacy. She could lean toward me to hug—in a restaurant, at the theater—and place her lips firmly enough against my neck to send chills down to my toes. Her fingers were light as feathers as she drew lines up my legs. "Sprinter's thighs," she would whisper from behind, having discovered the unbearably vulnerable spot at the back of my neck. She would hold me as if I were a drowning swimmer and she, the lifeguard, were bringing me back to shore. I loved the full width of her hand as it circled over my chest, particularly when we cuddled to listen to Billie after Lorene's fingers had unbuttoned my shirt. It was clear to me that for her, to love was to give, to offer, to comfort. Lorene had no reservations or bounds. She was a dedicated, focused bestower who murmured descriptive comments of purpose and intent that heightened the pleasure for both of us. "How does that feel?" Oh it felt great, Booby.

Could this be magic, as one of the groups had sung on the *Young Fellow*? Could I have been so lucky as to move from a relationship where the woman did not know how to reciprocate—to devote herself to our mutual enjoyment—to one who seemed to be obsessed with nothing less than a dedicated bestowing of bliss?

When she modeled for me at my apartment, patiently changing positions as I directed her and never complaining, she often wore a diaphanous red top that she had bought just for our sessions. I concentrated on taking advantage of the rays of declining sunlight as they filtered through my curtains and fell over her body. Yes I loved to watch the light hitting her clavicle and then spreading over the rest of her shoulders and part of her chest. But I enjoyed nothing as much as her lying on my chaise with her strong legs up against the wall. That first glance that I had of her calves in her office was now transformed to a full view that I could patiently enjoy while roaming over its features photographically. If legs could be perfectly shaped, she had proved it. Her knees were smooth accents that invited you to follow the tapering of her calf down to her ankle. How I cherished the trip made by my cheek along that solid shin of hers, baby smooth from a recent shave. Or looking above the knee, I marveled at how her leg flowed from the tight hamstrings into a thigh that itself widened into the curve of her hip.

Her legs were a geometric feast for me as a photographer, and I positioned them so that the light hitting them reminded me of various lunar phases—from the full curve of the half moon to the thinner sharper angle of the crescent. Her legs, like the real moon, were only reflecting the light. But like humans all over the world fascinated continually by the mysterious bright luster of the moon, I never tired of watching her legs, whether they were under the focus of my camera lens or purely being observed with my most appreciative eyes.

Well that was the wonderful component. The unfortunate part is that she had too much heavy baggage—parental responsibilities. What? I didn't mention the five little munchkins—four boys and a girl? They were cute when I first met them that snowy night, bounding toward their mommy with unreserved uproar as we opened the door, then tackling me at the knees after a quick introduction and crawling all over my body as I lay on my back trying to repel them affectionately while they introduced themselves, listed their favorite football players, inquired about my interest in playing a board game called Monopoly, and were intent on determining if I was ticklish under my arms when Lorene finally pulled them off me. I can't even remember their names now. Larry? Larue? Lionel? Lee? Laronda?

They were of various shades, from light-skinned to brown, because they didn't have the same father. Ages?—from five to 13 from what I remember. The oldest—her daughter in high school—took care of the boys until Lorene came home from work. She always seemed to be standing sideways as she spoke to you while preparing to bolt into another room.

But as the weeks progressed and I had more encounters with the spirited young tough guys, they transformed themselves into a formidable obstacle to the growth of any relationship between Lorene and me. I didn't think much of the loss of the dollar bills from my pants pockets that first night. Perhaps the money had fallen out during the unexpected wrestling match, and one of the boys just thought that the cash belonged to someone in the household.

No, it was the time and attention they craved that scared me away. They, of course, were looking for that male figure who had been missing for some years. Thinking that it was information Lorene would offer voluntarily, I hadn't inquired about the fathers. Did they ever visit, call, send a letter? I never found out. While the young girl flitted around us like a bashful spirit, stopping just for that second to smile or answer a question monosyllabically before disappearing into her room, they on the other hand were bodies of kinetic energy in constant motion seeking the same male bonding that I had sought from Yo-Yo. But I had been one little person, and they were four. That day in the park after a heavy snow, Larry, Lionel, Lee, Larue—they were all a blur—pelted me with such an unending barrage of snowballs that when I came to consciousness, a park policeman was bending over me asking if I could hear him.

"Is he dead?" one little voice asked. I thought I felt a hand going in my pants pockets.

They did want to destroy me, I realized one morning when my body ached from the previous week's escapades. A water gun fight had almost blinded me, and a kickball game in the apartment lobby had sent me hobbling up the circular staircase with the fearful sensation that my ankles would never support me again.

"My momma said she wanna marry you," Larue or Larry or Lionel told me between heaving breaths during the Saturday afternoon wrestling match that turned out to be our last. While they lay on their backs exhausted and looking at television cartoons, I rose quietly, ignoring the pain in my bruised ribs. As I tipped down the hallway toward the front door, I saw Lorene's leg sticking out as I passed her bedroom, and a shadow of her daughter moved across the kitchen wall. I put on my coat, closed the front door (did I see the daughter peeking out at me?), headed toward the stairway but then decided to take the elevator.

Lorene had definitely been a lifesaver for those six months, Booby, buffeting me from the storms that began with my being fired from *Week*. I thanked her for those wonderful comforting moments while trying to emphasize that there was no future for us. I couldn't give her and her family what they needed.

"You don't have to give us anything," she said. "Just be there. I just want you to be there. You know how much I care for you. I want to spend the life of my life with you." Her handsome face was pained, her smooth forehead showing a line I hadn't seen before as we sat in the busy café across the street from the hospital in Harlem. I tried to push those exquisite memories out of my mind that her gray eyes brought back to me. She would look straight into my eyes and then down at her napkin and then back into my eyes again. I could hardly swallow my food and kept hoping that she would just jump up and leave. When we walked out of the café and I watched her legs moving down the street, I had to restrain myself from calling her back.

"I think you made the right decision," Harvey advised me by telephone. "You put a lot of time into trying to make it work—as you always do. She really loved you from what you tell me."

She loved me more than we both thought. That's what her new voice told me a few days later. I heard a raspy metallic tone: "I can't live without you, and you don't deserve to live." After a pause, a deep intake of breath, she blurted out: "I'm going to kill you."

"Who me?" I should have remained silent or hung up, I thought.

"I have a gun. Sometime this weekend—I don't know exactly when—I'm going to shoot you between the eyes."

"But I won't be home," I whispered so softly that I wondered if she heard. "I said I won't be home."

"I'll find you," she said, voice trembling before hanging up.

Booby, I didn't have the same calm perspective that I have now nearing age 50. I was 33 then, and the prospect of death and even being killed sent my hands into a shaking unsteadiness. I almost dropped the phone on its receiver. I lay on the couch and stared at the screen on the ceiling. I was being lowered into the casket and only a few friends were looking down. Of course Harvey was there, but I couldn't make out the other faces—John Durham? David? How would they find out that I was dead? Who would speak at the funeral? Would they talk about my talent that was never really appreciated? Maybe my violent end would spark new interest in my work and I would be as popular as I had been during my first years out of college. At least Gahtsum had insisted on my making a will, so all of my prints and negatives were going to the black university in the nation's capital.

I sat up and looked out the window at a gray skyline. Standing up, I fell to my knees quickly and crawled over to close the shutters. I peeked through them: no sign of her. Then I crawled back over to the telephone.

"I can hardly hear you," Harvey told me. "Why are you whispering?"

"It's me. I don't want to talk too loud. Lorene just called. She said that she's going to kill me—shoot me—this weekend."

"This weekend coming? Darn, you can't come here because I'm going away—a short vacation."

"I don't think she's kidding," I said, but I wasn't able to say much more because Harvey had insisted that he could not talk long.

I could see the sky darkening as I lay on the couch listening to my racing heartbeat. She hadn't said that I had done anything—only that I didn't deserve to live. She was hurt, I was sure, but what good would it do to take my life? I was pleading with her in my mind when the phone rang.

Mrs. Dawson's voice was tearful, her words alternately halting and speeding when she introduced herself. She was sorry for disturbing me. She assured me that she had talked her daughter out of that crazy idea. Lorene was just upset, didn't even own a gun. Her voice took a sorrowful intake of relief, I thought when I told her that no, there wasn't another woman. She was sorry. She thanked me for my time. And I'm still alive.

And those storms that Lorene helped me weather? They continued for another year—almost two—without her being there for me. Although I still had access to the leaders of the movement and others whom I had met through Sylvester during my years at the magazine, I had no supporter like Wiles, who I learned moved to the West Coast to start another publishing venture. Nobody I approached—the publications, the galleries, the museums—cared about the movement, the turmoil, the upheaval.

"Why must you concentrate on black people?" they asked.

"Have you considered not concentrating on white people?" I replied. "You know, most of the world is not white," remembering one of Sylvester's favorite lecture topics.

"Yes I've heard that theory," the gallery director said, rising to exhale her cigarette smoke, "from those radicals clamoring for black power. And that wild man called Big Red—I hope you aren't listening to his incendiary rhetoric? Don't you see, our customers prefer the universal approach. We are just one mankind. We don't need these unnecessary separations," she said without a smile, putting on her coat to signal that the meeting was ending.

"What do you mean by universality? I wasn't aware that the entire universe felt the same about everything," I asked as she moved past me to leave me in her office. "Or, do you mean white Western universality? There is a huge difference you know."

I left with my jaws tighter than Dick's headband. When I went through the door of her downtown gallery, I saw one of their featured artists climbing out of a fancy red convertible. He had just been profiled with a cover photo in *Week*. He lived farther out on the island in a house whose walls of glass made it a bookmark of the new architectural approach spreading throughout the area. Thumbing through the *Week* pages, I saw him and his wife sitting in their living room and looking out at the floating herons that were enjoying the same view of the ocean. He was fabulously successful and was a millionaire from the sale of his photographs and magazine assignments that flew him all over the world to shoot the most beautiful women lying by pools with a large dog or a waiter at the knee. His photographs were pretty much template efforts produced with plenty of lighting and a huge staff of assistants, including a make-up artist. It was mostly mechanical work showing not an iota of interest in exploring the real nature of light—the photographer's main challenge. To him the camera and light did not represent a photographer's paintbrush. They were just two items in his vocabulary with two different definitions.

On some of those nights I didn't want to discuss with Lorene why I was so irritable. But she finally pushed away my frustration with, "You'll be recognized eventually," she told me. She was rubbing the back of my head so soothingly that I was transported onto a cloud of reverie where I too was a recognized artist living comfortably. And what did those terms mean—*recognized* and *comfortably*? Did I want to walk down the street with difficulty or not? Was I in search of those moments when you are stopped on the street by someone who has matched your face with a photograph of you and wants to make special contact through a smile, gesture, or conversation? What artist has ever had that experience? No, acknowledgment in the media that your work is important would do, that you are making a significant contribution, that it's not folly. Maybe your work is some of the most innovative undertakings ever seen.

And *comfortable*, what was that? Wasn't I comfortable? I didn't have a house by the ocean and an expensive car, but I wasn't uncomfortable at all. I was certain that Gahtsum would help me out if I had financial difficulties. No, I determined it wasn't the money so much that I sought; it was the recognition. At least acknowledge that I was more talented than most. So many of them made such an extravagant amount of money, proving that there was no relationship between ability and reward. Some of the most obviously untalented could hitch on to a thematic niche that was in vogue, and stick with it. Others could cultivate a clientele of art directors who would always call on them for jobs. Or they could propose some preposterously avant garde approach that, if marketed correctly, would guarantee them a dedicated audience.

It continued even after Lorene. For a few years.

Chapter 25

Then nothing went right after Lorene. True, the challenges lasted for only a couple of years. But when you are experiencing difficult times, each painful minute seems to drag out into interminable seconds stretching into netherland, and you wonder if there is any relief. A few minutes of discomfort is magnified in your mind as hours of anguish. Today is a welcome relief from yesterday's travail if for no other reason than you don't have to face ever again those 24 hours that have just passed. After the torment continues for weeks, you face the next month with gloomy pessimism. Before you know it, the nightmare has lasted for two years.

They didn't want my work anymore. "The market is flat, changing," they said. My images were too remindful of the problems we faced. They decided to take a break, a release from the painful reality that disturbed them. They didn't want my photographs of the real deal. Just a few years earlier my images showing the unrest throughout the country had been prominently displayed on the covers and the inside pages of *Week*. Every newspaper, magazine and television station had covered the movement diligently. The galleries, museums and theaters had almost burst from within as they proclaimed their support for this newest of the new. Booby, you should have seen all those special black art shows at the main museum, special black art exhibits at the galleries, special black poetry readings, special black theater events. I had covered them all— and even been invited to display my work in some of the group shows.

But now? All that excitement, enthusiasm, direction was somehow muted into only the most occasional outbursts that received national attention. Now the publication and everybody else was under new management with a new direction. And everybody else in the Apple seemed to be of the same mindset. No lie. Don't bother us, we aren't interested. We don't want to be reminded of the unrest and turmoil rummaging through the country by looking at the images of this agitation. Forget about those children in Beanton being hit by glass and bricks when they tried to register for school. Ignore those protestors attacked by construction workers just across the street from city hall. Yes, there was a riot at a correctional facility just a few hours away where 39 prisoners were killed by guards, but there are more pleasant situations to cover.

Then just as I was beginning to feel better, as if I had been refreshed or at least less depressed about my circumstances, I was attending Aunt Clara's funeral. The phone call from Gahtsum about her death really took the wind out of my stomach, and I curled up on my bed and cried all afternoon while relishing her voice that fluttered through my mind in so many scenes that begin with, "and look..." The disease that grows had zig-zagged through her, burning up her lungs after surfacing first as pneumonia. Without stopping, it rocketed up to her brain cells and destroyed them. By then...all this happening within the space of three weeks...she was being rolled into the hospital morgue.

When had I seen her last? Not in a year. I had been wrapped up in my own crisis, in touch with her only by telephone—and even then being assured by Aunt Clara that things would change if I just persevered. "After the storm there is sunlight," she told me, "guaranteed." Sitting on my bed after Gahtsum's call, I picked up my bird book, glancing through aimlessly yet hoping that something would stand out. I stopped at the illustration of the wren where one of the three birds stood at the top of the frame looking up for something. The other two were below, but their stance was clearly subsidiary to the drama of the wren at the top of the frame looking up for something. I felt like the wren at the top—looking up for something.

So I closed the book and lay that on its side, only to wander around the apartment until I was dragging the briefcase that she had given me out of the closet. My fingers rummaged through the compartments to pull out the clippings she had kept...that record of my growing up for which she was mainly responsible. There I was in all those stories –"in the paper more than Pete Lloyd"—that I had read myself many times. Other clippings were in a zippered section that seemed not to have been opened. I didn't remember them—yellowed, in a thick envelope secured by a rubber band. I unfolded the columns. And read them. The stories were all about a wealthy Brotherly Love couple on the mainline involved in a murder. A housekeeper was killed. "Infidelity" ran across the top of one piece. Had a child been born? If so, he had disappeared. A black housekeeper was involved with a wealthy white man. They had a baby. Then although I was reading the stories with studious attention, the details became a combination of foggy phantoms that could be blocked out or ignored. There was no reason to pay attention to that tale. I could skip over it. I could block it out.

Only a dozen or so friends were at her service. I recognized one gambler in dark glasses who may have tipped me a quarter during one of my visits to their dark sanctum. And I hated the wig that fell over her forehead. I kept a fairly stoic face throughout the ceremony and suppressed the sense of deep loss that boiled within me. Something in my stomach wanted to rise up like a flood. At one point I thought that I would not be able to submerge it any longer as the organ tones rose to their most solemn bars. Finally I was looking around once more to see if Mister Bat had come as Gahtsum and I were leaving the little room in the basement of the church and heading for the cemetery. Feeling Gahtsum's arm around my shoulders only intensified the rise, for it was that very expression of warmth that almost forced me into a whining recognition of how helpless I was now.

But nothing during the church ceremony could have been as overpowering as sitting on the folding chair at the cemetery as they lowered her casket into the ground. As I consider the ceremony that I must arrange for my Chinita, I wonder if I can endure seeing her go down—into the earth. I had no breath left, it seemed, and as I struggled for air with my mouth open and my knees bent forward, I wondered for an instant if I were going to die too. But I could hear myself whimpering—little half cries with deep intakes of breath. And then I couldn't suppress it any longer and simply let it all come out of me: babbling.

"She was your mother's best friend," Gahtsum said, his eyes looking at the clouds, his lips trembling. It was of the few times that the voice coming out of his stomach was not filled with soft power; it was softly somber instead. "And she was so special to me." He was standing a few feet away now watching the others move toward their parked cars. I could hear the thump of the doors closing. It was a nippy fall day, the wind rushing in from the east, from the shoreline. "I haven't heard from Anida, don't know where she is. I heard the Apple. You?"

"Nothing," I said, "haven't seen her since my divorce." I was thinking that I didn't have much of a family left. Mister William and Aunt Hattie had gone on with their lives somewhere without my knowing how to contact them. I stood to examine him more closely from the side. I had fallen back into the dream land that I usually inhabited whenever my mother became the topic. His thin lips formed the words coming out of his mouth but the sentences evaporated before reaching my ears. His nose was large and prominent. His eyes were earnest. It's the same face that I have seen countless times I told myself. But this time I searched over it for additional features to seal in my mind. A part streaked through his hair. Had that always been there?

"She thought of you as her own boy," he said, his hair illuminated by the rays of a falling sun. We were walking past a tall monument that had a horse and rider atop it. We stopped at the same time, turned and went over to it. He leaned against the base and faced me.

"She was just like a mother to me," I said. "I don't remember a time without her."

"Well you have a father...somewhere...that's for sure." He was looking at his toes.

"That's for sure," I said, speaking as if I had been transported suddenly to another realm where I could once again block out what did not seem discussable. Again I watched his lips move without hearing the words, the words that were telling a story about a married couple whose relationship was interrupted by a women who worked in the household. Then there was a baby born and then there was a murdered housekeeper. From there the details became increasingly less relevant as I pulled down the curtain on the stage in front of my mind.

"Your Aunt Clara was such a special friend to me. I knew that I could trust her to take care of you. And I've tried to make things as comfortable as possible for you both. But...it just wasn't a good idea for you to know everything...at least not immediately. There was a plan," he said, his voice at the lowest I had ever heard it. "And then the years went on and it became more difficult for me to tell you. The bird book was to be a way for me to begin the conversation. But you seem to have blocked it out, so we thought you needed time. We had an idea that you knew anyway. Did you?"

I kicked the ground with, "I guess I was just ignoring it, blocking it out," I said.

He came toward me and we embraced. I wanted to hold him tighter, squeeze my arms around his arms as if he were a relative visiting for the first time in years, imbibe more of the pleasant scent of his cologne. But I had never held him before and felt awkward.

The next morning I woke up early to catch the train to the capital to spend a week with Harvey. "I have some incredible news," I said to him, but I couldn't reach the next sentence before he interrupted me with his rapid-fire spurt of high-pitched complaints and mournings. I wanted to tell him about my discovery. But he was verbally irrepressible, boiling with emotion.

"Look at how they are acting up there. Attacking those poor kids trying to go to school. Worse than those crackers down in the Sip. At least when I went down there for that semester I knew that they didn't want us. They told us they didn't want us. But up there in the so-called cradle of liberty, they're supposed to have respect for human beings. All they do is smile in your face while they stab you in the back."

I couldn't argue with him although I kept looking for an opening to tell him about my discovery. Sylvester had disappeared and the Pumas had simply dwindled away. The movement leaders whom he had introduced me to had filtered off into individual initiatives or had just gone off into a world where they would blend in and not be noticed. Still I sensed that these men whom I had first met in that conference room in the back of the theater were in a state of redirection...on the edge of something—new, different? I was too depressed during this time to give Harvey much of a fight, so whenever he put on his radical mantle and began spouting revolutionary rhetoric, I listened with more than artificial interest.

Besides, he had just turned thirty I told myself while waiting for him to meet me at the train station. We were going to celebrate all week and do a lot of talking and drinking. He had decided to give up his private practice to work for a community action agency in the capital. They had started a street academy for kids who had dropped out of the public school system. "Well I wanted to give something back," he had explained, "and I got tired of trying to get my clients to pay me."

I knew that the same topics that had always electrified us would again be examined. We'd definitely talk about women. Harvey had always thought that my obsession with the company of females demonstrated some dangerous psychological undertones. On the other hand I wondered about his inability to be trusting again. He speculated about my being able to recover from an unfortunate relationship and then eagerly seek out another, confident that the next would be better. But of course he didn't know about my history with the Young Fellow and how the music had driven us mad with the need to stretch beyond the walls that stood in front of us.

Who could imagine it, a world without women, without that warmth, without that connection with your other side. I believed in a soul mate. I didn't want to be alone, I told him as we entered the elevator of his building. His mouth and eyes were open wide when he responded. "You mean you don't want to be without a woman?"

"Exactly," I said, keeping the rest of my thoughts to myself as he opened the door to his apartment. I didn't want to imagine myself without someone whose presence was indispensable, an extension of mine, like the mystical communication between Aunt Hattie and Mister William, Miss Rachel and Mister Arthur. I would be with her even when I wasn't with her, like the woman whose incarcerated mate is behind bars but yet at her side even as she (hundreds of miles away) stands in line at the post office about to send a letter to him. Oh no, I needed someone to share evening talk—about the man in the moon, the rainbow, the special moment that left a joyous impression earlier in the day. Who wanted to be without that touch, that sharing, that presence that although separate from you was part of you? No way, I didn't want to be subjected to those rough years without a soft comforting lap or a tender neck to lay my head against after the day's end. It wasn't just the physical connection; in many ways, it was the less palpable transmittal of affection—a look, a feel—that carried equal value. And had not Rachel and Arthur talked one night during a commercial about Miss Bernice who claimed that her dead husband Roland visited her in the evenings for a month after his burial? There at an age when the *Young Fellow* was just beginning to influence me, I reflected at night on that possibility—communication with a loved one after death.

"Well how do you know she won't leave you?" he wondered.

"There are no guarantees I guess," I answered. "You have to go with how you feel."

"Feel...." he began. "How can you feel when they won't let you?"

"What do you mean?" I asked, and Booby I remember that first evening as the beginning of his thinking that led to the court case he's been working on for years. We had gone to Mama's, a festive little soul food restaurant in northwest near his apartment and it was buzzing with Friday evening voices. The waitresses were zipping around and serving the special—fried chicken, collards and potato salad.

"I mean, we spend so much effort fighting oppression, we hardly have anything left in us to devote to love and affection. Those feelings are almost luxuries at the end of the day." He stared at me with a face that was flush with fervent certainty.

"Well they have made it hard. But maybe we just have to fight to make love happen, to make it less of a luxury," I said, catching the eyes of two well-dressed women in a corner. "If we can't find the energy to fight for love, what do we fight for?"

He looked down at his plate. "I can't think so much about love. I gave my heart to Sandra. There will never be another. I tried. But I will never feel that way again about a woman. You keep checking out those broads in the corner as if there's a possibility. But for me, it's a waste of time."

"That one with the short Afro is cute, you must admit. Professor Gut said once that we may have to kick love in their faces. I often wondered about that. Did he mean that we have to show them what love is—against their resistance to it? Maybe they don't know? Is that what he meant by tectonics bringing us together—bringing us together through love?"

"I can't even remember any of my professors. And I never did understand how you got involved with that tectonics stuff. Wasn't that some special concentration that isn't offered any more?"

"Well they can't remember you either. The only reason the dean knew your name is because it always showed up as absent at convocation."

"Look," he said, smiling as he held his glass of wine, "you were so much in love with that school, the group itself and their tradition—despite what they did to you—and us—they could have told you anything. Now I hear that they have recruited more black students and even have a few black professors."

"Harvey I did get my first job through a trustee, and that got me to the Apple. And look at you—you got into law school. I'm surprised that you read the alumni magazine. I didn't think you cared."

"I care all right. I care about what they did to us. And that's the least they could do is get you a job or get me into law school. I've done a lot of reading ever since you gave me those books Kwame stole from the archives. Those founders were something else, you know, making a fortune from the slave trade. Oh I'm keeping up with your renowned institution of higher learning that insists on…what is it…the usefulness of life? Getting you a job is just a drop in the bucket. Look at you now—hustling to make it as a photographer. Don't you worry. I'm trying to figure out a way to make them pay us.

"Pay us? Well I agree that it was a lonely experience…"

"Lonely? They fucking ignored and isolated us as if we weren't even there, drove one talented brother away and another mad, and you call it just loneliness? They did everything they could to show us that they didn't want us, and you call it loneliness?" His cheeks were tinged as he leaned forward: "And another thing, have you noticed that we are disappearing?"

"We are?"

"Well it's nothing new. Thank goodness Kwame forced me to go back and read more history. Our history. And it's obvious. They have done everything they could to control and destroy the black man. I think the country should pay us for all the black male lives they have taken."

"That sounds rather preposterous," I said. Well it did at the time, Booby.

"Does it sound preposterous that we were brought here enslaved?

That all those men in the South were hanged? That Sylvester and his group were gunned down by the police? That those prisoners were slaughtered by the national guard? That those innocent young boys were put in jail to remain until they were old men? That our high school friends were sent to be killed in a war? And what about the Dreamer? They killed him for what—being nonviolent?"

So the idea for reparations had developed naturally...beginning as a wild bold statement that was eventually examined thoroughly...to one that has more currency than I could ever have imagined.

As we stood to leave Mama's, the young lady with the short Afro came over smiling. "Did I see your picture in the paper?" she asked Harvey. "Aren't you the one with that drop-out program...it was in the paper. My name is Joyce Parker."

"Yes, I guess so," he said, introducing himself and me, and within seconds, her friend was standing behind her.

"Nice to meet you," she said, mispronouncing my name and almost close enough to Harvey to kiss him. "I'd love to find out how to volunteer for your program," she said, handing him a business card. "It sounds so exciting,"

Her companion, a taller darker woman with shorter hair stood still without speaking, her eyeglasses throwing off a reflection as she turned her head to look at Harvey and me.

"Well I'll give you a call," Harvey said, waving as we went out of the front door.

"Why don't you take it," he said, giving me her card after we got to his car.

"She was kind of cute," I said.

"Yeah, so maybe you should give her a call," he said. "I don't need the bother."

From there Harvey ushered me to several clubs where he was greeted by a number of friends who knew it was his birthday and insisted on buying us drinks. It became a night of stupefied vagueness, of visiting establishments that were different but yet not so different from those on the strip back home. As you entered, they all had one long bar going down the wall on the left and tables on the right. Blasting from the ceiling was the Kid's hypnotic beat or another pounding rhythm from the Wicked or some other performer whose spellbinding beat yanked people off their bar stools and pushed them on to the floor.

At one club, featuring a bandstand in the back, it was so dark that I could barely see anything more than the gray haze of cigarette smoke that was punctuated by red lights in the corners. As soon as I entered I noticed her sitting at the front of the bar. She turned and saw us and almost fell off the stool as she approached Harvey and me with wide arms. "Hey baby, it's your birthday. Who's your handsome little friend?"

"Where?" asked Harvey, looking at me, and the entire row turned to laugh.

"Let's dance, honey bunch before the band comes back," said Big Mama, "I love that song." While my mouth was open to say that I was going to the men's room, my wrist was in her hand as she spun me onto the floor and threw up her hands as if released from a grueling incarceration. Standing in front of me and shaking her hips, she yelled, "Come on, yeah—do the funky Broadway! It's party time." She knew the words by heart and sang almost louder than the Wicked's voice blasting from the speakers. That tune merged into another hit song that reminded her of yet another set of steps. She turned sideways and banged her hips against me with such power that I saw the wall coming toward me. "Hey where you goin' sweet thing, don't you know the bump?"

"Bump?" I heard somebody in the back scream. "That look more like collision."

"Oh my goodness, here come one of my favorites, time for the hustle, you know it?" She grabbed both my hands as if we were in grade school playing paddy cake. Then she twisted my arms around her neck and then over her shoulders until we were entangled in a near tango. I was close enough to see the glint of a gold tooth in her upper mouth. Next I was two feet away, then pulled toward her, then thrown to the side.

"Thanks," I said to Big Mama, the song finished and a slow drag starting; and "Oh no, I won't," when she told me not to forget her. I limped away, joining Harvey at the bar with some friends who were fascinated by his statements about making somebody pay us for what they had done to us—all black men.

"You fuckin' right, Harv man, they owe us!"

I had another drink and another, at different clubs, and everything began to melt into one uninterrupted sequence of hazy events, only a few unforgettable seconds of which remain in memory. I know that at one club we sat at a table with two attractive women attorneys who insisted that we celebrate with champagne. But they got into an argument, started calling each other bitches, and stood up at the same time with purses poised to strike before we were able to separate them. Then the mouths whose teeth were set to eviscerate each other became pursed into apology; they hugged and started crying. I was tearful too for some reason. But before I could even pull out my handkerchief, I heard, "Duck." A gun shot whistled through the club and a man came running unsteadily from the rear. "Hey put that damn thing down before you hurt somebody," the bartender shouted, his head just high enough above the bar to expose his eyes.

I'ma hurt somebody all right, just you wait," waving his pistol in the air and turning in a circle so that everybody in the club ducked in order. "I'ma hurt somebody all right, just you wait." He started the sentence again but in his third rotation crumpled to the floor before getting to "wait."

Then reassembling in the rear, the band started playing and everybody in the club was raising his drink to toast Harvey's birthday. It reminded me of the pep rallies back in high school. "I don't know half these people," he whispered to me, his face red, his eyes blurred.

"Big strong line!" somebody said, and soon we were all holding on to the person's hip ahead of us as we marched around the room ("Hey wake up, wake up, get in line") proclaiming Harvey a jolly good fellow. The band played faster, the line got longer, and soon we had strutted through the front door of the club and were marching down the street, the horn players following us, some dogs at the fringe of an alley barking and threatening to attack us, cars slowing down for drivers to look out curiously. One club, two…four? I can't say, Booby.

The bartender at the last club had insisted that he send us home in a cab. So exhausted, we had collapsed in the back seat. By the time we got to Harvey's building, we were stumbling like invalids, holding on to each other for support ("I got you, don't worry…wait, not so fast…where are we now?").

"What was it you wanted to tell me, anyway?" he said, his voice slurred and slow, looking at my profile as I held him up. Inside the elevator, we fell against the wall.

"My father," I said. "He's white." I could hardly keep my eyes open, and my voice sounded far away. I expected him to say that I was drunk and didn't know what I was talking about.

"You mean Gahtsum?"

"You knew?"

"Well I read those newspaper clips that were in the briefcase with Kwame's material. It didn't take a genius to put it together. You mean all this time you never figured out why he gave you that damn bird book?"

"What about the bird book?" I said.

"You didn't know that the mother of the most famous bird illustrator in the world was a Jamaican?—and his father was a white sailor?"

I was looking at the panel of elevator buttons when he said that, wondering when the door would open. Then we both realized that we had been talking and leaning against the wall for fifteen minutes without having pushed a button.

Chapter 26

When I returned to the Apple I knew that Gahtsum and I would have to meet. For two days I rehearsed what I would say and guessed what he would to say to me. I'd have to be careful. I could accuse him. But then he could accuse me also. He had given me as much as he could—and that was a lot. All I had done in return was accept his generosity and companionship while blocking out those inconvenient facts. Were they inconvenient? Why?

I was mulling over that very question, actually scratching my head as I stood in front of the display case surveying the fish and wondering if I would broil or bake when the shopping cart crashed into the hip that Big Mama had bumped repeatedly a week earlier.

"Oh I'm so sorry," I heard a voice. But it wasn't directed at me.

"No don't worry," he said "you hit this young man over here," pointing at me.

"Oh." Its tone was eerily familiar, and then I recognized the face. She removed her sunglasses and looked straight at me. "I don't believe it. Is that you?"

Why the invigorating surge through my body—despite the aching hip? Why the relieving sense of comfort? Why did I feel like a lost hiker who had discovered the path that would lead him out of the woods? "Yes it's me," I said. "Is that you, Phyllis? Don't tell me you live in the Apple."

She had grown more beautiful I told myself as I watched those luscious lips spill out the details of her life since we had last talked. Her cheeks had that same luster too. Although we were rolling our carts down the aisle together, I could tell through sideways glances at the lower part of her body that her small but shapely hips were twisting forward with the same distinctive flow as they had in high school. "Stacked like a brick shit house," Wayne whispered once as we watched her go down the hall between classes. And in my rambunctious attempt to explore as many adventures as possible, we had lost connection—and then I married Atlanta.

Well yes she had been in the Apple for just more than a year, "working in publishing, and I get to talk a lot." She seemed very earnest when she expressed her regrets that the marriage with Atlanta had not worked out: "She didn't seem your type." And somebody had told her about my aunt's death, she noted with a cheerless gasp and a finger at the corner of one eye. Yes she lived all the way in the northern part of the city—beyond Harlem—and had traveled 45 minutes on the subway to my part of the Apple to shop in this special delicatessen. It had the best desserts and best fresh fish in town; didn't I know? Before I could respond she was stymied at the checkout. "What? Oh my goodness, I can't believe it. This isn't my cart—look, cereal and canned beans and...where is my swordfish?" We all turned to look behind us as if we were responsible for locating the cart of Phyllis. I found it finally in a corner by the ladies room. In it lay a small box of French chocolates and a package of swordfish.

A light rain had started on that windy April afternoon; the streets were shiny with dampness. I was still trying to process the barrage of information that still spilled out from those sweet lips when suddenly she gave me her package and dashed to the middle of the street to stop a cab. "Do you want to come see my place?" she yelled, her hand in the air, a truck's horn blaring on the other side of the street. For a visually marvelous second as she slid into the back seat, her skirt was pushed above her knees. She beckoned me with a curling finger. "Broadway and One-Eighty-Six," she instructed the driver. "And take the bridge over to the west side, don't go through Chinatown." She exhaled deeply, sinking her body into the corner of the seat and wiping the rain drops off her forehead. She stared at me with a smile that turned the memory clock in my head.

"I live just a few blocks away," I said.

"Oh don't be ridiculous. I haven't seen you in ages. You come uptown and look out from my new apartment. You can see Connecticut—or maybe it's New Jersey. You aren't working at night are you?"

My memory clock said that I knew her, that I could trust her, that she was capable of spreading the balm of Phyllis, a most soothing emollient for one so scarred as I. Had she not introduced me to the fullest possibilities of the kiss? Why on earth had I let her escape? We never even had an argument. Oh a sea of jubilation was entering my life again, washing away the waves of desolation and anguish that had preoccupied me. Snuggled in the corner over there was euphoria itself, as happy to see me as I was in need of a truly desirable presence.

"Come over here little boy," she said, reminding me of how engagingly mischievous, how creative in the most upbeat manner she could be. "Put your head down," spreading out her legs to form the most welcoming lap. I shifted, kicking our packages on the floor. I was on my back looking out the window and enjoying the warm massage of her fingers against my temples. Through the window I looked upward at the steel cables of the bridge leading to the financial district and lower downtown. Then we were on the bridge itself as Phyllis brought me up to date.

She wasn't exactly in publishing. She sold magazine subscriptions by telephone—from her apartment. "People need to know that they can have access to all the best that's thought and written and filled with useful advice if they subscribe to *Ladies Journal, Fisherman's Monthly, Pictorial Mechanics, Friday's Morning Post*, and others," she explained. "I thought what's-his-name who lived in the inlet and wore those dreadful looking pants without pleats was crazy going around, selling magazines door-to-door. But do you know he made a fortune?"

"You mean Swing?"

"That clumsy boy was a millionaire almost," she declared. "He had much more sense than that dullard David, who he hung around with." She had lived for a year and almost been engaged to Vincent the Mustache whom I remembered meeting on the beach, but... "he put me out for a young thing in college. God, you should have seen her makeup—it was everywhere. Well wait until you see my white nurse's outfit," she chuckled. "I do that on the side for extra money. It's good preparation for a modeling career, don't you think? Well I guess you must be rich making all those photographs for *Week*. Are you?"

Did I fall in love or fall *back* in love? Had we just been separated for some unaccounted period? Had our relationship been simply interrupted from a normal state of development and now was there for us to reinitiate? Were we destined? Oh the more she talked, Booby the faster my heart thumped.

We dated for just a few months before I realized how quickly she had recaptured me. Through a strange reversal, I needed her more than she needed me. I hadn't moved in to her apartment, but I was spending practically every night with her, losing all resolve to leave after her morning routine finally wore me down. Standing in a robe in the morning, exuding the scent of a fresh bath, on the verge of tears, she would ask, "Are you leaving? You can stay, you know. You can stay as long as you like."

Did I say engagingly mischevious? Oh how she loved to create the most inventively amorous landscapes, highlighted by excited out-of-breath giggles. She loved shouting, "Come in now, it's ready!" I would open the bathroom door to a hot steamy room and a beaming face as she spread open the shower curtain for me to enter. Massaging my chest from behind with soapy hands, she would whisper, "Are we squeaky clean yet?" When we turned carefully to exchange positions, I enjoyed the slippery slide of my hands over her breasts and stomach even as I dropped the soap. In her other favorite bathroom scene, I would enter the same steamy space—mirror fogged, wall sweating—to see her lying in the tub, bubbles up to her neck, a hand beckoning me to join her: "Nice and hot." And somehow—my elbows hurting, our bodies twisted, her knees up to my shoulders and moving ever so carefully—we were linked, thrashing like sinking swimmers. When we finished, lying still and breathing hard yet contentedly, the water had drained out and we were shivering from the chill.

"Shall I get on my knees?" was more a declaration than a question, usually made when she detected a falling mood, a diminished confidence. If I recounted another disappointing meeting with an art director or pointed out a magazine or newspaper story featuring a photographer who was affluent and well-known, she might force me to sit in a chair or keep me standing as she knelt to pull off my pants. By the time she had finished her ministering, my disposition had experienced a thrilling metamorphosis, my body shaking with gratification.

"Oh you're a brilliant photographer. Don't let those white people tell you otherwise." Phyllis would tell me as I fumed while looking at magazine article profiling two photographers. One had received a prestigious foundation award allowing him enough money to live abroad for a year. Another had produced a new book of portraits from Africa. He stood smiling by the same editor who had rejected my portraits of black women with church hats. He didn't think anybody would be interested in it. "Besides," white women don't look as good in hats, so they wouldn't buy the book."

The African volume was filled with shots of topless natives. They were colorful, technically perfect photographs, and I knew that the magazine paid handsomely. But where was the art, I would bemoan. Where was the play of light and shadow, the concern with composition? Weren't these just technically adept photographic efforts without a slice of artistic input?

Let me think now...when was the pivotal moment? Oh yes, the week that she had proudly dressed herself in starched white cap, starched uniform, white silk stockings and polished white shoes to work in a Connecticut home. "Oh I love the Van Allens, but they don't allow me to make phone calls. You won't hear from me for a week, poo." I had no assignments that week and stayed in her apartment. In the evenings I would look out from her living room at the polka dots of lights across the river in New Jersey. Maybe it was the combination of not having any photo projects and missing her that sent my mood southward. I would stare out from her twentieth floor perspective at that most breathtaking view that so few in the Apple would ever enjoy, and yet the full dimension of that visual advantage meant nothing to me. Searching for a semblance of her presence—a whiff of perfume, her laughter bouncing off the walls, her smile in the mirror—I ambled through the rooms. I felt her arms around me when I sat on the couch where I identified with all the blues laments that the Young Fellow had played in the last part of his show. She had sailed away from me, and I was left ashore unable to make contact. Who was it, Booby in high school who described it: "She got your mind."

Stricken, yes I was, and in an unexpected but desirable role of wanting to be there for her. It was the reverse of what Lorene had done for me. Now I was her Lorene, wanting to do everything I could to care for Phyllis. I needed her more than she needed me.

I needed to be closer. I needed to be closer so that I could touch her, reach her sensual core, mysteriously bring her back to shore from her aimless sailing toward the horizon. She was on the edge, just a few seconds ahead of the spot or moment where I was. If we were children swinging side by side, she would always be a little ahead or behind me, either kicking her legs to speed up or bending them to slow down. Could I just reach out and touch her as the scuba diver touches the flitting yellow fish that stops for a second, or would I be left instead with seeing it disappear into the dark dissolving ocean? Once during a glorious climactic moment, tingling and fully satiated, I looked down at her frowning brow as she twisted her body and pushed me away, moaning, "No Daddy, no Daddy." I turned sideways and embraced my hurricane-turned-into-light-puffs-of-wind. I held her even tighter, kissing her protesting lips shut, kissing the tip of her perspiring nose, trailing my hand down the center of her back, basking in the afterglow of our intimacy.

What did it mean? Who was this nightmarish visitor interrupting our connectedness? Was Daddy a former lover, the nickname of an abuser? Was she calling me big daddy? Maybe she had meant *dandy*? Or was I her daddy, the man she had never really seen much of, the man whom every little girl first loves and cherishes. It was a combination, I learned.

Her parents were not really living together in that house on the west side when I first met her, she told me. Phyllis's father had forsaken them, running off to the Midwest with Reverend Colson. I almost choked. Hadn't I photographed the reverend with the Cat during that civil rights assembly? After the divorce, her parents argued over who should take custody of Phyllis. Neither had time for her. They made an arrangement with an elderly neighbor whom we all referred to as her grandmother. Her mother never forgave Phyllis. For what? Phyllis never knew. Her mother would summon her to stand by the dining room table. Then she would point a finger at Phyllis and say, "You." In her other hand would be a wedding photograph. Then she would turn to go upstairs. Or she would leave the house—for months at a time, telephoning from cities West, Northeast and South.

No, I needed to be on the scene just as that warbler's mate was there—perched attentively on guard, eyes straight ahead. Do you know that is one of the few illustrations in the entire book where one of the two birds is upside down? It's a most natural position for our acrobatic feathered friends who, defying gravity, twist, turn and teeter on quivering twigs and branches. But when our upsides are down, it is not usually by design. My Phyllis was often downside up, and I chose to be in the branch below, able and committed to bringing her back to whatever balance was possible.

She could never become the model she fantasized about or the model I wanted. Her poses themselves were striking—in stylish dresses with makeup that accentuated her lips. But she couldn't stay in front of the camera. She flitted out of the scenes that I had arranged before I could focus and shoot. I would tell her to stand with hands on hips and she would—but only for a second before remembering that the water was boiling for tea. In the nearby park she would stop to pet anything on a leash or scurry after a squirrel that hopped just fast enough to escape. Invariably my focusing was interrupted: she had to sneeze, her toe was itching, eyeliner was dripping, a "wait—hold it just a second" would be uttered for many reasons.

Frustrating? Not so much as tantalized, fascinated by her innocent eccentricities and off-centered *modus operandi*. "Sounds like a cuckoo to me," advised Harvey when I told him about Phyllis' fastidiously pinching out and eating the center from her bread before leaving a perfect ring of crust—to discard of course. Scurrying about her apartment to water her plants and organize her magazines, Phyllis would often emit a loud "ouch," alerting me to her having bumped yet again into a door frame, table, or chair. She was at her feeblest when caught in a revolving door with her open umbrella, turning with a wide-eyed, "Hey, I'm stuck, help me!" Inside the department store, I had to hold her hand as we went up the escalator: "My eyes are closed, are we there yet?"

She had wandered away from me one weekend at the photo show in New Jersey. When I found her later—after I had examined the telephoto lenses at several tables—she was standing near the ladies room, back against the wall, a rivulet of tears heading south on her cheeks. "I thought you had left me," she said, her little body shaking, her voice softer than I had ever heard it.

"Now why would I do that?" I asked, holding her against me. "Why would I leave my little poopo?"

"All the others did," she said, holding my hand tightly.

"Well they didn't love you," I replied. "Those men were phony. They couldn't leave you if they really loved you."

"That's what I thought," she said, almost losing balance while stepping around a shopper with a tripod hanging from his shoulder. "But do you think my daddy didn't love me? He never even sent a letter. I would never abandon Killer like that."

"Oh I'm sure he loved you," I said, sitting on a blanket with her in Central Park one Saturday. I held her around the shoulders while her nose nestled its cool tip against my neck. We were watching a father run after his two sons and their boat. The boys ran along the edge of the pond to watch the vessel while their father hustled behind them. "He just didn't have the time to spend with you," I told her. "He probably wanted to…well other things came up. Who knows what he had to do."

"Did your dad spend time with you? Wasn't he a paratrooper or something?"

I wanted to tell her the truth, but I didn't think I was quite ready. I would have to say that I had lied to everybody and that I had deliberately blocked out the facts in my own mind. I had held my father responsible for my mother's death and I never even knew her. I'd have to tell Phyllis that my father was wealthy and had taken care of Aunt Clara and me and kept us quite comfortable. My mother was a maid who worked in his mansion: that's I all I knew from the clippings. If I missed spending time with him, it was only because I had deliberately decided to limit our encounters. I still had a father who supported me. That's more than Phyllis could say—or even David or Swing or Danny Bunn.

I searched for the words that would comfort her. "He was there in my mind," I told her. "He wasn't there physically for me, but his presence was strong, I could feel it. I knew I had a father." As she squeezed me tighter around my waist and pressed her face against my cheeks, I knew that this was a response that she could live with. And maybe, I considered, that's what I needed to say to Gahtsum when we had our conversation—that he had been there for me and I appreciated his presence. Love? I don't think so. He and I didn't have that kind of relationship, and I didn't feel the closeness, the sense of connection. But there was something. And maybe it could grow, I thought, as we turned our heads to look for the screams. Farther to our left in an open area of grass a father was guiding a little boy's hand as he held a kite. The child sent out a wild shout of amazement while looking up at each dip, each soar, each change of direction of the kite.

"We'll have to go kite flying," she said. "They're having so much fun. Can we?"

She had never flown one in her life, and she was so eager that we decided on the next weekday—an overcast Monday in July that barely had enough wind to keep a kite afloat. I had no photo assignments, and Phyllis had decided to postpone her telemarketing until early evening. I felt like one who had come down the chimney and delivered presents the day before Christmas when I heard her let out a soft scream as the kite took to the air.

"Pull back...move forward...loosen up a bit," I commanded. I stood behind her to guide her movements. Soon she was in complete control of the kite and our bodies were as close together as two spoons. I pressed myself against her white shorts so that my knees were glued to the back of her knees, and each step ahead for her was a stride forward for me also. When she turned her waist or hips, I responded with the same motion—making sure that there was no loss of adhesion between us. So when the kite dove suddenly and she let out a huge sigh, pushing her backside against me, I stood my ground. Her neck fell against my lips. I encircled her waist. Oh Booby, our first kite flying event turned into an unexpected sensual treat for us. I say for us because I had first thought of it as a most pleasurable tango of body contact that I had unknowingly fallen upon yet slyly accepted. But soon I realized that her movements were not so accidental and that we were in consort; she was enjoying the dance as much as I. "Oh my goodness," was the statement—half sigh, half laugh—that alerted me. It was after a sudden circular movement of her hips against me. I responded by rolling my torso in the same direction. By the time we had finished our ride and exclaimed at the most recent flapping sounds of the kite against the wind, I was exhaustedly fulfilled. I felt wonderful.

"I did too," she said when I confessed, looking around the park to see if we had been too obvious. "It felt good to have you rolling against me." Yes she had become a participant in my hastily conceived little skit,

Clandestine Grind from Behind on Behind without acknowledging it.

"Oh I feel like a little girl again, protected and loved," she said, now skipping along the sidewalk that led us under the tunnel to the west side. She held the kite in the air like a saber. "I bet you would protect me all the time. Wouldn't you?" Don't ask me how, but my little skit with the kite was expanded into a one-act romance that attracted a group of onlookers as curious about our situation as they would be about the couple that quarrels in the middle of the street. I saw the pedestrians walking past, but I could also feel a knot of them gathered around us and waiting for me to answer: the father holding his son on his shoulder, the couple licking their ice cream cones, the gentleman in short pants leaning against the light pole. They lingered, almost circling us. Phyllis came closer and licked her lips, faced me.

She smiled, they smiled, and I smiled too when I saw that my answer had caused us all to smile. "Well of course I would protect my poopoo. I would always be there for you."

She threw her arms around me (barely missed my forehead with the kite) and hugged me tightly. I heard murmurs of gleeful assent from the circle. "Oh, let's get married. Let's get married now! Then you can protect me always. Can we?"

I could feel the question gaining a palpable presence as if its response would be recorded, considered, and distributed throughout the park by those supposedly busy with their own affairs but obviously on attentive edge about the resolution of our scene. From the side, I saw the man who was leaning against the pole bend down to tie his shoes while looking at us. The wife's ice cream cone stood unlicked in her hands.

"Well...of course," I heard from my lips. And I proposed. I asked her to marry me. Did a few pedestrians clap or was that the swoosh of the cars rushing through the tunnel?

"Congratulations," came a voice from behind a tree. "You've got less than two hours."

"Right now?" I asked, hoping that my cracked voice didn't sound like a whine. "A ring. Don't we need a ring?"

"Here, I have one from the Cracker Jack candy box." Emerging from the throng was a small lady in a flowered dress. "I've been saving it. It shines just like gold, see?"

"It's beautiful," Phyllis said, grabbing it and sticking it on her finger. "Thank you so much," pulling me up the sidewalk. And I do mean pull. I didn't know that she was so strong. She led me through the tunnel to the other side of the park—our pace sending pigeons scurrying—past the museum on our right, past the old stately apartment buildings facing the park, and finally to the subway where we nearly tumbled down the steps to the turnstile. "Are you there?" she asked, staring in my eyes and walking backward. The dropped kite had already been abandoned in the middle of Central Park West as we dashed between the cars. On the train, Phyllis held me tightly around my waist with a strength that surprised me.

"City hall?—across the street," directed a friendly co-passenger climbing up the steps with us. "Hey watch out lady! You better catch her before she gets hit."

Transformed into an Olympic sprinter, poopoo in white shorts was across the street and had taken the wide marble white steps by twos before I caught up with her at the huge door—the entrance that I had seen from a distance from Wiles' office. And down the hallway we scurried to the license bureau. Then we continued through a breathtaking forty minutes of paper signing and climbing stairs and waiting for creaking elevators until...we were married. A man congratulated us and shook our hands.

"We'll have to go back to my place and celebrate our wedding night," she told me, squeezing my fingers. Frankly Booby, I had been stunned into semi-consciousness since the little lady in the park had bestowed the wedding ring on us. As the cloudy trance began to lift away and I was able to feel my eyes blink again, I considered what had happened. It had started with a kiss when we were kids. We got separated, I married Atlanta. We rediscovered each other a few months ago and now we had committed ourselves to loving each other for the rest of our lives. Only death would set us apart. How would I explain this second matrimonial alliance to Harvey, Gahtsum? To myself? But she wasn't Atlanta, I parried, walking proudly down the hall with my new bride. I knew Phyllis; there were no hidden agendas. I needed her. I would take care of her.

When we got off the train at her stop and walked toward her apartment, she swinging my arm and singing a childhood ditty, my restored consciousness now focused on our upcoming celebration as husband and wife. The drunken splendor that I had first experienced with her at age thirteen would be relived in a few hours as husband and wife. I would wallow in the treasures of her lips, those shining sweet petals. No it would not be our first time; but it would be our first time as man and wife. Our inebriated spirits sent us laughing and stumbling down the street—neither fully in control of our faculties nor aware of how far away we were from sobriety.

We sang out some cheers from our high school athletic events. "Oh remember when we beat Camden finally," she laughed, shooting an imaginary basketball toward the darkening sky. Then Phyllis decided that she would become a cheerleader. She jumped in the air—maybe her feet were 12 inches from the ground—and swung out her arms like Lenora had done while wearing the blue and the white during the state championship series. I noticed that a few heads were looking our from windows to capture Phyllis' spontaneous take-off from the sidewalk. She was in the middle of the street. We were definitely playing Camden and I think she was urging them to "push 'em back, push 'em back, waaaay back." Then I believe the bassoons and trumpets from the band lifted her spirits higher than she had ever experienced—or expected. But it wasn't the band she heard—the high school marching band with the full complement of instruments including John Durham's trombone. No it was the blaring yell of the taxicab's horn as its driver had determined a few yards ago that he was in danger of not braking in time to prevent his running her down in the middle of her pushing back.

Booby, that was the last time that I saw Phyllis as my wife. Oh yes, I saw her—in the hospital less than an hour later—and for the rest of the summer almost daily. My sweet little poopoo lay that evening with a slight concussion, able merely to turn her head wrapped in bandages from side to side. She wasn't able to talk for weeks, so my first visits were spent sitting by the bed and holding her hand, ever hopeful that she would awaken, smile, and say that she was feeling better. Maybe she would ask, "Where am I?"

Instead, when I walked into her hospital room for the first time to see her sitting up awake, my poopoo! smiling, I heard this after holding her hands: "Who are you?"

"Who me?" I thought she was joking.

Amnesia is common after a concussion is sustained. That's how the physician described her condition to me. His hands were folded behind his back and he looked up to the fluorescent lights when I asked him if she would ever remember me again. "I wish I could tell you, but I don't know," he replied.

By the end of that summer I forced myself to accept the frightful truth. During each visit, she smiled and thanked me for coming, but she insisted that she did not know who I was. "You seem to be the kind of man I might marry," she told me. "But I don't know you well enough." The rhythm of her giggle was one that I hadn't heard before, as if she had taken on a new personality with altered features.

I couldn't tell the nurses and interns that I wasn't coming back. Their smiles had already expressed far too much sympathy. I'd have to listen to them try to convince me that there was a chance she might recover. Then they would stare at me—all of them would. They would be sad, and their sadness would pull out all the anguish that was lodged within me and I'd stand there shaking. Nay, Booby. Instead of that scene, I chose another. I chose a Friday to go in and begin our tête-à-tête with the thought that I'd try one more time and that would be it. And of course that was it, Phyllis being just as delightfully curious and amnestic as before without reversing her condition miraculously. Only two of the nurses were on duty when I left Phyllis' room for the last time. "See you tomorrow," I waved at them.

Chapter 27

Back in my own apartment that I hadn't slept in since the spring, I was once again looking through my bird book for solace—this time for a representative creature standing alone and ruminating about its condition just as I was. Funny, but most of the pages featured two birds, as if that were the natural thing—to be with another, not alone. When I turned to the eagle, it seemed far more stately and regal than I was feeling—its strong claws ready to grasp its prey, its eyes invincible and fearless. The cuckoo was preening itself and looking to its rear, I was sure, in a temporary state of solitude before joining its mate. The hawk's demeanor seemed too imperial, and so did the crane. And the gorgeous white pelican—how could it possibly be intimidated or subdued with its formidable stance accentuated by a beak shaped like a canoe. None of the portraits of single birds gave me what I was looking for—a psychological cohort, a partner in my aloneness. They were far too strong while I felt—well I felt drained. The bird book was filled with togetherness, not aloneness.

At first, not even the visual benefits of the park across the street that had kept me engaged on so many evenings and weekends were enough to enlighten my spirits: the squirrels that scampered up and down the tree trunks, the toddlers who thought that they could catch them, the woodpecker who had once awakened me with the thought that some construction crew was at work, the new trio of serenaders by the bench—none of them. I would sometimes pick up my camera with the idea of capturing yet another version of the same subject, and then overtaken suddenly by despondency, ask myself why bother and put down my camera.

One neighbor did supply the communion of aloneness that I sought.

He was known, according to some I had heard at the subway station to have lost it in the last Asian war we had fought. They said that his name was Hector and that he lived with his aunt in one of the brownstone rooming houses. "Good thing she taking care of him 'cause you know the poor thing can't do for himself. I think he got a hand shot off but you ever notice his sleeves so long you can't tell?" He walked around the park every day at the same time, emitting monosyllabic sounds like the cawing of a crow. Nobody laughed at or bothered Hector. Even the children simply looked and smiled sympathetically, just as I did from my window, enlisting myself as a partner in his sadness.

By the end of the week I realized that it was time for me to come out of my brooding and connect with the rest of the world. Talking to myself one night, I rehearsed my discussion about my plight with Aunt Clara as I walked around my apartment. I listened to her philosophical assessments about life's being no crystal stair, about if it ain't one thing it's another, about...and then I was brought back to the realization that she was dead. I couldn't talk to her anymore with my legs swinging in the kitchen chair to the rhythm of her wise sentences. Nor could I even nod my head supposedly in agreement with Aunt Shirl. I could hear her now: "That hussy ain't forgot nothing. She lying." For what purpose? Aunt Shirl didn't go that far in her indictments. Purpose and motive were not her areas of expertise.

I needed to talk to Gahtsum. A resounding reminder echoed through my mind: he is my father. The block had been removed, remember? I needed to talk to someone whose affinity was closer than friendship. Harvey was a dear friend. But Gahtsum was my father who had supported me as far back as I could remember, whose identity was my identity.

Before dialing his number, I rehearsed the various ways I could describe the situation—that my second wife had forgotten that we were married and it didn't seem as if she would recover from the amnesia caused by the accident—on our wedding night. Its succinctness surprised me, as if I were writing an essay for a class. All the elements were there, in order. Before I could think myself out of making the call, I picked up the receiver and almost hoped he wouldn't answer, that he was traveling, getting ready for the fall season. But it was his voice I heard.

"I'm not going back any more," I said. It's no use." Then I was lost, watching the words that I had practiced running ahead of me and disappearing. I could hear my own breath gasps, unable to continue.

"You sound hurt, my son."

Oh yes, I was. Oh yes, I was so relieved that he could tell. "Yes," I barely whispered it out. And I was glad that he had called me son. Thank goodness he kept talking so that I didn't have to muster the strength to stop my lips from trembling in order to respond. His words were soothing, supportive, the voice powerful yet caring. Now he was coming to visit me—for the first time. Was it over the bridge and then a left on Lafayette to Fort Greene? That must be a nice calming environment, he assured me. Be right there.

I went to the window after I said goodbye. It was a view I had lately not seen so much of. Instead of looking across the river from Phyllis' living room at the lights of New Jersey, I was peering down at tree leaves turning yellow and at people who were within shouting distance. They formed a blurry screen of activity that I watched without really paying attention. A man holding a leash and waiting for his dog to finish stood on the grassy edge while the loud voices of two young men went by them. A police cruiser crawled down the street and from the passenger side a flashlight's circle swept over the trees. When I saw Gahtsum's gray sedan angling to park, I went down to meet him. Hand adjusting his hat, he glanced down the street before starting up the steps. I opened the door and stood at the landing of the brown cement steps.

"Hey mon, let me have that hat," yelled out a man walking past with two laughing partners. "It looks better on me."

Gahtsum was smiling when I closed the door behind him. Before going up we hugged—for the first time that I could remember, although as I held my arms around his gray suit and took in his cologne, I sensed that in another moment in the past I had done this with him before, and that he had picked me up and thrown me above his shoulders.

"Very nice view," he said, upstairs now looking out the windows. "You must have gotten a lot of candid shots."

"Oh yeah, I have," I said, thinking of the series I had started before moving in with Phyllis of the serenading couples on the bench. And I still enjoyed looking at the portraits taken of Lenora with the shadows formed by the shutters. I sat on the couch and he sat next to me, both of us looking straight ahead at the wall of framed photographs. We were almost elbow to elbow.

"Well you get a divorce and move on," he said, crossing his legs. "I'll have somebody at the office handle it for you."

"Yep, another divorce," I responded. He took a seat next to me and we both stared out at the wall where I had hung some of my portraits.

"Don't take it too hard. Life goes on. Better to have loved and lived you know."

"You only married once, you were lucky," I said.

"Yes but I only loved…only your mother. We just met at the wrong time. But at least her memory is still alive." He patted my forearm. "She would be proud of you. Even if you aren't a lawyer." We both chuckled, and I snatched a look at his profile, searching for some semblance in the features but finding only those thin lips and the nose that jutted out like a little beak.

"That doesn't seem like such a bad idea sometimes," I sighed.

"But the important thing is that you gave your heart," he said. "Not many people have had that experience, that elated feeling of being on cloud nine. What is love but the ability to find the best in the other person? But then again you know all that stuff"—he turned to look at me, his lips curled into a smile, "Aunt Clara always thought you were a little Romeo. In fact I was afraid you would be too distracted by all those girls chasing after you—or you chasing them—but you kept your focus on your studies."

"Yes, and now I'm a freelance photographer with a degree in tectonics and no regular job," I said, standing up to go to the window. "I guess you were right keeping me from majoring in photography."

"Well, you chose to be an artist. That's a special calling, and I respect it. It's unfortunate that most of you have to suffer before you are recognized. Even your artist friend"—he pointed to the bird book on the cocktail table—"had a hard time of it. And then of course, I guess some never get recognized for their talent." He got up from the couch to look closely at my photograph of the Brim sitting alone in a dark corner of the jazz club. "That's a great shot; it captures mood beautifully."

"Nobody seems to be interested anymore in how I capture mood," I said, "especially if the subject isn't white. We had a movement, everybody was protesting, people were interested in changing things. I was the leading photographer at *Week* covering it all. And then they got tired. I can't even get an assignment that features us. They just want to see slick mindless images, shallow statements that cater to the unthinking." We were both standing, I by the window looking alternately at him and the silhouette of blackbirds squatting on the telephone line across the street, he on the other side of the room.

"My boy," his nose pointing upward as he sighed and faced me, "you must focus more on the inside and not the outside. The outside is just image, surface. Inside is what counts—how you feel about it right here." He came over to me and jabbed his finger against my chest. "Your task is to develop your art and believe in it. Keep producing and don't worry about its acceptance outside. Talent is always recognized eventually. And one thing is for certain." He put his hands in his pockets and looked in my eyes. He waited for me to lead him on.

"What's that?"

"The tides always change. What's in today will be out tomorrow and vice versa. If I were you," his head went up as he chuckled, "I wouldn't throw anything away. Just hold on and have faith."

I felt a wave of comfort flow through me, a wave that I had identified before but had ignored, pushed away. It had seemed too convenient—this same answer that Gahtsum was offering. It was a confirmation of what I had thought all the time but had not the confidence to accept. It's what Lorene and Sonja had told me. Phyllis had told me too. Booby, it's just hard to believe in yourself sometimes. But when will the tide change, I wondered to myself. We walked toward the couch and sat.

"The tides may change for you romantically too," Gahtsum said. "Don't be afraid to look for that soul mate you yearn for. She may still be out there. For me, no. There can be nobody to replace your mother in my heart. She was too special. Neither of us cared about color or social rank. We were just two people who loved each other. But I was married." His voice was softer as he crossed his legs and faced the wall of photographs again. "I've devoted myself to another love—helping to resurrect that marvelous church uptown—the one near the apartment that you and Atlanta lived in. It's been unfinished for more than a century. Who knows, maybe it will remain unfinished like us. But I'll give it a try. Remember it?"

Remarkably, I had a vision of my first day in the Apple and the beggar near the subway who insisted that the church would never be finished. And then I recalled Professor Gut's despondent throwing up of his hands after his slide lecture about the cathedral.

"Well yes, in fact my tectonics professor talked about it—but always in a pessimistic tone. But we never really understood why," I frowned.

"It is pessimistic if you consider the challenge," Gahtsum replied. You obviously didn't grasp the full meaning of what your visionary instructor was professing," he chuckled. "Let's just say that it's a symbol of how we can come together. Its founders in the nineteenth century thought of the cathedral as a place of worship for all people, a unifying center. But after Pearl Harbor and our entry into the war, construction stopped. Can you imagine, that wonderful building has been sitting there unfinished for decades. We're having a committee meeting in a few days. I've dedicated myself to help raising as much money as I can."

Booby, we talked all night. "My goodness, it's three in the morning," looking at his watch, he said as he rose to leave. Later I lay in bed sleepless for another hour or so considering all that we had discussed. Somehow he had become another Young Fellow, bringing me yet again to the exploration of that mysterious realm called love. But Gahtsum had suggested that my understanding of it—despite my ability to let my heart fly—was still limited. "True love is finding the good in a person," he said, holding his middle finger in the air as if lecturing. But there was a larger dimension, he insisted, and I realized that he had been leading me down it kicking and screaming for as long as I could remember. I had spent so much time blocking out the truth about him and my mother and being vindictive that I had missed the fact that he had orchestrated much of my edification. He had encouraged me to major in tectonics for a reason, and now lying in bed that morning I understood fully what Professor Gut had been trying to show us. We needed to come together—all of us. That's why Gut kept showing us the globe and declaring that the land masses would fit together again like the interlocking of fingers.

"Imagine if you eliminated all the water," he said. "Then the land would all join together like this"—he linked the fingers of both hands. And we had sat there taking notes and winking at each other and not truly understanding.

Gut had been trying to get us to consider that there was something larger yet than the passion that generated the scary electric fluttering of my heart when Phyllis first kissed me. Is that why his most frequently quoted poetic line was, "We must love one another or die."? Yes, he meant that we needed to expand, go beyond ourselves—love our neighbors.

Listening to Gahtsum, I was transformed as the churchgoer is whose belief becomes even more rock solid and firmer after hearing a pastor's spellbinding sermon. And like that same believer, I was able finally to release from within me a surging itch that had been repressed too long. He had gone down the brownstone steps and turned sideways, placing his hand to the side of his hat. I yelled, "Hey dad." He turned to look at me. "I love you," I said. He smiled, waved and went toward his sedan. I could feel my heart thumping as I went back up to my apartment.

What I hadn't been able to resolve—and still haven't as I sit here talking to you and waiting for Harvey—is how to reconcile what both Gut and Gahtsum had proposed with Harvey's grand design. Weren't their approaches at odds? Wasn't Harvey's solution—like mine *had* been—based on an unforgiving demand? Wasn't he being unnecessarily vindictive?

Gahtsum had also convinced me that I would benefit enormously from a change of scenery. A friend of a friend had just started a magazine featuring local personalities in the Virginia Tidewater area. Gahtsum was sure he could persuade James Towne to take me onboard as a staff photographer. "He's got enough investor funding to keep him afloat for awhile," Gahtsum advised me. "And I'll get my office to find you a nice place that you can rent on the beach. You go down and refurbish your spirits and then see what develops. Remember your Aunt Clara used to say that things can change overnight."

So Booby I'm taking it to the bridge, don't get lost now. That's how I got to that little Virginia town on the bay before finally moving to the capital to join *Ontime* two years ago. And then I met Chinita.

Before I knew it I had been in Virginia for eight years or so, and one day I realized that I was in my forties. Oh it took me only a few weeks after unloading my furniture, books, and camera equipment to regain my spirits and confidence. Before I knew it, I was on the hunt again for my soul mate. Before I knew it, the memory of Phyllis had dissolved into a hazy set of indistinct scenes that became increasingly difficult to recall. Before I knew it, I was looking for that famed Virginia ham, that fabled beauty with the thick thighs and red-brown skin described in Johnson's pool hall. "Lemme tell you, they got some hammers down there in Virginy," I remember Wally promising a regular who was holding up a wall and whose travel, like most of those listening and appearing not to, had obviously been limited. "Legs like you never seen. I mean them girls down there got some hamstrings"—he patted his own thigh. "And skin the shade of smoked ham. Them pretty womens down there will hurt you." He racked the balls with a loud enough emphasis to make a few in his audience jump away from the wall.

At any rate, between my stint with the magazine published by Gahtsum's friend's friend and my freelancing years featuring the lovely Vixoria, I found time to enquire about the Virginia ham as well as other potential intoxicators.

The very first was an actual Virginia ham whom I met at a conference I was shooting for that infamous magazine that had lured me to the area. Rachel exhibited all of the features that not only Johnson had prophesied about, but also that I could testify about with my own eyes. Her legs and arms, as I watched her move smartly among the project managers and focus group directors, had that rare baked sun tint that contrasted like an explosion against her black skirt. Her lower torso blossomed, and her hip was as plenteous as your imagination. But she was married, I learned by the fourth or fifth paragraph, so the invitation to join her for drinks—"I'm thinking of starting my own newsletter"—seemed appropriately innocent and proper. She was a country girl—she made no bones about it—but at the same time she must have expected me to see that she was a country girl with a big city attitude.

We agreed to meet at a hotel bar on the bay where redevelopment of the city was taking place. Within minutes I was drawn to her. Was it the fact that I was having difficulty understanding her accent and kept moving closer each time I asked her to repeat herself until suddenly my eyes were only inches from hers? They were clear and intense and they were looking right back at me. She used an *e* for an *a* and vice versa. So her *ayes* were looking into my *ayes* and she thought we might *tek* a walk along the pier.

The more I listened, the more I became convinced that the marital ties between them had dissolved years ago and that she and her husband were just living together until they could afford to get a divorce. There was no marriage being broken up here, I determined as she pushed her dark glasses over her nose to look at me more intently. "Oh he doesn't care what I do," she laughed softly. "But as soon as I get enough saved, I'll be leaving to do my own thing."

He did care that she come home every night, so our rendezvous were limited to the hours we could share after she sped from her office and came to my apartment. I would open the door and she would brush past me with a kiss, and sprinkling her shoes, her dress, and her bra on the steps, proceeded to skip up to my bedroom. "You bringing the wine?" she'd ask from the top of the stairway. From below, I watched the two firm posts that were her Virginia hams spread apart and twist. I hardly heard the rest. By the time I had pulled out some cheese and crackers and strawberries to go with the wine and leaped up the steps, she would be under the covers with the remote control aimed at the television.

"Hurry up, you know I can't stay forever," her eyes had a special twinkle that would disappear with the rest of her body as she slid under the sheets. Through my window I could hear the soothing sounds of the breakers hitting the beach, the gulls declaring and the children screaming. I liked to hold Rachel tightly and stare at her. She couldn't stand it. She couldn't stand the impulses that the intense eye contact generated within her. She would have to close her eyes finally—after much frowning and resisting, and even stretching her toes. Nothing mattered for us but those moments. How easy it was to toss the bag of worries and concerns out of our lives—out the window—to concentrate on just the two of us. We were directing our trip of pleasure on a flying, floating rowboat that made us oblivious to the everything else for those sacred moments. Goodbye, editor Dempsey; farewell, husband Oscar, and so long, everybody else.

How could I possibly be concerned with not being able to pay my rent, of the number of black men—according to Harvey—who were dying of a new virus brought over from the motherland, of Gahtsum's difficulty in rebuilding that cathedral building, of my next assignment, of some rumblings that True Washington might even run for president? Nay, get thee gone, outside world of pesky worries. I was far more occupied with holding on to Rachel, holding on to the possibility of...of an attachment? Could this thing last? Could this be magic? Let us continue to inebriate ourselves, stumbling and soaring with fingers clasped together, ignoring those sounds from the outside planet that we had—hadn't we just left it?

Booby, my faithful good man, I ran into a problem after the first few wonderful encounters. Rachel did not need the cuddling and holding that nourished me. After our love boat would return to shore, I craved lying next to her, my hand free to gallop down the center of her back and over those thighs while our cheeks pressed together. I liked rubbing my nose against hers and tickling her chin with my tongue. But she would twist away as if she had been entwined like a prisoner and then jump up, pick up her scattered clothes and begin dressing. Even that evening of the terrible storm when all outside was gray and the wind whistled madly and I had lit two scented candles, she did not sense the special opportunity for a lingering aftermath. While dressing, she talked fast about a dinner to prepare, a book that I should read, a co-worker at the office. And then she was down the steps, at the doorway, outside, her car door slamming shut. Oh how sweet that short haircut with the few strands against her forehead looked as she pulled away from my garage. I would turn from the kitchen window with an empty feeling and return to the bed where the sheets and pillows still held the scent of her thighs.

More, I needed more, Booby! I wanted my earth angel to remain with me after our memorable voyage, not rushing off to the Alps to assist Hannibal and leaving me like a forsaken vagabond, hands reaching out to touch no one, memories of our cruise to share with no one, lips pursed to kiss no one. No, I could not stand it any longer—this sense of being deserted—and I told her that when we met at the same bar where we had begun.

"Well..." She was silent after that syllable, eyes blinking away tears and looking upward, moving her glass from left to right. We both stared out at two gulls sitting on posts. She was still silent when the waitress asked us if everything was all right. "I don't know how to be any other way," she said finally. So we remained friends, and I heard after I left for the nation's capital that she had divorced her husband and moved in with a wealthy optometrist.

I was still aware—despite our circumscribed world of after-work liaison at the darkest and smallest restaurants and bars we could find— that there were rumblings afoot in that outside world. Of course it could hardly match the ferment of those tumultuous times during my last years in college and later when I lived in the Apple. The new rumblings were not those of militant blacks demanding radical changes. No student groups threatened to take over our universities. The activity was more sophisticated now, based on methodical analysis and planning. "That pork chop nationalism of the sixties didn't get us anywhere," declared Harvey. "Those brothers thought that we could get our freedom by eating soul food, wearing African garb, and speaking Swahili. No, you've got to be more sophisticated than that to beat whitey," he insisted as he described the trips he had taken to help with political activities. "You know we've got black mayors elected in the Windy City, the Motor City, right here in the capital and elsewhere. And brothers coming out of college are being recruited by top corporations. We're breaking down all those barriers that they set up through their slick systems. I'm telling you it's about the money, dude. And when I present my case, even money won't be a problem any more."

It sounded outlandishly fanatical when I first heard it, even though I was accustomed to listening patiently to his harangues. Wasn't he the same Harvey who stuck his thumb out at attending college in the group (never once went to convocation!) but still took advantage of that prestige to go to a top law school? Hadn't he gone to the Sip to work with the movement? And hadn't he left his law practice to work in the street academy? So there was nothing that new. Yet it seemed totally preposterous. I don't know when it came to him at first. Had it begun as a wild thought not to be entertained, and then to be considered seriously? And then did it seem less outrageous as he discussed it with more people who agreed with him? And then did obsession set in and the idea become a dreamy proposition that pulled and pushed him around as he slept at night? "It's a simple matter of getting repaid for injustice," he explained to me one weekend when I was in the capital for a quick assignment covering a marathon race. "Somebody has to pay, that's all I can say. Look at what they've done to us. I refuse to disappear." Always at this part of his speech, the blood surging in his cheeks would darken his freckled face.

I was actually cogitating on that very prospect—of disappearing— while waiting for my session with Vanetta to begin after her victorious singles match. But when she fell out of the locker room—white shorts, huge smile brighter than light bulbs—my mood changed immediately and *I* was almost apologizing for *her* tardiness. What really caused the fluttering butterflies in my stomach? It was her walk. I thought that she was losing her balance and falling to the side while in fact she was merely moving in her own inimitably fluid style—like a tightrope walker leaning precariously from one side to the other. She continued toward me with perfect balance after each step-tilt so that by the time she was within a foot and could shake my hand, I had seen a full runway's worth of her walk. What, I wondered, would this wondrous rhythm of hip and leg look like from behind?

"I know you must be mad at me," she said, holding out her hand. "I'm sorry but I just couldn't decide on which lipstick. This is going in next week's issue, right?"

"Well if we can finish the shoot before next week," I said, thinking of how I would pose her standing by the net. Then I described the earlier assignment that afternoon where I had shot a player who had switched the racket from one hand to the other instead of using a backhand and had accidentally banged the racket into his mouth and knocked himself down. I shot him sitting, knees up on the court, touching his bleeding lip. She laughed heartily, her head back, shoulders heaving.

And that was the signal that I needed. My mind left my body again and began mumbling to itself. I was talking and shooting and directing her to pose in real time, but my mind had transported me to a movie scene in a South African veldt thousands of miles away. Me hunt prey. Uhmmm me see prey. But me walk around as if prey not there. Me spout goody goody words—anecdotes, puns, maxims—as if no interest in more than nice guy. Me nice guy with words. Looksee, me have many funny words. You relax, laugh, sip kola nut juice. You laugh and laugh until you lose resistance. You trust nice guy. Then nice guy swoop. You be mine.

"Well of course we can go to dinner; I'd love to, she said at the end of the shoot, having just begged me to "stop those hilarious stories, you're killing me." And so Booby, that assignment with Vanetta the tennis player—or should I say the impressionable tennis player—turned out to be the start of something new. She wasn't a professional tennis player. Her real employment was as a real estate agent. She lived an hour away in the town that had been the Confederate capital during the Civil War. The state had just elected a black governor, and I promised Harvey that I would photograph him whenever I saw the white-haired phenomenon.

"I can't believe you live that close to the Confederate capital and haven't seen the governor all these years," he shouted in the phone one night. "I bet you see lots of Confederate flags and hear good old boys talking about the good old days when we had slavery," he chuckled.

At the time I was getting a secure stream of assignments from a sports magazine based in the Apple before they went out of business, and so Vanetta and I both had to wait until the weekends to be with each other. We spent most of that summer—my last before coming up to the capital—laughing and talking our way through parks, restaurants, clubs, museums. Anywhere that held the promise of being a topic of conversation was a place that would qualify for a visit from us. And oh did we laugh. And oh did I love to see her tantalizing tilt-walk—up a stairway, down a stairway—it didn't matter; just walk child.

She lived in a section of older brick homes that was going up in value rapidly as many in the surrounding areas were joining the trend of moving back to the city. The living room floor planks were solid oak, I remember, and she had two lovely antiques—a butler's table on which we usually placed our cocktails, and a Tiffany lamp—given to her by a deceased aunt. We had behaved as if we were close friends and nothing more for the first month. But I could not bear for long her pull, her magnetic energy bundled up in a powerful small frame. She would bounce off the court when I met her there and run in my direction as if I were the source of limitless trust and wisdom. I always held out my hand to slow her down because her run was nothing compared to her walk.

And it was during one of those approaches—at her house, leaving the kitchen and coming toward me with two glasses of wine—that she seemed to transform herself into the dream that I had longed for. I rose to kiss her as if to celebrate our union, and before I knew it she had placed the glasses down and settled within my arms. It was as if each of us had been waiting for the other to make a commitment—beyond friendship. We both wanted a home. Mmmm back in the veldt, me hold her tight tight. Me tell her me do all the things. Me take good care. Me nice guy always. Me protect: hold back flood, fire, storm.

And then I told her that my tongue would leave no part of her body unbathed. She looked at me curiously, her eyes sad. Quiet as it's kept, Booby I had used that jewel of a romantic promise before—first gathered at one of the bars that I visited during my summer treks. "Well you may not want to go that far," she said, taking a seat on the couch next to me.

And no I didn't, I found out. She had undergone surgery—something she had told me about at least once. I had been too busy preparing to toss off another quip to have comprehended all the specifics of that conversation. But some of the facts whirled hazily in my mind as she held my hand to lead me to her bedroom. In fact tennis had been the driving force of her recovery. They had cut inside, but her legs and arms were strong still. I did remember her saying, "By strengthening my limbs and keeping my championship form, I was able to appear normal." She had tossed that off in a sequence of silly assertions we were throwing around in a loud pizza parlor. She seems perfectly normal to me, I thought as I lay naked on the bed, waiting for my own Althea Gibson to return from the bathroom. I heard the water running, the cabinet doors opening and closing, the toilet flushing, and some cellophane crackling before the radiance that was her face appeared at the doorway. She moved toward me in a white silk negligee and was soon on the mattress crawling on hands and knees toward me.

Her toilet water had a strong scent, I considered as I pulled her on top of me.

"Careful. Oh darn, wait." She slipped out of my arms and moved toward the bathroom. I heard the water running, the cabinet doors opening and closing, the toilet flushing, and then suddenly thought that I should study the poster hanging over there on the side of the bed rather than monitor her bathroom sounds. Her hands were behind her when she came out again. "I think I should have a standby," she said, looking at me with the oddest expression, as if it were a question. Or maybe it was a plea? Now in her hands was the replacement bag that looked like a rubber glove without fingers. It was part of the apparatus that kept her alive since they had removed most of her insides, she explained. "I got tired of my old bladder, kidneys and esophagus, so I got them to make me some rubber substitutes," she said, trying to laugh. But her voice was too plaintive, almost shaking. "It doesn't have an odor, does it? Sometimes I can't tell."

"It's fine," I said. "I mean they are fine." I lay on my back and held her hand. She was sitting on the side of the bed and looking at the poster.

"Do you want to leave?" she asked.

"Yes," I said. I squeezed her hand and then pulled her toward me. I bet sweet Vanetta would have no problem cuddling. She'd probably stay in bed with me all day if I asked. I felt a small rubber strip as I slid my leg between hers. Her eyes were still shining, but I wondered if they were moist too. I didn't want to stay. But I couldn't leave like that, as if I wanted no part of her. Yet I had already shown that I didn't want to be there. Everything that I loved about her was still lovable. But I couldn't love her the way I wanted to love a woman. There was an additional requirement here, wasn't there? More love was needed here than I was capable of giving. So what kind of love, how much love could I give anyway? Did I even know what love really is? What could I do? What should I do? My heart was beating fast against her breasts. I didn't want any part of part of her; and I wanted every part of the other part. Booby, I was getting a headache. I knew finally that I should do anything to make her feel better. Leaving would not help.

"I'm really so tired," I said.

"You must be," she said. "You've had a long day."

"Yes. Hey do you mind if I sleep here tonight? I don't think I can drive back."

"Sure," she said. "You can sleep here anytime," nestling her head against me.

Chapter 28

It all went so fast. I'm almost 50 Booby. Is that all I have done? Did we just cover my whole life in five hours? High school, college, ten years in the Apple, another seven in Virginia, and almost four here in the capital. I'll be an old man soon Booby.

Vanetta was my last relationship before I finally met Chinita, my true earth angel. She and I continued to meet for impromptu lunch and dinner dates. But a different atmosphere surrounded us after that night. We both sensed that everything had changed back to friendship just as suddenly as we had taken our good relations beyond its companionable plateau to become intimate. There was no need to articulate the change. She knew that I didn't want her. We didn't kiss goodbye, we didn't hold hands at all. We were stunted almost, frozen by the new roles of being mere platonic friends, and I was grateful for the sweet little tennis vanquisher's cordial acceptance of my—well, was it simply cowardice? Is that why I couldn't see myself with a soul mate who was challenged with disabilities? What kind of definition of love was I relying on anyway, I asked myself a few times during a sleepless thoughtful night. If my love had restrictions about who was worthy, then what did it say about me?

I left that alone, especially when Harvey suggested that I was the typical romantic artist, far too self-indulged to apprehend the larger picture surrounding my personal dilemmas.

"Look," he told me, just before they repossessed my car in Virginia, "I know that you are having a tough time making it as a photographer, especially after those years of being a celebrity in the Apple. But you ought to take time to look around and see what's happening. We've got serious problems is all I'm saying, my brother," he told me during our usual Sunday evening phone call. "Something else is afoot," he whispered as he usually did when the subject to him was of great consequence. "Our brothers are dying like crazy from a strange virus. Where did it come from? And while this is going on, you are spending all of your extra hours running after some bitches."

"I usually run after one at a time," I corrected him. "It would be much nicer to come home at night to a warm tender human being," I said. "If you want to return to an empty home at night, that's fine with me. But I'm not discouraged because of two divorces. "

No, I wasn't Booby, and when I met Chinita for the first time at the banquet, I wasn't at all fearful of losing my heart again. I was thinking of the bright future, not the dark past. Now sit back up. I know you've been listening for several hours. I'll be quiet soon.

Even when I saw Chinita slipping away from me in sickness I refused to give up hope. One day everything was fine. We were listening to the Caribbean crooner describing a lifetime in spring, and then she was ill and never recovered, as if his words about its being fatal for him to be alone were warnings for me. The decline was as swift as the discovery. I see the change now as a fast-moving film where the individual scenes keep you engaged by the minute, and then suddenly the end is announced. Then time passes and it places more and more distance between the scenes and you, and suddenly it was a long time ago when the scenes took place. But the long time ago still feels like yesterday, Booby.

It was just yesterday when my *Neeta* and I lay together on Sunday morning, the remnants of Goddess still lingering, she having turned toward me instinctively to bury her chin against my neck. She eased her knee between my thighs and her breasts lay against my chest. My mission, suddenly handed down to me by my subconscious, was to hold her as tightly as I could. I wanted to melt into her body, turning us into one indivisible committed set of souls who had momentarily relinquished ourselves for the other. *It was just yesterday* when I came home early and saw her standing in her favorite classroom outfit, a blue dress. Her hand was on the closet door. Frantically desiring the promise that her lipstick held, I pressed my lips against hers as if it would be our last, pushing her back into the dark closet, where despite our elbows and knees banging against walls, hanging clothes pushing against our shoulders, and acrobatic bends and leans, we managed to connect with most of our clothes still on. *It was just yesterday* when we played character. She said that Daddy had been a bad boy and that he would need punishing. Suddenly the phrase, the idea of *Daddy* was a bad *boy* took on stimulating significance. I became tantalized by her imagination. My entire being seemed captive to her whispered utterings from a voice that was both hefty and soft, both innocently sweet yet seasoned and capable. If I were a real bad boy, then it would be my responsibility to atone for my inexcusable behavior, and I was maniacally committed to showing her, through the most tender expressions that I could create, how much I adored her and how I had not meant to be a bad boy. Finally it would mean clasping her toward me so tightly that she would gasp.

Hold up for a moment, Booby. Is there something wrong with me? Who me? Of course not, but I have wondered if those uncontainable urges I had were...were normal. I would be driven to the point of lunacy when I was near Chinita, as if the full moon had hijacked my senses as easily as it forces an uproarious rise of the oceans. Lunatic, mad man, madcap, screwball; call me any of those. I simply had to have some tactile connection! And no, poor perverse obsessed devotee of the sensual, I couldn't talk about these...these needs with anybody. Can you imagine how Harvey would respond? Well what did it matter anyway? My partner in lunacy, my sweet angel of the earth accepted and encouraged my fixations, her eyes always bright.

As I was saying, *it was just yesterday* when I had sent her into a moaning swoon by pulling on each individual toe before kneading the instep with my fist as I massaged her feet, sore from a day of standing in front of the classroom; just yesterday when her soothing palm ran down the back of my neck while I was driving through the city; just yesterday when we were caught in the storm while walking along the mall and laughed like fools as we pointed at each others drenched faces; just yesterday when I found on my desk a letter from her describing how proud of me she was.

And then those scenes seemed to have been blacked out suddenly, Booby, as if the director had decided that the film needed to be shortened. The three of us were having dinner on that evening when I had agreed to assist Harvey further in his project after he saw my photos of Mazique in prison. "These are extraordinary," he said after dessert. "God he looks so defeated with his head down like that. I didn't know you had these. And the chicken was delicious, Chinita," he told her as she left us in the living room to prepare for her morning classes. "And you have others?"

"Yes, I probably took a half-dozen rolls when I visited him in prison," I said. We were side by side on the couch.

"You can really help with your photos," he said, turning to look me directly in the eye. "When are you going to put up some more of your shots on the walls?"

"We're still redecorating the apartment," I said, standing up, "and I haven't found all of my negatives."

"We need the photographs to help us with our case," he said. It was the beginning of February and the first snow flakes of the winter were fluttering past the living room window, the same window that I had looked out just a year earlier when I was calling my sweet earth angel to profess my love while listening to the Tender Force. Chinita loved to look down at the busy movement on the avenue.

Frankly, I had become amazed when I learned that Harvey had been working on his case for almost the entire time that I was in Virginia. Ten years of commitment he had made, steadfastly concentrating on completing his mission. I admired his resolve, his vision, his courage, and yet it was...well frightening in its enormity of scope. But I had agreed to let him store the boxes of papers right downstairs in the garage. It had been during one of our lunches at the Grille near the college where he had finally stunned me with the details—what he and his student volunteers had been developing. I sat there in a blurry mixture of confusion, fear, and pride.

"It's not getting any better," he told me in a low voice, the freckles hidden almost in the dark rear of the restaurant.

"You don't like the biscuits?" I wondered.

"We are not just disappearing, we are being exterminated. There's only one thing that they will understand and one thing that will bring them down—money." He looked at me, still silent, knowing that he was just at the introduction. "They need to pay us for every penny we have lost because of their mistreatment of us. They have enslaved, tortured, killed, and dehumanized us since the beginning. It just continues—look at Mazique, the kid shot in the alley, even the Plane. Now they have to pay. Their time is up." His eyes glazed with anger.

"The Plane? What did he do?" I asked, wondering where I had stored those negatives.

"All we get is demeaning images of ourselves; that's all they show. That's part of their dehumanizing. He hasn't made a damn shot yet, and they make it seem as if floating in the air is all he does. No, they have got to pay, my brother."

"You want them to pay us?" I questioned.

"We're suing the government for 136 gazillion dollars based on our calculations of what we would have right now had they not enslaved, tortured, discriminated against and killed so many black men. They focused on the male because if they exterminate us, how can we reproduce? If they kill us off, they kill off the race." He was looking up at the ceiling as if reviewing his calculation.

"That's an amazing amount, Harvey," I said. "I don't even know what a gazillion dollars amounts to."

"A gazillion dollars is equal to 2.54 trillion dollars," he said calmly, his lips twitching in a smile. The way I see it, we practically own the damn country."

I could hear my heart thumping. I felt as if I were in a suspense movie as I looked around at the photographs of the distinguished alumni staring at us from the walls and watched the determined steps of the students moving in and out of the restaurant who may have been bringing in some new detail or item of information for the project. And Harvey's freckled cheeks kept moving in and out of the room's dim lighting. "It sounds incredible," is all that I could muster. "But of course I will help. What are the chances?"

"They did it for others, why not for us? The Japanese and Jews got reparations. I've got the numbers and copies of the agreements.."

And now, in my living room, he was telling me that he wanted more—wanted to use my photos as supplementary proof of how the black man had been reduced from the time that we were in charge of mighty kingdoms to where we are now. "Your photographs will be presented as supporting evidence of the historic pattern of extermination," he explained. "Your photos are the real deal. You have captured the essence of the black man's predicament, my good brother."

"Who me?" I felt myself being pulled into a world that was more complicated than it had ever been. The window of snow flakes tumbling downward reminded me of the time that I was sitting on the floor in front of Yo-Yo and dividing my concentration between the first snow of the winter and a newspaper column that Yo-Yo had circled. It was the black weekly with the colored pages (were they pink?) that I had usually ignored, preferring the shiny magazines. This column described a mighty warrior named Hannibal. From that moment on I picked up the weekly regularly to read that column, "Great Men of Color." Once there was Estevanico. Then there was Dumas, then Pushkin, then Touissant. These were the men about whom Harvey was talking—men of African descent whose extraordinary exploits had been legendary. But why had I not heard about them since those newspaper articles? Where had they gone? Or had they gone anywhere?

Should I be pulled farther into this firestorm that he had created? Actually I was feeling more comfortable about his position than I ever had been before listening to what I termed his revolutionary prattle. And although I may not have realized it then, the answer is transparently clear now. I was happy. As I listened to him that evening, my earth angel was in the other room. I would soon be joining her. Problems I had with Taney at the magazine: totally negligible! I could leave the office, leave those others who moved about like shadows and whose talent I thought was no more than mediocre anyway, and forget them all until another day. My earth angel would be there for me. Because I knew she was there, I was oh so confident that I could sustain any challenge. Yes my attitude had changed, and that outside world that before had seemed to threaten to erupt in thunder and lightning as soon as I closed my door was now a sky of bright blue possibility, urging me to smile. Another part of me had been released, giving me the freedom to see things through a different, less restricted lens.

I wanted to know more. It was exciting. I was feeling a buildup within me, forcing me to think that I had to do a great deal of rethinking. I wanted to describe it all to Chinita at breakfast the next morning, but it was a secret. I had promised Harvey. I wanted to discuss it with Gahtsum, but I couldn't—not yet.

And just as Aunt Clara promised, things changed overnight. My sweet angel returned from school that afternoon with a headache. A stressful situation had developed. A student had been sent home, the parent objected, the principal berated the parent, the parent called the teacher's union, a counselor who had sent the student home was a union official, and...she was lying on the bed fully clothed. I pulled off her shoes, threw a blanket over her shoulders and patted her head. "Don't worry, get some rest." Chinita slept through the night, turning side to side so that I could pull off her clothes and put her under the covers. She was breathing in a deep sleep immediately.

Did she go into a dream and take me with her? It seemed as if time had swept us up and sped us along and then spit us out as if we were dice in a cruel joker's hand. If it were a dream that we had been collected into, it must have been a nightmare version. Her headache got worse and became daily headaches. It was no longer a lingering discomfort for a few days, but a week, then weeks. She needed to take a leave from teaching.

Gahtsum went with us to the medical center that was dedicated to treating military personnel and elected officials. He had made contact with some specialists there. It was only a few miles away from our apartment, on a campus of winding lanes and iron security fences off Sixteenth Street. After the evaluation, the doctors told us that they had identified the problem. "She needs rest, some medication, the handsome Dr. Phoenix told us. You can pick up the prescription downstairs. Nice to see you Gahtsum—friends of yours?" And before he could answer, "I hear that Tony left Tufts to start his own practice. Imagine that, on his own in Beanton."

"He was always a risk-taker," Gahtsum responded.

It only took a month for her condition to worsen. After another month, the physician was more definitive. As I wheeled her down the hallway, I noticed that her head would tilt to the side in a quick nap. "It's clear that there is a danger of her having the sickness that grows," Doctor Phoenix told me. "We'll do what we can to arrest it. But sometimes it moves so fast..." His eyes turned from mine to look at Chinita sitting, half asleep in her wheelchair.

It only took a few more weeks after the meeting with Doctor Phoenix before her condition worsened. I remember each instance of her growing discomfort as a separate scene, as if I had left the apartment momentarily and returned to face a new model to photograph. In one pose at dinner I noticed that Chinita's cheeks had sagged into a thinness that seemed to narrow her face. In another she turned her head sideways to say something and I noticed that her eyes were cloudy. Then the pain became more frequent, growing from soreness in her limbs to which she could point, to a more penetrating burning that she couldn't point to, that sent her lying on her back and tossing her head from side to side, inhaling deeply. When I had to pick her up to take her to the bathroom, she always nestled her now bony face against my cheek, once complaining, "Oh look at the mess I've made in the bed. You must hate this. I'm so much trouble."

"Maybe you should call her mother," Gahtsum advised me by telephone one night when I described Chinita's deterioration. He too was having his challenges, and it was one of the first times that I detected weariness in his voice. "She may need something more than medication," he suggested. "Who knows what her mother might know based on old Indian lore. I sure wish she could find some powwow medicine for us."

"You aren't losing faith, are you young man?" I said with a deep tenor imitating his voice.

"Well not exactly. But we hadn't raised half as much money as we needed before the fire," he said. "You read about it of course—the whole transept is gone. Now we face greater rebuilding expenses. We have to stop construction again. That lovely church was meant to be a unifying center, but I begin to wonder more and more if there are enough of us really interested in coming together."

I had remembered, but frankly with the fast-moving tide of affairs that I was swept up in—running back and forth between the office and home; facing Taney's inevitable dispassionate assessment of my photographs, and meeting with Harvey to select the photographs—I had pretty much obliterated the outside world to concentrate on my own preoccupations. After all, I was barely able to get from sun up to sundown, as Aunt Clara would say, handling my own affairs. But a kernel of conversation did surface within my memory. I did remember overhearing Taney tell one of the writers that she did not need to go to the Apple to cover that story, that a fire in "some big old church" wasn't something *Ontime* needed to highlight

"But sir, it is the largest gothic cathedral in the world," the young writer had told Taney. "And I found a lot of history about it in the archives. Its doors have the same bronze that's used in the Statue of Liberty." She was just out of college with a girlish voice and young-at-heart enthusiasm. "And did you know that"—her tone really accelerated to the pitch of a bluejay—"that it was open the same year that the immigrants started arriving on Ellis Island?"

But I was passing by at that point, so he invited her inside his office and closed the door, the words, "it's not the image we want, my dear," trailing behind them.

"I didn't realize that the fire was at the church that you have been raising money for," I told Gahtsum. "I'm sorry. And I lived up the street from it and when I first moved to the Apple. It's an imposing structure."

"Well you have enough on your mind, my son," he said. "But I would see if you can get Chinita's mother to come out."

She had been planning to suggest it anyway, she told me on the phone, and when I saw her little figure standing at the airport baggage return, I could feel a ton of cares lifting from my shoulders.

"I was wondering if the plane would ever land," I said, trying to express a familial affection that I hadn't taken time to cultivate after her husband's memorial service. They had never found his body.

"I was wondering if it would ever land too," she said, reminding me of her penchant for repeating what you said. We hugged for a long time, and then I had to hold her longer because I could feel her shoulders trembling. I took a deep breath to keep my knees from shaking and to suppress the whining impulse to ask why this was happening.

"She's such a sweet little thing," she said, sneezing in the crook of her elbow when we stood apart. "Quick, there it is." I bent to grab the handle of the suitcase. But she began uttering the same phrase, "there it is" until I had grabbed and spun around and placed more than a half dozen suitcases, boxes and bags on the floor in front of us. "I checked with Chief Tame Bear who is retired, before coming. He suggested some herbs that I wasn't familiar with. I figure you can't have enough."

But despite the diseases and ailments and maladies that so many chiefs and medicine men and healing squaws had ministered effectively in the past, none of them worked for my Chinita. Her mother, with her arsenal of suitcases, cardboard boxes and cloth bags of mixed sizes, spent countless days and evenings administering her concoctions of inner bark tea, rose petals and orange peel. I came in one evening to see her standing over her daughter in full buckskin regalia. She held a bow and spear that I learned was a substitute for shooting black arrow in the air to kill evil spirits. And whenever Rosalie felt the impulse, she might jump up from her chair and begin calling to the animal spirits, her hands cupped over her mouth like a cheering fan at a basketball game. And oh yes, our bed was surrounded by a throng of protective plants painstakingly chosen from the rows and rows of offerings at a suburban Maryland landscaper. "Look at these leaves—eaten by gnats," dismissing that potted philodendron with a disdainful hiss.

No Booby, it did no good. Her condition didn't improve, and it seemed that the tide wrapping me up was becoming stronger and stronger, throwing me around like the waves that I had dived under as a kid in the world's playground. Sometimes instead of gliding the few yards to a floating stop where I would stand up thrilled to have ridden the breakers that far, the surf would push me with so much unexpected force that my stomach would scrape the sand and I'd come to an abrupt, painful stop at the edge of the beach. Yes, I had to consider that our merry-go-round was coming to an unanticipated halt. A montage of wonderful moments passed through my mind. Together—almost two years—we had circled about in paradisal bliss while the rest of the still world watched us—so we thought. But was the rest of the world really still and not moving also? Were we the only two spinning while the rest of humanity remained stationary? Or had we just been oblivious to the planet beyond us? Was that what my physics teacher in high school kept insisting—that it was all relative, that the rest of the world was moving also? We just weren't paying attention. Perhaps if they were watching us circling in our own little cocoon, we might be considered stationary because they were moving even faster? And if it was all relative, did that mean we were all related?

I was thinking about all of this on the morning that they moved her to the hospital. Or maybe I was trying to think about it. It did seem that the fog that I was in when I first lost my mind falling in love with Chinita had returned to encompass me under entirely different circumstances. Dr. Phoenix felt that the sickness had eaten too much of her, that she needed more support than we could give her at home. "We will try to arrest it with chemotherapy and radiology," he said. "That's all we can do with this darn thing—try to kill it. We have no cure, just technology and instruments" he sighed, patting me on the back. Rosalie and I watched as Dr. Phoenix directed two nurses who were hooking up Chinita's arms and legs with various tubes and hoses.

Half-walking down the hospital's bright white hallway, the intercom sending out a flurry of pages and calls, I wondered how I would get through the day. Both Taney and Harvey had called the previous evening. If it's not one thing, it's two. Taney had been unusually sympathetic, giving me days off and keeping my travel assignments to a minimum. "You're under a lot of pressure, my boy, your face shoes it." But he needed to see me right away. And Harvey had interrupted a prayer session with Chinita's mother to ask me to come to the Grille. He needed to talk about some photographs.

As I rode the elevator up to Taney's office I reminded myself that I needed to mention to Wilma that the herbal cures had not worked so well. "Those old world remedies may be better than all of this new medicine," she had suggested. But who was this?—a new receptionist? She introduced herself while brushing the hair from her forehead when I came up to her, smiled broadly, mispronounced my name and stood to lead me in to his office.

The rising sun's rays were just hitting the Capitol when I walked in. This time his smile-frown was all frown, and he leaned so far forward that I thought his chin would bang against the desk. "So you're involved! I couldn't believe it. And you were this close to getting a damn office with windows!"

"Who me?" I was already so tired I could hardly think.

"Yes you! And that damn ungrateful injun lass we hired and tried to expose her to a civilized lifestyle. She told me about your photographs. To think that you would be involved in such outrageous shenanigans!"

"What...how...? I don't understand what you're talking about." I stood staring with my hands at my sides.

"We found out about the law suit that malcontent friend of yours and Wilma are preparing. Seems like she left some notes in the ladies' room and one of our editors brought it to me. Gazillions of dollars huh? You think you and them will bankrupt the country. I can't believe it," standing up, and with his back to me, facing the Capitol.

Was he saying that Wilma was involved with Harvey's case? Is that why she wasn't at the reception desk? How had she found out about it? I tried to follow every word, but my legs started shaking and my eyes felt strained, as if I had been squinting through a telephoto lens for hours. I knew that this was important, that he was angry, that I myself might soon erupt at his anger, but for some reason the sight of the Capitol that he was staring at brought back the Sunday that Chinita and I had walked around its majestic marble steps and terraces, pointing at the statue at the top, looking out over the gardens, the pond, the city, feeling as if we had been kidnapped by happiness. Then he was saying something about *Ontime* had a responsibility for exposing the devious plot, that it would no longer be a surreptitious conspiracy designed to bring down the very republic itself. Once exposed, the villains would be destabilized, discredited, left powerless and hopefully homeless. He banged his fist twice on the desk as he pronounced the last word.

I heard him but I was thinking of the impending cold nights when I will turn to hold her and she won't be there. Or when I awaken in a sweat from the fiend who had chased me in a dream to face a pillow without a dimple. What about when I can't sleep and won't sleep because of the tumble of memories that gnaw at my mind, tossing me left and right. Will she return and talk to me without your hearing, Booby, as Miss Bernice said that Roland came to her on certain evenings—at least for the first four months after his death? Will her voice echo in the shower, in the closets, over the music? Will she be a ghost in pink floating over my bed, knocking over a lamp, beckoning me with a curled finger? I had to prepare for her imminent leaving, and it was a dreadful prospect. *I didn't want to lose my Chinita* became an echoing refrain, filling my brain like a foghorn. I felt the moisture trickling down my checks when he turned to face me. "Well, I guess I should be looking for another job," I said, wiping my eyes.

"Ha! Absolutely not! And I see I've frightened you to tears. No, if we fired you our whole image would fit right into their scheme. No, we're finding you an office with windows. And we're doing a special on Truman Washington with some of those photographs of yours. We found out he's fathered a child by that lady…what's her name. But we're not going to mention it."

"Well it seems as if…" I didn't know what to say after that. It seemed like the proper introduction to something appropriate. But I was a tired sleepwalker, a disoriented drunk, a weak feather floating downward, barely aware of where I was.

"Yes we have covered our bases, and we're prepared. You tell your cohorts that. We are prepared to protect our republic from all transgressors. Is there anything else?"

I wanted to sit down—lie down really—and rest, wanted to wave away the bothersome distractions, but I nodded no and turned to make my unsteady way back to my office. Heads peaked out of entrances and then disappeared behind slammed doors. My breath was coming in short gasps as I sat staring at the clock on the wall. In an hour I was scheduled to meet with Harvey. Putting my head on my desk, I wondered if I could just fall asleep for a minute. But no, I needed to get back to the hospital after meeting with Harvey, so I dragged myself to my feet and reached for the door knob. I was floating down the hallway past another set of prize-winning mediocre photographs—one by a staffer who had actually spoken to me as he jumped in a cab one rainy day. He was going to a black tie awards dinner sponsored by a local press association.

By the time we had driven two blocks I had fallen asleep in the cab and awoke to hear the chapel bells and a parade of students chattering and taking the hill to classes. "You a student or a professor?" the driver asked, looking bewildered when I shook my head to indicate yes. The lunch crowd had not yet started, so most of the tables were empty when I opened the door to the Grille.

"You okay? You haven't been drinking already have you?" Clyde asked, and then, "sorry about Chinita man. Hang in there. Your boy's in the back."

Stumbling almost, fighting off the vertigo of confusion, despair and lack of sleep, I made my way to the back toward the waving hands that were connected to Harvey and Wilma. Their words too floated in the air like dreamy songs as I fell to my seat at their table. "We met at the street academy. She came to volunteer. And before you knew it, an observation here, an opinion there, and we were united in the struggle." Their faces turned toward each other like two teammates agreeing simultaneously on a strategy. "Next thing we knew, she had brought a new dimension to the entire project"—this in a whisper so low I had to bend forward. "We're joining forces." I wondered what that meant. "After she saw those pictures you took of the statue of liberty that showed the woman to be white and not a Native American as everybody has been led to believe, she understood better how they distort the truth. Oh it was just more of the same, show the positive side only, even if it's untrue. Then she started doing her own little research. Well my brother, we have upped the ante. We're not suing just for the defilement of the black man. We're suing also for all the land taken from her people." Harvey held up the writing pad in front of his face for me to read. "Look at those gazillions." I couldn't read the numbers, but they spread across the entire pad and had lots of commas. "So we have to get the papers from your garage in a few days before they start their campaign against us. We can't wait to gather any more evidence. They've already begun to prepare."

I heard and yet I wasn't sure I heard; it made sense and yet it didn't make sense. I was awake and strong enough to feel conscious, and yet I didn't feel as if I were fully in control of whatever I felt. Harvey and Wilma were going to sue the country for what it had done to the black man and Native Americans. The damages would amount to gazillions of dollars. "I have to get back to the hospital," I said, and then looked behind me. Had I uttered those words?

"Clyde, bring him some water. Hey you want some hot soup? Have you eaten? You really look tired, man."

"No I just have to get back to the hospital," I said. "I have to make a decision. What time is it?"

"Don't worry, we'll take you back."

"No," I said, rising, "I'll grab a cab. "And let me know when you want to meet me at the beach for the papers."

"One other thing. A professor at the law school has already told us that we will bankrupt the country if we win. They won't have enough money to pay the judgment when you add up the gazillions they have taken from the black man and the gazillions that the land is worth that they stole from Wilma's people."

"We'll own the country," I said, pushing back my chair and standing on the same tottering legs that had barely held me when I had listened to Taney's harangue just an hour previously. It was a phrase I had heard Harvey use on several occasions and it appeared in my mind like the lines an actor suddenly sees who is stumbling to remember what comes next.

"Well they don't have enough in the treasury to pay us." I was almost to the front door when he said that.

I had remembered that there was a pay telephone booth nearby. I needed to talk to my daddy, Booby. That's all I could think of as I skirted around the students coming toward me. "My dad will kill me if he finds out," I heard one coed tell her friend as they paused to walk around me. "Oh just turn at the corner there," she told me without breaking her pace, "it's on the right across from the car lot." And suddenly the phrase *talk to my daddy* kept drumming itself into my consciousness as if I were a child again and needed an answer to a monumental question like *is that right?* or *what should I do, Daddy?* I was a little boy lost, like the child in that memoir who follows a parade until he finds himself miles away from his home, in some unknown town. I saw the empty phone booth when I turned the corner and increased my pace before anybody could beat me to it. I slid the door shut and watched an old dog across the street in the car lot perk up at the sound. A voice told me that the line was disconnected. I must have dialed incorrectly and tried again. This time Gahtsum's secretary picked up and transferred me.

"I was wondering where you are," he said. "Where are you?"

"Can you come over, Dad?" is all that I could muster. My shaking voice sounded so low that I had to repeat it. "I wanted to see you before I go to the hospital."

"Sure son; sure thing,"

When I opened the telephone booth, the old shepherd limped across the street toward me. His scraggly gray coat was covered with large spots of black oil. "Poor boy," I said, "were you lonely too?" I knelt to pet him when the cab wheeled around the corner and chased him back. I got in and turned my head to see my hobbling almost friend. His one good eye was focusing on us as I gave my address to the driver.

When I go to my apartment, I washed my face. In the mirror, my eyes looked red and small. Glad to have an opportunity to rest, I was sitting on my couch nodding when Gahtsum arrived. "This traffic is getting worse," he said. "We need to eliminate cars altogether and go to bicycles. What's new? Hey you look tired."

"I have to make a decision about Chinita," I said. "She's not getting any better. She's just lying there suffering. She's not even technically alive according to Dr. Phoenix."

"Yes I spoke with him a few days ago," Gahtsum replied.

"I may ask them...I may ask them..." The air left my stomach and I couldn't finish and so I stood up to go toward the window. "It's all falling apart," I said. "She's dying, Harvey's got me further involved with his law suit, and I could lose my job—again. I needed to talk with somebody. I needed to talk with you. I've got a terrible headache."

"Well I'm glad that you called me. That's what fathers are for. You have a lot on your mind. Don't worry, it's not falling apart. You just have a lot to deal with and you feel overwhelmed."

"I don't think I'm going to continue with her on that respirator," I said. "Her mother feels the same way. She's almost a vegetable." I turned to see him sitting on the couch in his suit, staring out the window behind me.

"It's tough losing a loved one, under any circumstances," he said, standing to take off his jacket and fold it on the arm of the couch. "And it always seems unfair, making you ask why it has to be you to be so unfortunate, to have to suffer."

He knew exactly what I was thinking. I was trying to sort out the other disturbing events that were packed into compartments of my mind. I said, "Now Wilma, the secretary at the magazine has joined with Harvey. They're planning to expand the suit to include Native Americans. They're talking about gazillions of dollars—I can't even count that high."

"Yes I heard through some contacts at the magazine. They're furious—but scared too. A fascinating idea I must say. We'll have to see what happens. Maybe we will come together, who knows. Frankly I think the prospects are more unlikely than ever. I certainly don't think we'll find the money to finish the church—after a half century of its being incomplete. I guess this just isn't the time. You and I have had our turn, and maybe we should be grateful and recount our blessings."

What was he talking about? I whirled to face him and listened as he continued, sitting down now, waving his hands as he had done so many times when dispensing advice to me or Aunt Clara. I sat too in the chair by the window and tried to follow his statements that jumped from subject to subject. No, the country could not pay all the money that Harvey and Wilma insisted on if they won their case. They would bring the country to the brink of insolvency—it would be broke. "Do they love Caesar more than they love Rome?" What did that mean, I heard myself asking. "It's my Shakespearian twist. Do you bring down the entire country because you love your own more than you love the country?" I wasn't sure why not; but Harvey had made some convincing arguments, and look at what's happening to us even today. When will it stop? my mind asked. Look at my son—frightened back into history, gone. And all of Gahtsum's friends who were to help me—what happened? "The answer is that Caesar and Rome must come together, that's the only way. That's all that Professor Gut ever meant. That's all that the church stood for. But you see that Gut couldn't get support for his thinking, and we can't raise enough money to rebuild that marvelous church, and your good friend Harvey would rather bankrupt the country." Yes, I thought, but maybe Harvey's idea that the country should be bankrupt to teach it a lesson isn't such a bad proposition after all. Maybe you have to fight before you come together. Didn't a poet say that we had to kick law into their teeth? As if already considering the thought Gahtsum said, "We can't continue to solve our differences by conflict and warfare."

"So we just can't come together," I offered, my head becoming somewhat clearer since I had made a pot of tea while he sat with knees crossed on the couch.

"My son, you and I may have come as close to Professor Gut's ideal as possible. Remember, the poet said that we must love one another or die. You and I have had at least the experience of a deep fulfilling loving relationship. I had your mother. You had Chinita. How many can say that they lived so many wonderful moments—even if they were shorter than we wished. Maybe that's as close as we can get. Should we not be grateful?"

Of course the answer was yes, Booby. But I had to go to the hospital, I told Gahtsum. I wanted to go by myself and give the instructions. Then I would wait to see how Harvey's law suit progressed. I'd take a personal leave from *Ontime*. I'd wait to see how they responded to Harvey and Wilma. By now I knew that it was all about image. It wasn't the truth that was so important, it was how you presented your version of reality and sold it as *the truth*. Well they had hoodwinked me for quite a while, making me think that their image is the one that I should accept. But they hadn't stopped me from pursuing my romantic ideal or of finally finding my earth angel. Of course I should recount my blessings.

So I gave them the instructions to take Chinita out of her misery. And then the good Dr. Phoenix suggested that I take some time to think and rest—with you, Booby. I know, you must be exhausted listening to me recount almost 50 years. I'm tired myself. Go ahead, lie down. Here, you don't have to sit up. Lie down Booby. There.

Printed in the United States
70761LV00003B/4-24